MY VIDEO GAME ATE MY HOME-WORK

DEWEY JENKINS
13 YEARS OLD - TWIN BROTHER

BEATRICE JENKINS
13 YEARS OLD - TWIN SISTER

RONALD FERGUSON
12.5 YEARS OLD - ALWAYS HUNGRY

KATHERINE ORTIZ
12 YEARS OLD - SUPER LOYAL

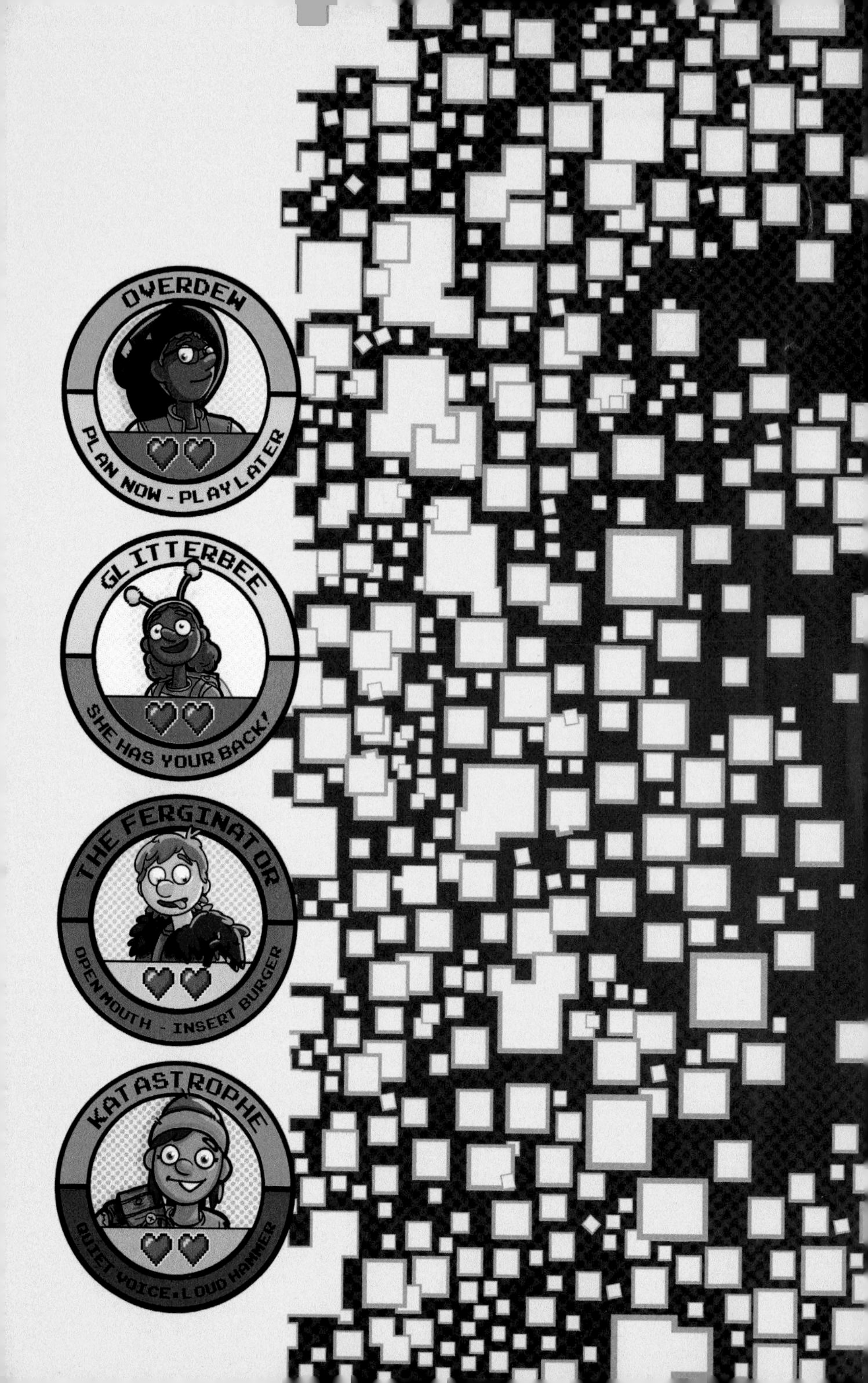
OVERDEW
PLAN NOW - PLAYLATER
GLITTERBEE
SHE HAS YOUR BACK!
THE FERGINATOR
OPEN MOUTH - INSERT BURGER
KATASTROPHE
QUIET VOICE. LOUD HAMMER

MY VIDEO GAME ATE MY HOME- WORK

Written and Illustrated by

DUSTIN HANSEN

Lettered by Corey Breen

JIM CHADWICK Editor
DIEGO LOPEZ Associate Editor
STEVE COOK Design Director - Books
AMIE BROCKWAY-METCALF Publication Design

BOB HARRAS Senior VP - Editor-in-Chief, DC Comics
MICHELE R. WELLS VP & Executive Editor, Young Reader

DAN DiDIO Publisher
JIM LEE Publisher & Chief Creative Officer
BOBBIE CHASE VP - New Publishing Initiatives
DON FALLETTI VP - Manufacturing Operations & Workflow Management
LAWRENCE GANEM VP - Talent Services
ALISON GILL Senior VP - Manufacturing & Operations
HANK KANALZ Senior VP - Publishing Strategy & Support Services
DAN MIRON VP - Publishing Operations
NICK J. NAPOLITANO VP - Manufacturing Administration & Design
NANCY SPEARS VP - Sales
JONAH WEILAND VP - Marketing & Creative Services

MY VIDEO GAME ATE MY HOMEWORK

Published by DC Comics. Copyright © 2020 DC Comics.
All Rights Reserved. All characters, their distinctive
likenesses, and related elements featured in this
publication are trademarks of DC Comics. The stories,
characters, and incidents featured in this publication
are entirely fictional. DC Comics does not read or
accept unsolicited submissions of ideas, stories,
or artwork. DC - a WarnerMedia Company.

DC Comics, 2900 West Alameda Ave.,
Burbank, CA 91505
Printed by LSC Communications,
Crawfordsville, IN, USA. 3/13/20.
First Printing.
ISBN: 978-1-4012-9326-0

PEFC Certified
This product is from
sustainably managed
forests and controlled
sources
PEFC/29-31-337   www.pefc.org

Library of Congress Cataloging-in-Publication Data

Names: Hansen, Dustin, writer, illustrator. | Breen, Corey, letterer.
Title: My video game ate my homework : a graphic novel / written and
    illustrated by Dustin Hansen ; lettered by Corey Breen.
Description: Burbank, CA : DC Comics, [2020] | Audience: Ages 8-12 |
    Audience: Grades 4-6 | Summary: Dewey Jenkins wants to have the top
    science project in class to avoid summer school and win a
    state-of-the-art virtual reality video game, but after his friend Ferg
    accidentally breaks the console, they accidentally trigger the device,
    finding themselves transported inside a video game.
Identifiers: LCCN 2020000363 (print) | LCCN 2020000364 (ebook) | ISBN
    9781401293260 (paperback) | ISBN 9781779503657 (ebook)
Subjects: LCSH: Graphic novels. | CYAC: Graphic novels. | Virtual
    reality--Fiction.
Classification: LCC PZ7.7.H362 My 2020 (print) | LCC PZ7.7.H362 (ebook) |
    DDC 741.5/973--dc23
LC record available at https://lccn.loc.gov/2020000363
LC ebook record available at https://lccn.loc.gov/2020000364

MY VIDEO GAME ATE MY HOME-WORK

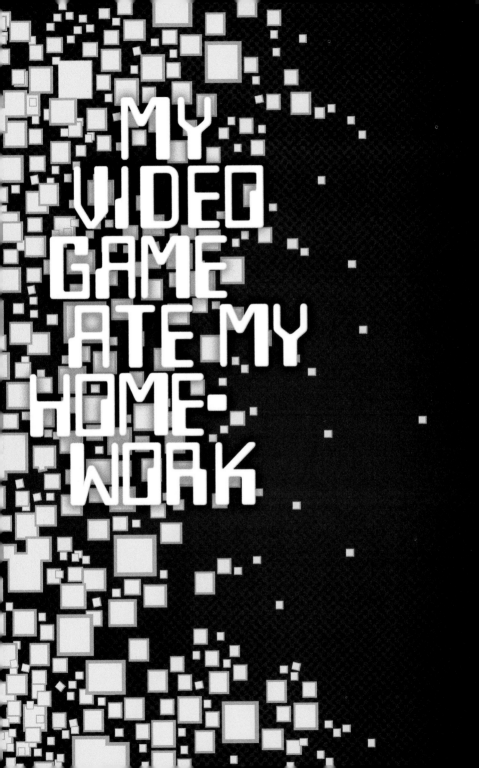

For my hero and best friend, Davis,
who faces adversity like an adventure.
—Dustin Hansen

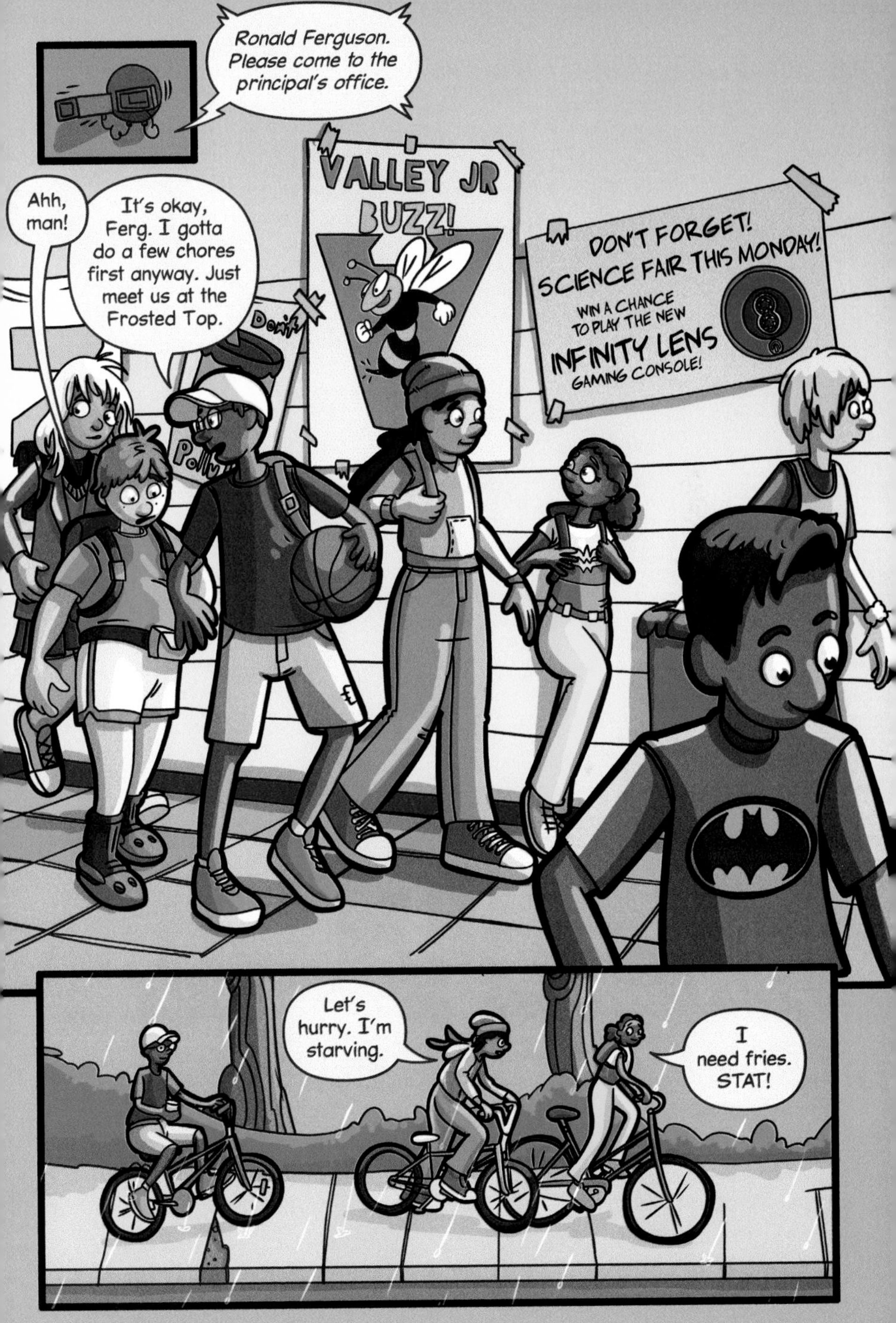
Ronald Ferguson. Please come to the principal's office.
VALLEY JR BUZZ!
DON'T FORGET! SCIENCE FAIR THIS MONDAY!
WIN A CHANCE TO PLAY THE NEW
INFINITY LENS
GAMING CONSOLE!
Ahh, man!
It's okay, Ferg. I gotta do a few chores first anyway. Just meet us at the Frosted Top.
Let's hurry. I'm starving.
I need fries. STAT!

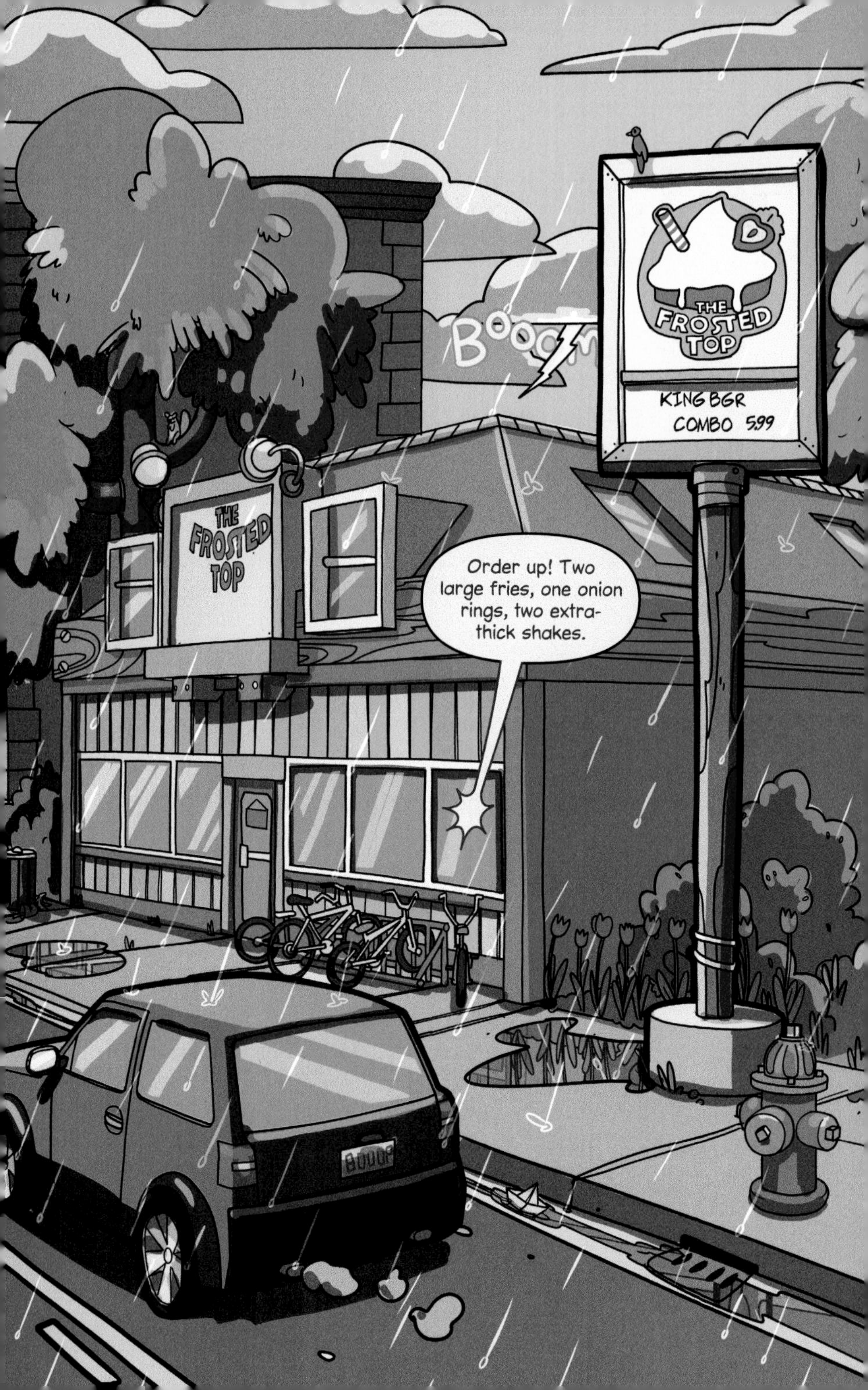
THE FROSTED TOP
KING BGR COMBO 5.99
BOOOM
THE FROSTED TOP
Order up! Two large fries, one onion rings, two extra-thick shakes.

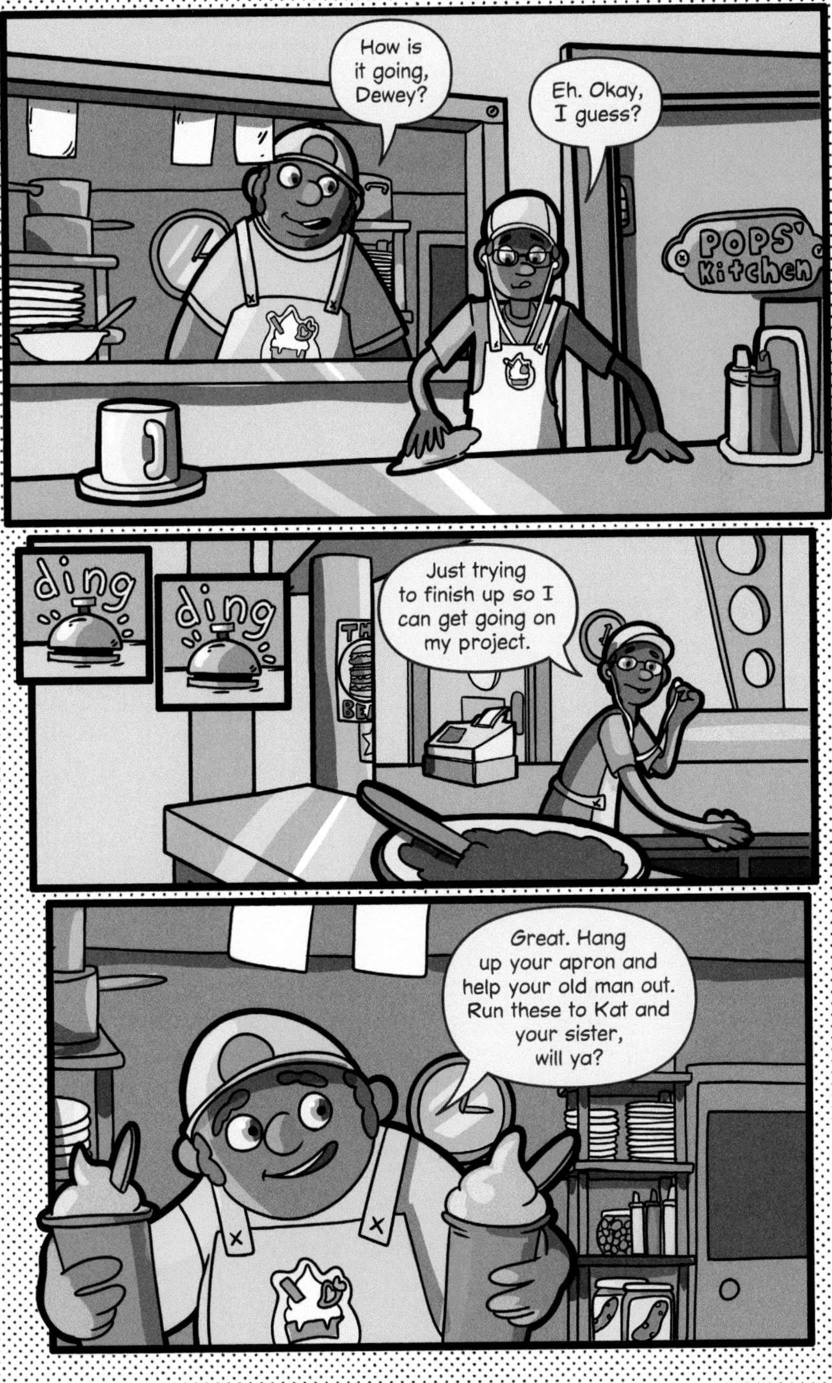
How is it going, Dewey?
Eh. Okay, I guess?
POPS' Kitchen
ding
ding
Just trying to finish up so I can get going on my project.
Great. Hang up your apron and help your old man out. Run these to Kat and your sister, will ya?

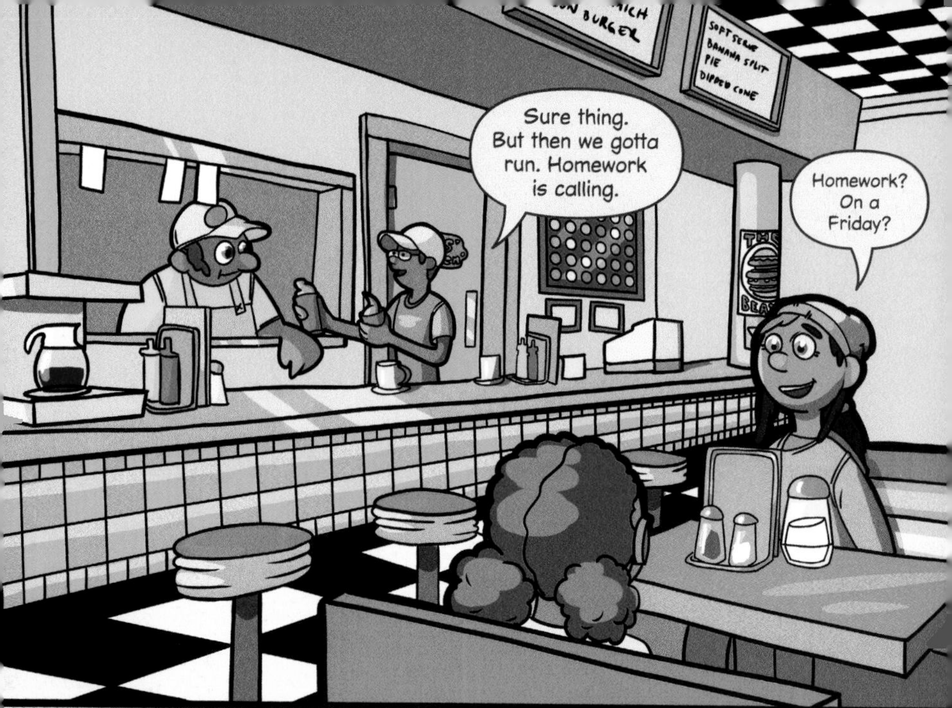
SOFT SERVE
BANANA SPLIT
PIE
DIPPED CONE
Sure thing. But then we gotta run. Homework is calling.
Homework? On a Friday?

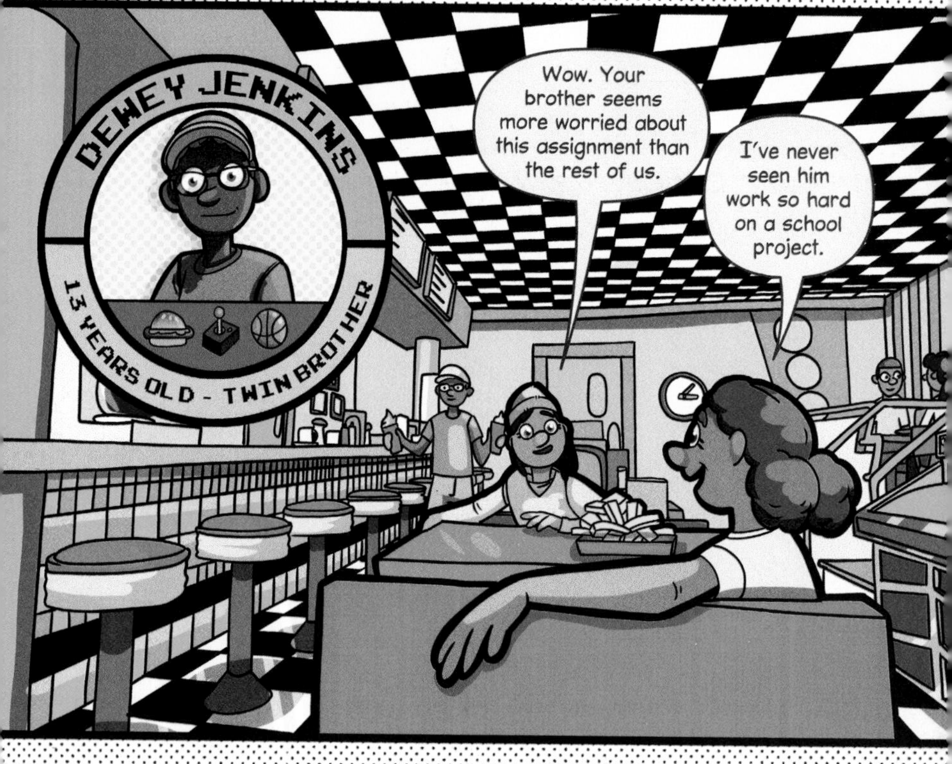
DEWEY JENKINS
13 YEARS OLD - TWIN BROTHER
Wow. Your brother seems more worried about this assignment than the rest of us.
I've never seen him work so hard on a school project.

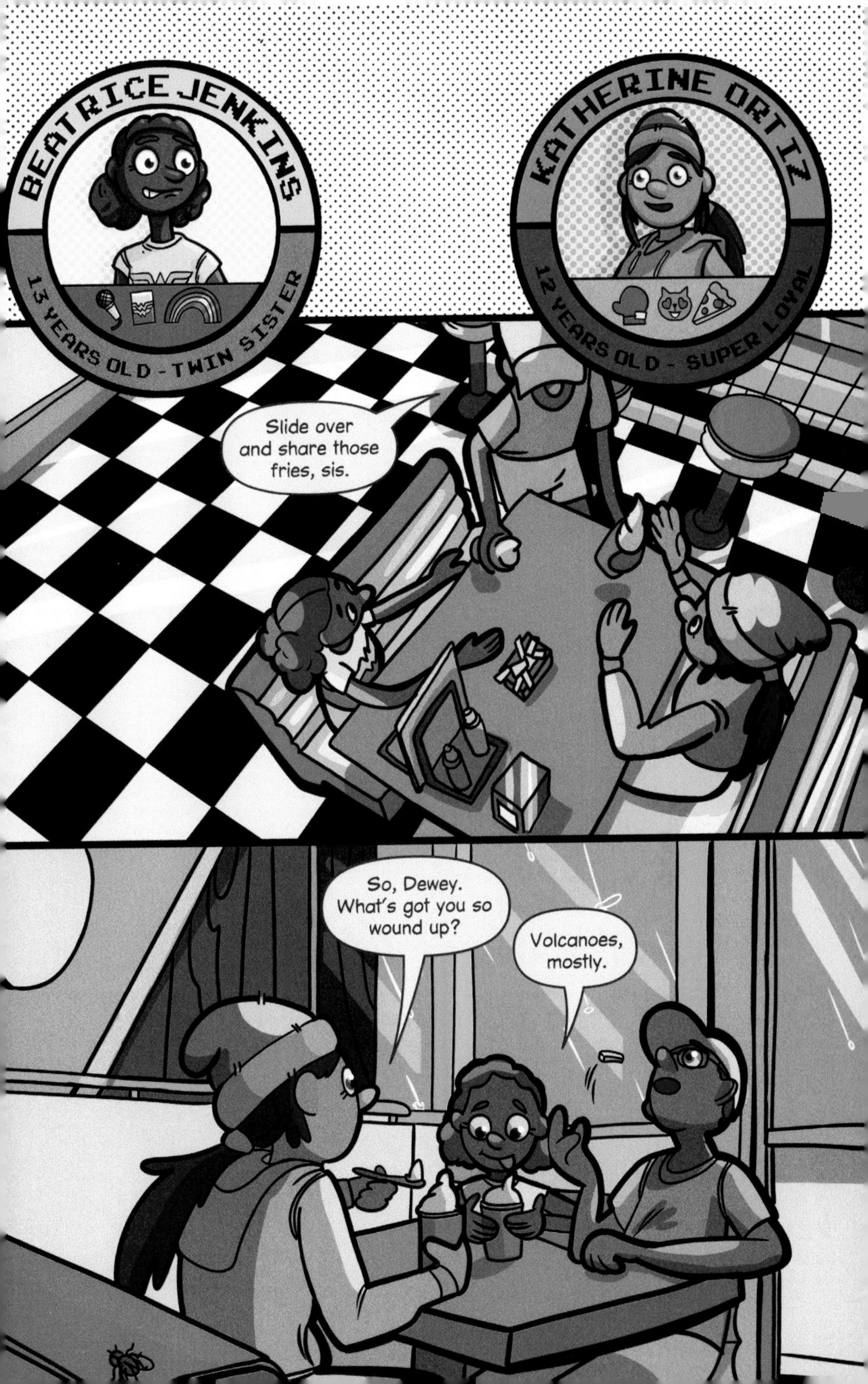
BEATRICE JENKINS
13 YEARS OLD - TWIN SISTER
KATHERINE ORTIZ
12 YEARS OLD - SUPER LOYAL
Slide over and share those fries, sis.
So, Dewey. What's got you so wound up?
Volcanoes, mostly.

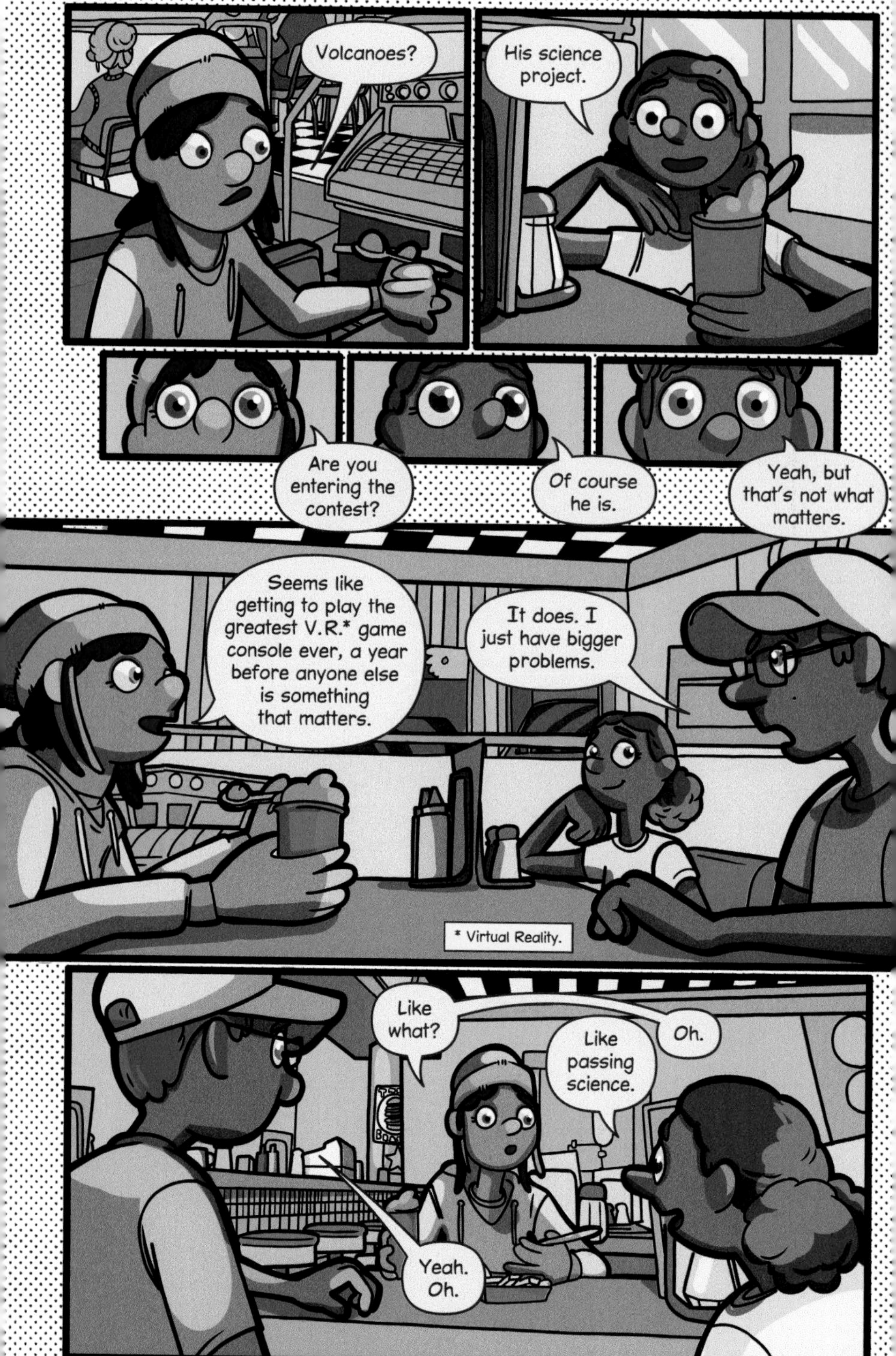
Volcanoes?
His science project.
Are you entering the contest?
Of course he is.
Yeah, but that's not what matters.
Seems like getting to play the greatest V.R.* game console ever, a year before anyone else is something that matters.
It does. I just have bigger problems.
* Virtual Reality.
Like what?
Like passing science.
Oh.
Yeah. Oh.

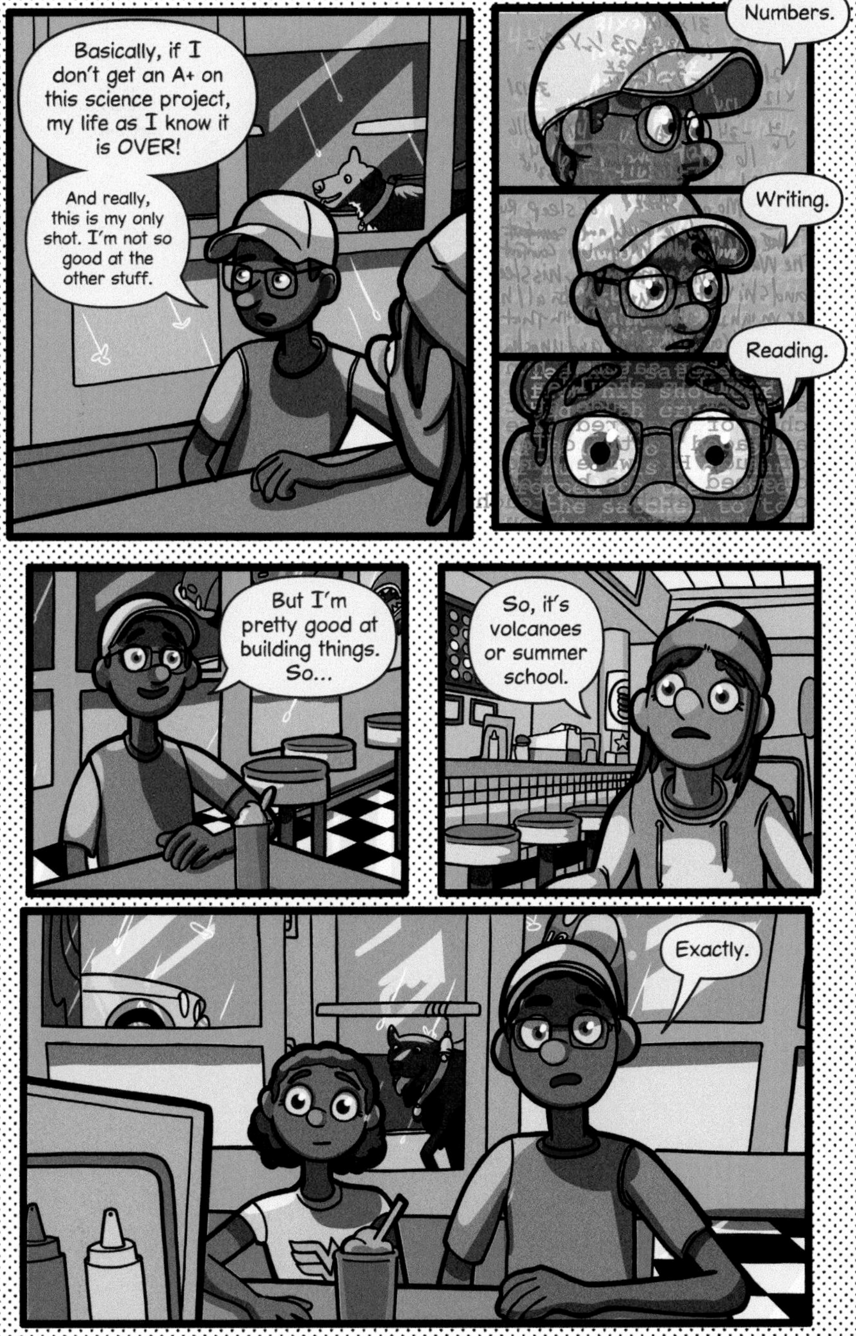
Basically, if I don't get an A+ on this science project, my life as I know it is OVER!
And really, this is my only shot. I'm not so good at the other stuff.
Numbers.
Writing.
Reading.
But I'm pretty good at building things. So...
So, it's volcanoes or summer school.
Exactly.

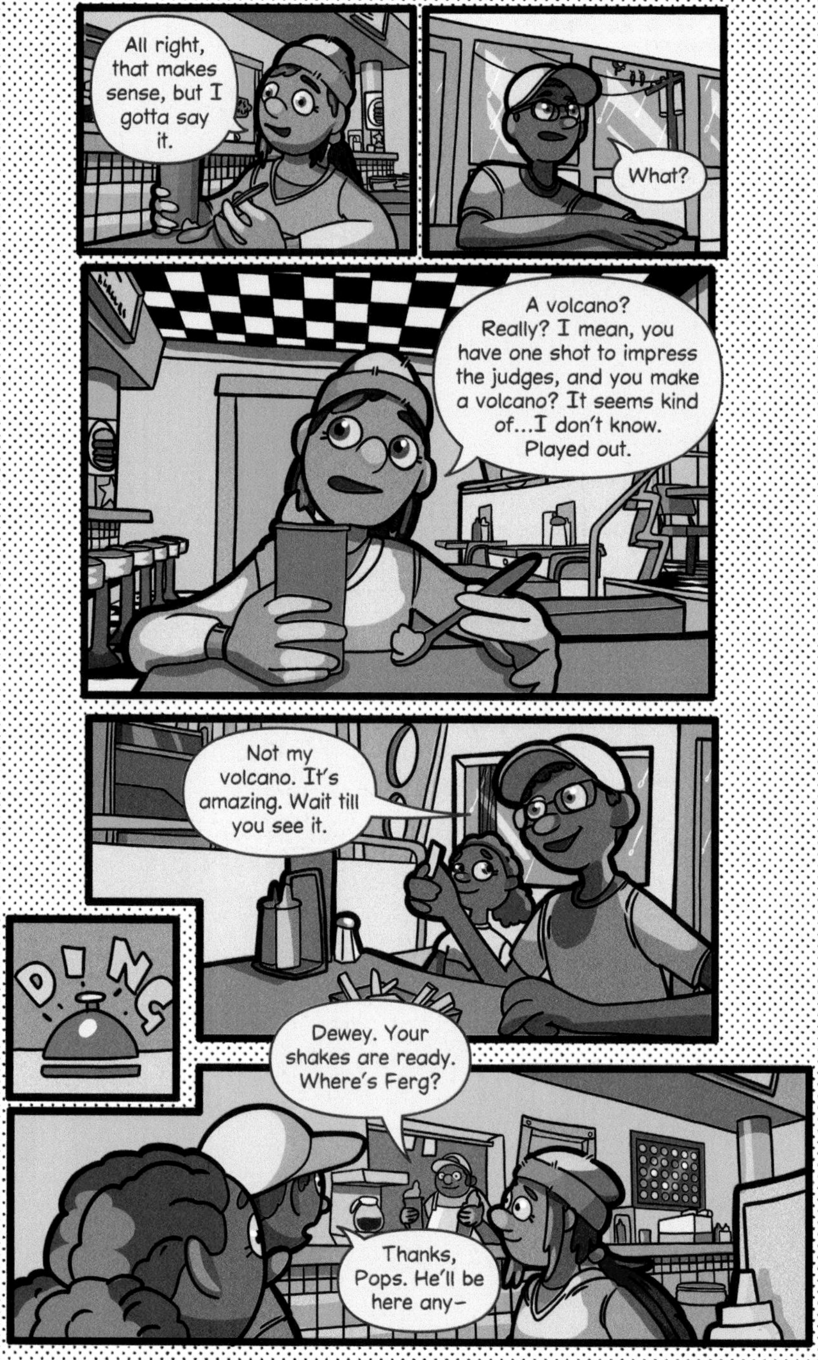
All right, that makes sense, but I gotta say it.
What?
A volcano? Really? I mean, you have one shot to impress the judges, and you make a volcano? It seems kind of...I don't know. Played out.
Not my volcano. It's amazing. Wait till you see it.
DING
Dewey. Your shakes are ready. Where's Ferg?
Thanks, Pops. He'll be here any–

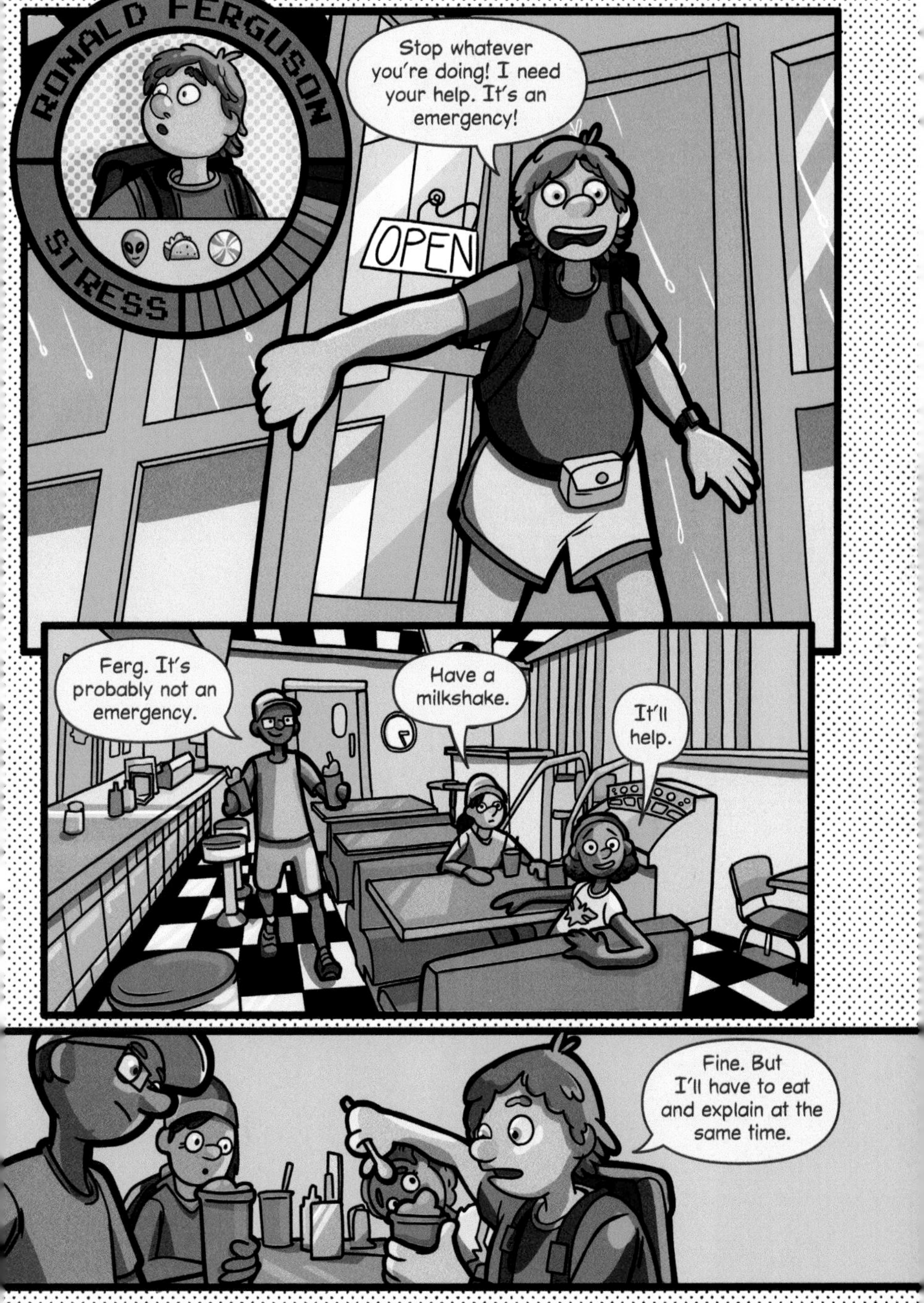
RONALD FERGUSON
STRESS
Stop whatever you're doing! I need your help. It's an emergency!
OPEN
Ferg. It's probably not an emergency.
Have a milkshake.
It'll help.
Fine. But I'll have to eat and explain at the same time.

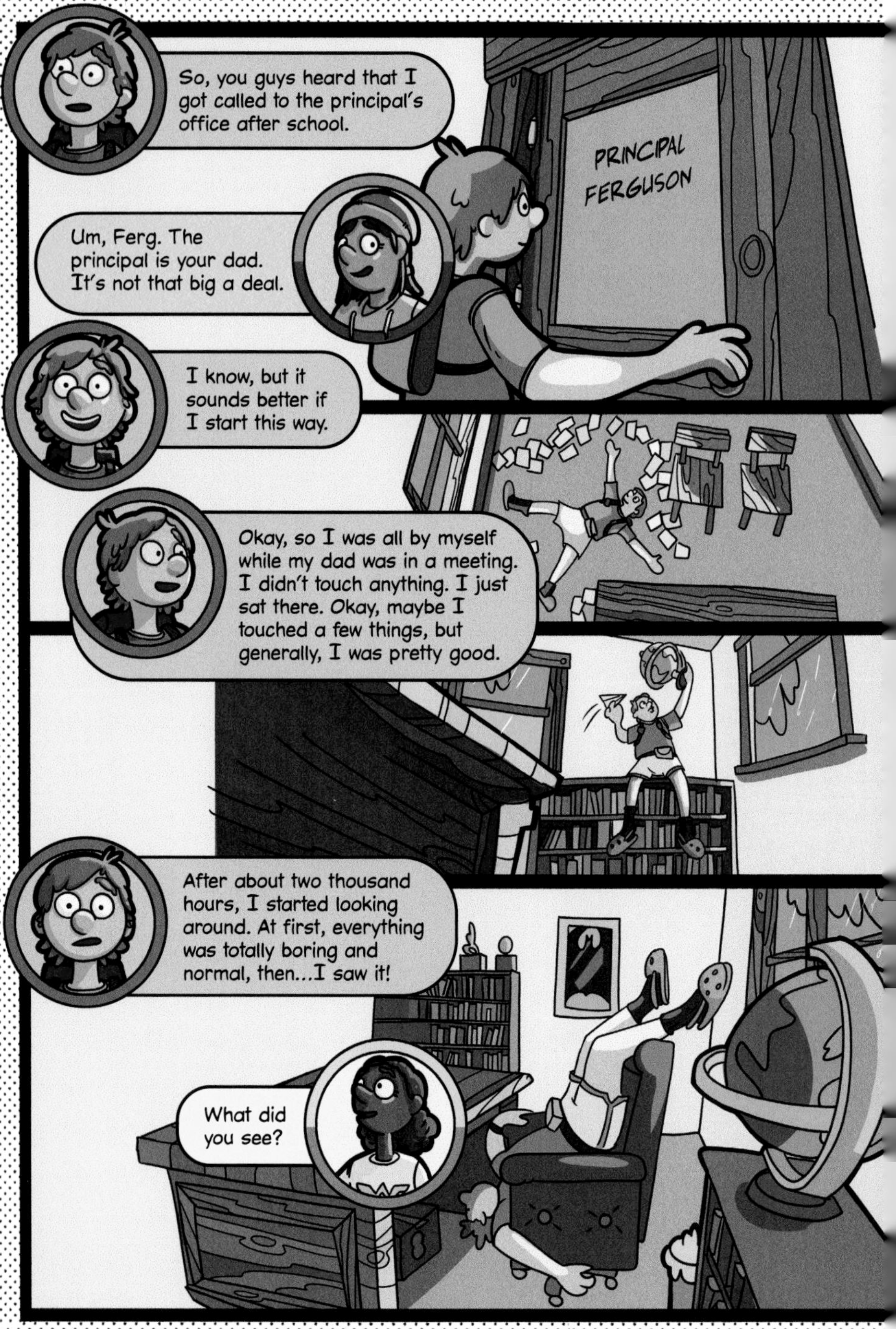
So, you guys heard that I got called to the principal's office after school.
PRINCIPAL FERGUSON
Um, Ferg. The principal is your dad. It's not that big a deal.
I know, but it sounds better if I start this way.
Okay, so I was all by myself while my dad was in a meeting. I didn't touch anything. I just sat there. Okay, maybe I touched a few things, but generally, I was pretty good.
After about two thousand hours, I started looking around. At first, everything was totally boring and normal, then...I saw it!
What did you see?

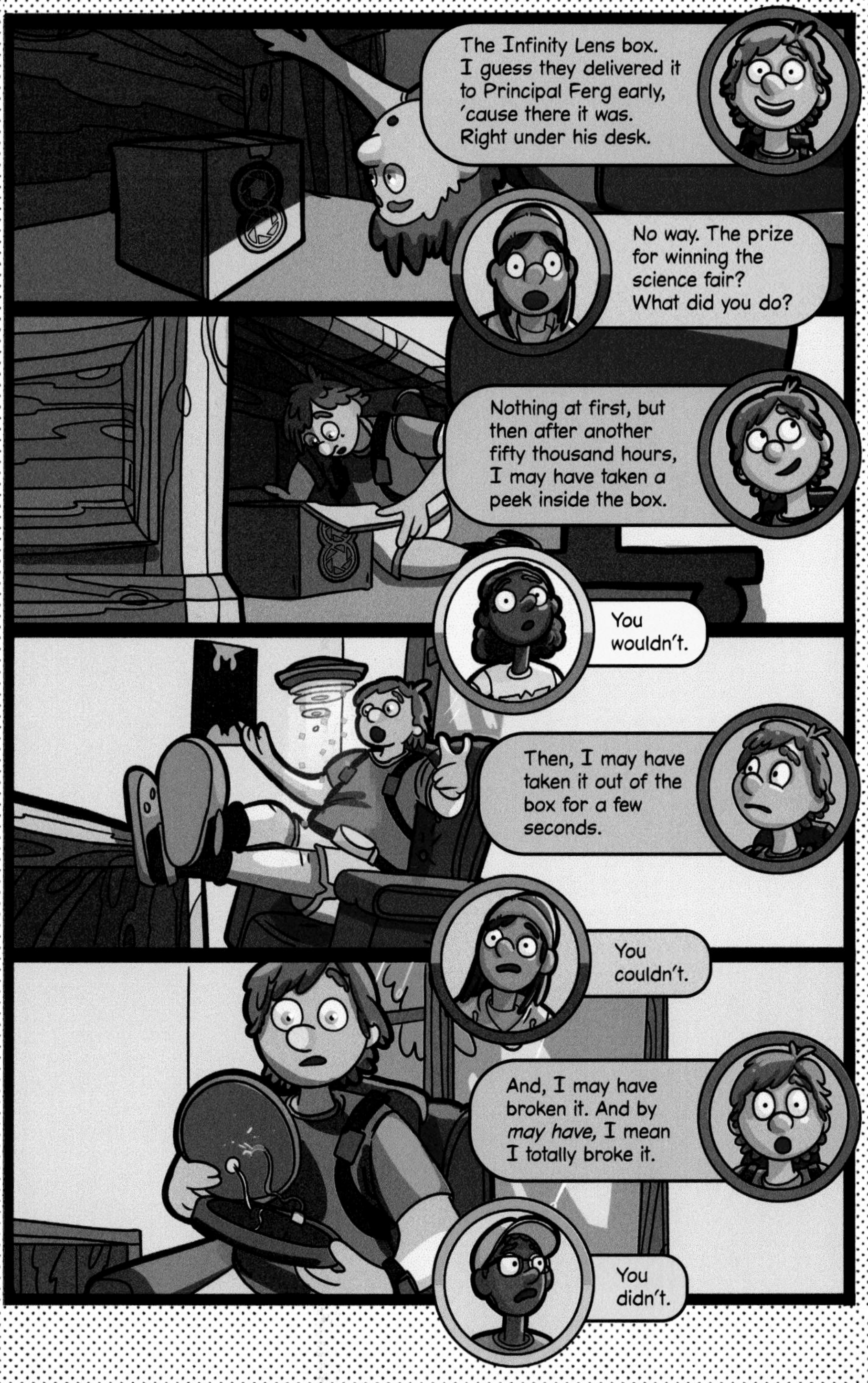
The Infinity Lens box. I guess they delivered it to Principal Ferg early, 'cause there it was. Right under his desk.
No way. The prize for winning the science fair? What did you do?
Nothing at first, but then after another fifty thousand hours, I may have taken a peek inside the box.
You wouldn't.
Then, I may have taken it out of the box for a few seconds.
You couldn't.
And, I may have broken it. And by *may have,* I mean I totally broke it.
You didn't.

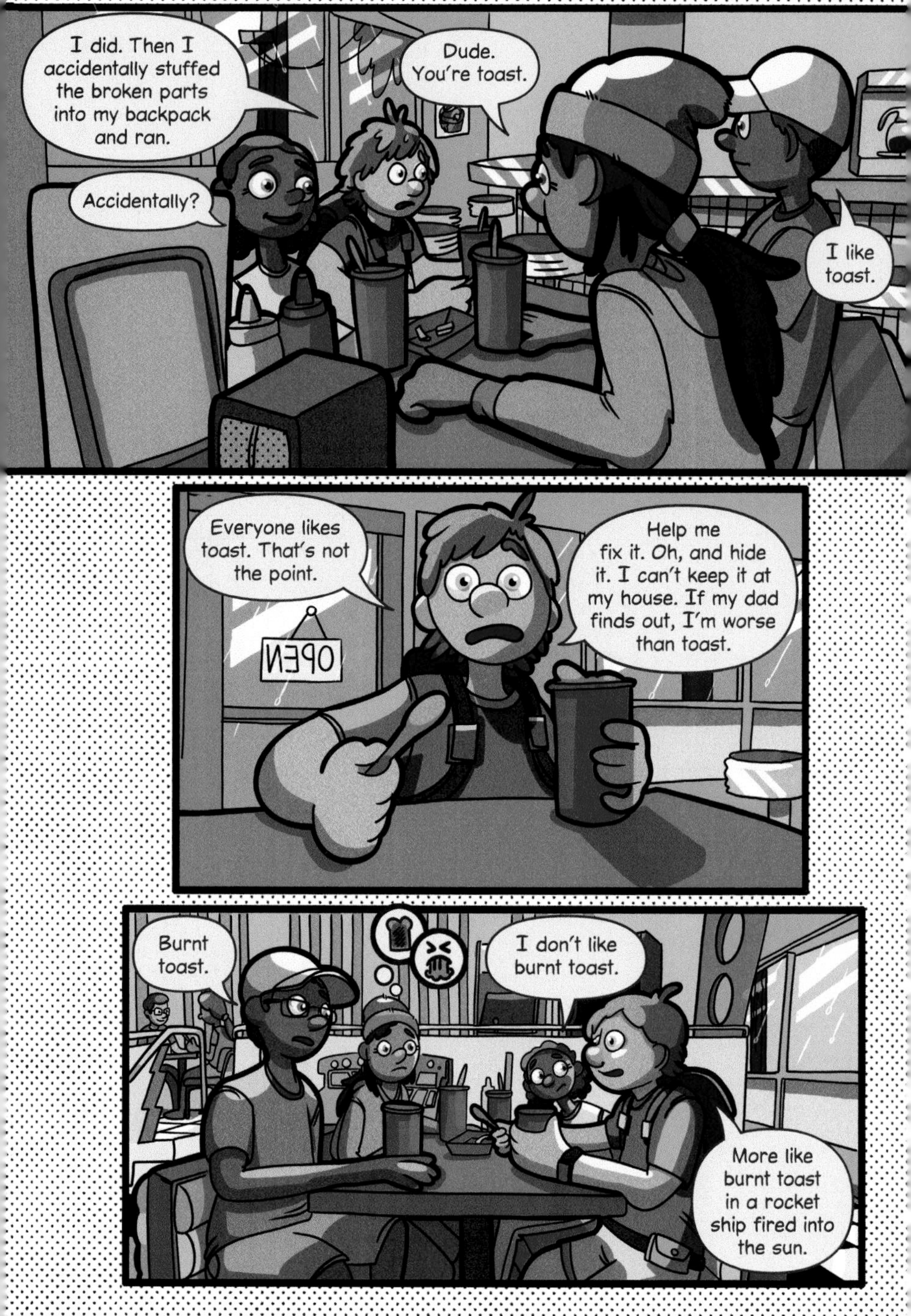
I did. Then I accidentally stuffed the broken parts into my backpack and ran.
Dude. You're toast.
Accidentally?
I like toast.
Everyone likes toast. That's not the point.
Help me fix it. Oh, and hide it. I can't keep it at my house. If my dad finds out, I'm worse than toast.
OPEN
Burnt toast.
I don't like burnt toast.
More like burnt toast in a rocket ship fired into the sun.

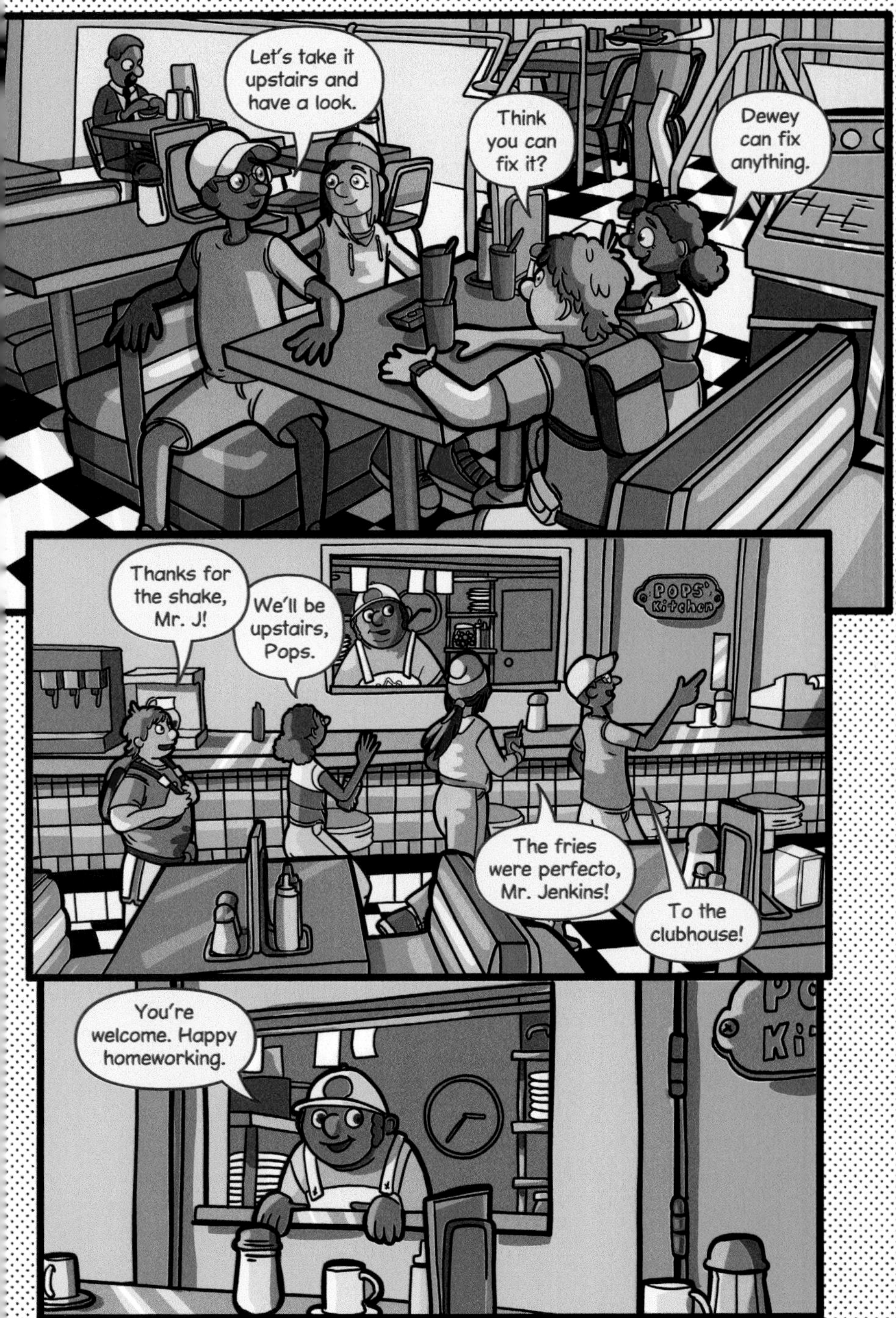
Let's take it upstairs and have a look.
Think you can fix it?
Dewey can fix anything.
Thanks for the shake, Mr. J!
We'll be upstairs, Pops.
POPS' Kitchen
The fries were perfecto, Mr. Jenkins!
To the clubhouse!
You're welcome. Happy homeworking.

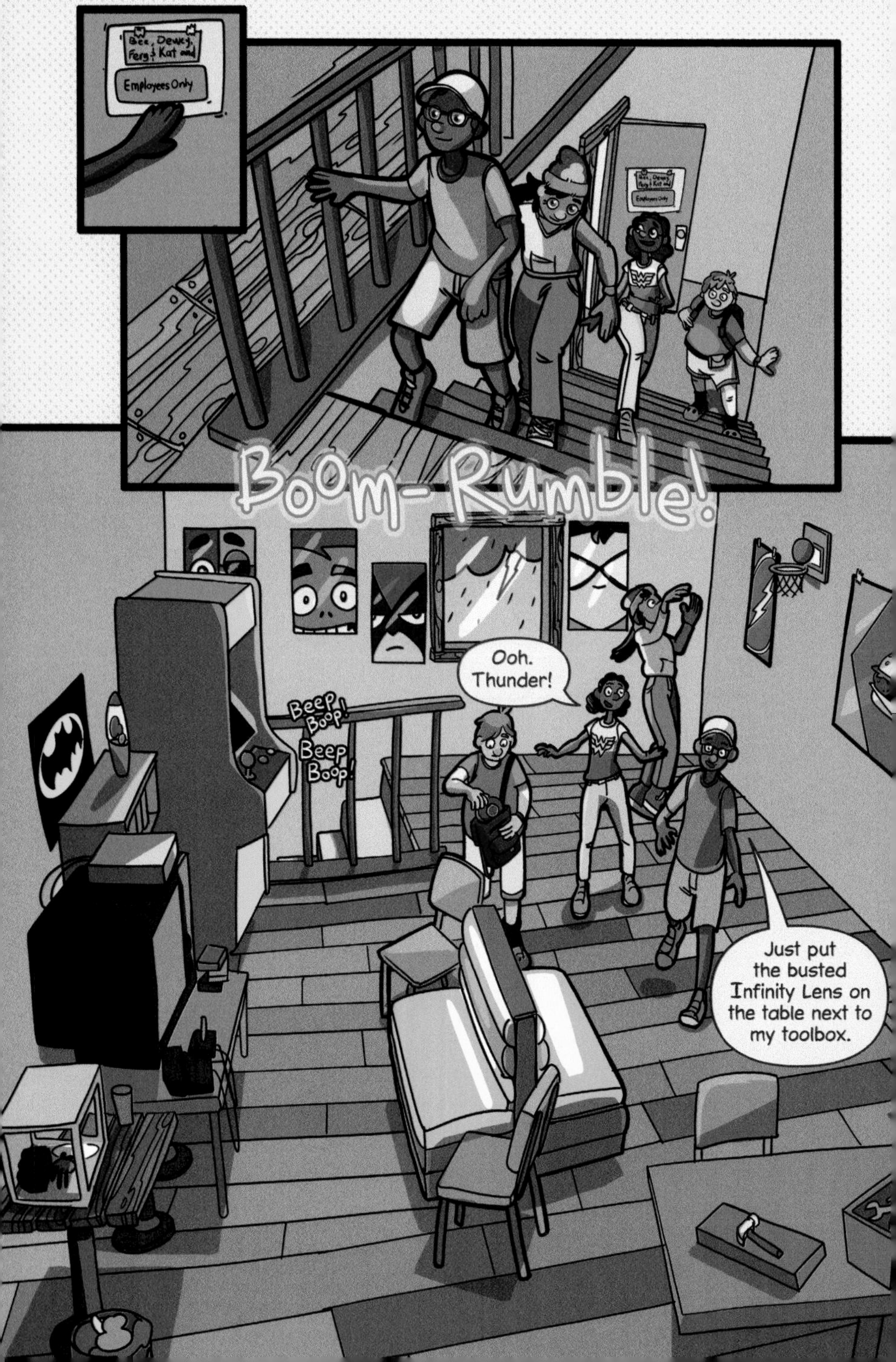
Bee, Dewey, Ferg & Kat and
Employees Only
Boom-Rumble!
Ooh. Thunder!
Beep Boop!
Beep Boop!
Just put the busted Infinity Lens on the table next to my toolbox.

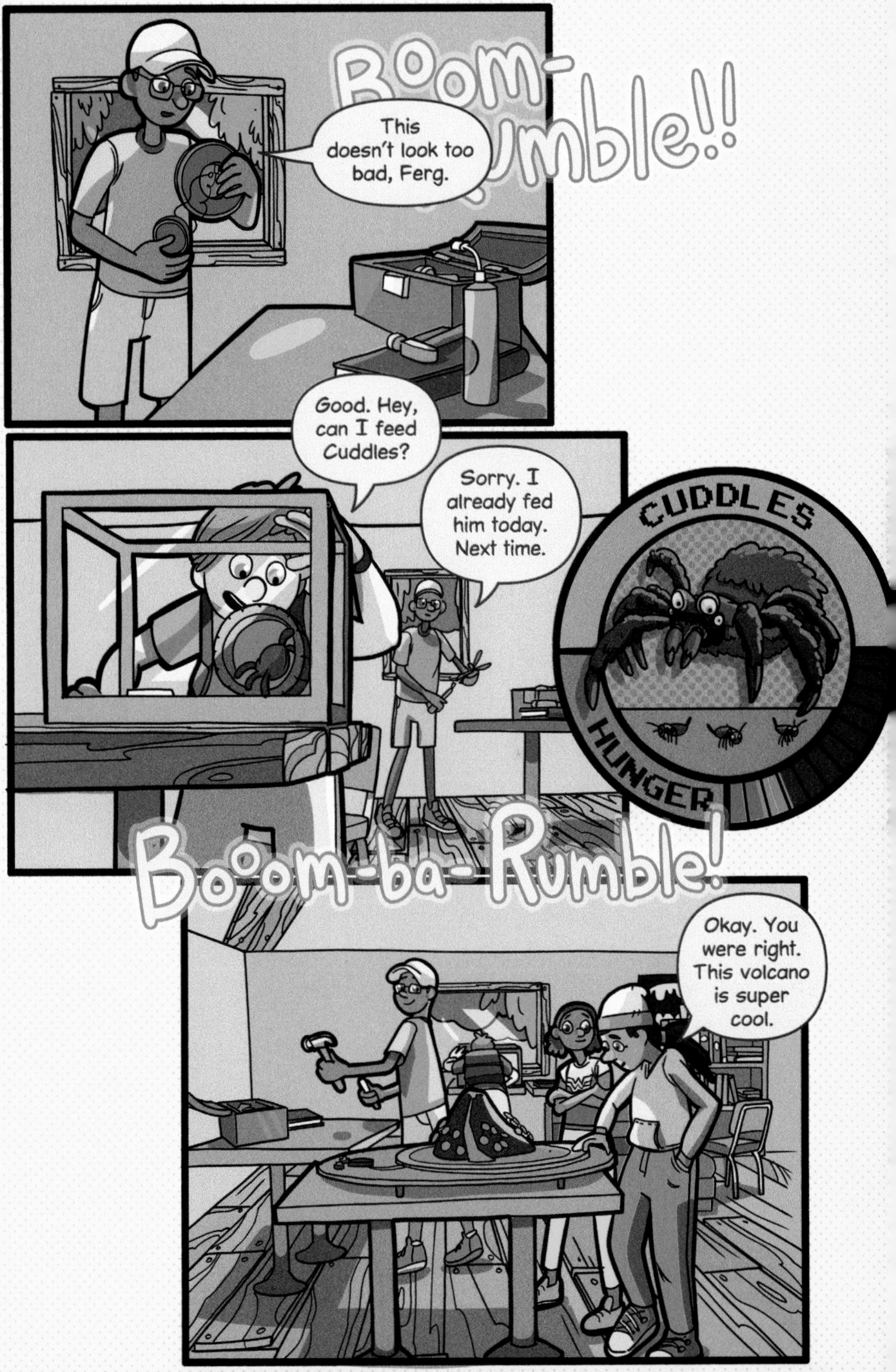
Boom-Rumble!!
This doesn't look too bad, Ferg.
Good. Hey, can I feed Cuddles?
Sorry. I already fed him today. Next time.
CUDDLES
HUNGER
Bo-om-ba-Rumble!
Okay. You were right. This volcano is super cool.

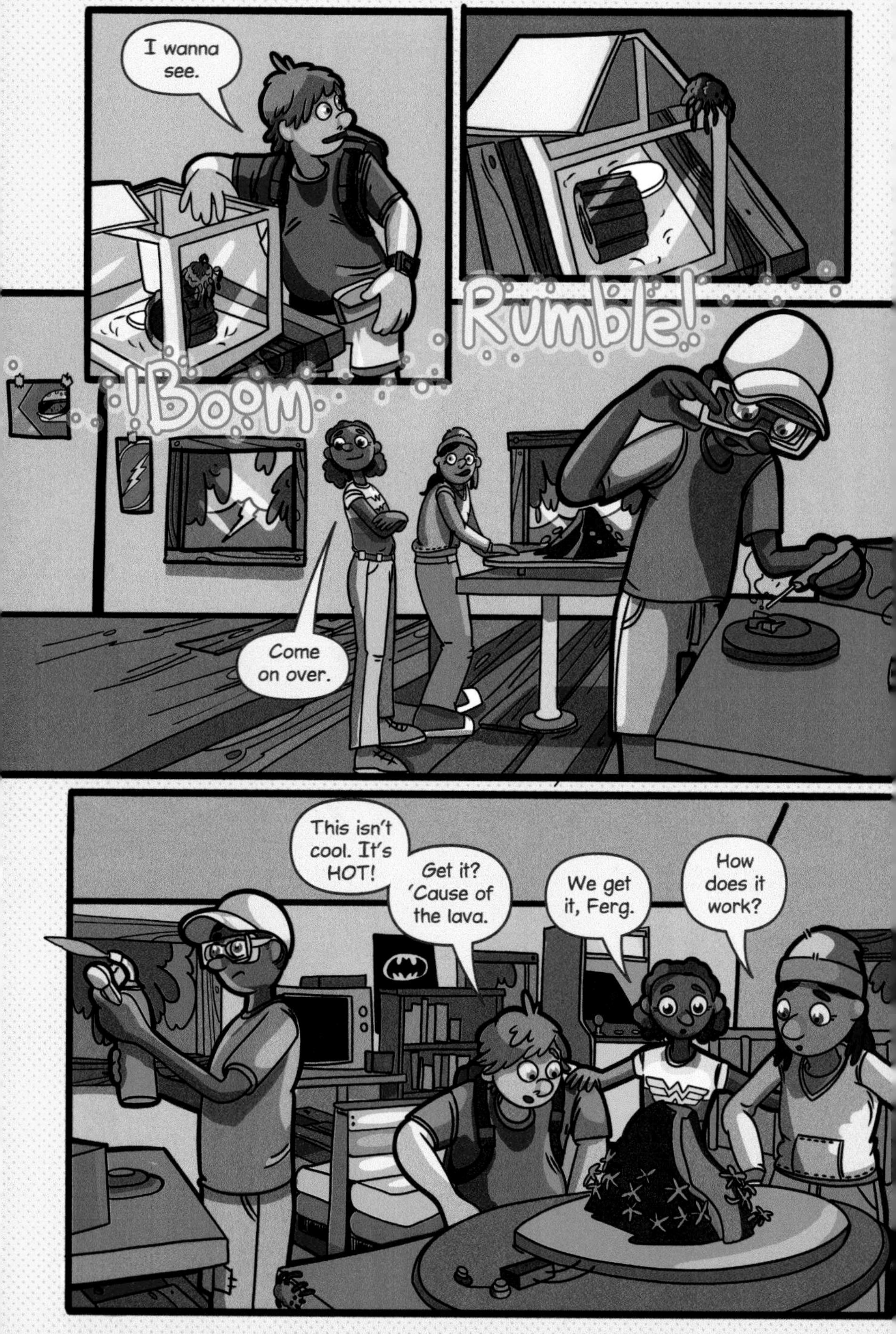
I wanna see.
Rumble!
Boom
Come on over.
This isn't cool. It's HOT!
Get it? 'Cause of the lava.
We get it, Ferg.
How does it work?

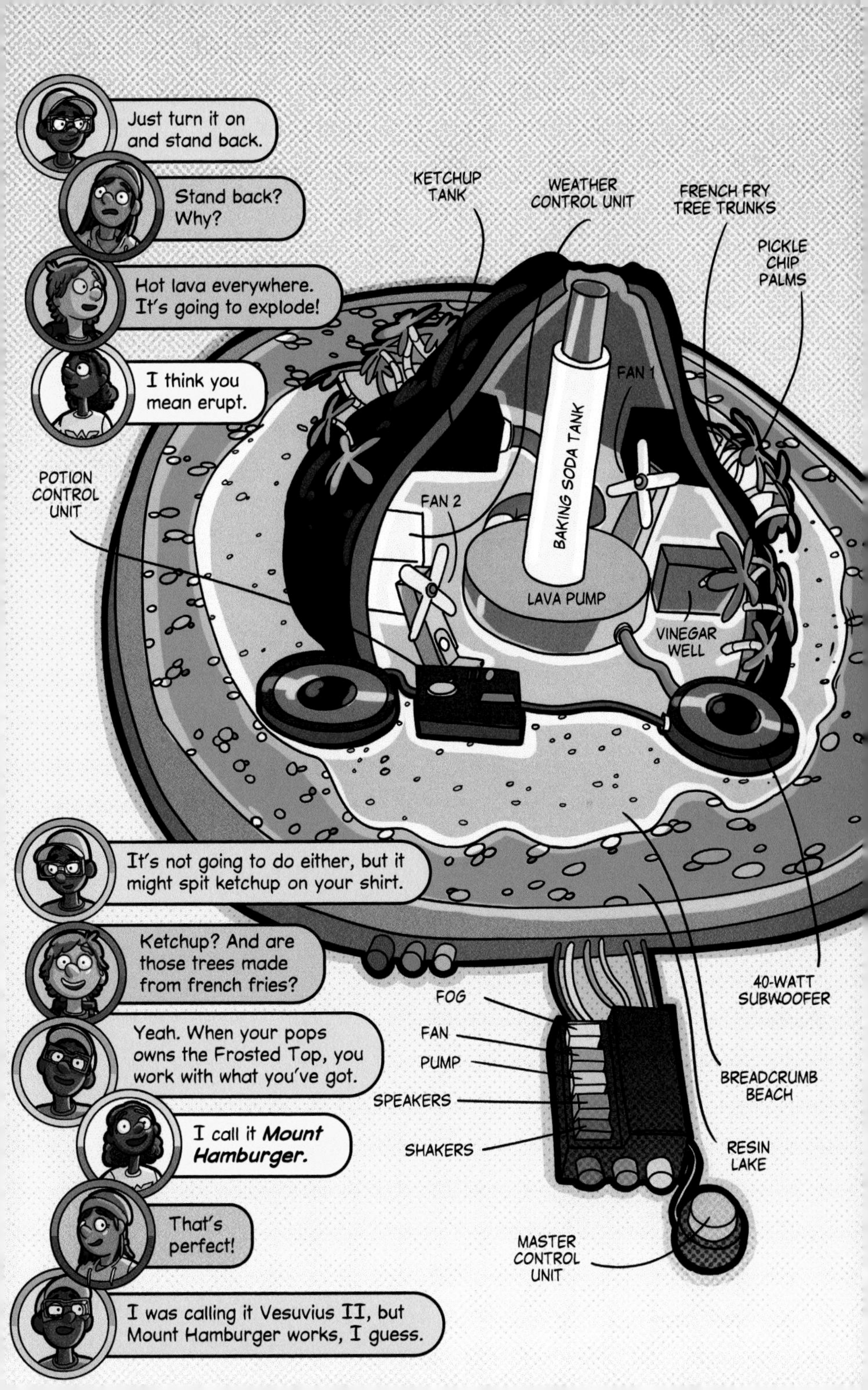

Just turn it on and stand back.
Stand back? Why?
Hot lava everywhere. It's going to explode!
I think you mean erupt.
KETCHUP TANK
WEATHER CONTROL UNIT
FRENCH FRY TREE TRUNKS
PICKLE CHIP PALMS
FAN 1
BAKING SODA TANK
POTION CONTROL UNIT
FAN 2
LAVA PUMP
VINEGAR WELL
It's not going to do either, but it might spit ketchup on your shirt.
Ketchup? And are those trees made from french fries?
Yeah. When your pops owns the Frosted Top, you work with what you've got.
I call it *Mount Hamburger.*
That's perfect!
I was calling it Vesuvius II, but Mount Hamburger works, I guess.
FOG
FAN
PUMP
SPEAKERS
SHAKERS
40-WATT SUBWOOFER
BREADCRUMB BEACH
RESIN LAKE
MASTER CONTROL UNIT

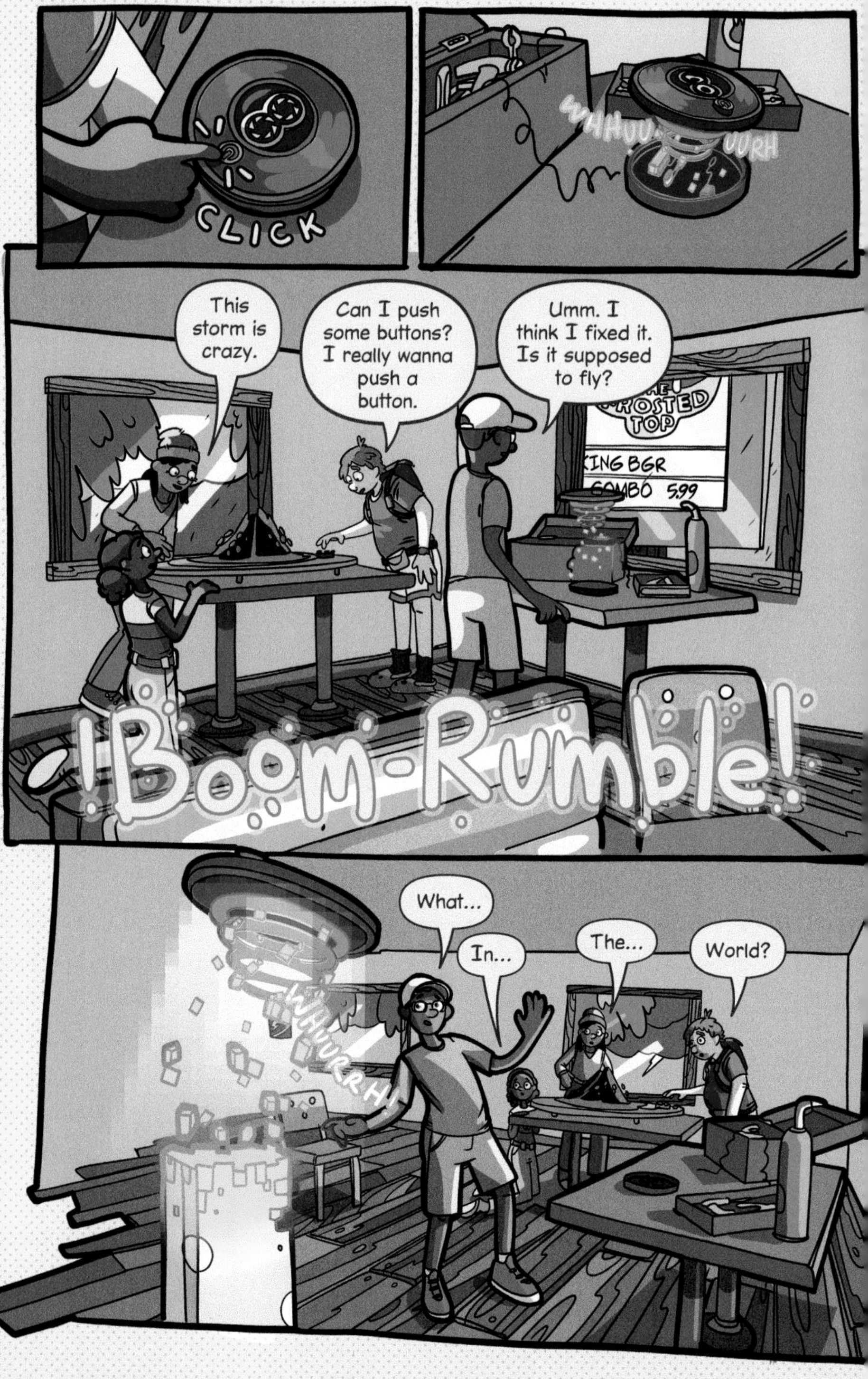
CLICK
WHHUUURH
This storm is crazy.
Can I push some buttons? I really wanna push a button.
Umm. I think I fixed it. Is it supposed to fly?
THE FROSTED TOP
KING BGR
COMBO 5.99
!Boom-Rumble!
What...
In...
The...
World?
WHHUURRH!

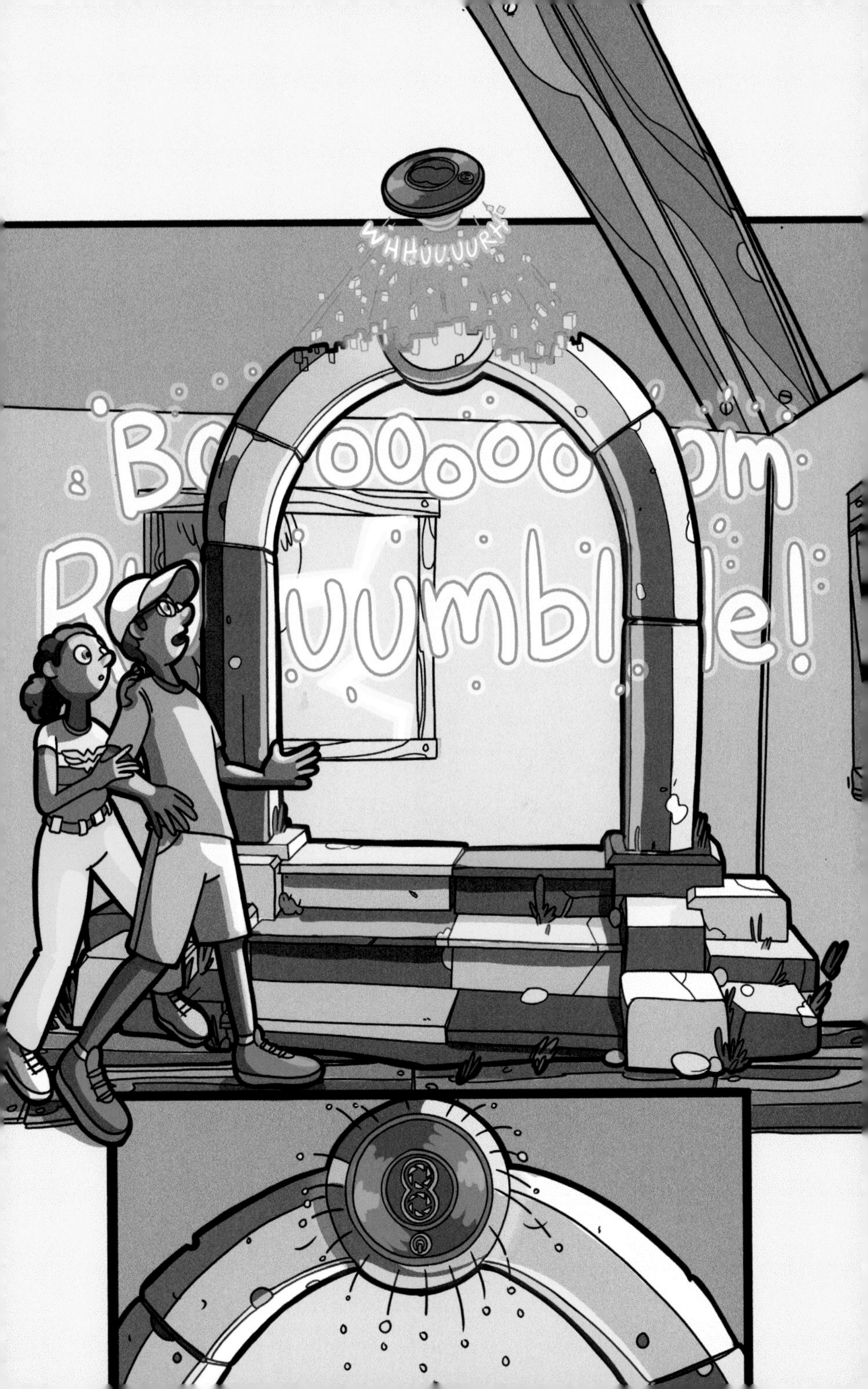
WHHUUUURH
Bo…OOoOOO…om
R… uumbl…le!

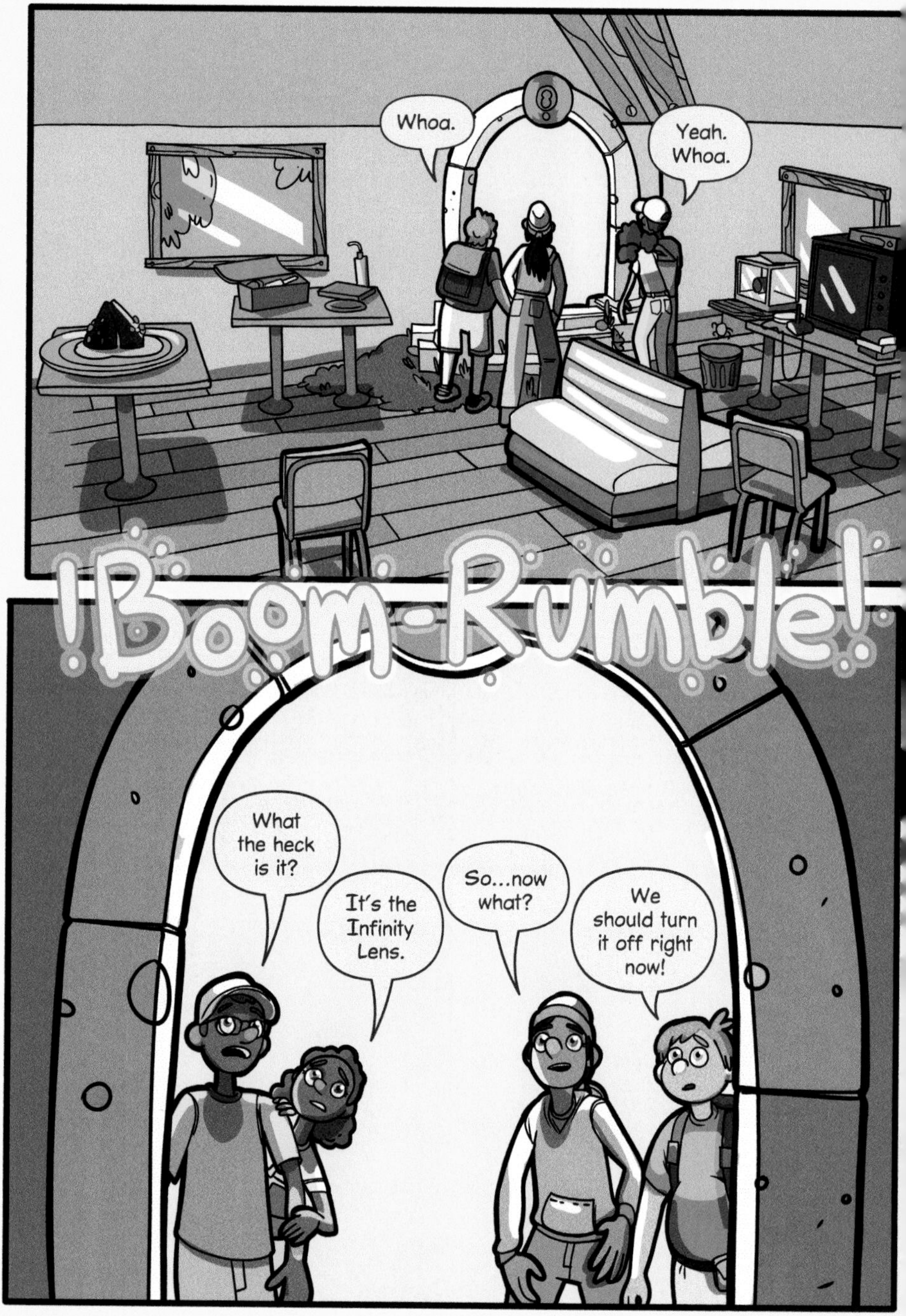
Whoa.
Yeah. Whoa.
!Boom-Rumble!
What the heck is it?
It's the Infinity Lens.
So...now what?
We should turn it off right now!

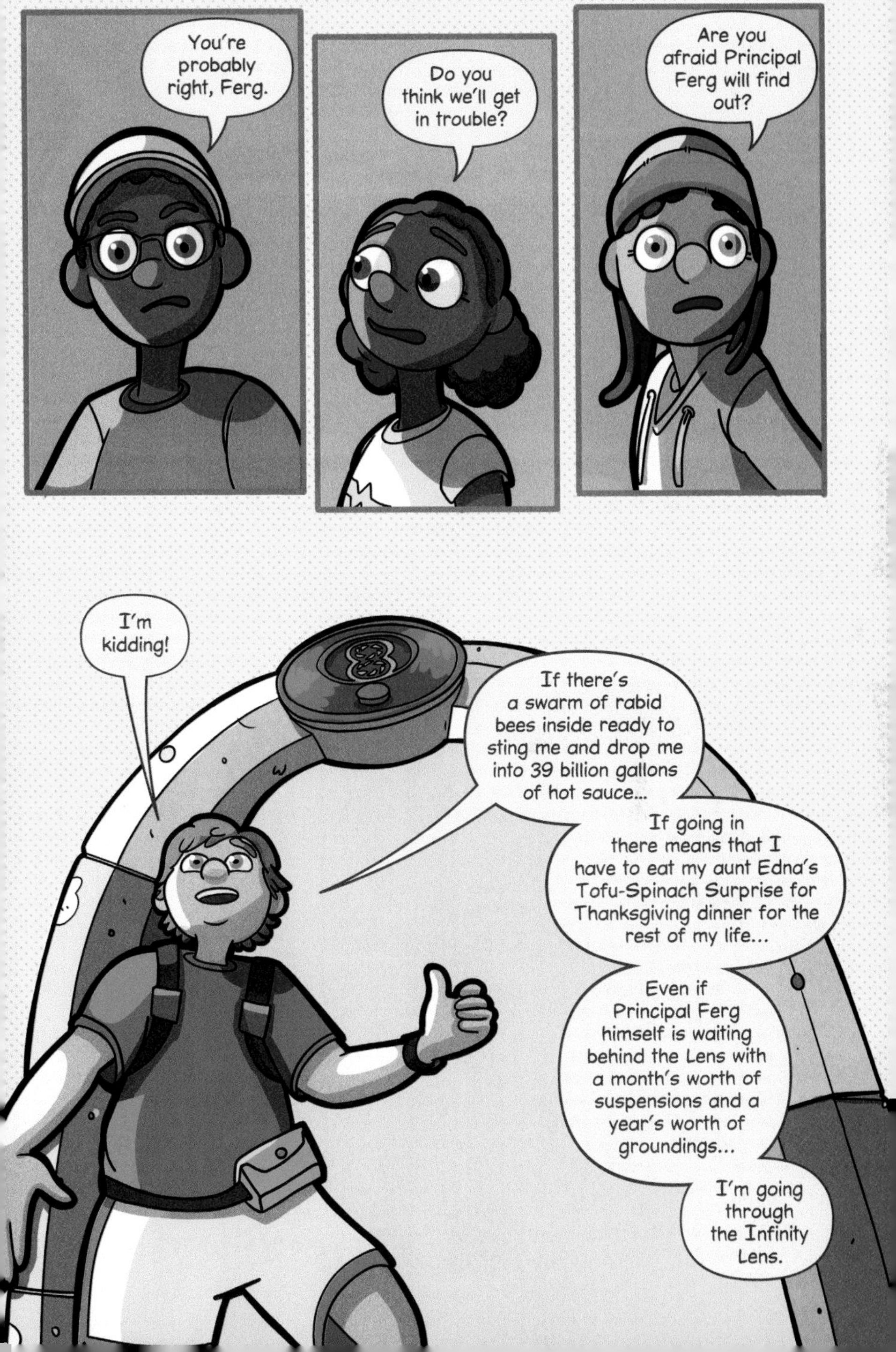
You're probably right, Ferg.
Do you think we'll get in trouble?
Are you afraid Principal Ferg will find out?
I'm kidding!
If there's a swarm of rabid bees inside ready to sting me and drop me into 39 billion gallons of hot sauce...
If going in there means that I have to eat my aunt Edna's Tofu-Spinach Surprise for Thanksgiving dinner for the rest of my life...
Even if Principal Ferg himself is waiting behind the Lens with a month's worth of suspensions and a year's worth of groundings...
I'm going through the Infinity Lens.

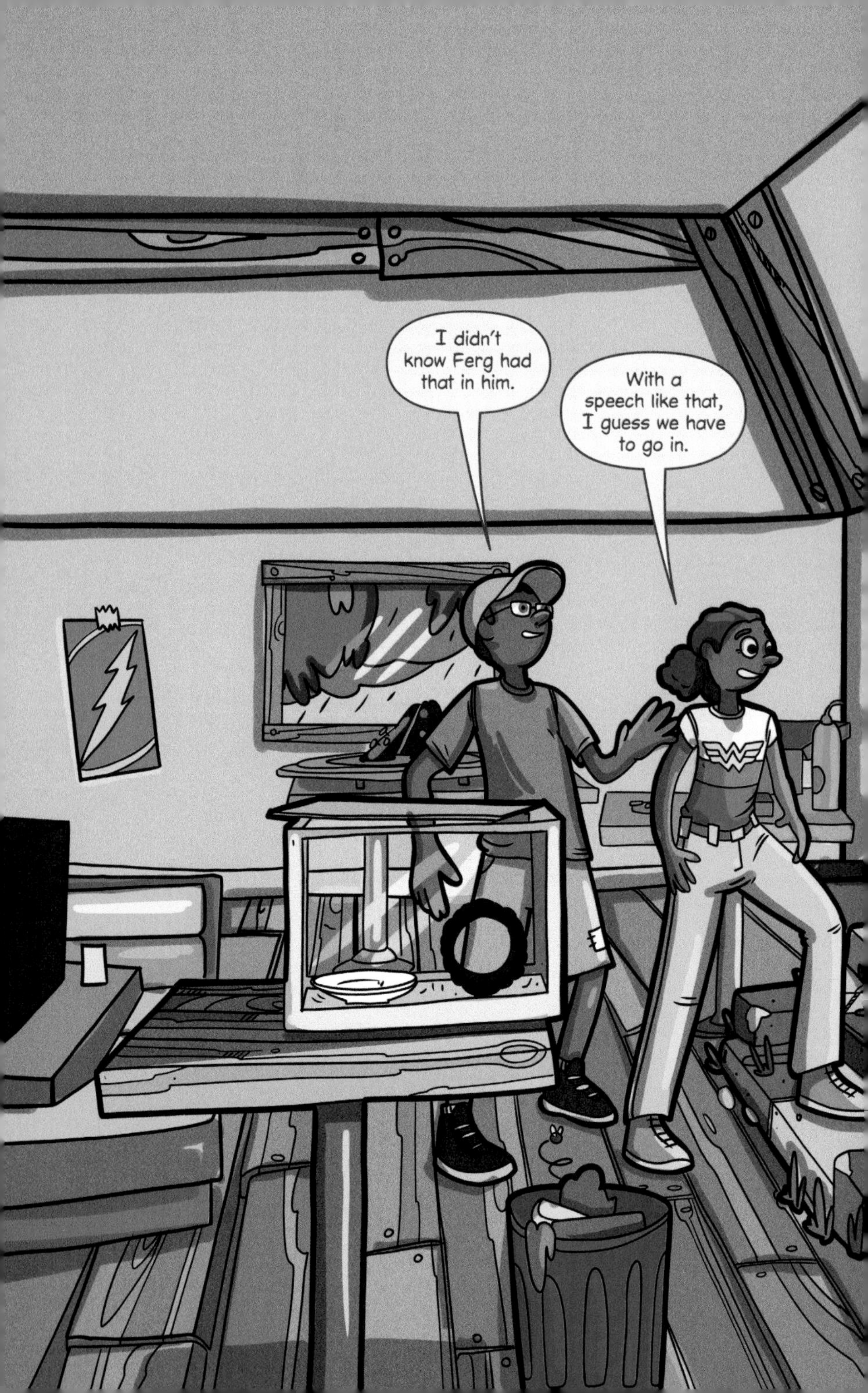
I didn't know Ferg had that in him.
With a speech like that, I guess we have to go in.

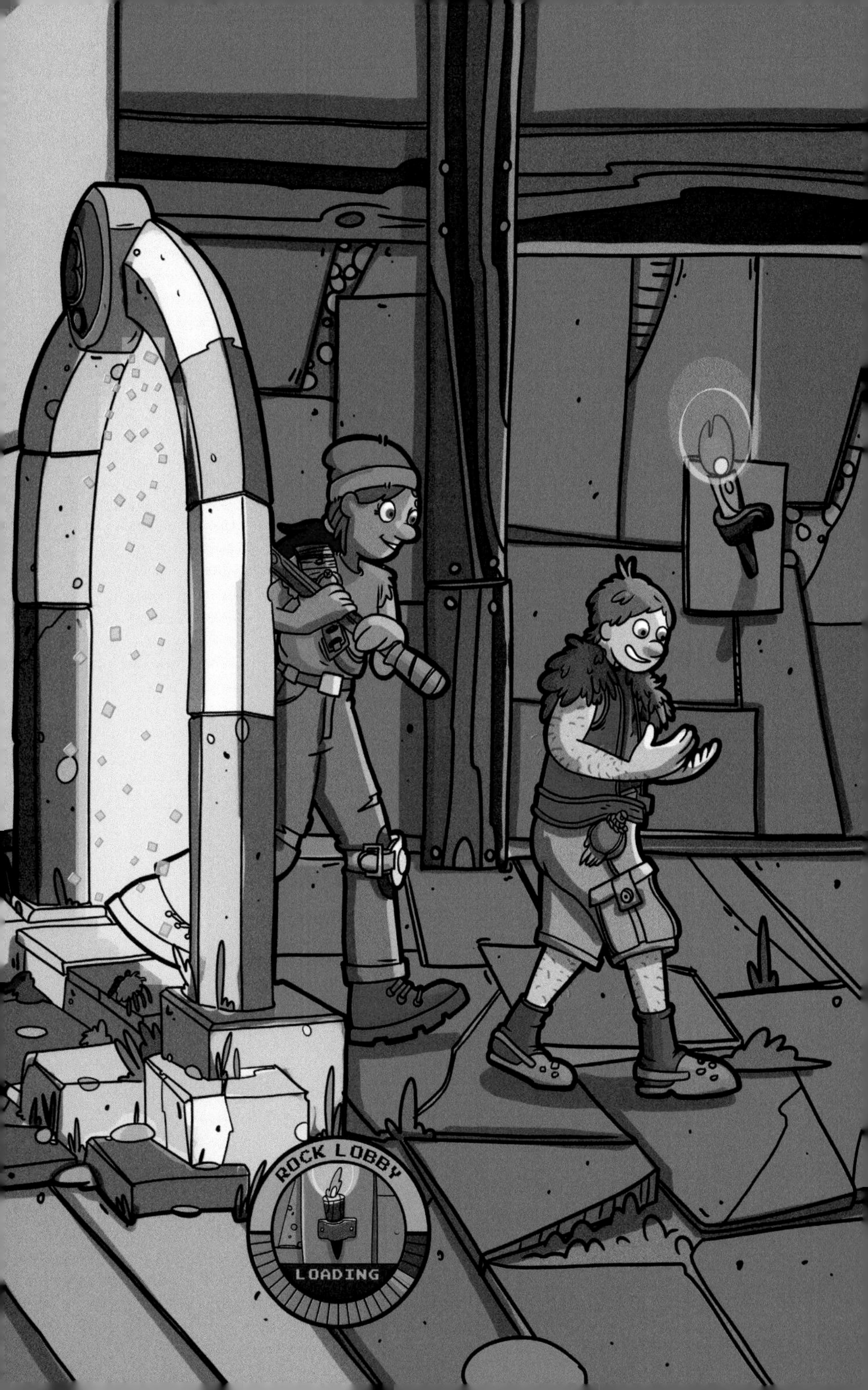
ROCK LOBBY
LOADING

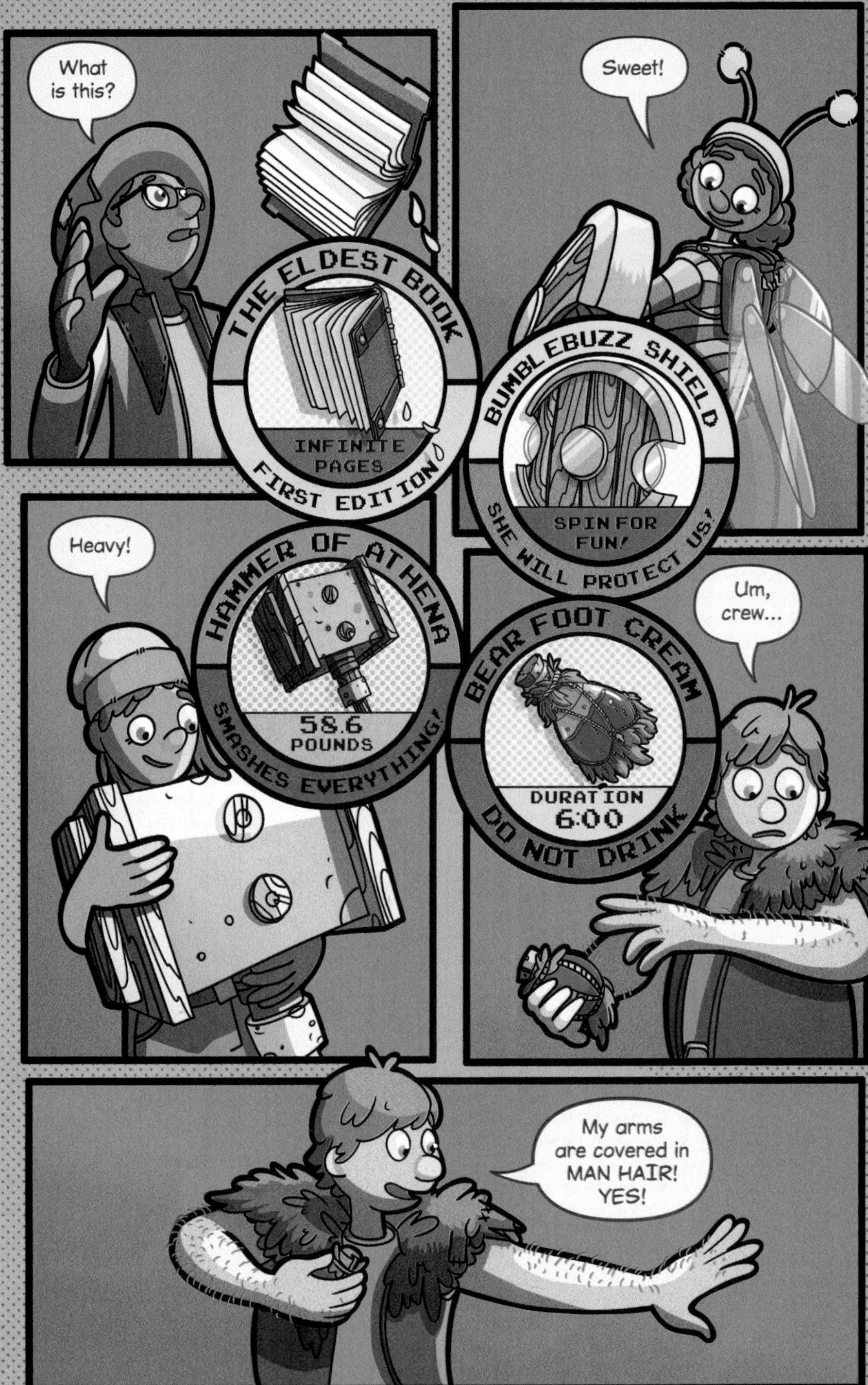
What is this?
THE ELDEST BOOK
INFINITE PAGES
FIRST EDITION
Sweet!
BUMBLEBUZZ SHIELD
SPIN FOR FUN!
SHE WILL PROTECT US!
Heavy!
HAMMER OF ATHENA
58.6 POUNDS
SMASHES EVERYTHING!
Um, crew...
BEAR FOOT CREAM
DURATION 6:00
DO NOT DRINK
My arms are covered in MAN HAIR! YES!

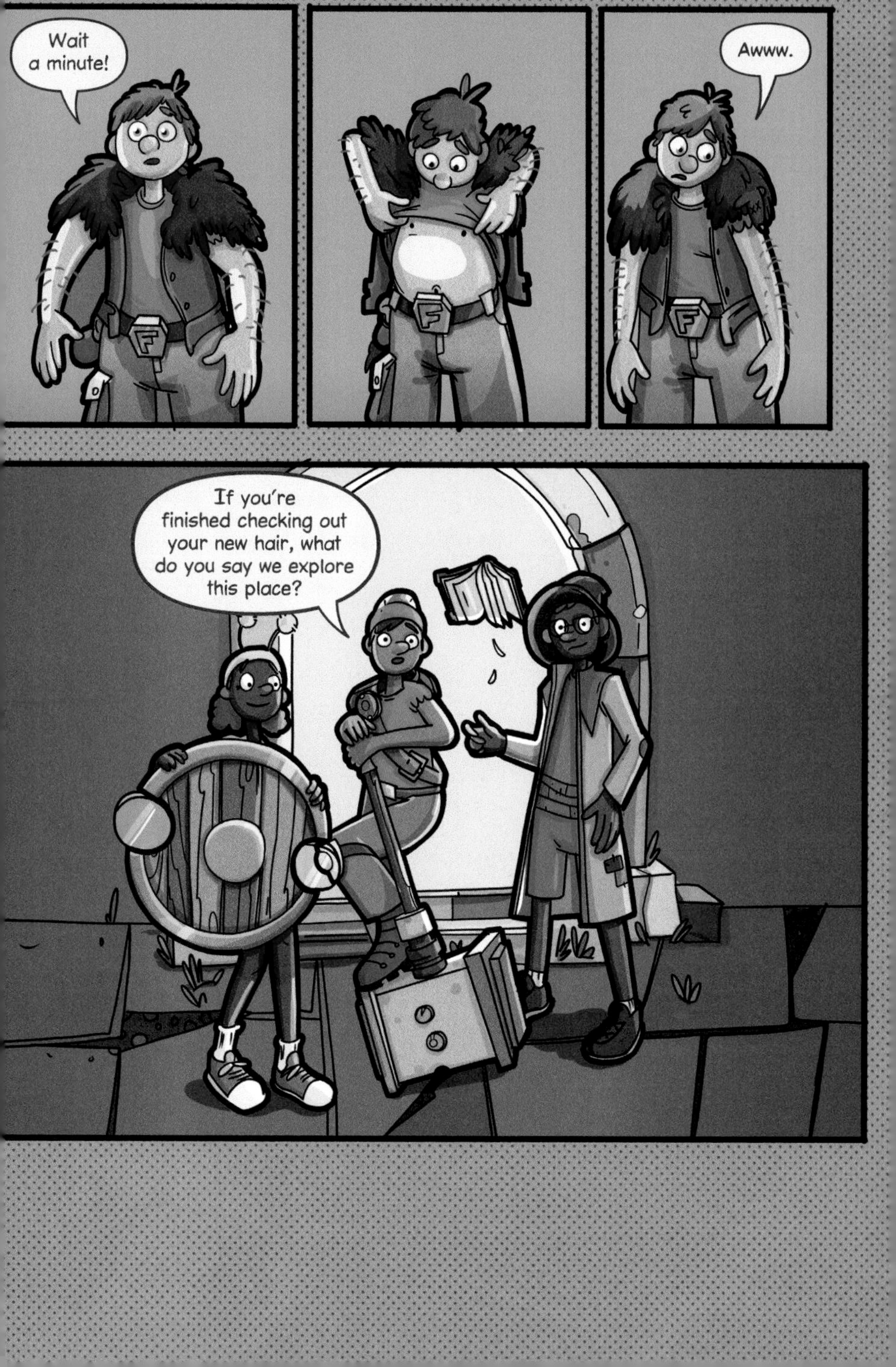
Wait a minute!
Awww.
If you're finished checking out your new hair, what do you say we explore this place?

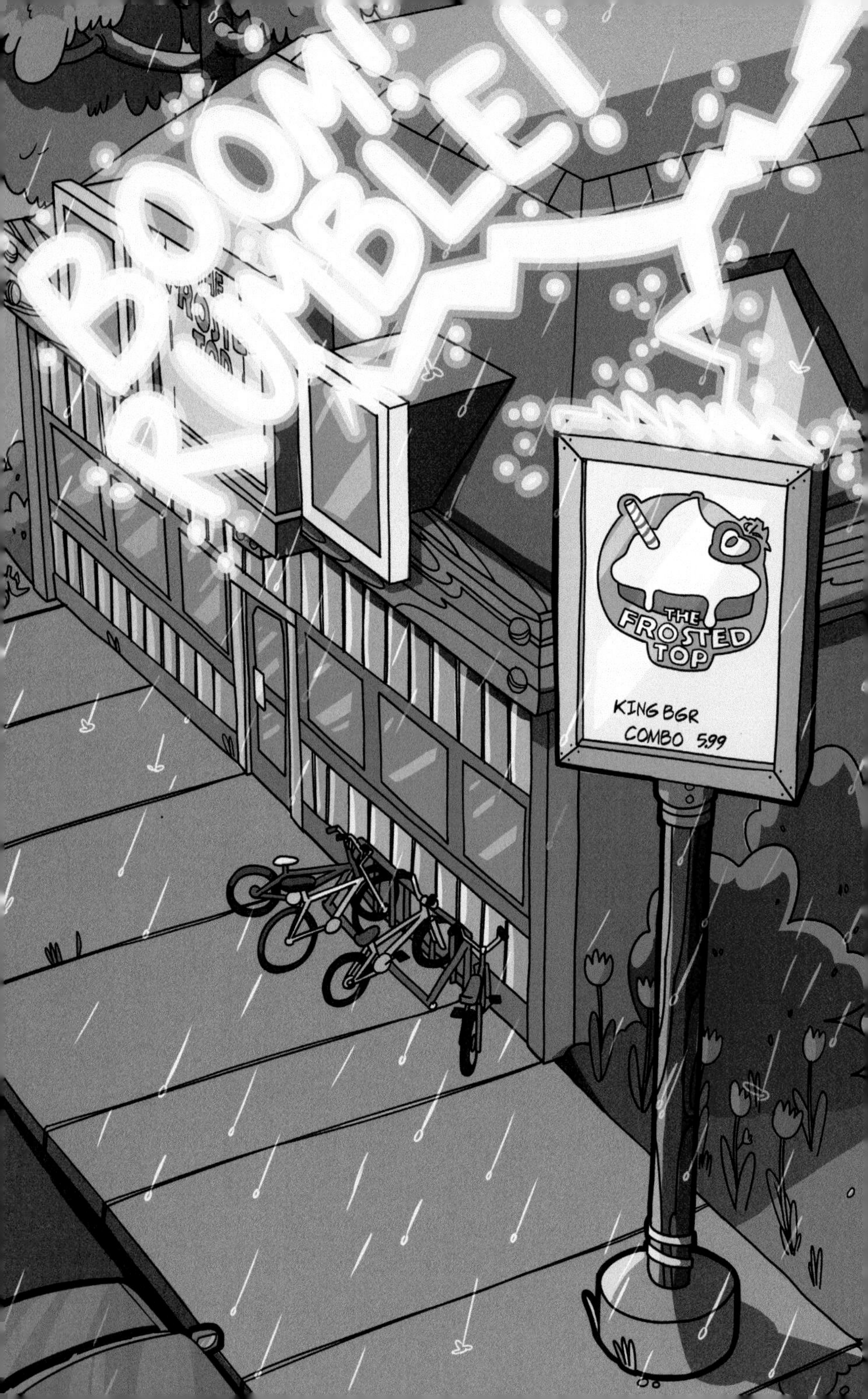
BOOM! RUMBLE!
THE FROSTED TOP
KING BGR
COMBO 5.99

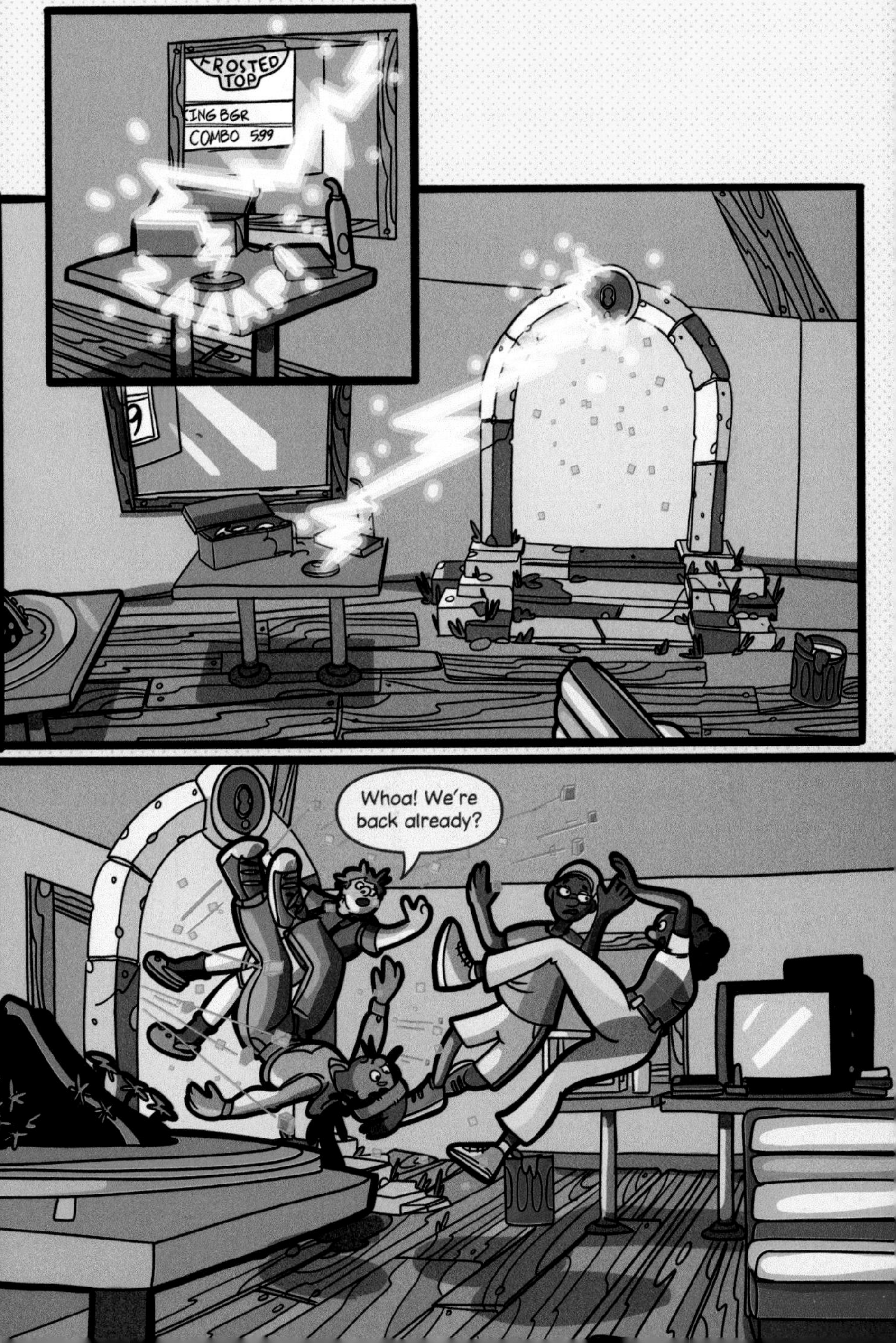
FROSTED TOP
COMBO 5.99
Whoa! We're back already?

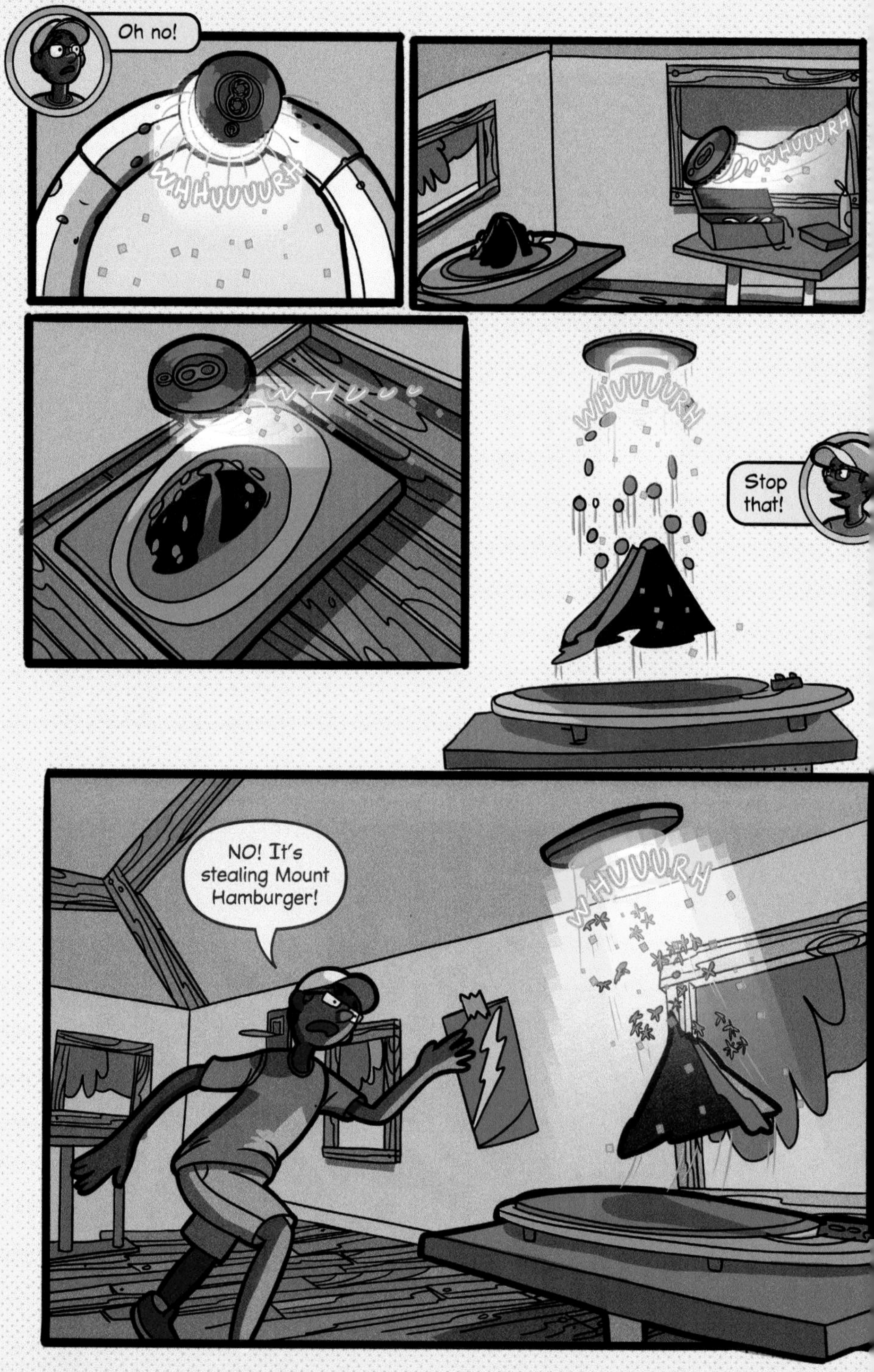
Oh no!
WHHUUUURH
WHUUURH
WHUUU
WHUUUURH
Stop that!
NO! It's stealing Mount Hamburger!
WHUUURH

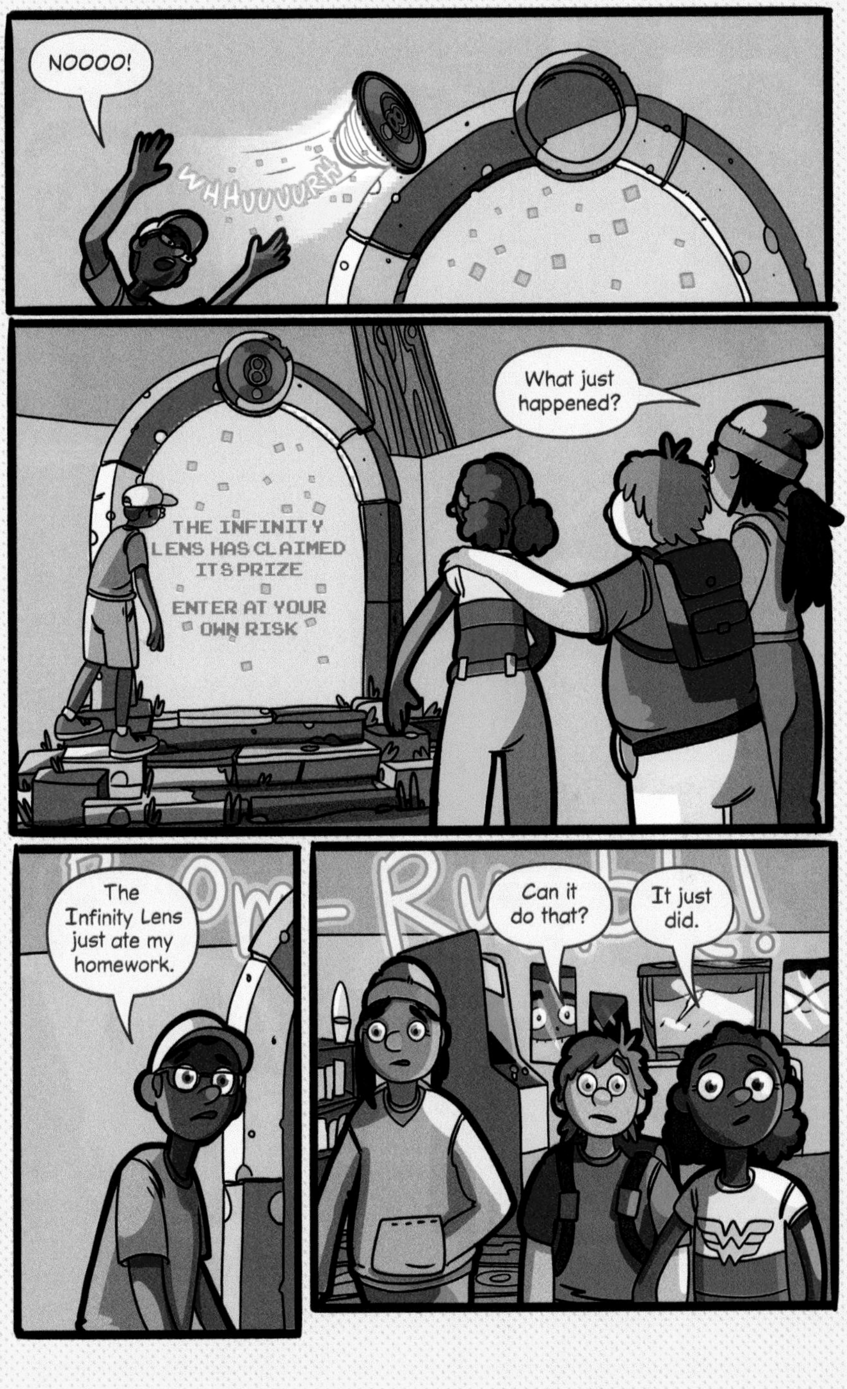
NOOOO!
WHHUUUURH
What just happened?
THE INFINITY LENS HAS CLAIMED ITS PRIZE
ENTER AT YOUR OWN RISK
The Infinity Lens just ate my homework.
Can it do that?
It just did.

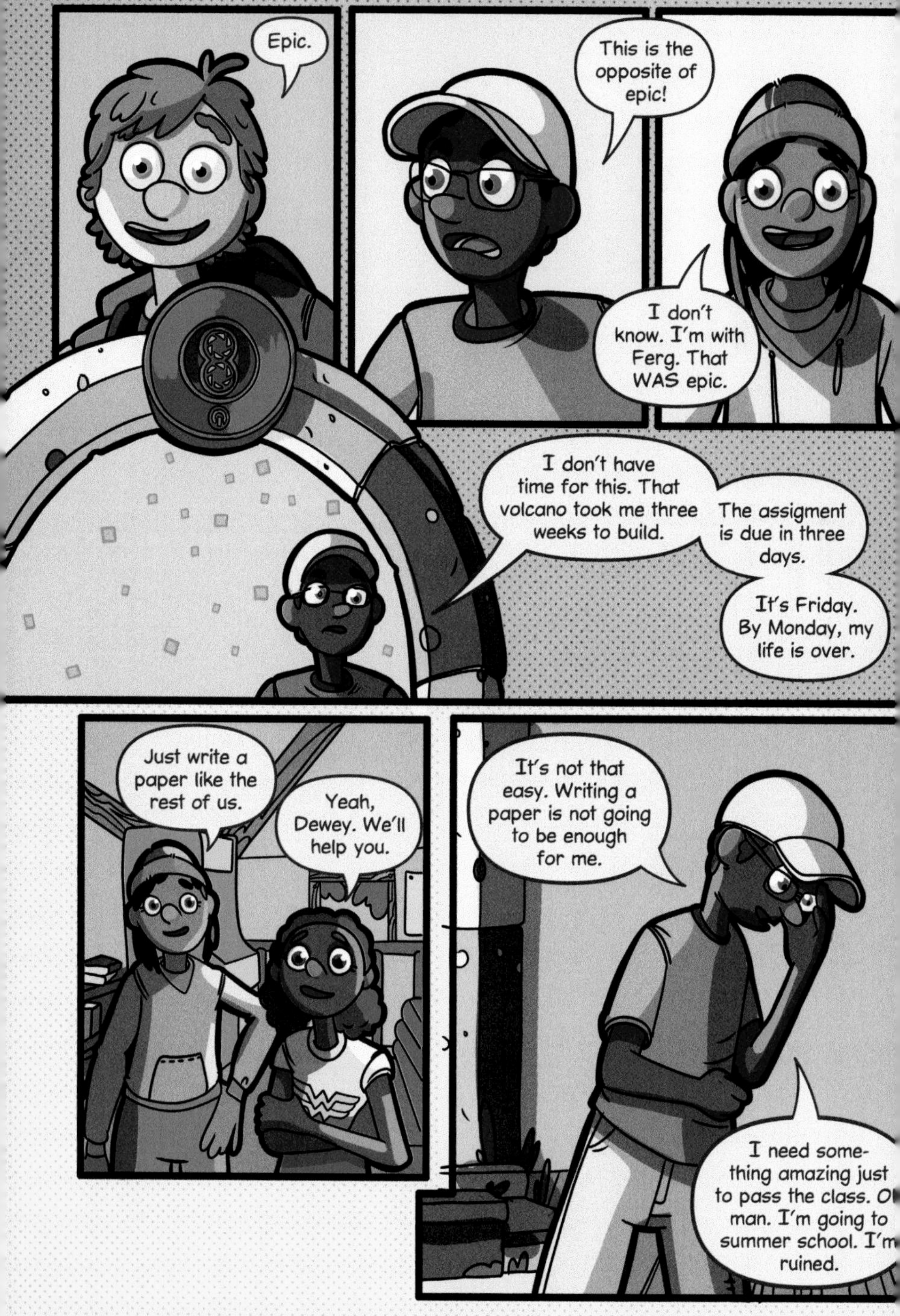
Epic.
This is the opposite of epic!
I don't know. I'm with Ferg. That WAS epic.
I don't have time for this. That volcano took me three weeks to build.
The assigment is due in three days.
It's Friday. By Monday, my life is over.
Just write a paper like the rest of us.
Yeah, Dewey. We'll help you.
It's not that easy. Writing a paper is not going to be enough for me.
I need something amazing just to pass the class. O man. I'm going to summer school. I'm ruined.

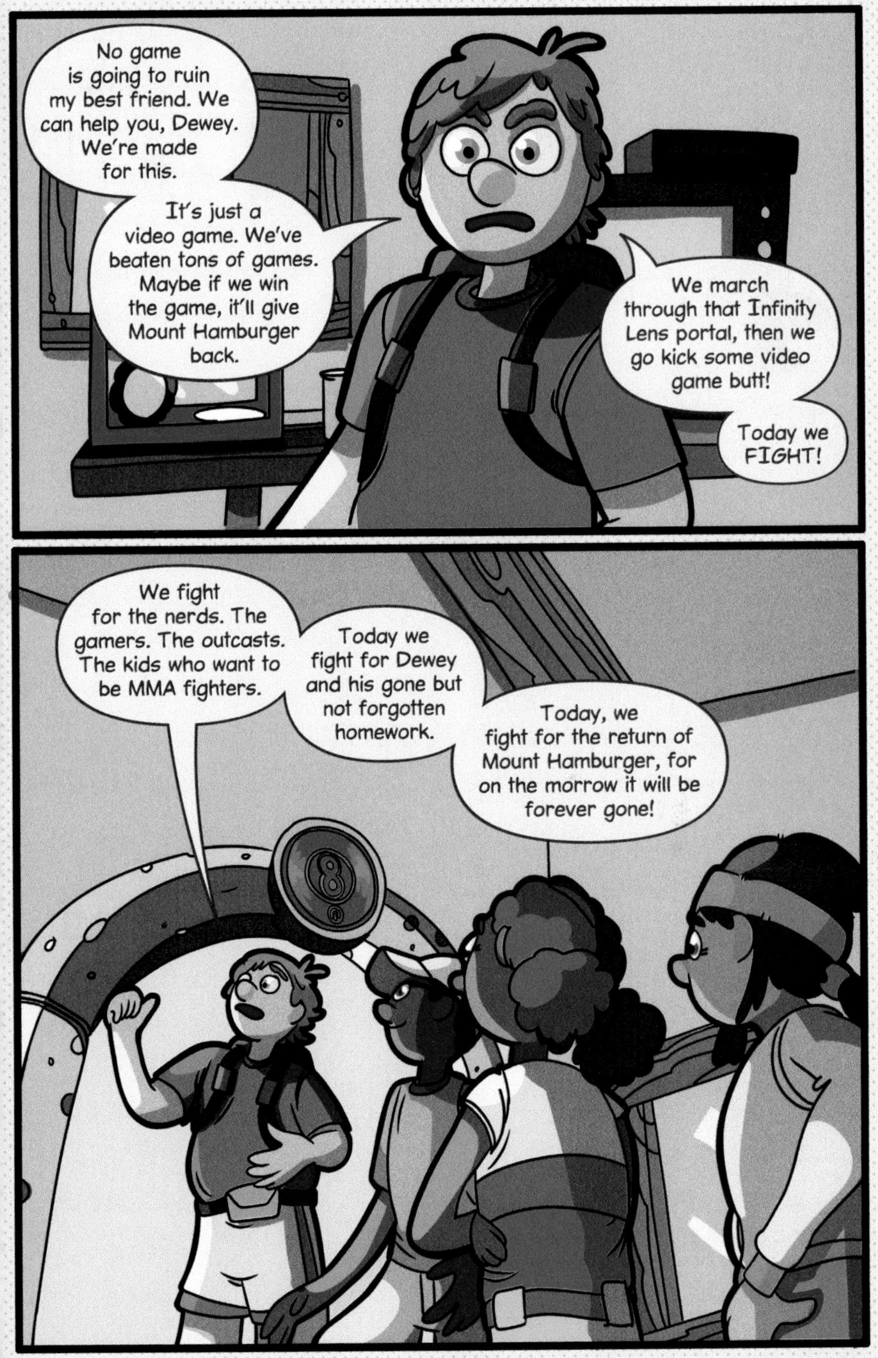

No game is going to ruin my best friend. We can help you, Dewey. We're made for this.
It's just a video game. We've beaten tons of games. Maybe if we win the game, it'll give Mount Hamburger back.
We march through that Infinity Lens portal, then we go kick some video game butt!
Today we FIGHT!
We fight for the nerds. The gamers. The outcasts. The kids who want to be MMA fighters.
Today we fight for Dewey and his gone but not forgotten homework.
Today, we fight for the return of Mount Hamburger, for on the morrow it will be forever gone!

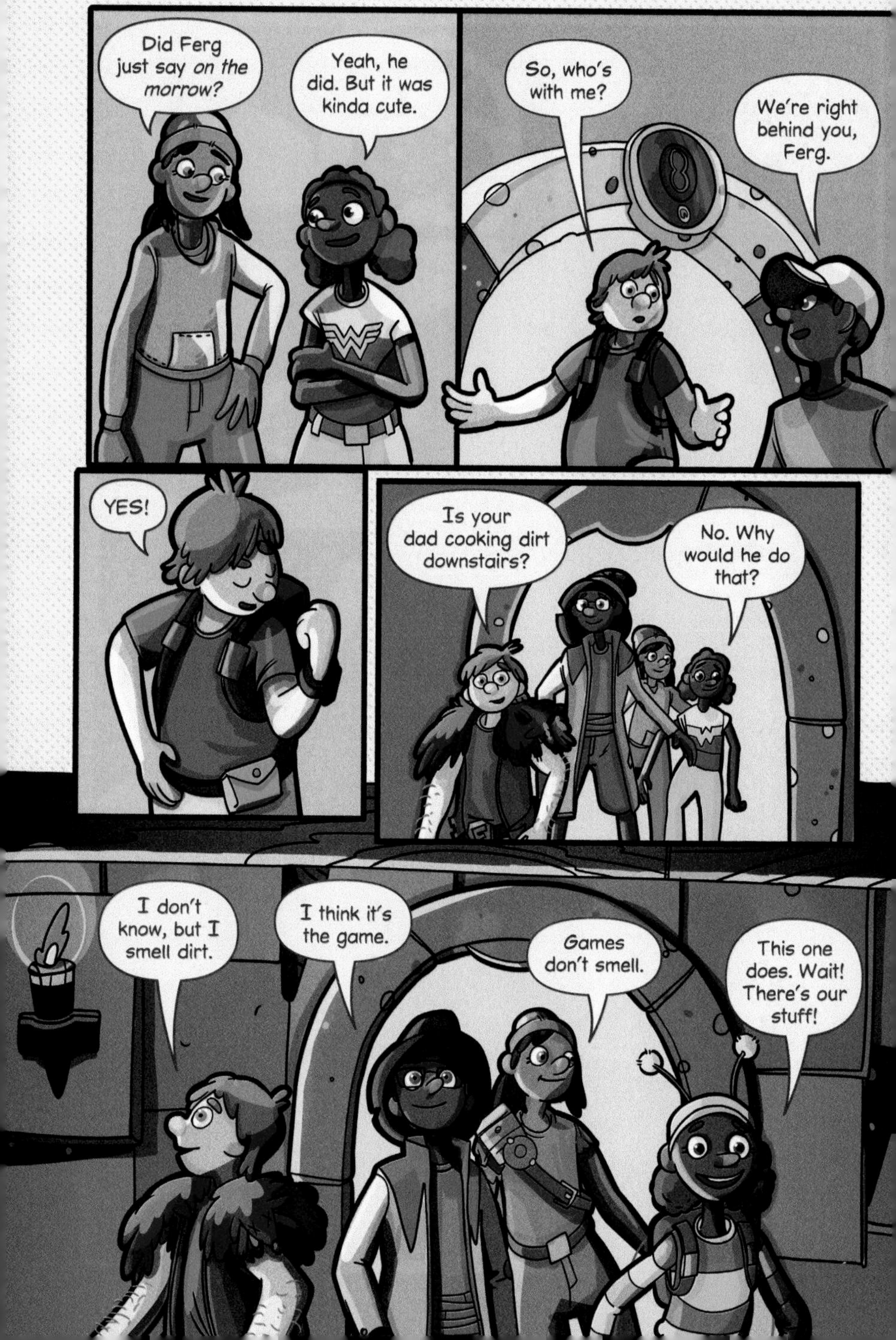
Did Ferg just say *on the morrow?*
Yeah, he did. But it was kinda cute.
So, who's with me?
We're right behind you, Ferg.
YES!
Is your dad cooking dirt downstairs?
No. Why would he do that?
I don't know, but I smell dirt.
I think it's the game.
Games don't smell.
This one does. Wait! There's our stuff!

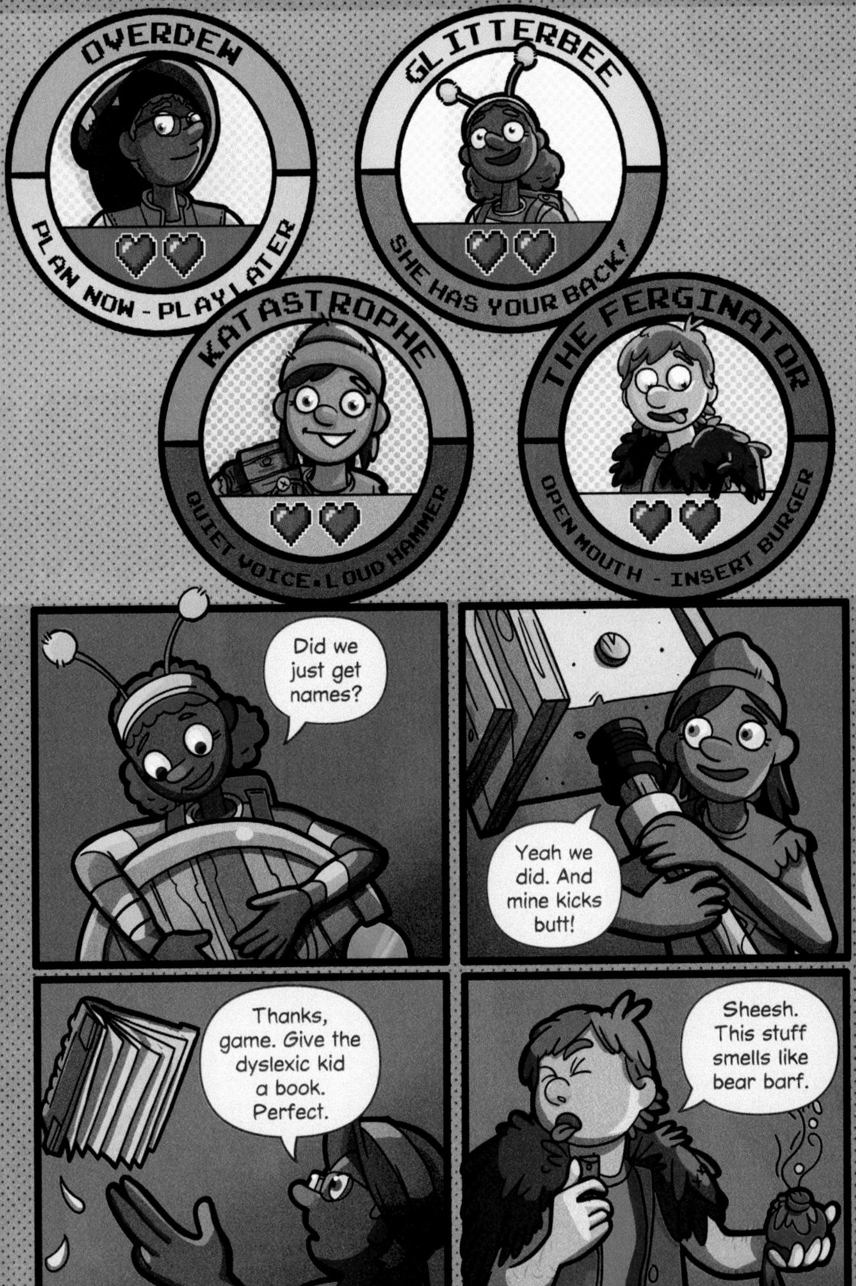
OVERDEW
PLAN NOW - PLAY LATER
GLITTERBEE
SHE HAS YOUR BACK!
KATASTROPHE
QUIET VOICE • LOUD HAMMER
THE FERGINATOR
OPEN MOUTH - INSERT BURGER
Did we just get names?
Yeah we did. And mine kicks butt!
Thanks, game. Give the dyslexic kid a book. Perfect.
Sheesh. This stuff smells like bear barf.

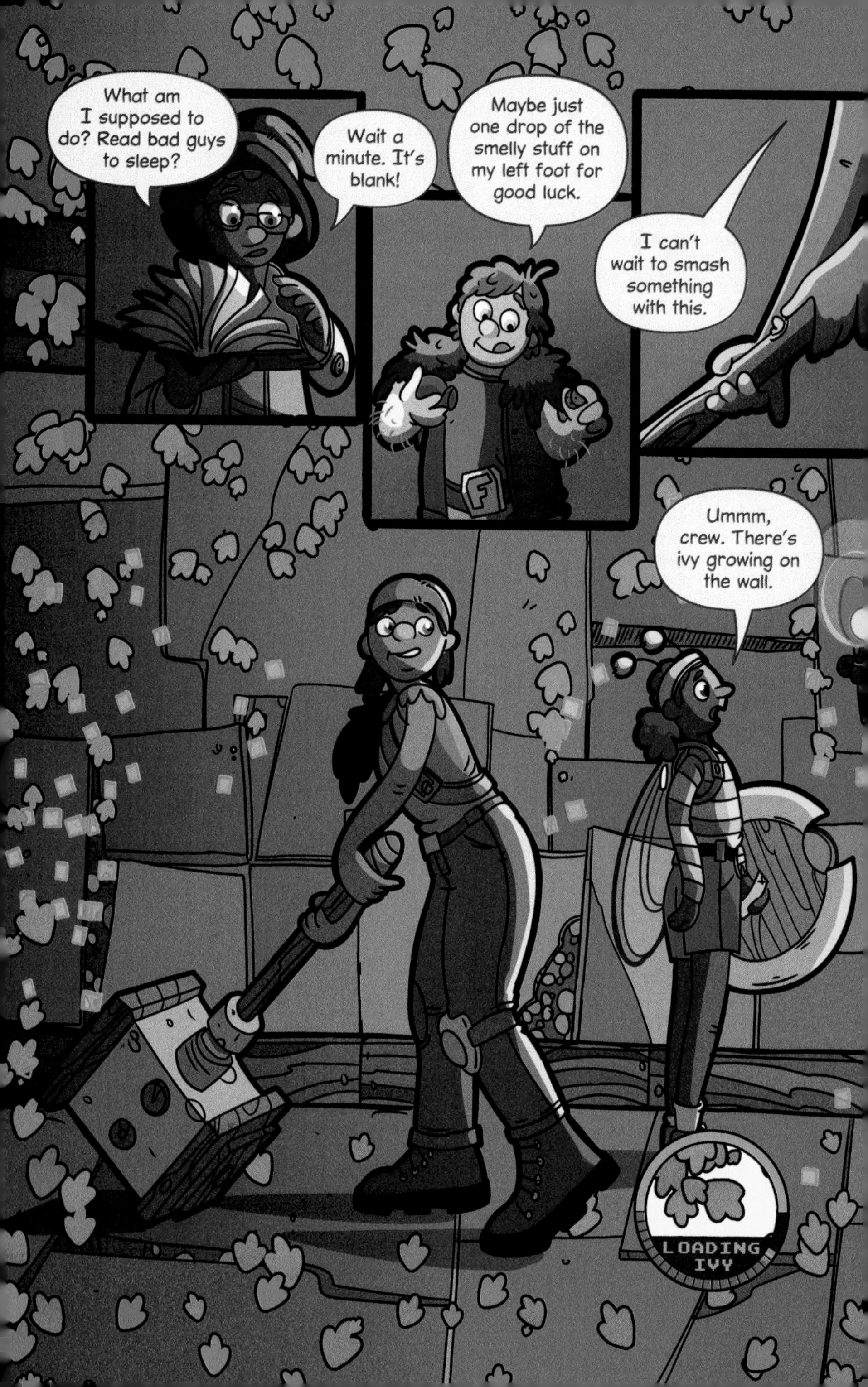
What am I supposed to do? Read bad guys to sleep?
Wait a minute. It's blank!
Maybe just one drop of the smelly stuff on my left foot for good luck.
I can't wait to smash something with this.
Ummm, crew. There's ivy growing on the wall.
LOADING IVY

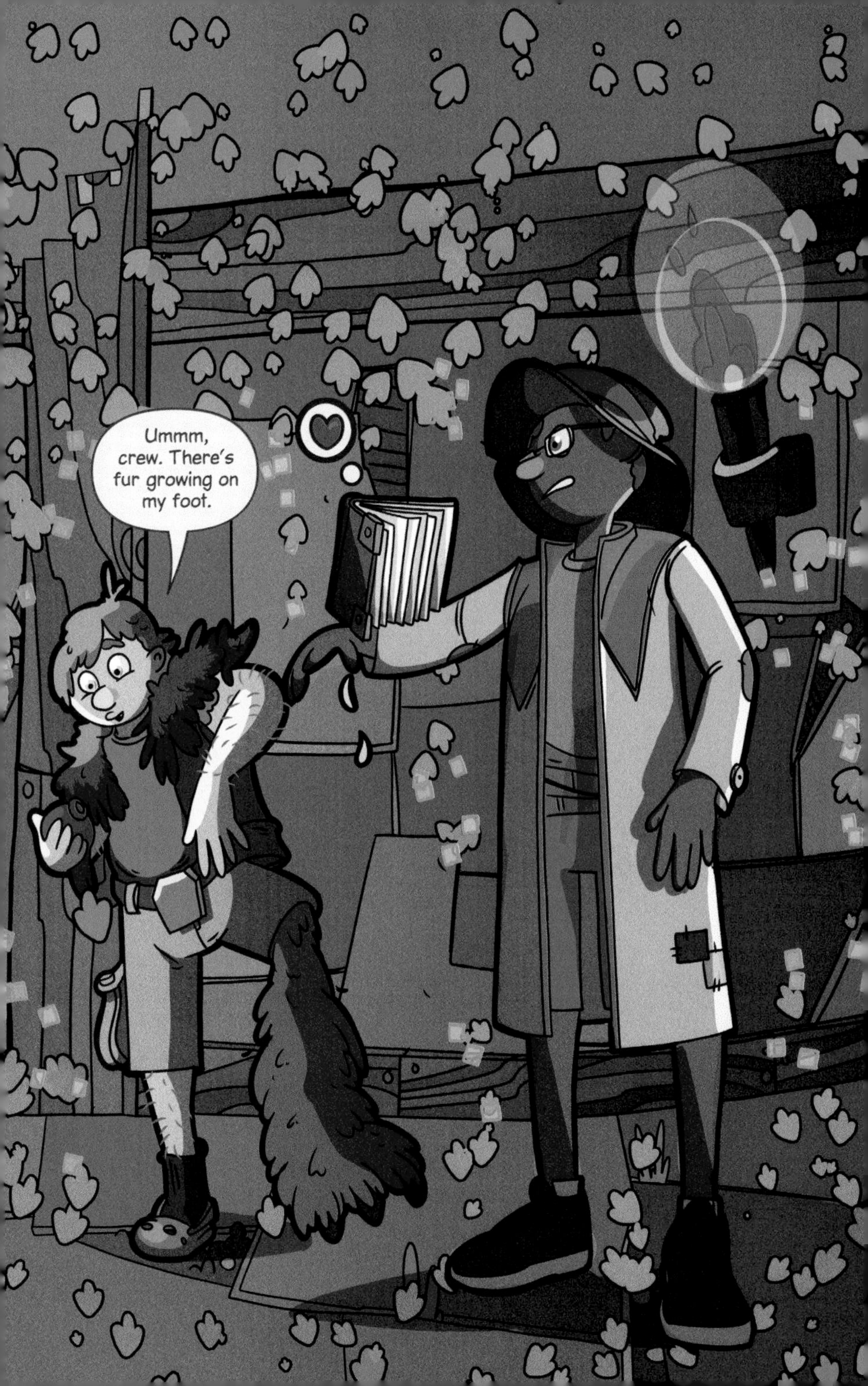
Ummm, crew. There's fur growing on my foot.

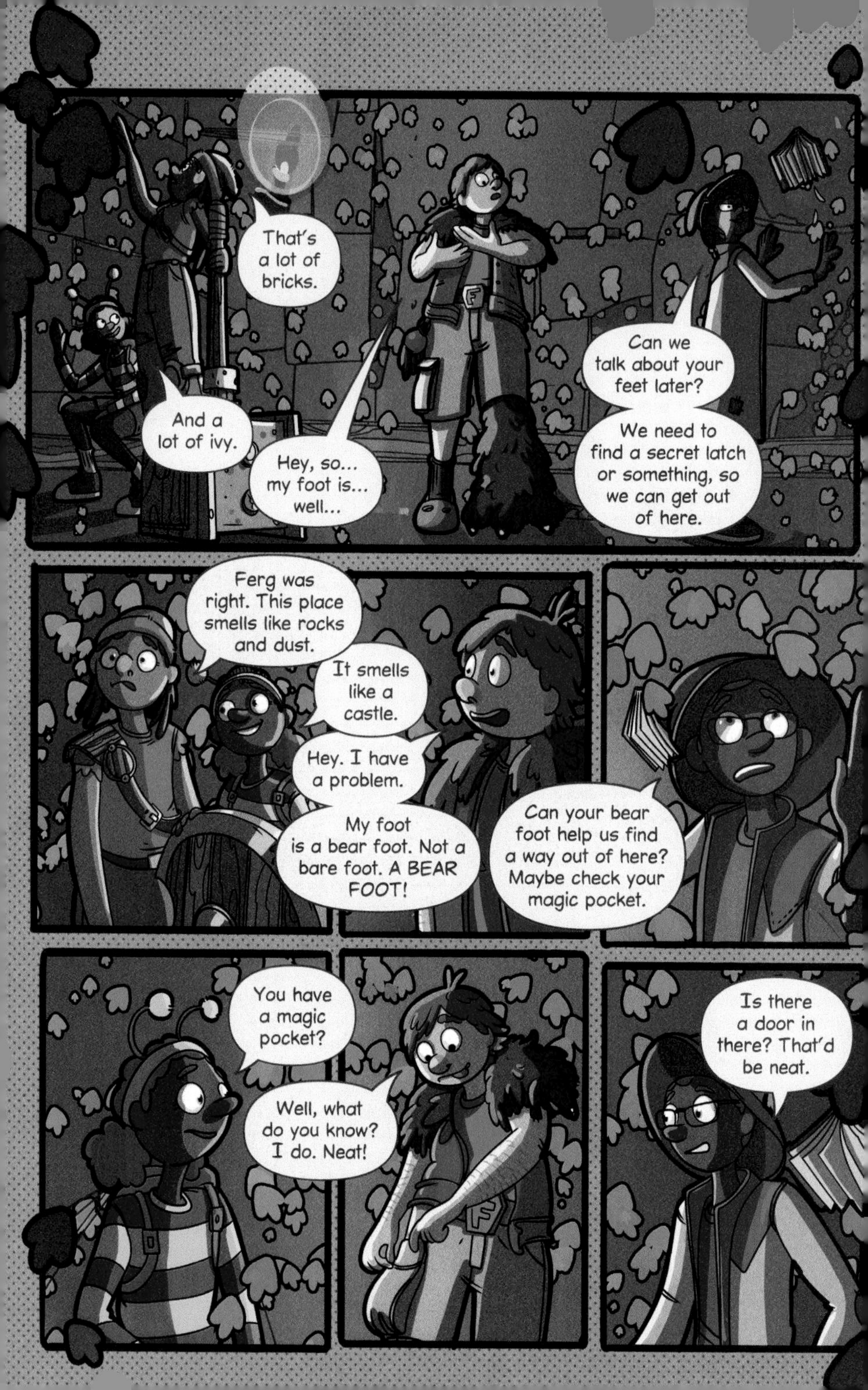
That's a lot of bricks.
And a lot of ivy.
Hey, so... my foot is... well...
Can we talk about your feet later?
We need to find a secret latch or something, so we can get out of here.
Ferg was right. This place smells like rocks and dust.
It smells like a castle.
Hey. I have a problem.
My foot is a bear foot. Not a bare foot. A BEAR FOOT!
Can your bear foot help us find a way out of here? Maybe check your magic pocket.
You have a magic pocket?
Well, what do you know? I do. Neat!
Is there a door in there? That'd be neat.

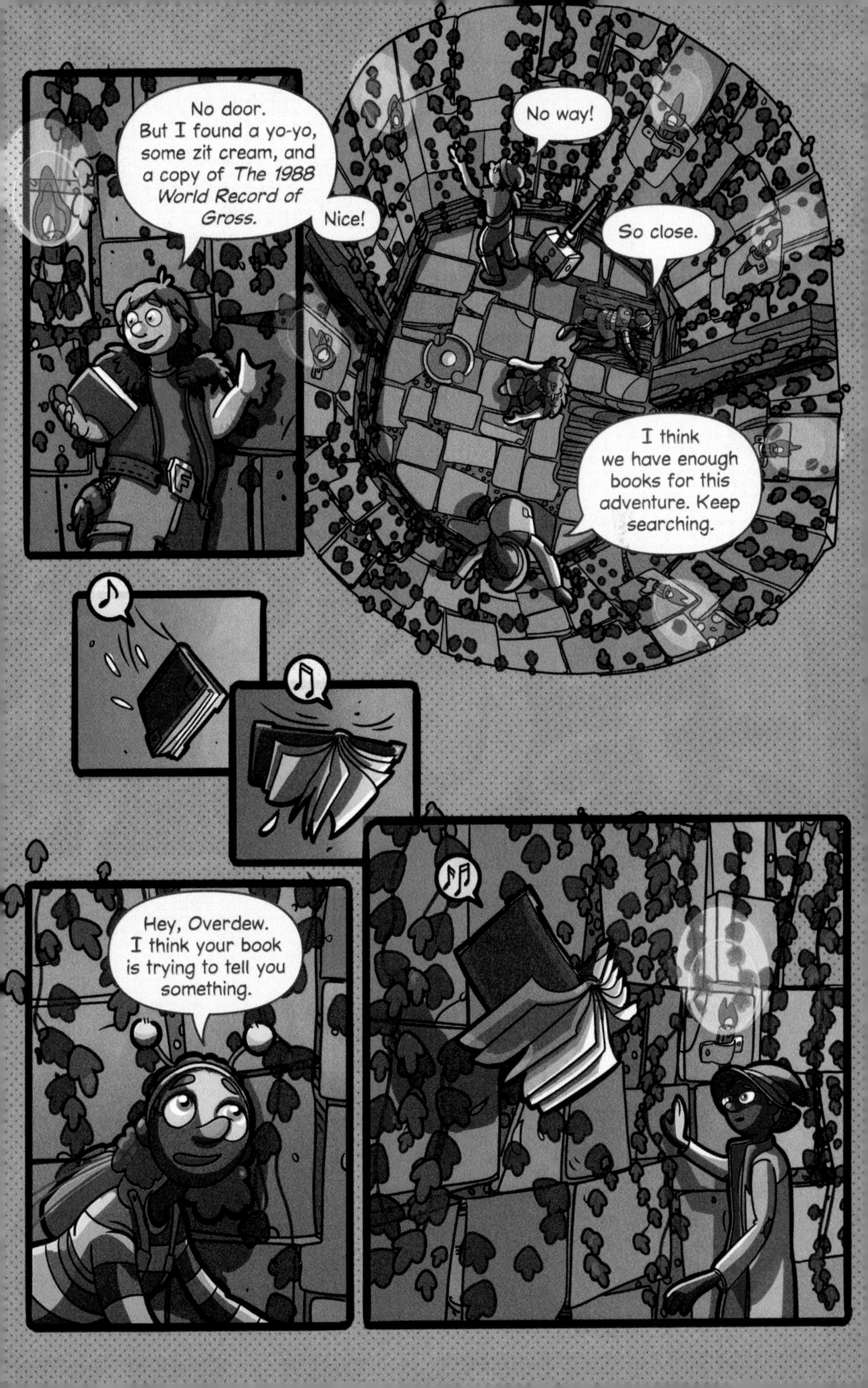
No door. But I found a yo-yo, some zit cream, and a copy of *The 1988 World Record of Gross.*
Nice!
No way!
So close.
I think we have enough books for this adventure. Keep searching.
♪
♫
Hey, Overdew. I think your book is trying to tell you something.
♫

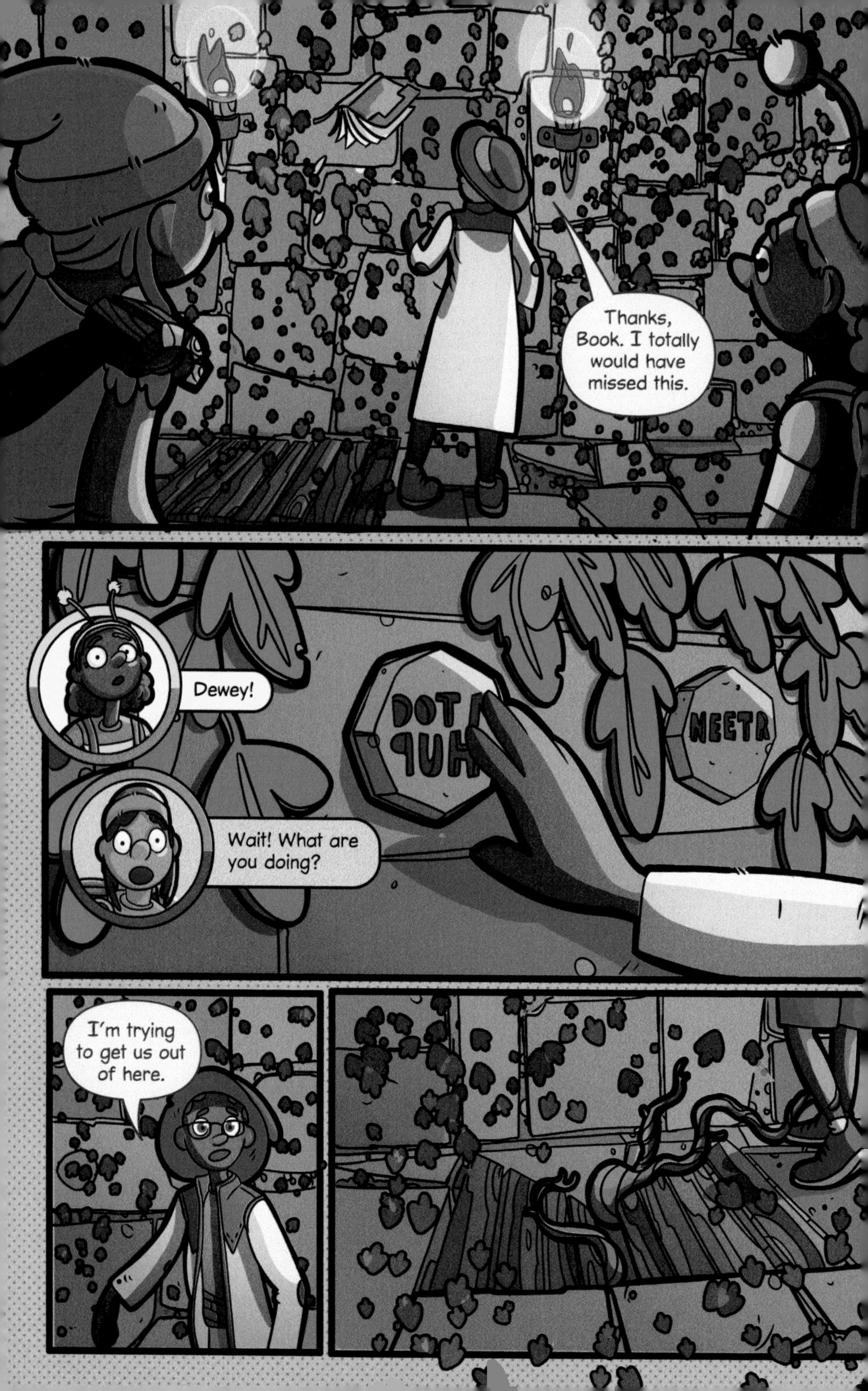
Thanks, Book. I totally would have missed this.
Dewey!
Wait! What are you doing?
I'm trying to get us out of here.

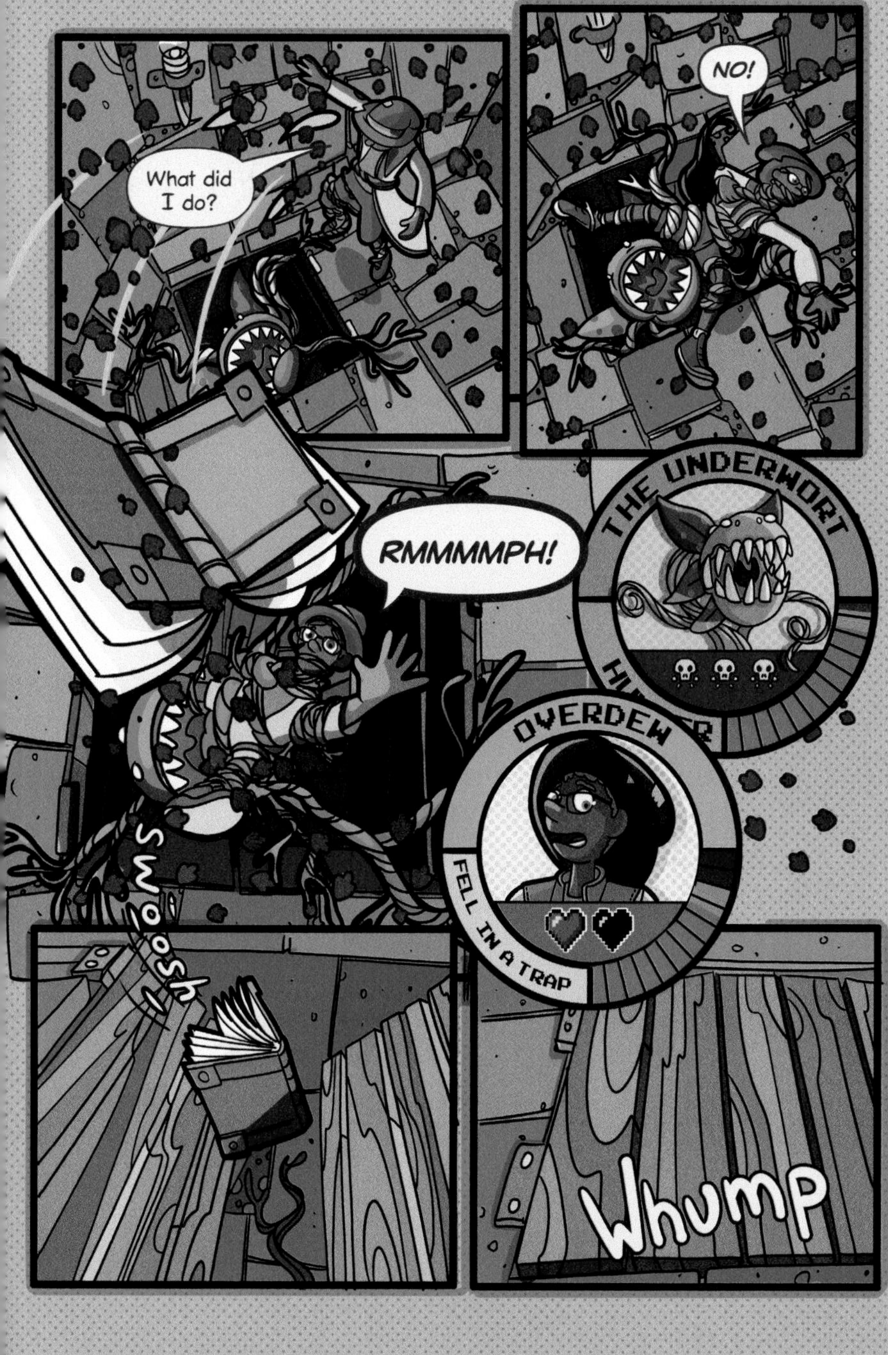
What did I do?
NO!
RMMMMPH!
THE UNDERWORT
OVERDEW
FELL IN A TRAP
swoosh
Whump

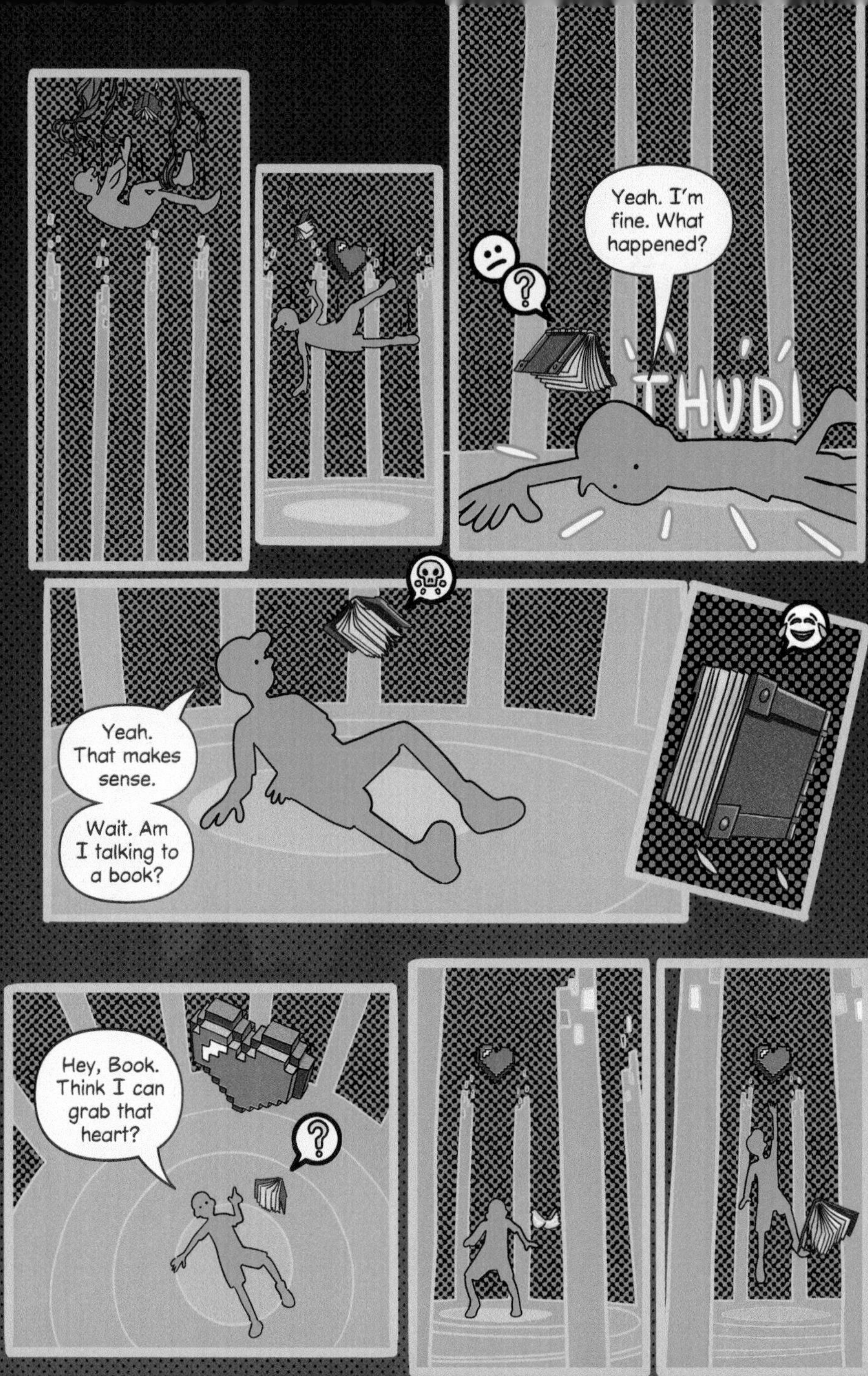
Yeah. I'm fine. What happened?
THUD!
Yeah. That makes sense.
Wait. Am I talking to a book?
Hey, Book. Think I can grab that heart?

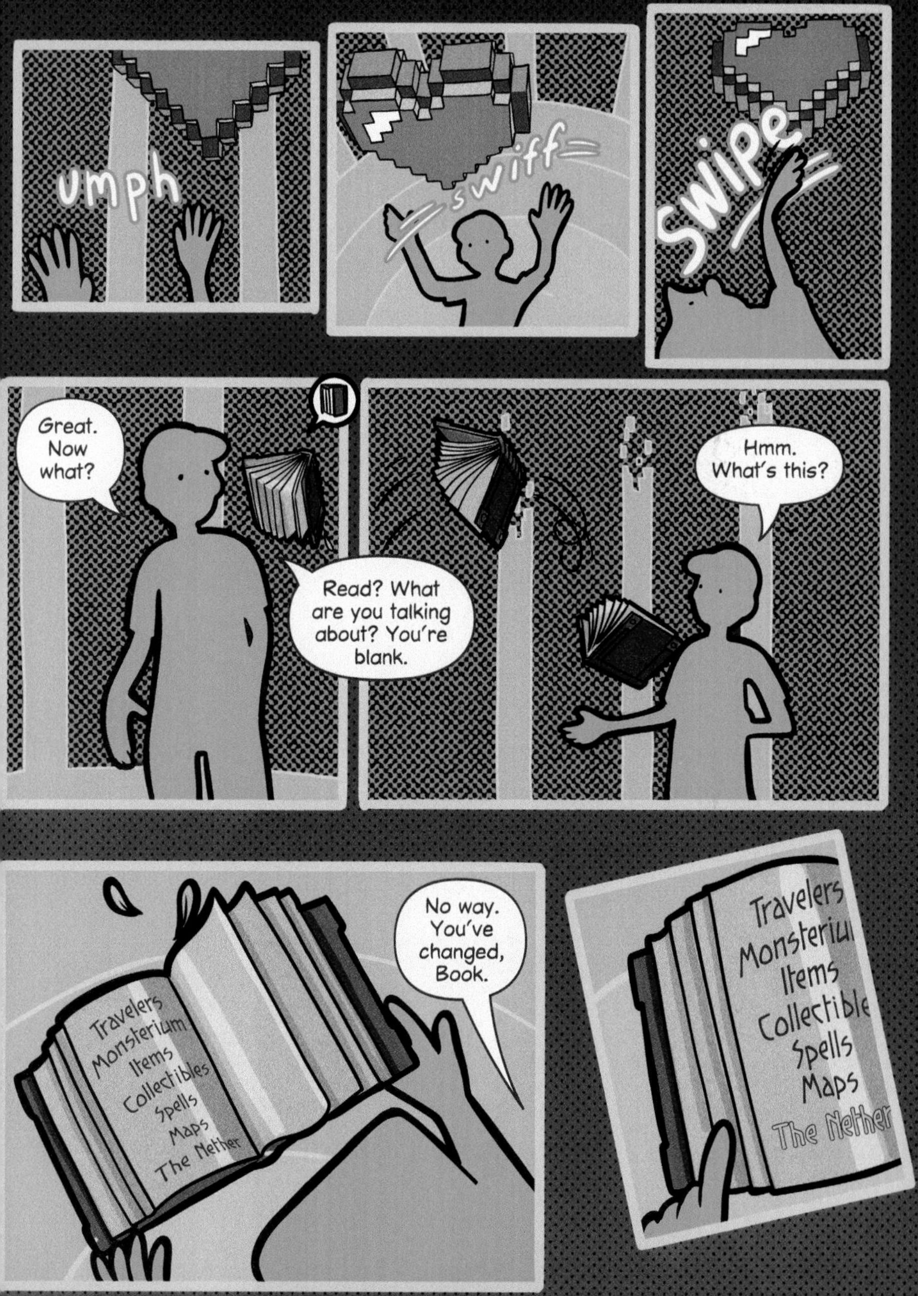
umph
swiff
swipe
Great. Now what?
Read? What are you talking about? You're blank.
Hmm. What's this?
Travelers
Monsterium
Items
Collectibles
Spells
Maps
The Nether
No way. You've changed, Book.
Travelers
Items
Spells
Maps
The Nether

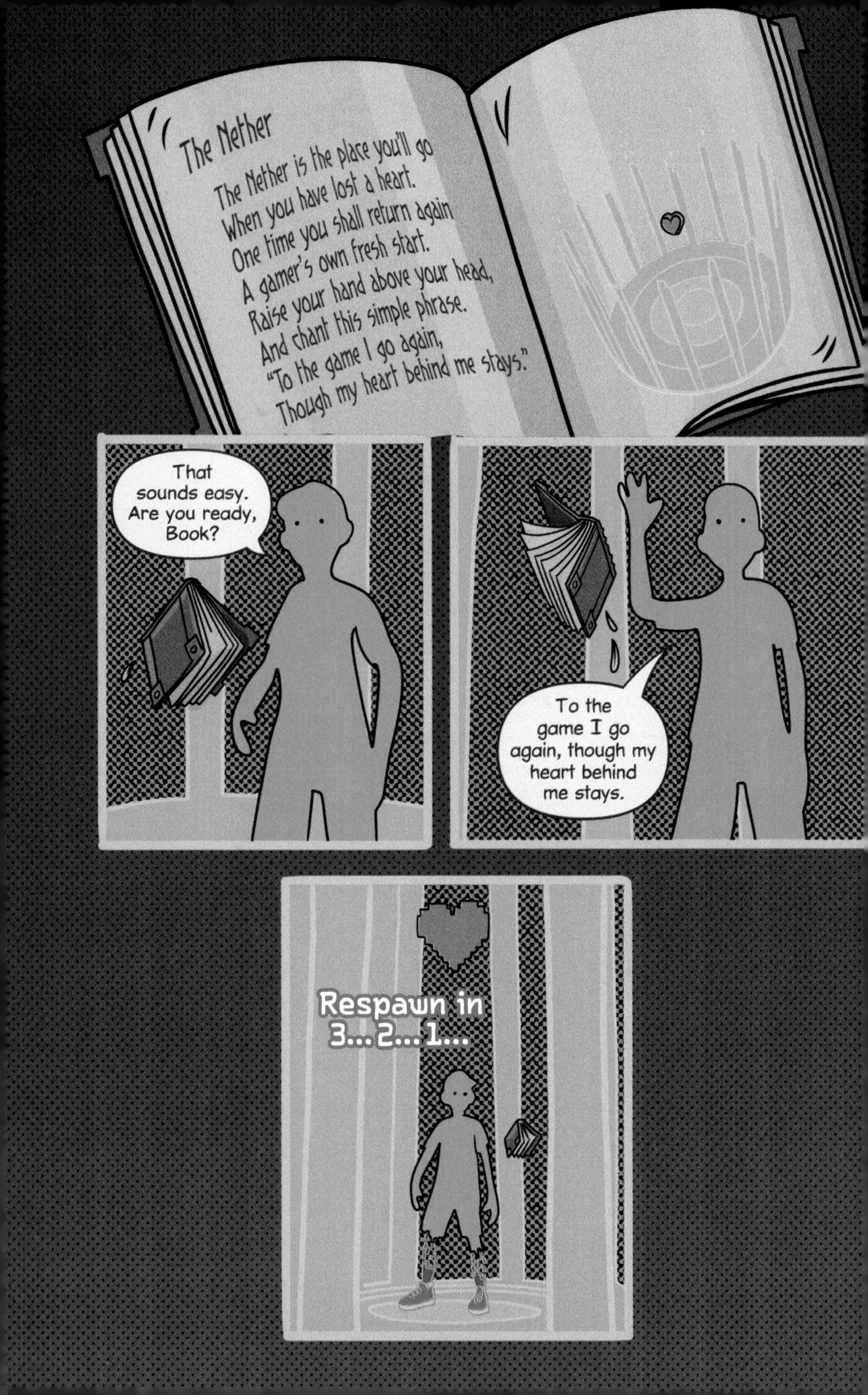
The Nether
The Nether is the place you'll go
When you have lost a heart.
One time you shall return again
A gamer's own fresh start.
Raise your hand above your head,
And chant this simple phrase.
"To the game I go again,
Though my heart behind me stays."
That sounds easy. Are you ready, Book?
To the game I go again, though my heart behind me stays.
Respawn in 3... 2... 1...

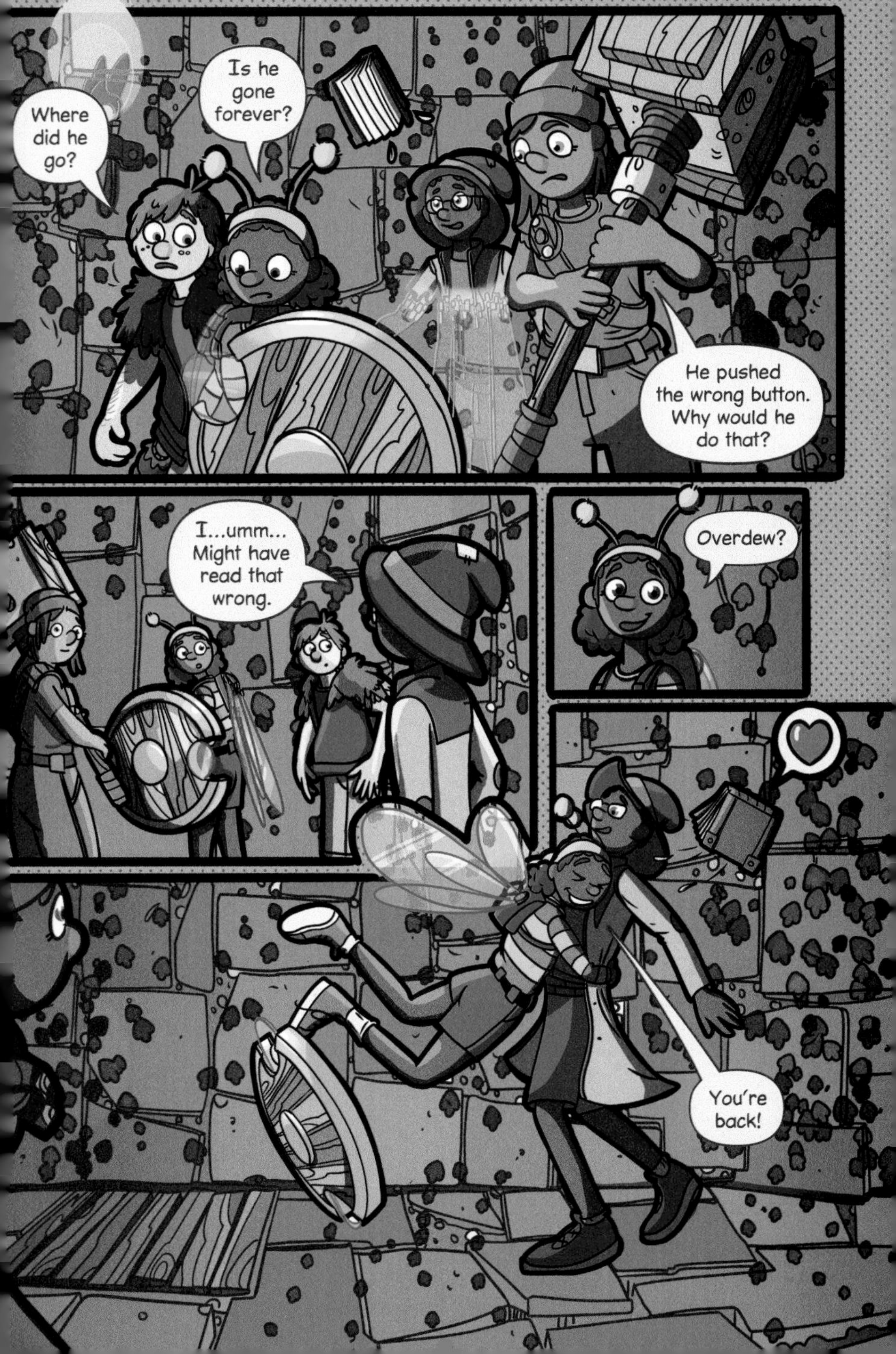
Where did he go?
Is he gone forever?
He pushed the wrong button. Why would he do that?
I...umm... Might have read that wrong.
Overdew?
You're back!

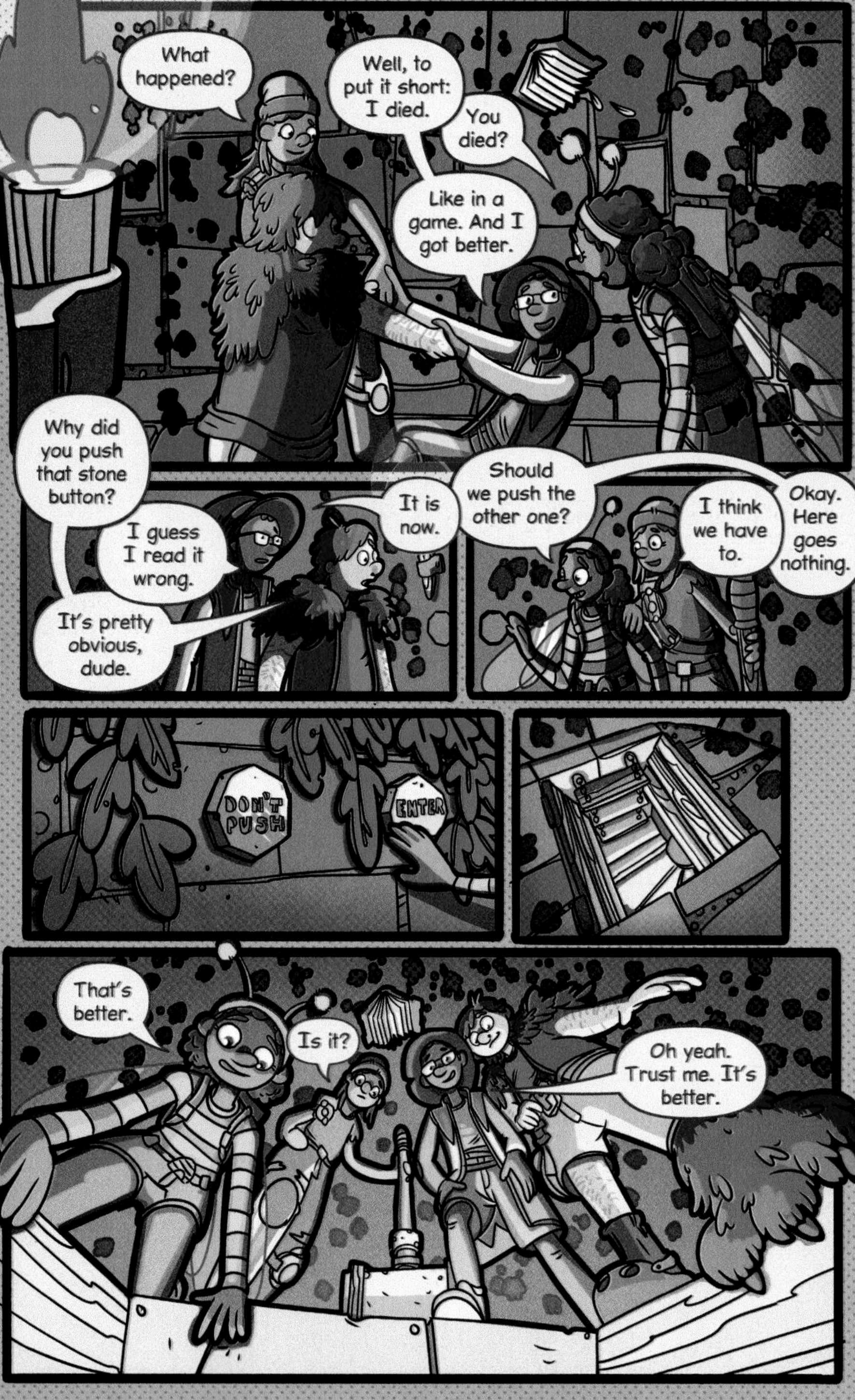

What happened?
Well, to put it short: I died.
You died?
Like in a game. And I got better.
Why did you push that stone button?
I guess I read it wrong.
It's pretty obvious, dude.
It is now.
Should we push the other one?
I think we have to.
Okay. Here goes nothing.
DON'T PUSH
ENTER
That's better.
Is it?
Oh yeah. Trust me. It's better.

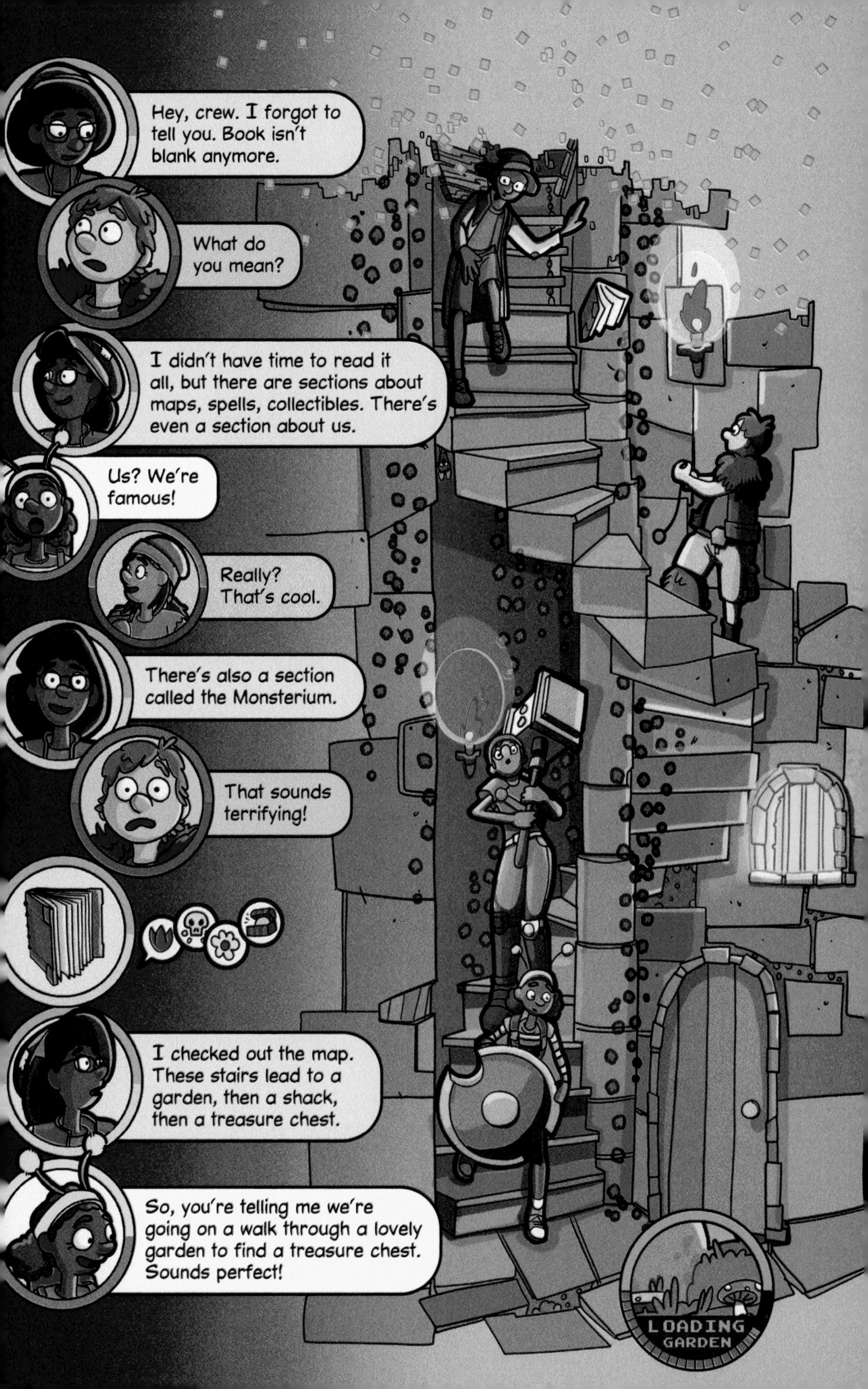

Hey, crew. I forgot to tell you. Book isn't blank anymore.
What do you mean?
I didn't have time to read it all, but there are sections about maps, spells, collectibles. There's even a section about us.
Us? We're famous!
Really? That's cool.
There's also a section called the Monsterium.
That sounds terrifying!
I checked out the map. These stairs lead to a garden, then a shack, then a treasure chest.
So, you're telling me we're going on a walk through a lovely garden to find a treasure chest. Sounds perfect!
LOADING
GARDEN

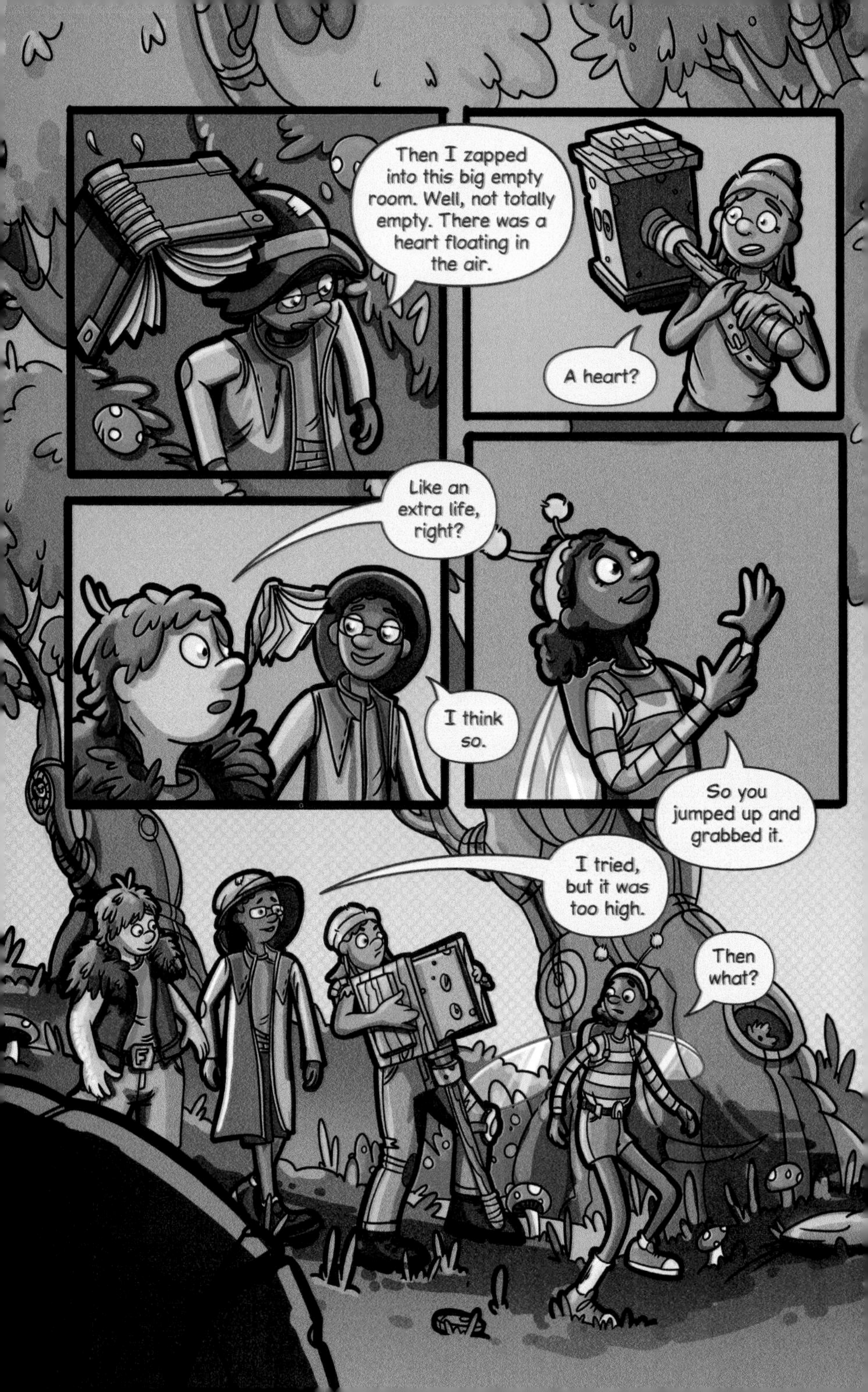
Then I zapped into this big empty room. Well, not totally empty. There was a heart floating in the air.
A heart?
Like an extra life, right?
I think so.
So you jumped up and grabbed it.
I tried, but it was too high.
Then what?

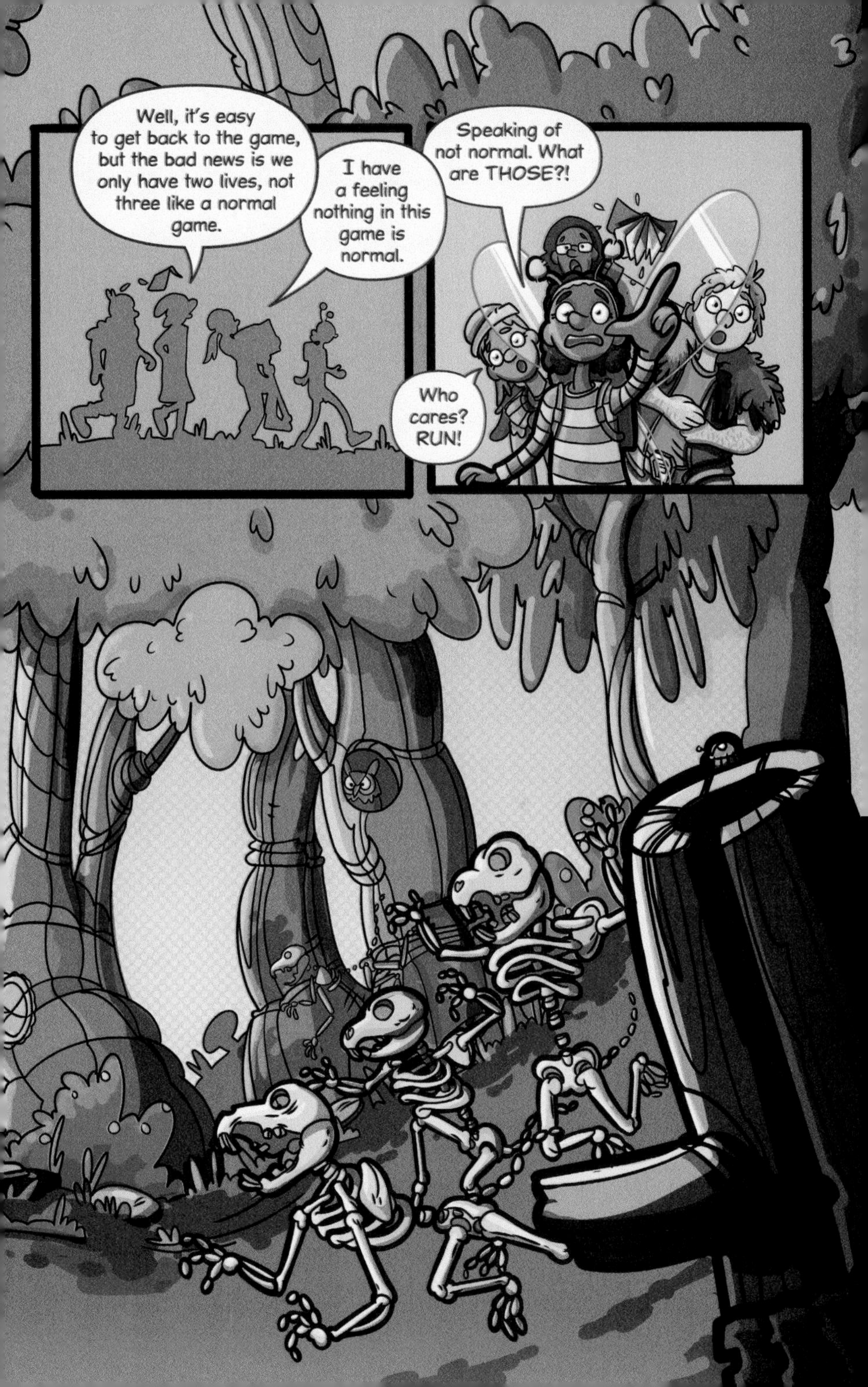
Well, it's easy to get back to the game, but the bad news is we only have two lives, not three like a normal game.
I have a feeling nothing in this game is normal.
Speaking of not normal. What are THOSE?!
Who cares? RUN!

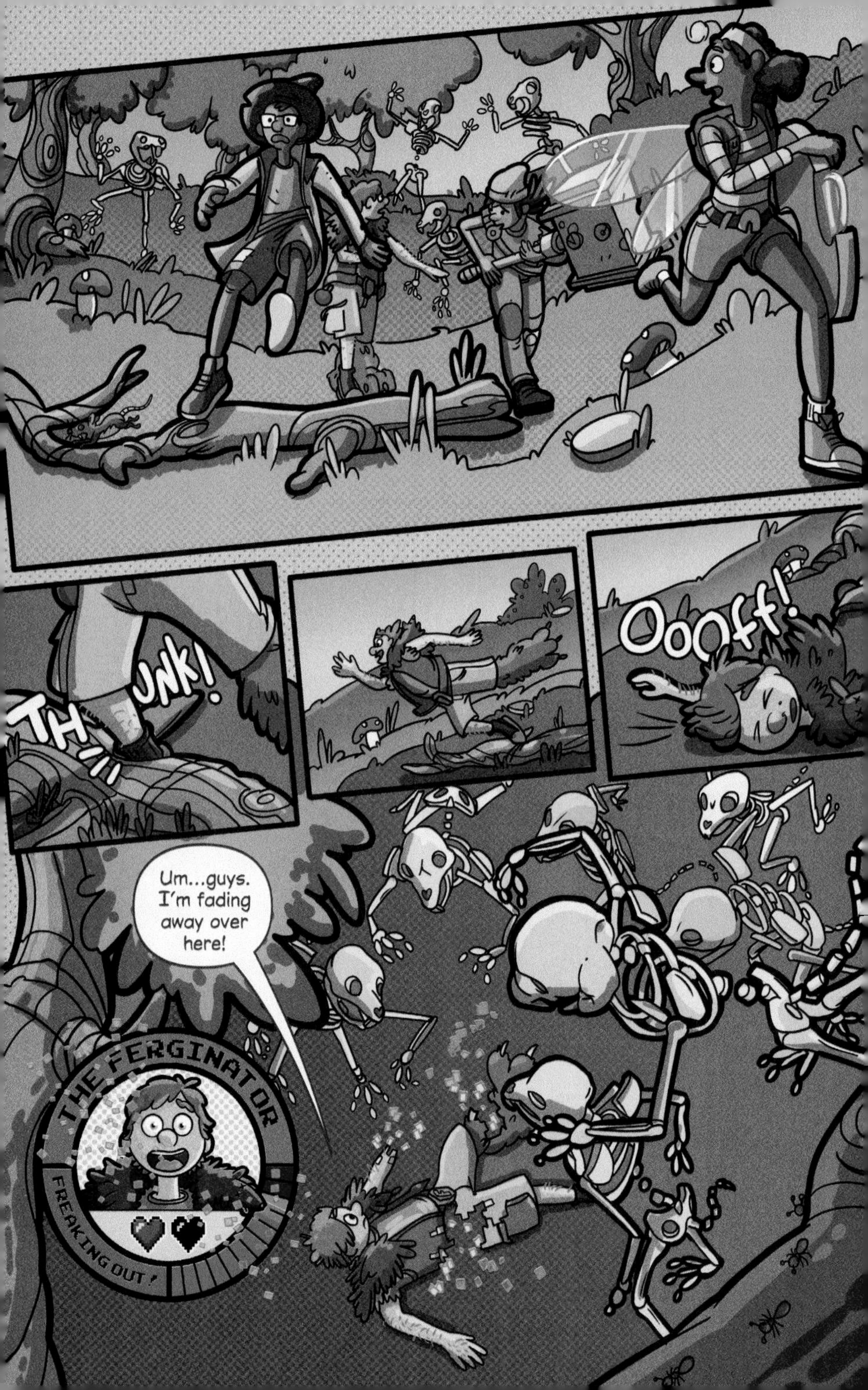
THUNK!
OOOFF!
Um...guys. I'm fading away over here!
THE FERGINATOR
FREAKING OUT!

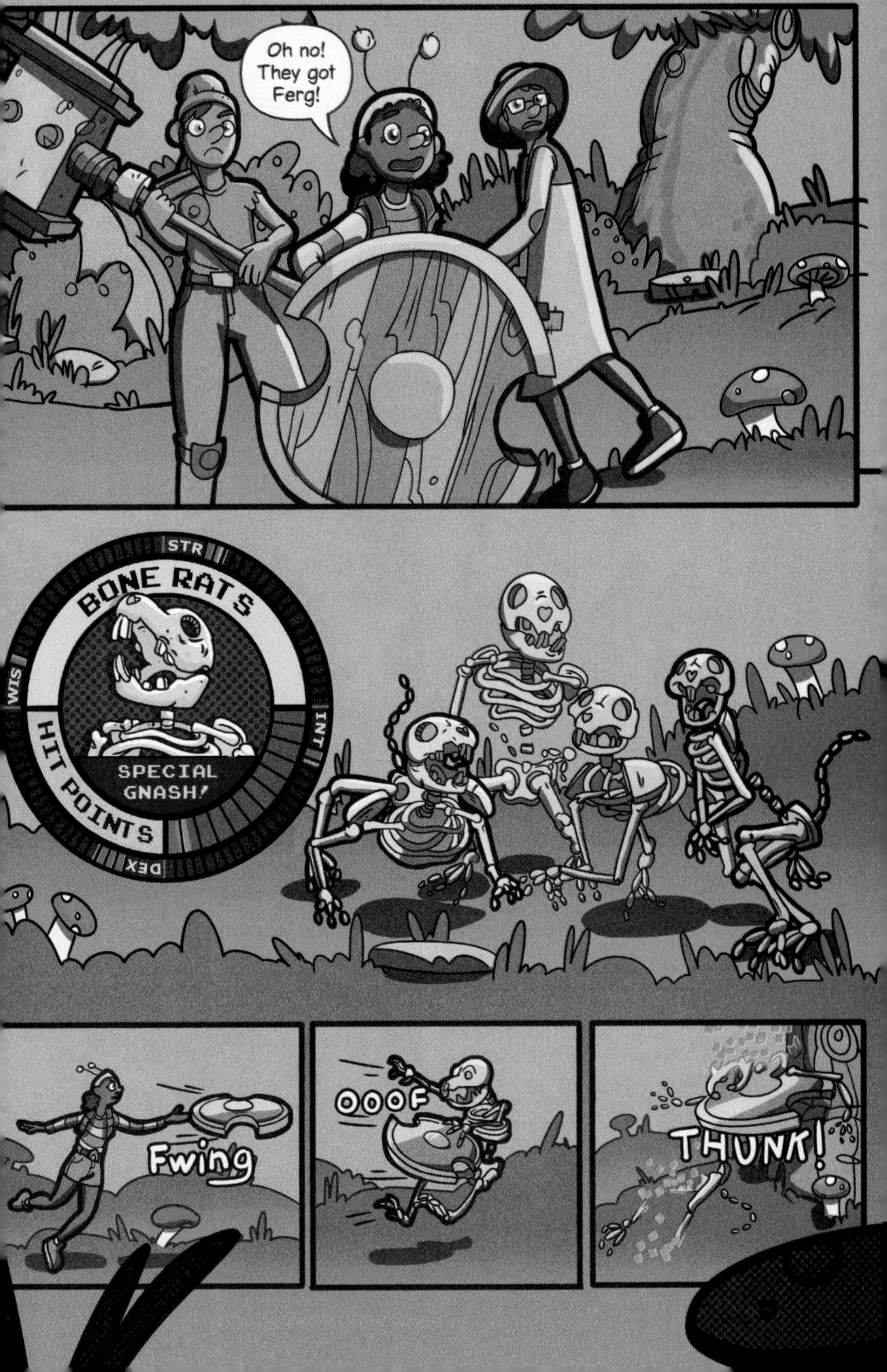
Oh no! They got Ferg!
STR
BONE RATS
WIS
INT
HIT POINTS
SPECIAL GNASH!
DEX
Fwing
OOOF
THUNK!

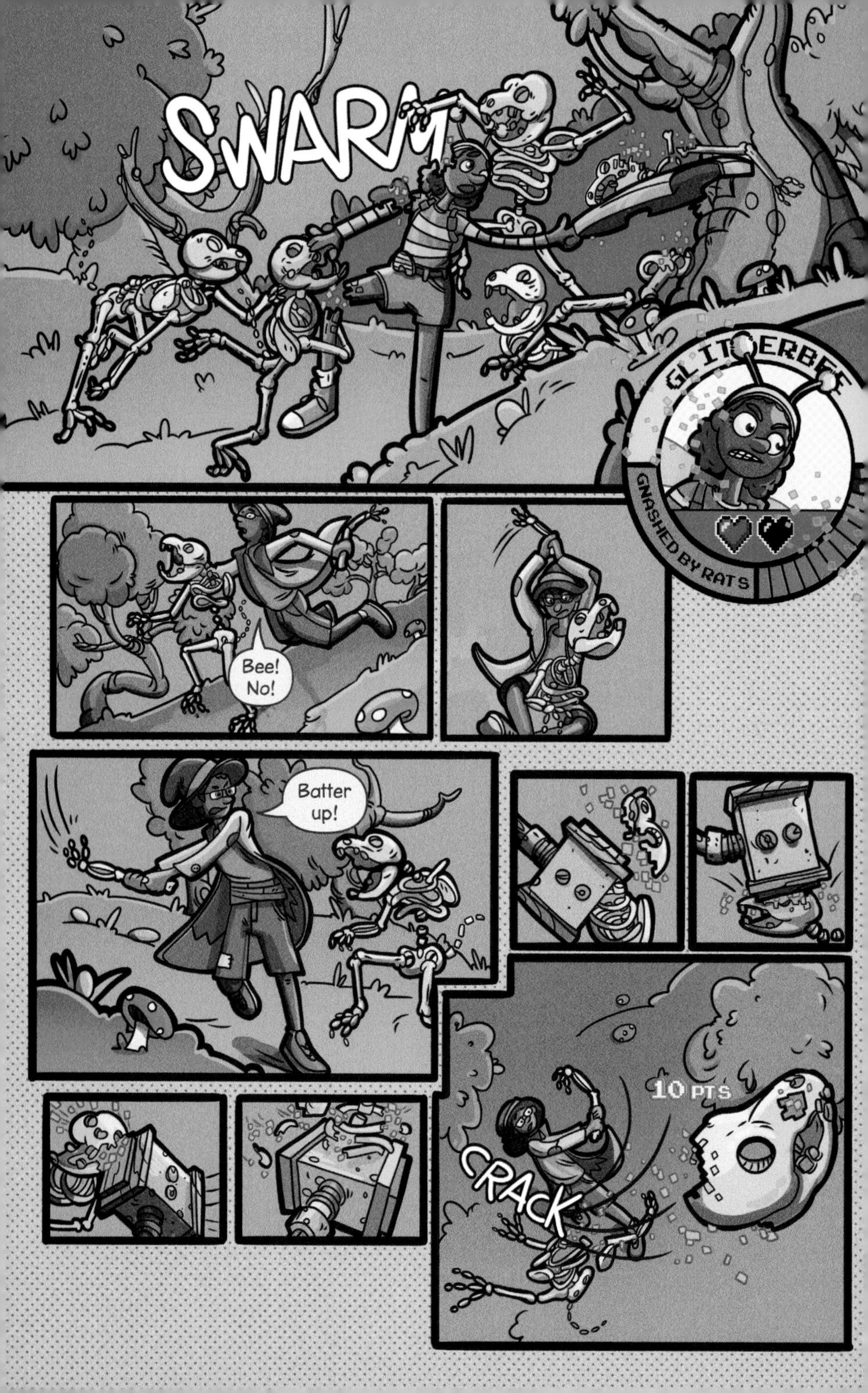
SWARM
GLITCERBEE
GNASHED BY RATS
Bee! No!
Batter up!
10 PTS
CRACK

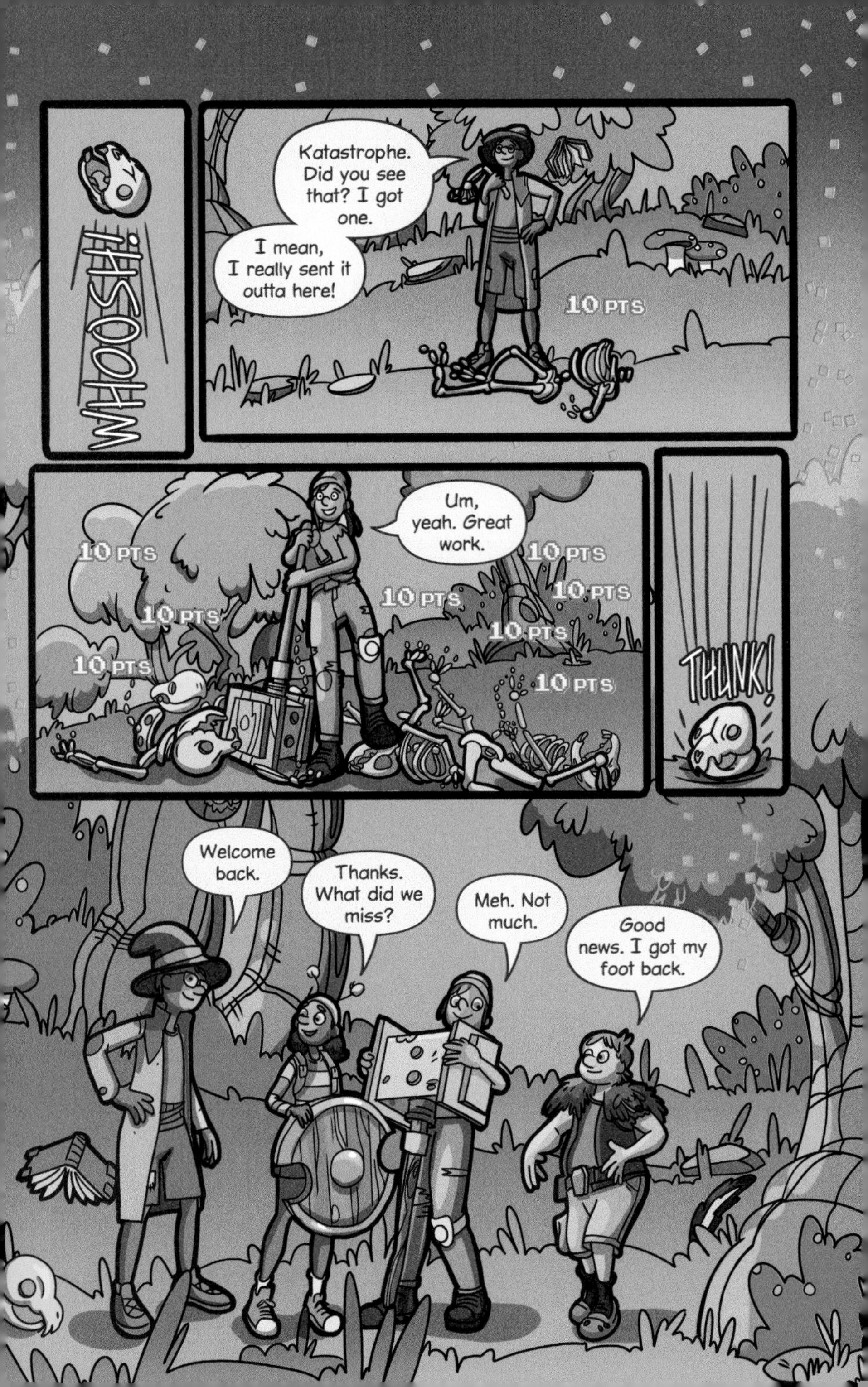
WHOOSH!
Katastrophe. Did you see that? I got one.
I mean, I really sent it outta here!
10 PTS
Um, yeah. Great work.
10 PTS
10 PTS
10 PTS
10 PTS
10 PTS
10 PTS
10 PTS
10 PTS
THUNK!
Welcome back.
Thanks. What did we miss?
Meh. Not much.
Good news. I got my foot back.

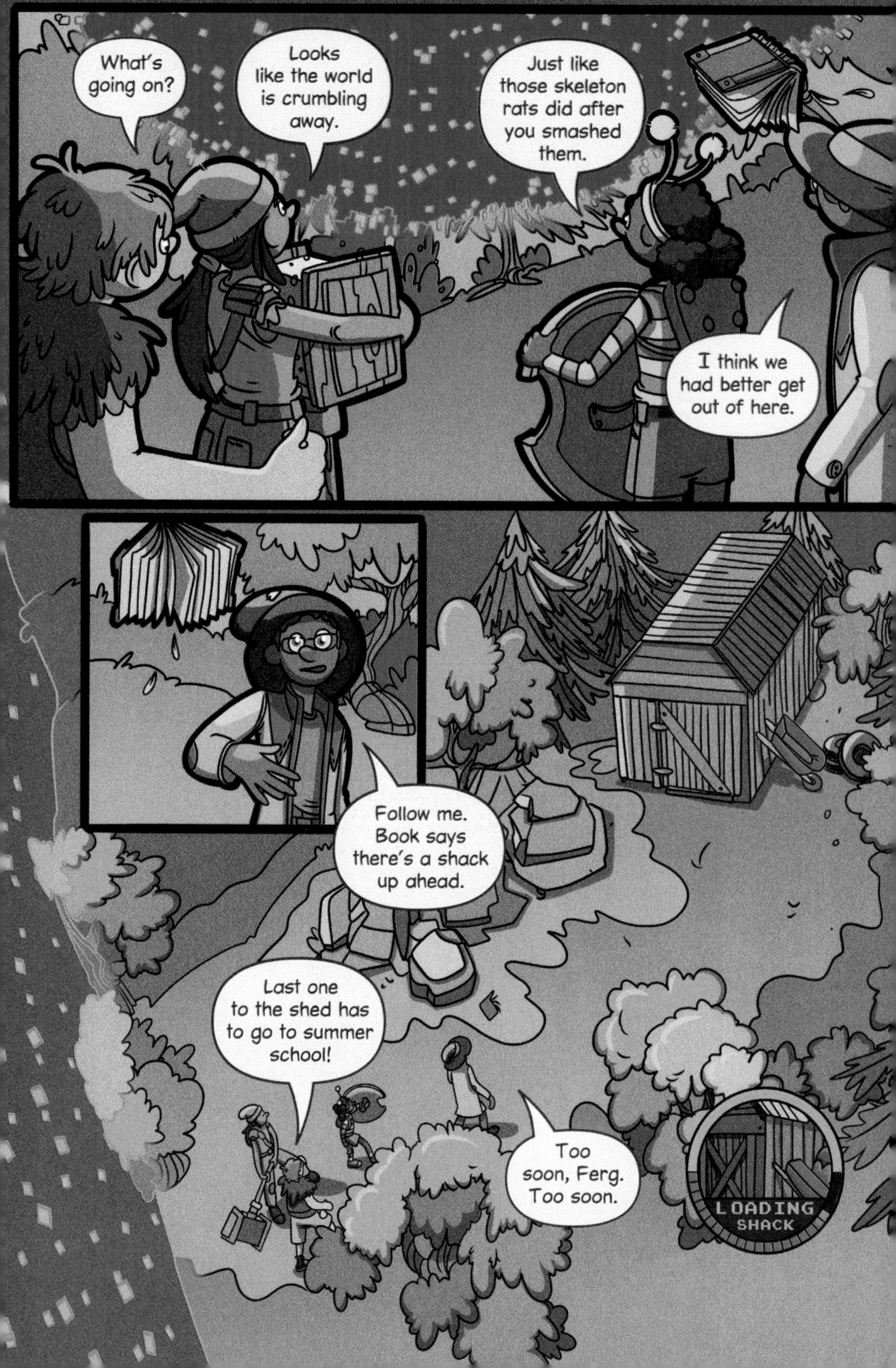
What's going on?
Looks like the world is crumbling away.
Just like those skeleton rats did after you smashed them.
I think we had better get out of here.
Follow me. Book says there's a shack up ahead.
Last one to the shed has to go to summer school!
Too soon, Ferg. Too soon.
LOADING SHACK

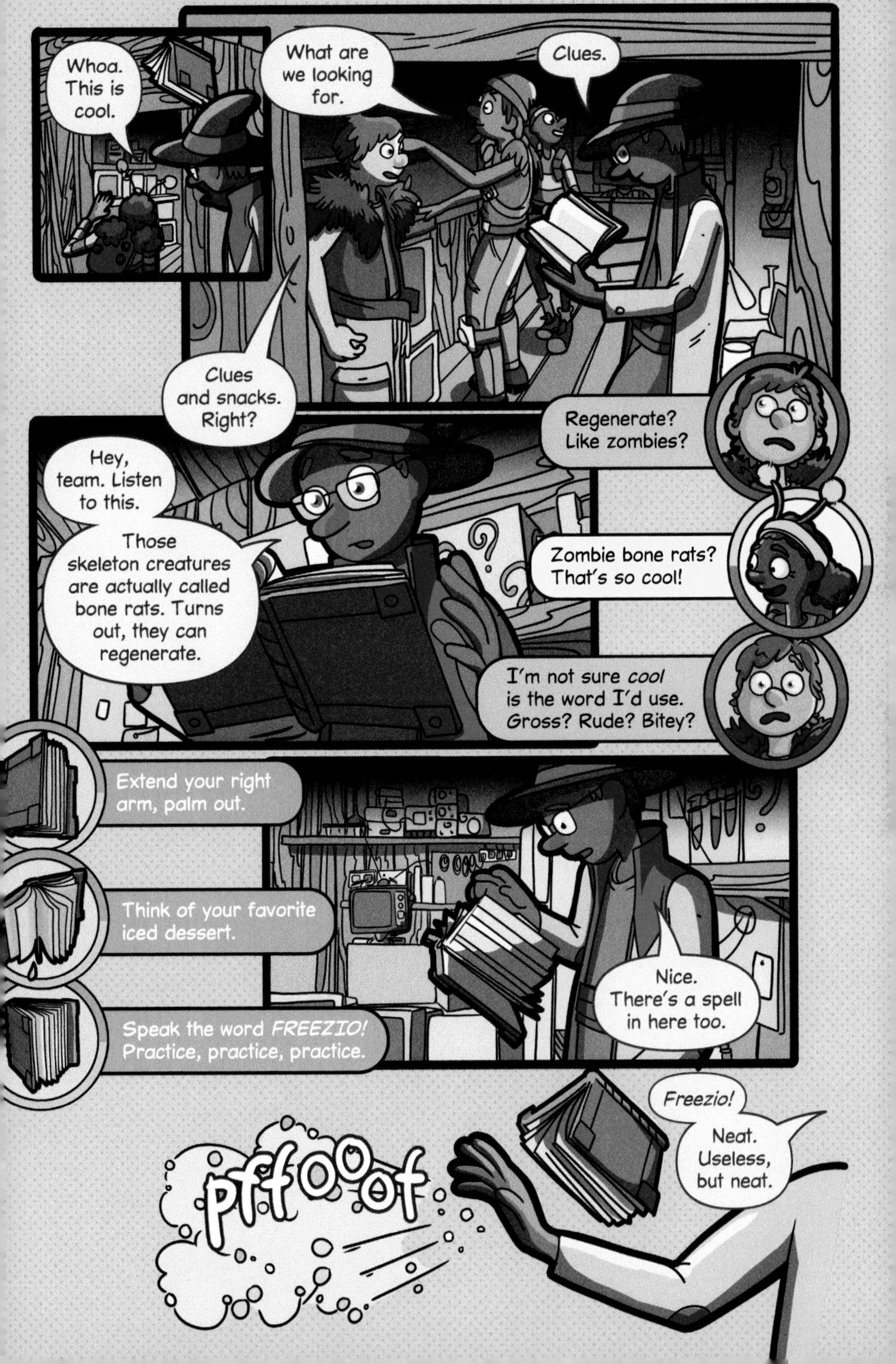
Whoa. This is cool.
What are we looking for.
Clues.
Clues and snacks. Right?
Hey, team. Listen to this.
Those skeleton creatures are actually called bone rats. Turns out, they can regenerate.
Regenerate? Like zombies?
Zombie bone rats? That's so cool!
I'm not sure *cool* is the word I'd use. Gross? Rude? Bitey?
Extend your right arm, palm out.
Think of your favorite iced dessert.
Speak the word *FREEZIO!* Practice, practice, practice.
Nice. There's a spell in here too.
Freezio!
pfOOof
Neat. Useless, but neat.

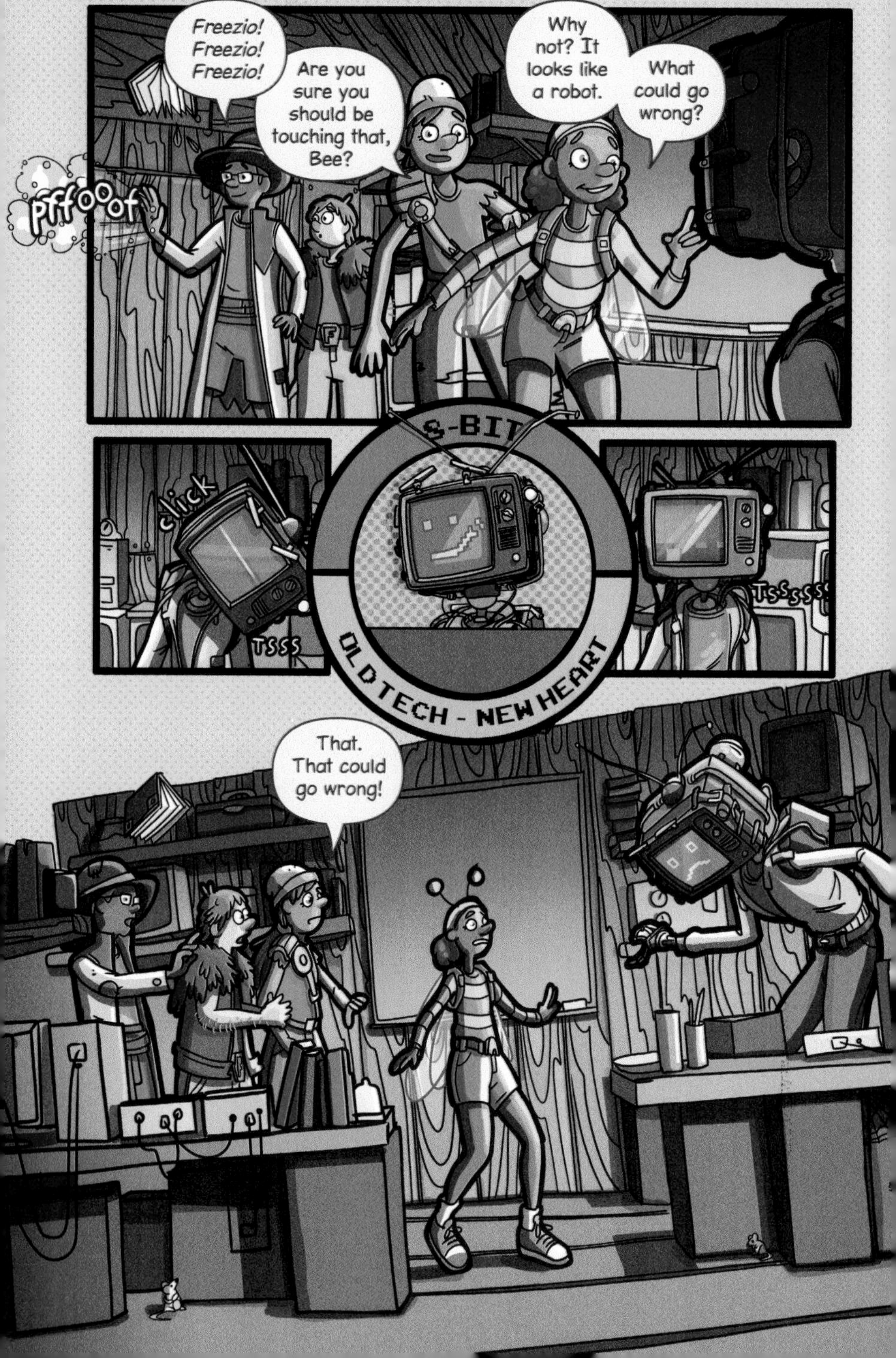
Freezio! Freezio! Freezio!
pffoOof
Are you sure you should be touching that, Bee?
Why not? It looks like a robot.
What could go wrong?
click
TSSS
8-BIT
OLD TECH - NEW HEART
TSsssss
That. That could go wrong!

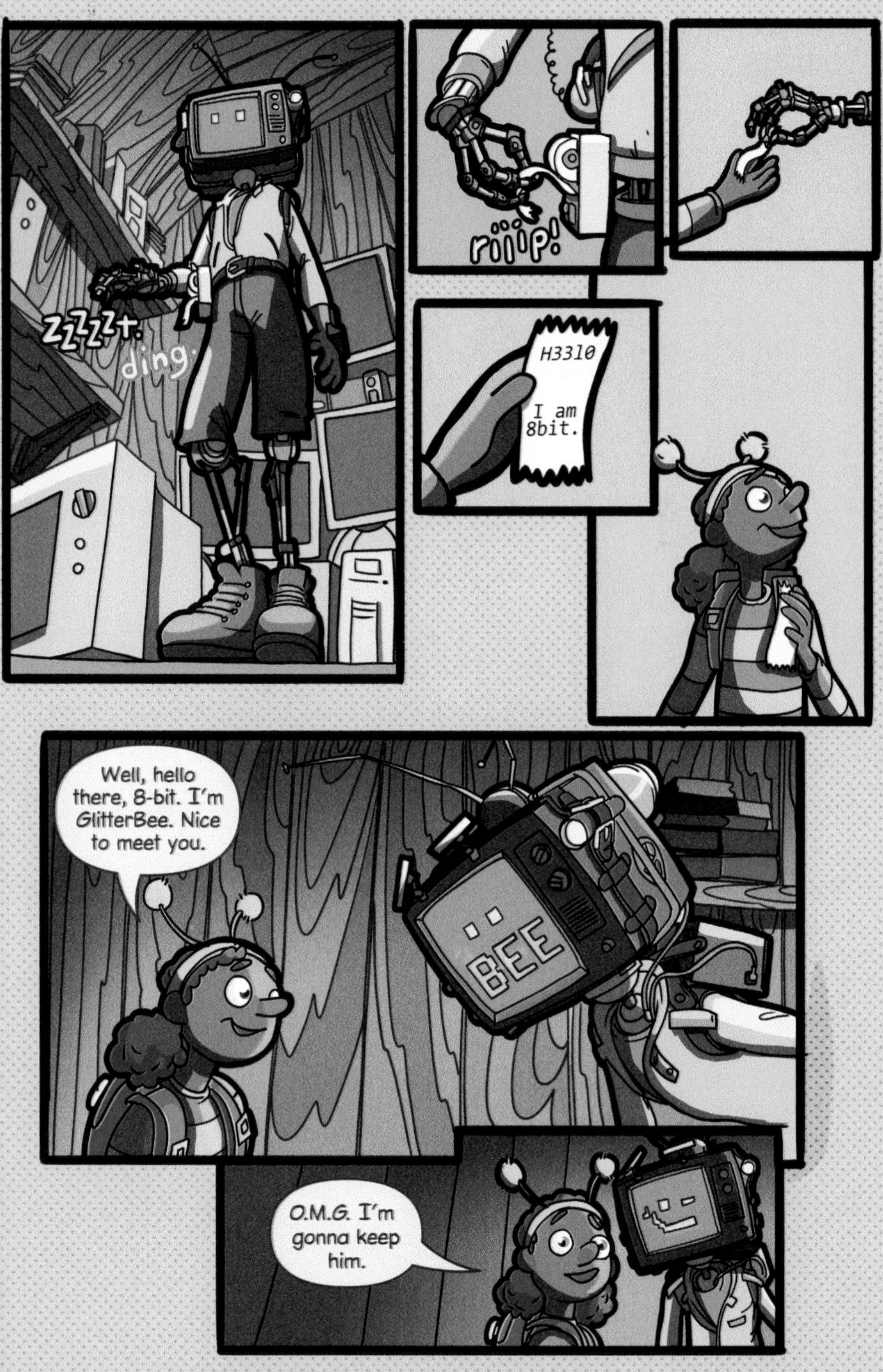
zzzzzt.
ding.
riiip!
H3310
I am 8bit.
BEE
Well, hello there, 8-bit. I'm GlitterBee. Nice to meet you.
O.M.G. I'm gonna keep him.

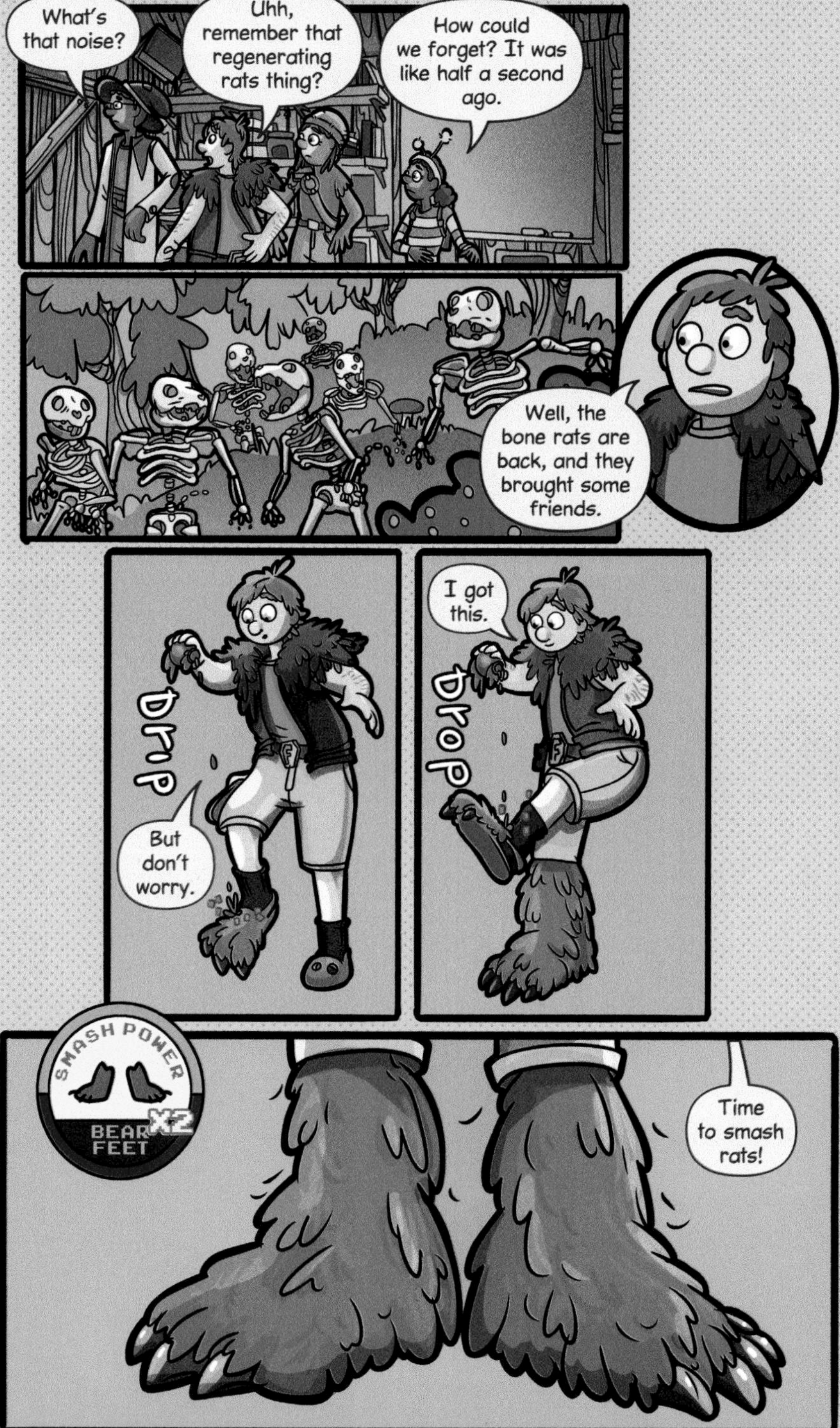
What's that noise?
Uhh, remember that regenerating rats thing?
How could we forget? It was like half a second ago.
Well, the bone rats are back, and they brought some friends.
DRIP
But don't worry.
I got this.
DROP
SMASH POWER
BEAR FEET
X2
Time to smash rats!

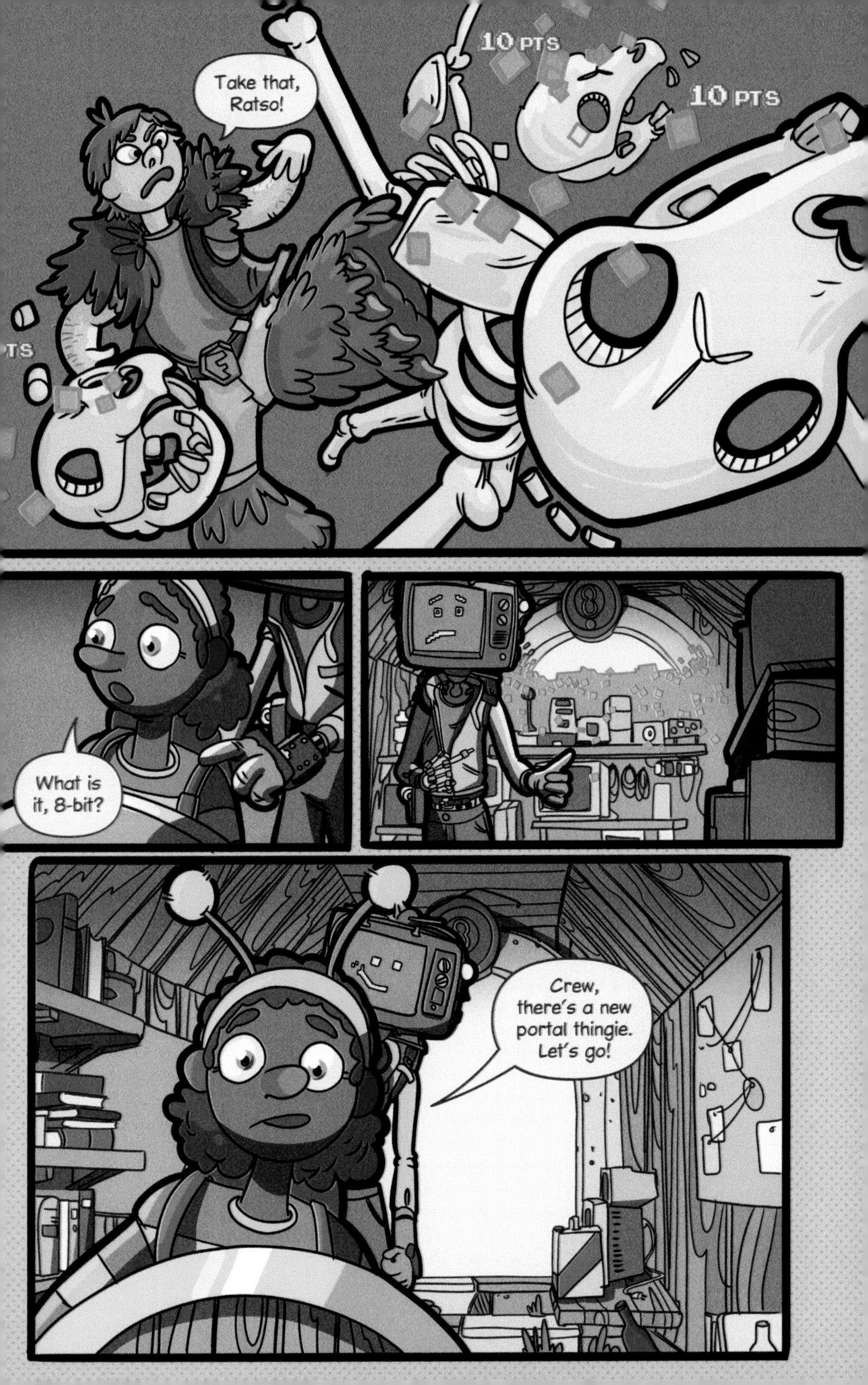
10 PTS
10 PTS
Take that, Ratso!
TS
What is it, 8-bit?
Crew, there's a new portal thingie. Let's go!

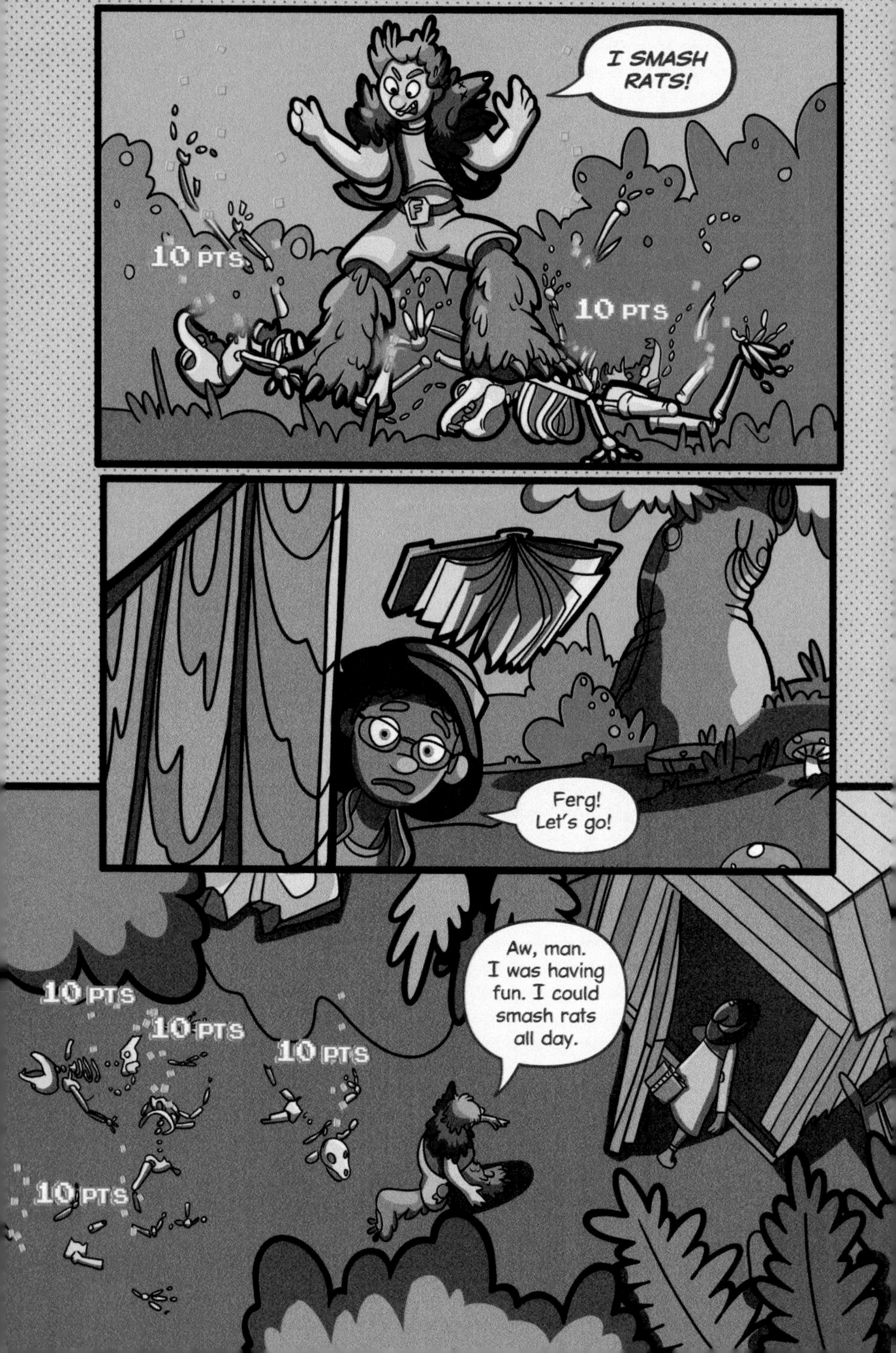
I SMASH RATS!
10 PTS
10 PTS
Ferg! Let's go!
Aw, man. I was having fun. I could smash rats all day.
10 PTS
10 PTS
10 PTS
10 PTS

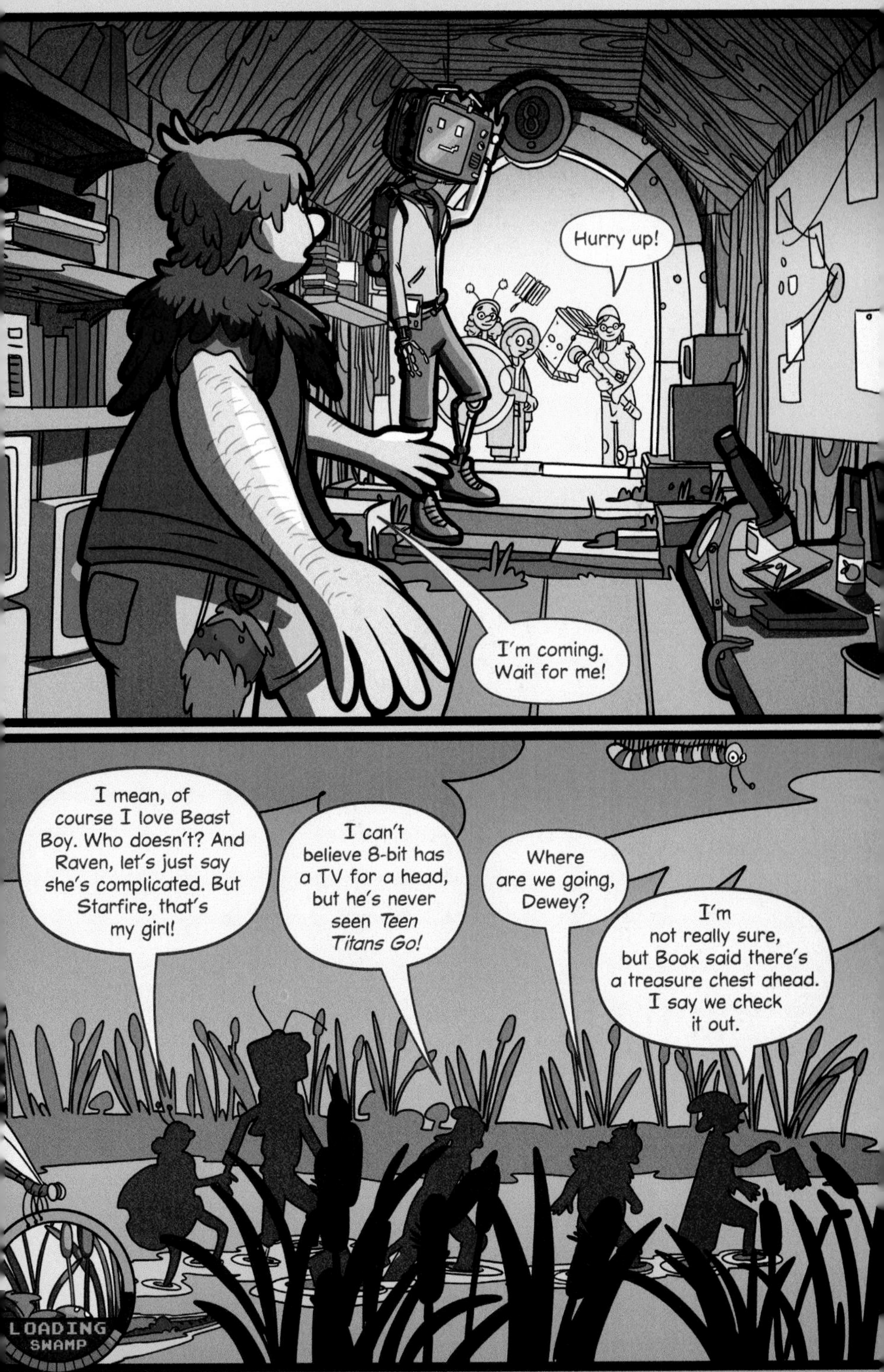
Hurry up!
I'm coming. Wait for me!
I mean, of course I love Beast Boy. Who doesn't? And Raven, let's just say she's complicated. But Starfire, that's my girl!
I can't believe 8-bit has a TV for a head, but he's never seen *Teen Titans Go!*
Where are we going, Dewey?
I'm not really sure, but Book said there's a treasure chest ahead. I say we check it out.
LOADING SWAMP

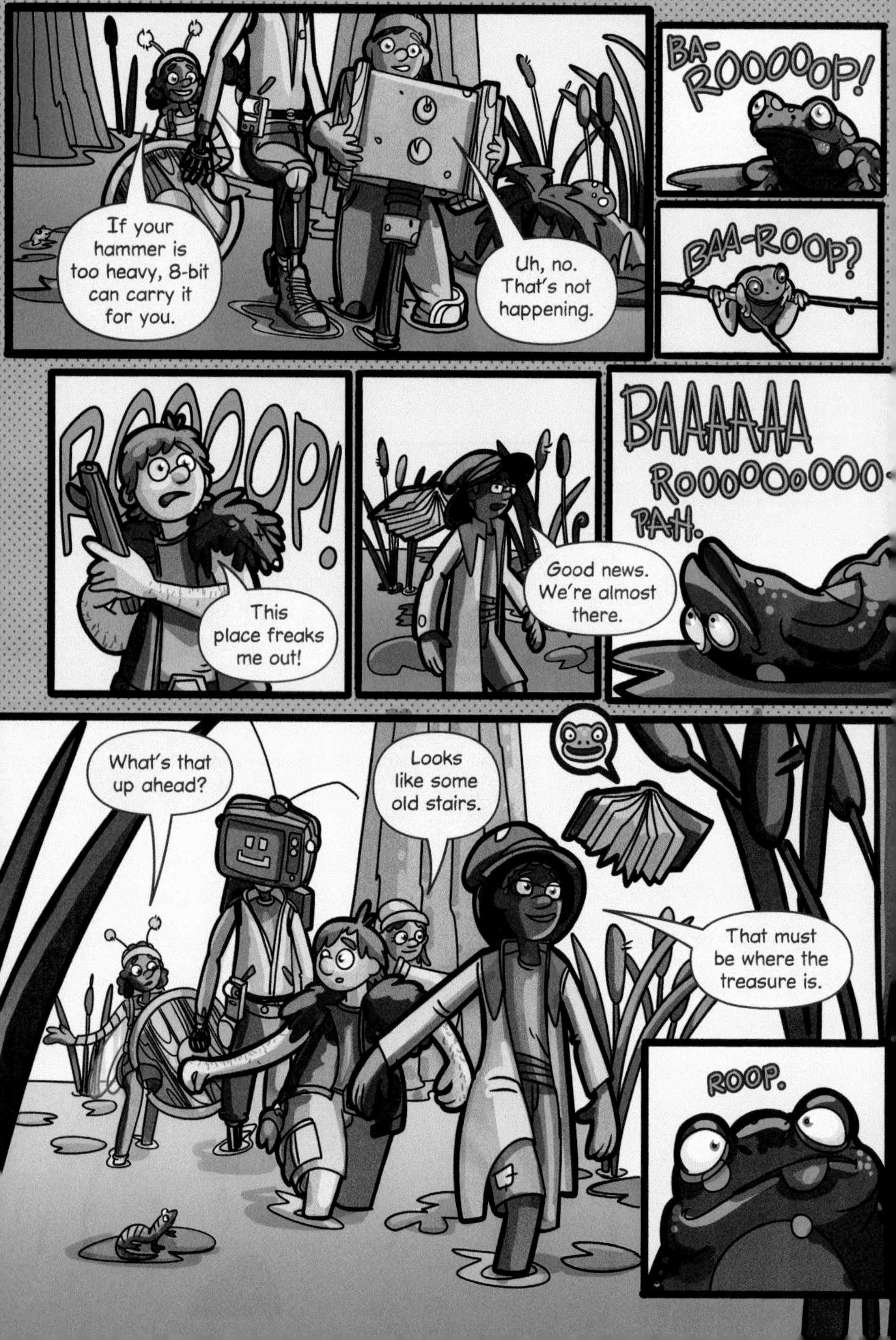
If your hammer is too heavy, 8-bit can carry it for you.
Uh, no. That's not happening.
BA-ROOOOOP!
BAA-ROOP?
ROOOOP!
This place freaks me out!
Good news. We're almost there.
BAAAAAA ROOOOOOOOO-PAH.
What's that up ahead?
Looks like some old stairs.
That must be where the treasure is.
ROOP.

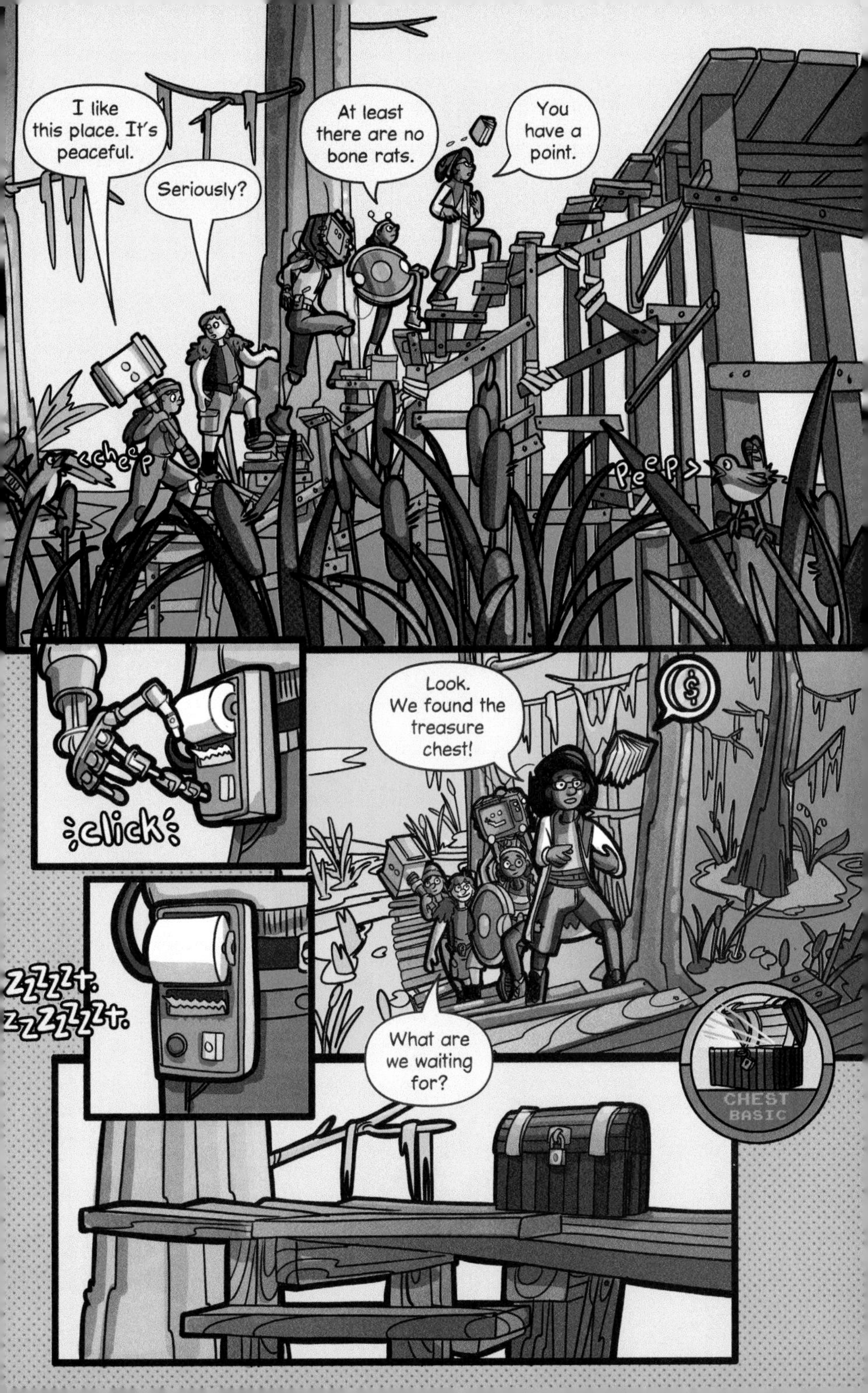
I like this place. It's peaceful.
Seriously?
At least there are no bone rats.
You have a point.
<cheep
Peep>
:click:
zzzzt.
zzzzzzt.
Look. We found the treasure chest!
What are we waiting for?
CHEST
BASIC

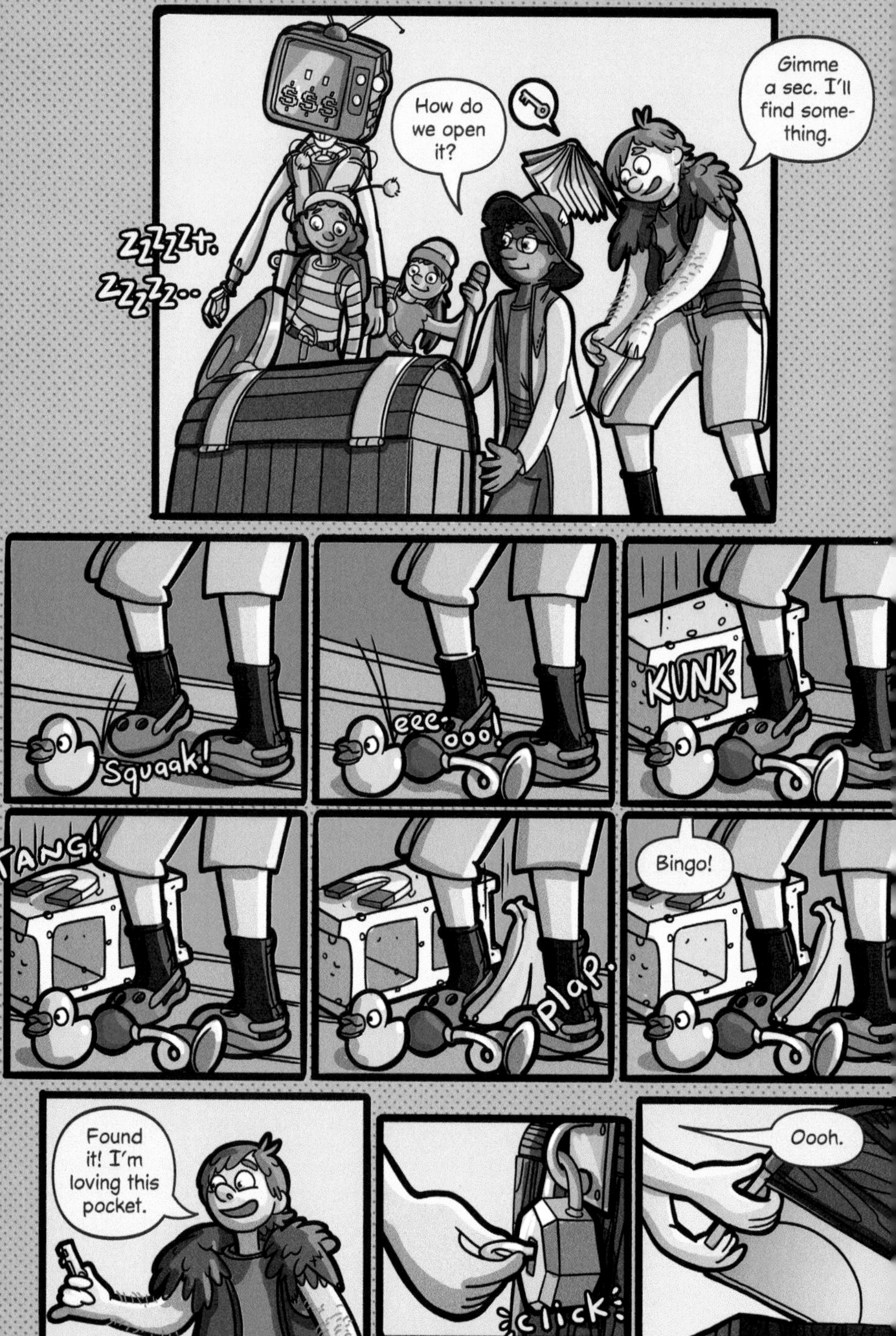
ZZZZZT.
ZZZZZ..
How do we open it?
Gimme a sec. I'll find some-thing.
Squaak!
eee-ooo!
KUNK
TANG!
Plap.
Bingo!
Found it! I'm loving this pocket.
click
Oooh.

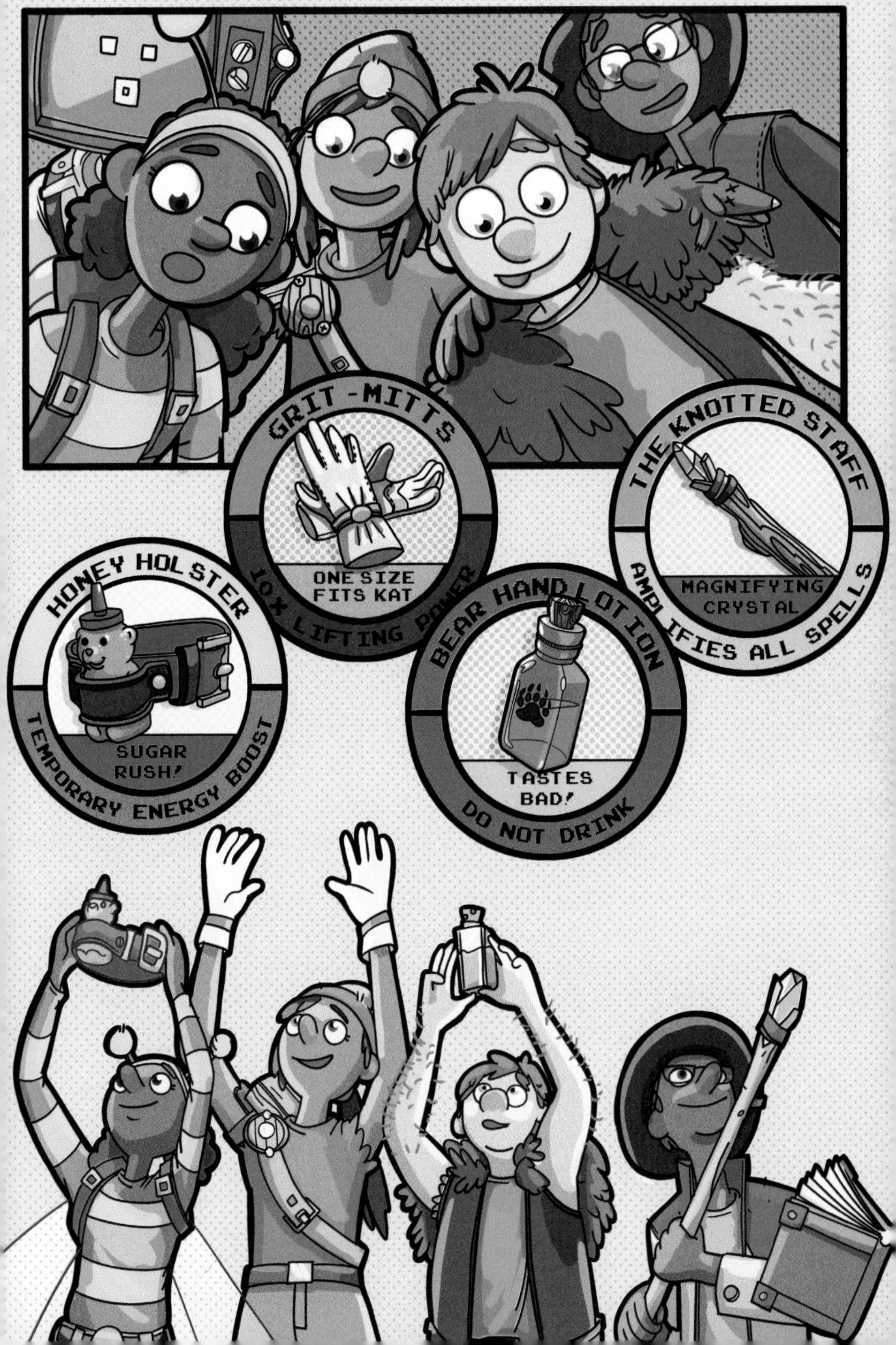
GRIT-MITTS
ONE SIZE FITS KAT
10X LIFTING POWER
THE KNOTTED STAFF
MAGNIFYING CRYSTAL
AMPLIFIES ALL SPELLS
HONEY HOLSTER
SUGAR RUSH!
TEMPORARY ENERGY BOOST
BEAR HAND LOTION
TASTES BAD!
DO NOT DRINK

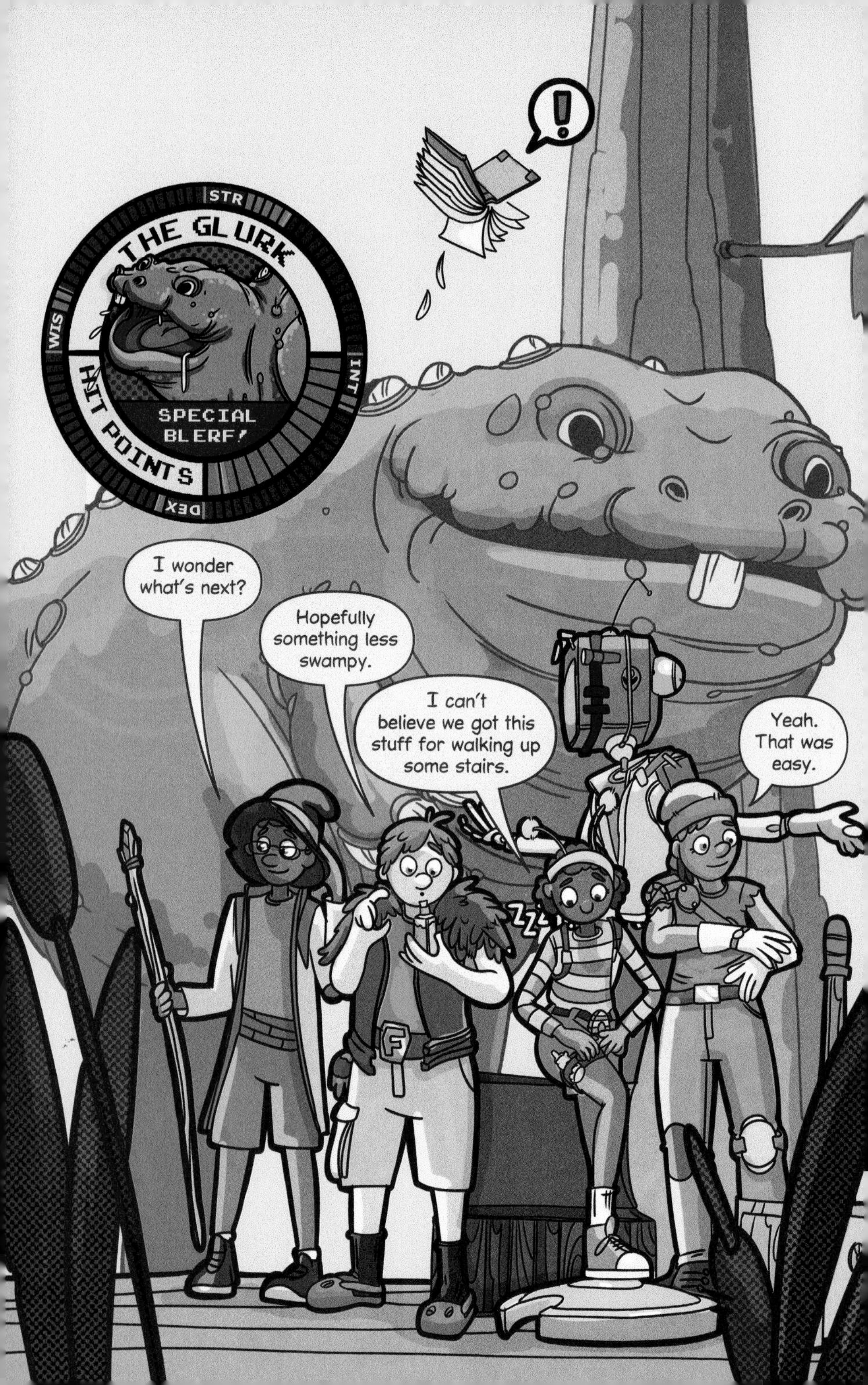
!
THE GLURK
STR
WIS
INT
DEX
HIT POINTS
SPECIAL BLERF!
I wonder what's next?
Hopefully something less swampy.
I can't believe we got this stuff for walking up some stairs.
Yeah. That was easy.
ZZZ

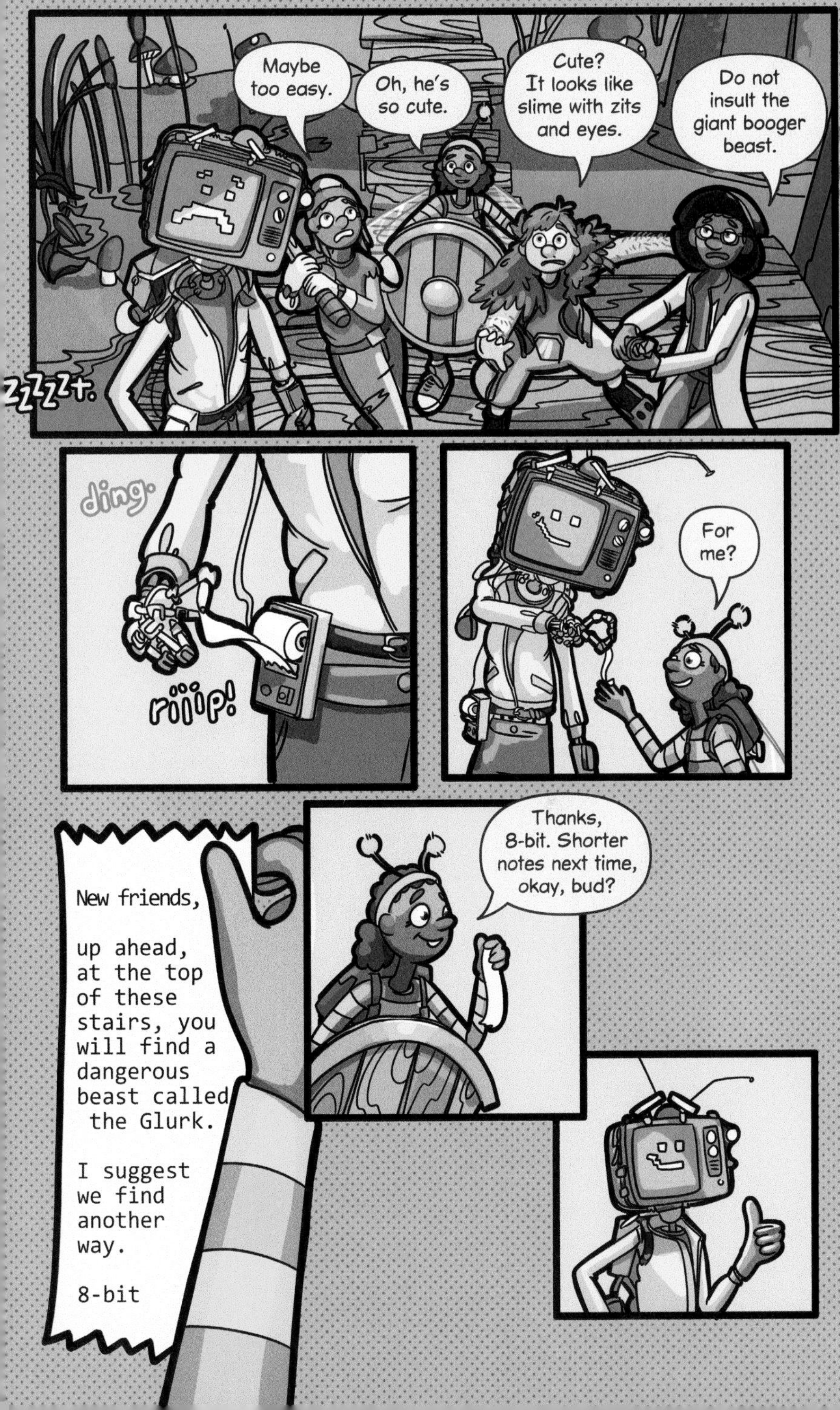
Maybe too easy.
Oh, he's so cute.
Cute? It looks like slime with zits and eyes.
Do not insult the giant booger beast.
zzzzzt.
ding.
riiip!
For me?
New friends,
up ahead, at the top of these stairs, you will find a dangerous beast called the Glurk.
I suggest we find another way.
8-bit
Thanks, 8-bit. Shorter notes next time, okay, bud?

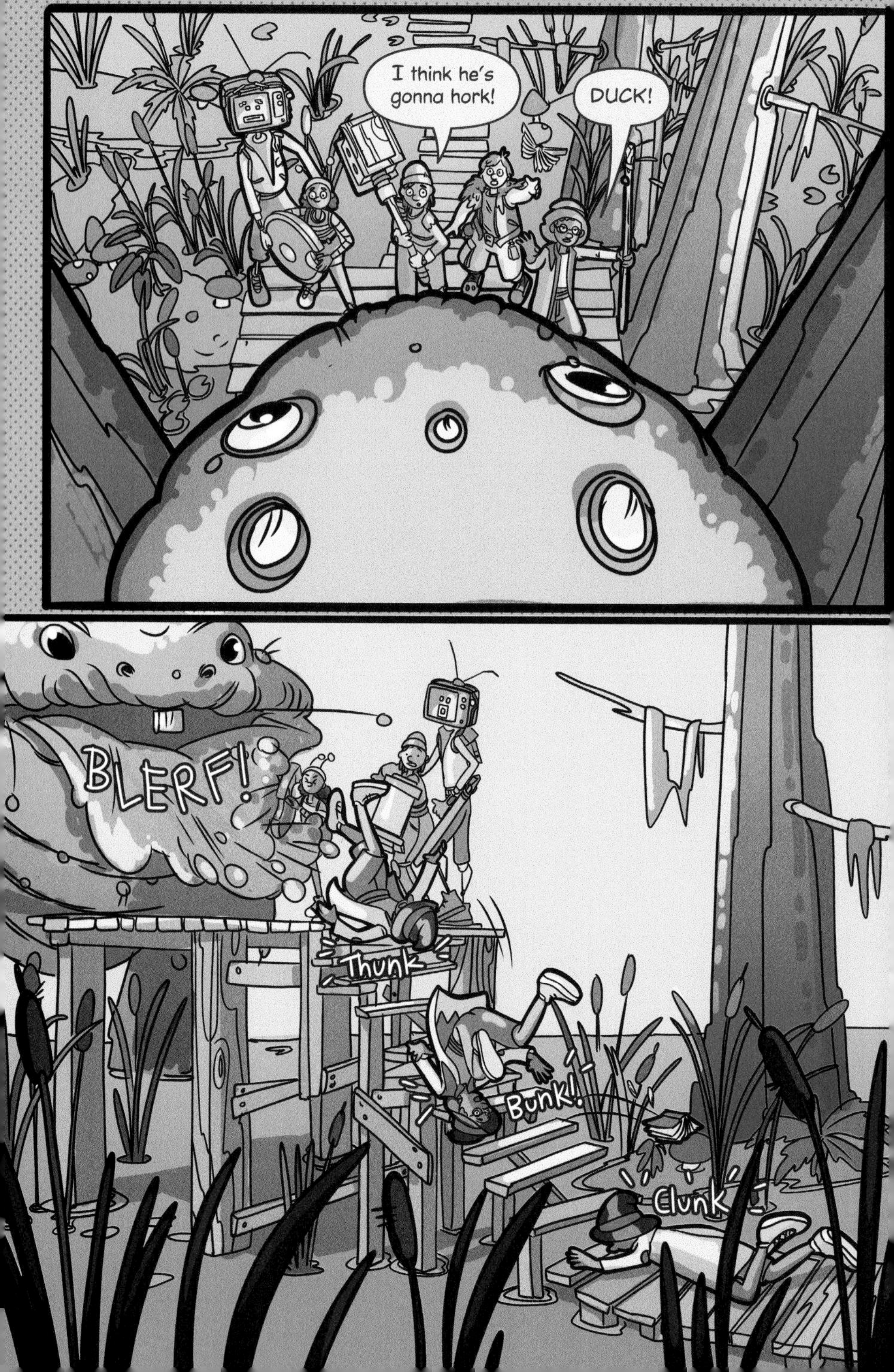
I think he's gonna hork!
DUCK!
BLERF!
Thunk
Bunk!
Clunk

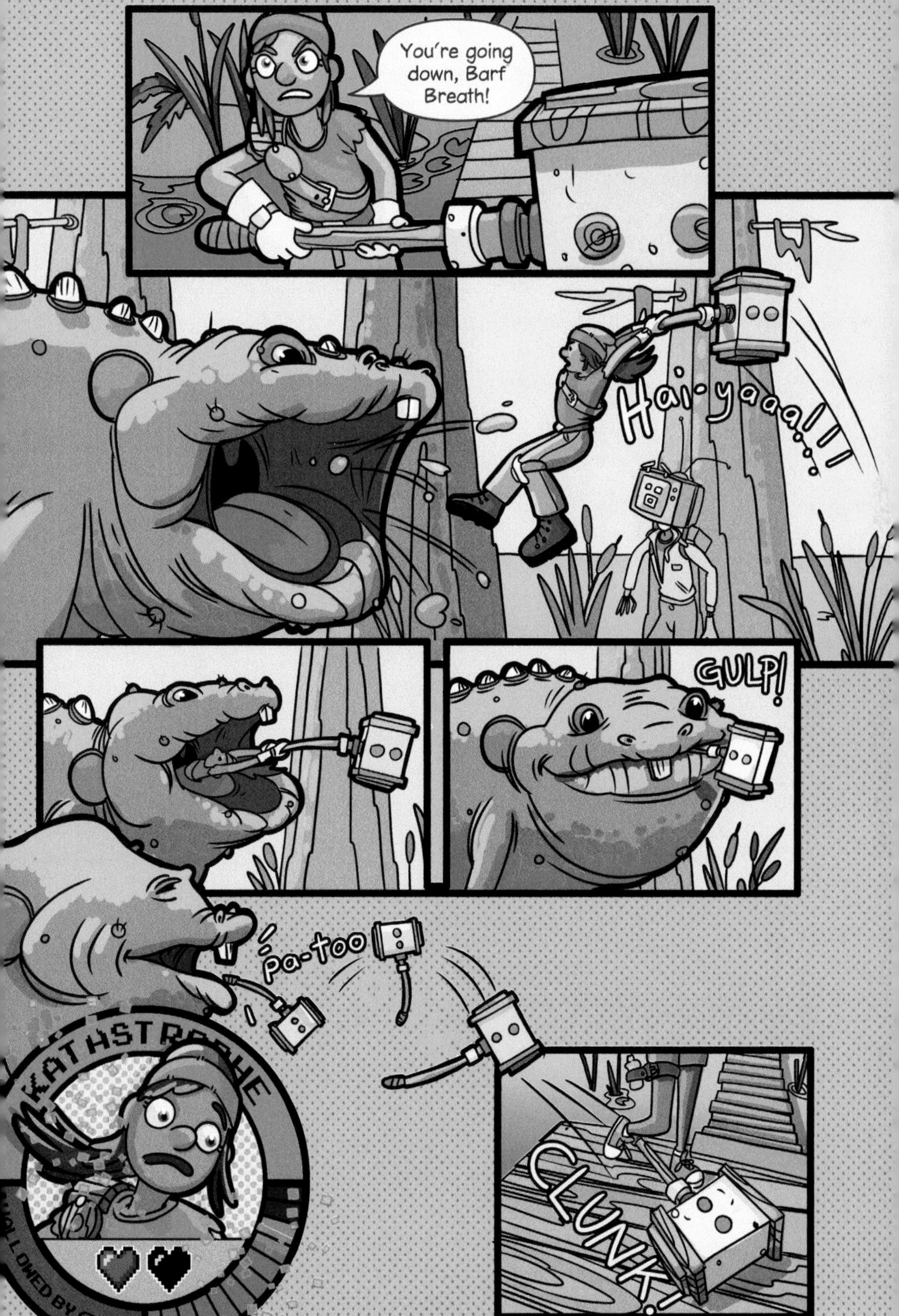
You're going down, Barf Breath!
Hai-yaaa!!!
GULP!
pa-too
KATHSTR
HE
LLOWED BY GL URK
CLUNK!

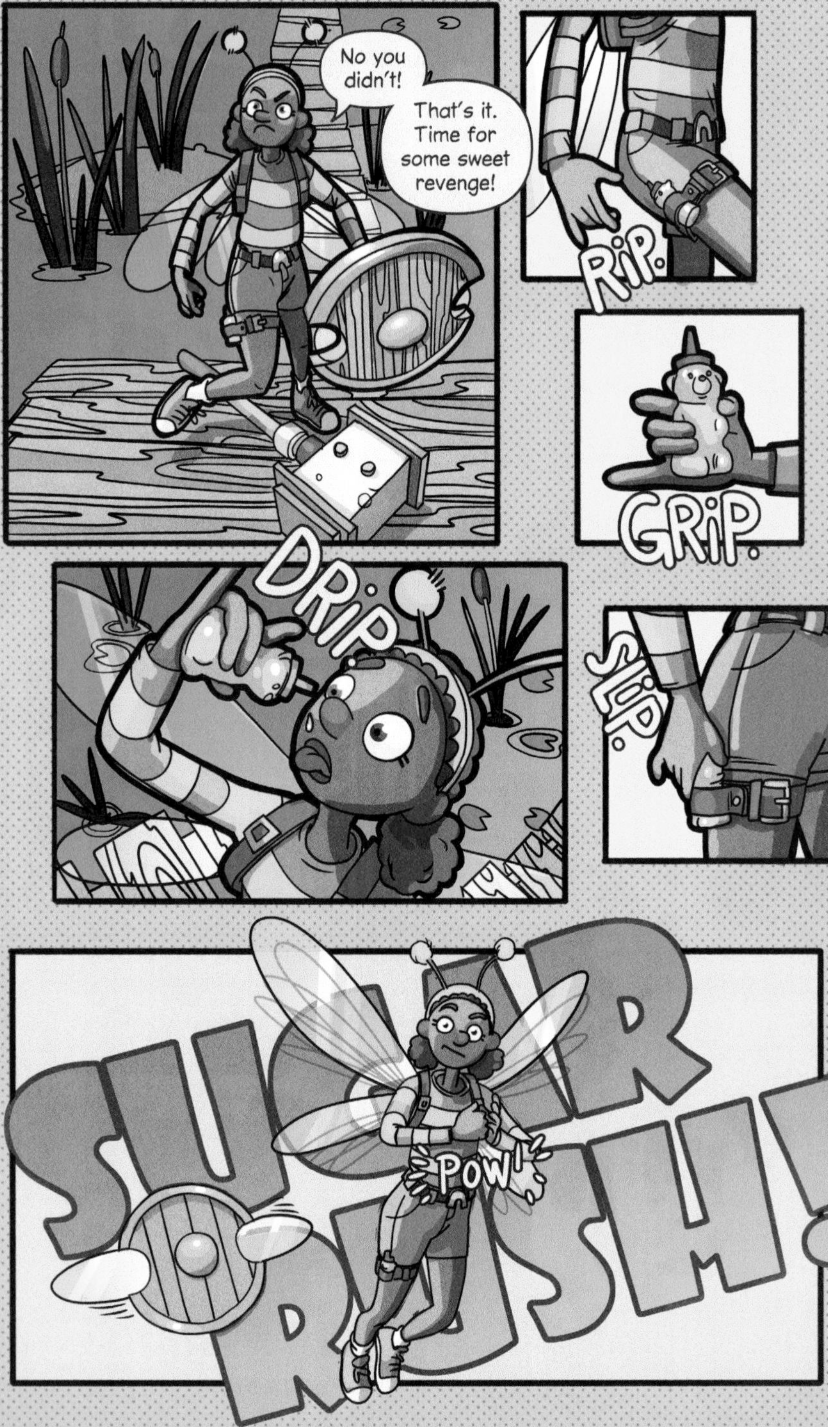
No you didn't!
That's it. Time for some sweet revenge!
RIP.
GRIP.
DRIP.
SLIP.
SUGAR RUSH!
POW!

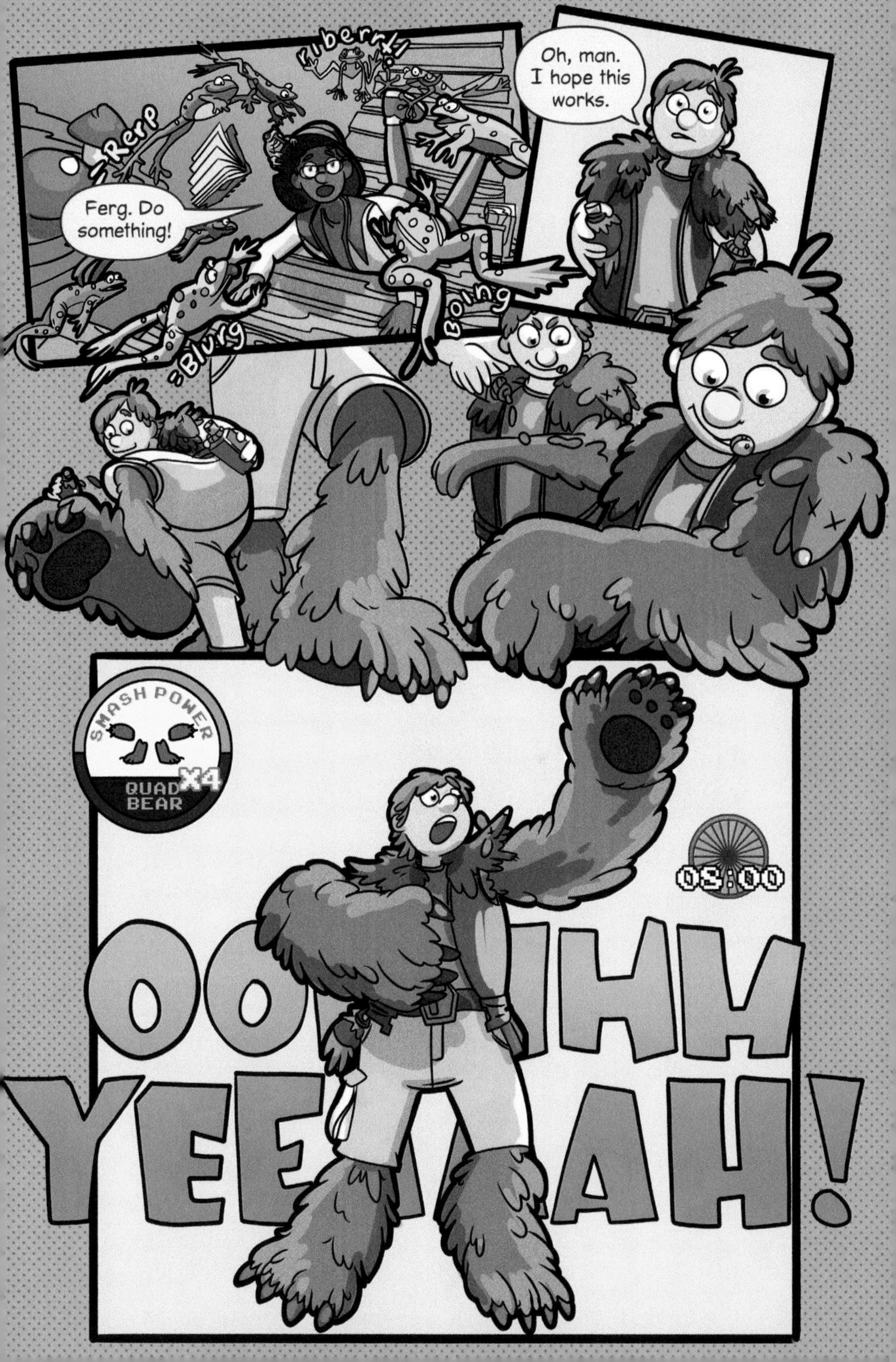

Rerp
Riberrt!
Ferg. Do something!
Blurg
Boing
Oh, man. I hope this works.
SMASH POWER
QUAD BEAR
X4
05:00
OOHHM YEEAAH!

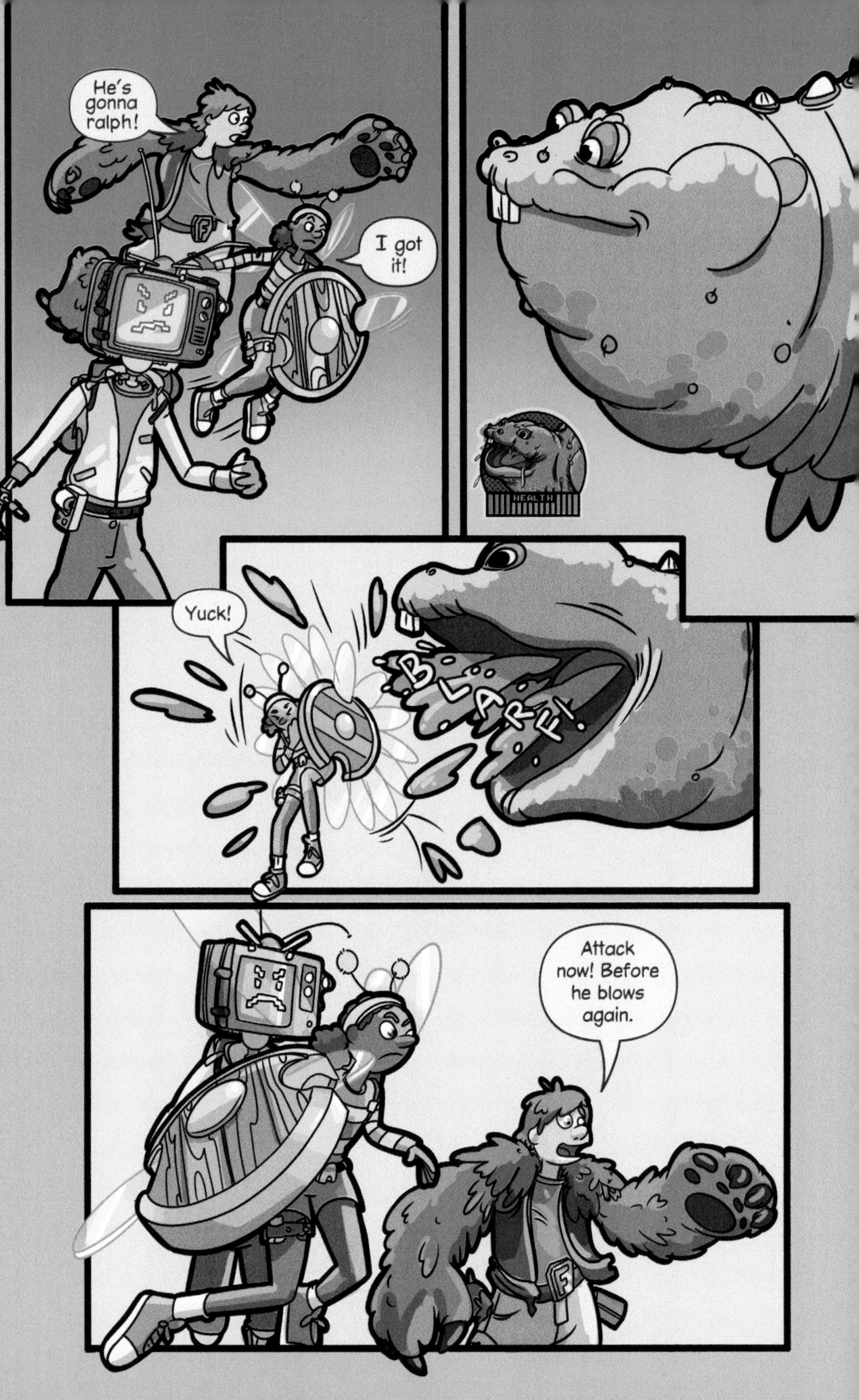
He's gonna ralph!
I got it!
HEALTH
Yuck!
BLARF!
Attack now! Before he blows again.

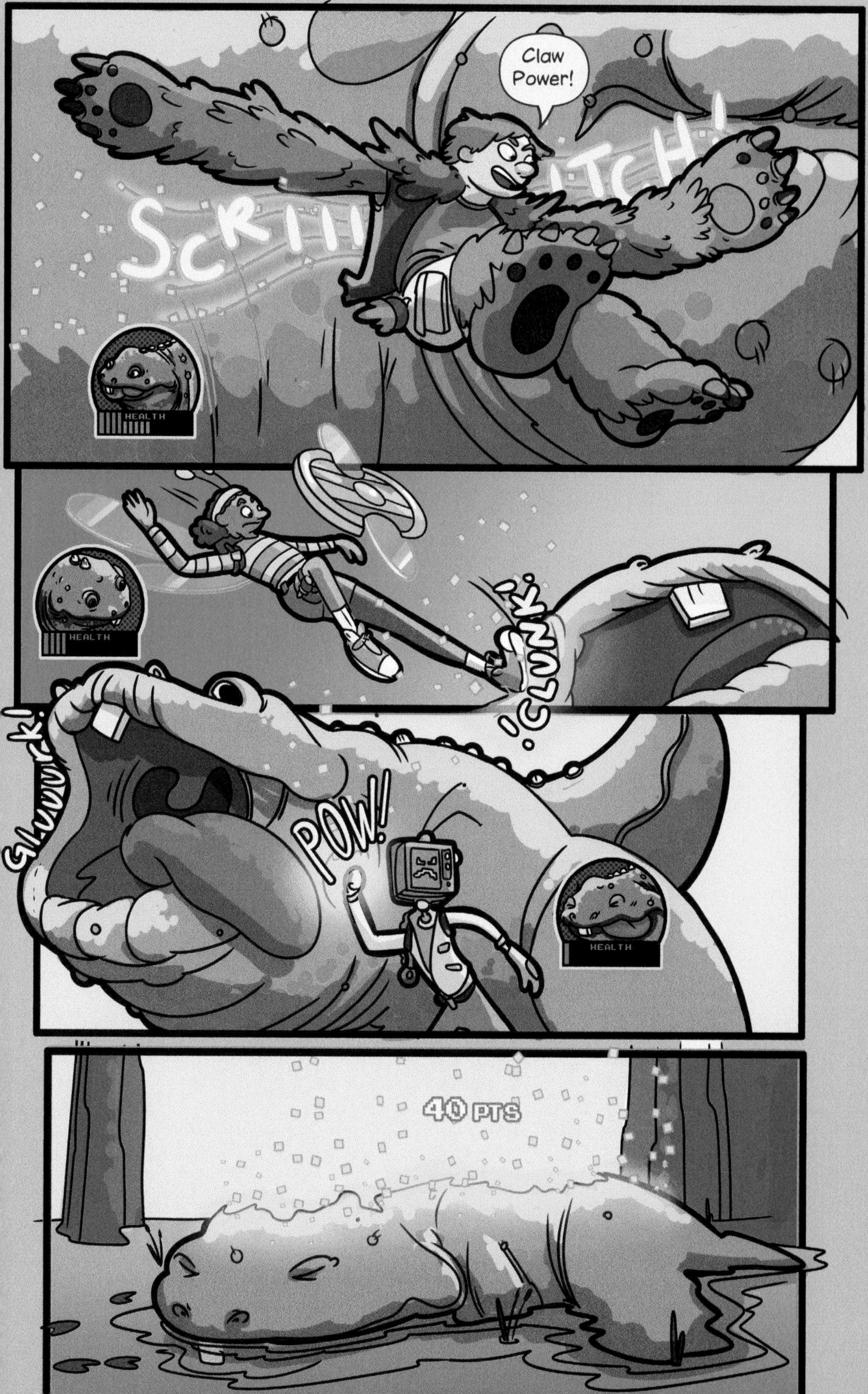
Claw Power!
SCRIIIITCH!
HEALTH
HEALTH
CLUNK!
GLUUUURK!
POW!
HEALTH
40 PTS

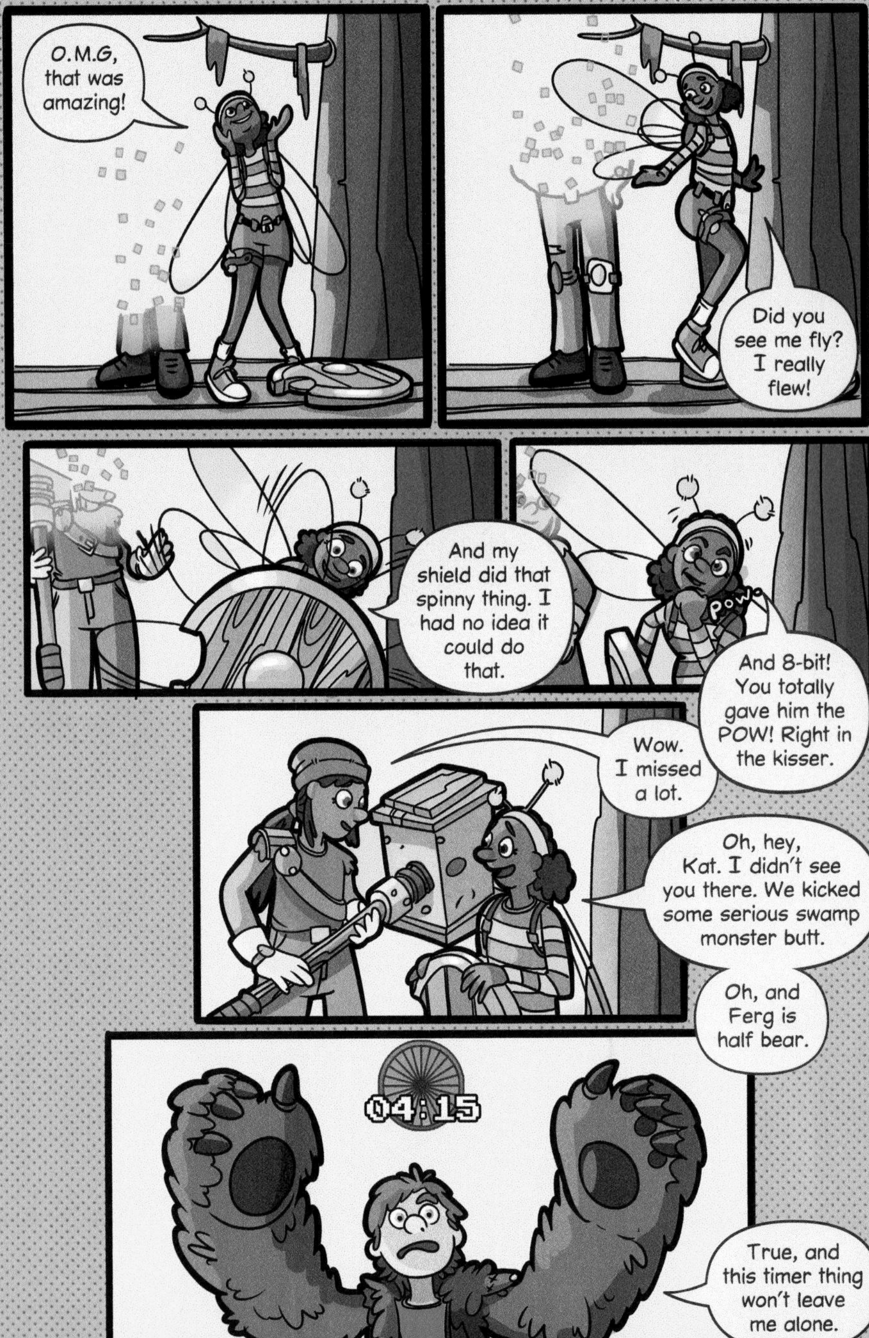
O.M.G, that was amazing!
Did you see me fly? I really flew!
And my shield did that spinny thing. I had no idea it could do that.
POW
And 8-bit! You totally gave him the POW! Right in the kisser.
Wow. I missed a lot.
Oh, hey, Kat. I didn't see you there. We kicked some serious swamp monster butt.
Oh, and Ferg is half bear.
04:15
True, and this timer thing won't leave me alone.

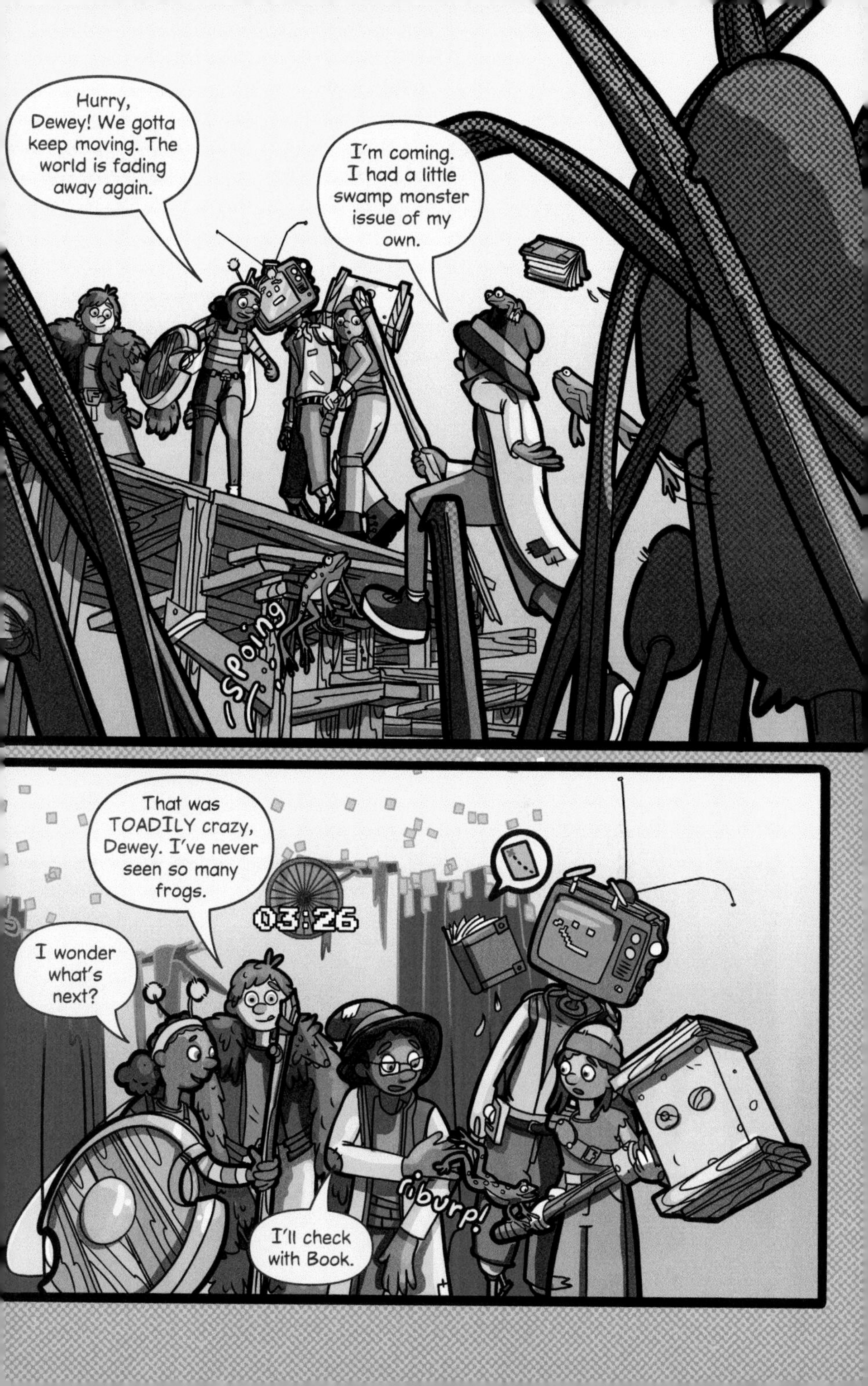
Hurry, Dewey! We gotta keep moving. The world is fading away again.
I'm coming. I had a little swamp monster issue of my own.
SPOING
That was TOADILY crazy, Dewey. I've never seen so many frogs.
03:26
I wonder what's next?
I'll check with Book.
riburp!

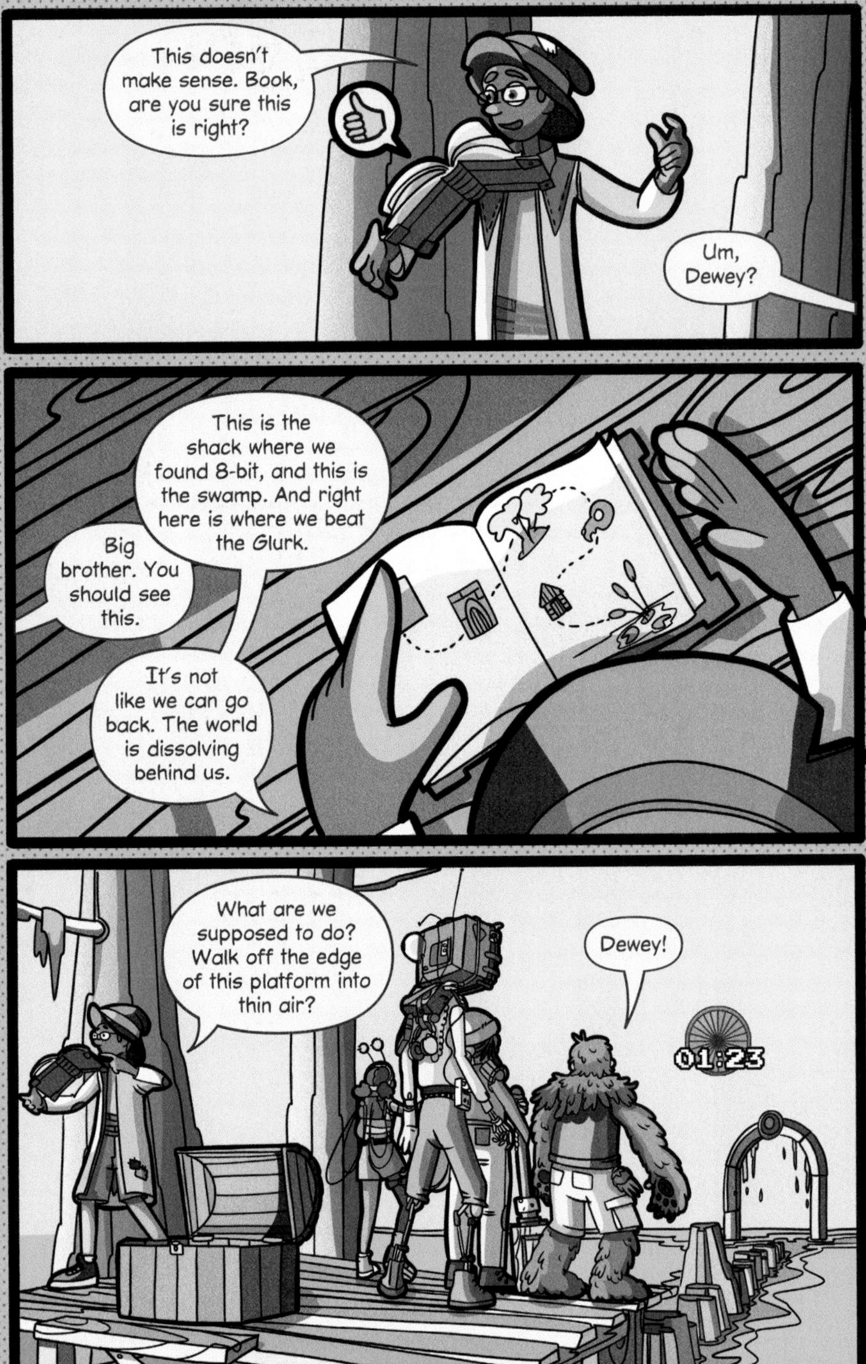
This doesn't make sense. Book, are you sure this is right?
Um, Dewey?
This is the shack where we found 8-bit, and this is the swamp. And right here is where we beat the Glurk.
Big brother. You should see this.
It's not like we can go back. The world is dissolving behind us.
What are we supposed to do? Walk off the edge of this platform into thin air?
Dewey!
01:23

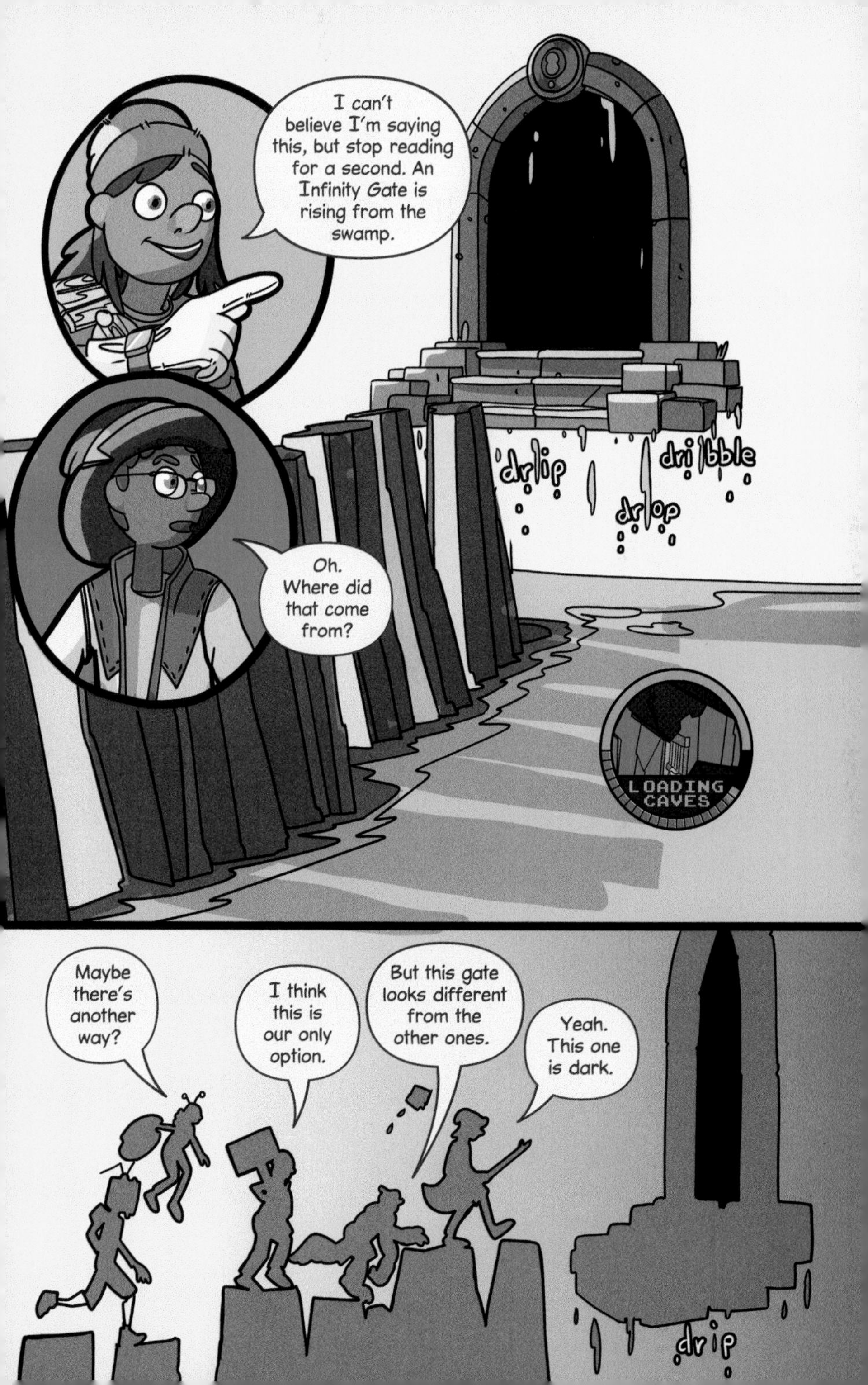
I can't believe I'm saying this, but stop reading for a second. An Infinity Gate is rising from the swamp.
Oh. Where did that come from?
drip
dribble
drop
LOADING CAVES
Maybe there's another way?
I think this is our only option.
But this gate looks different from the other ones.
Yeah. This one is dark.
drip

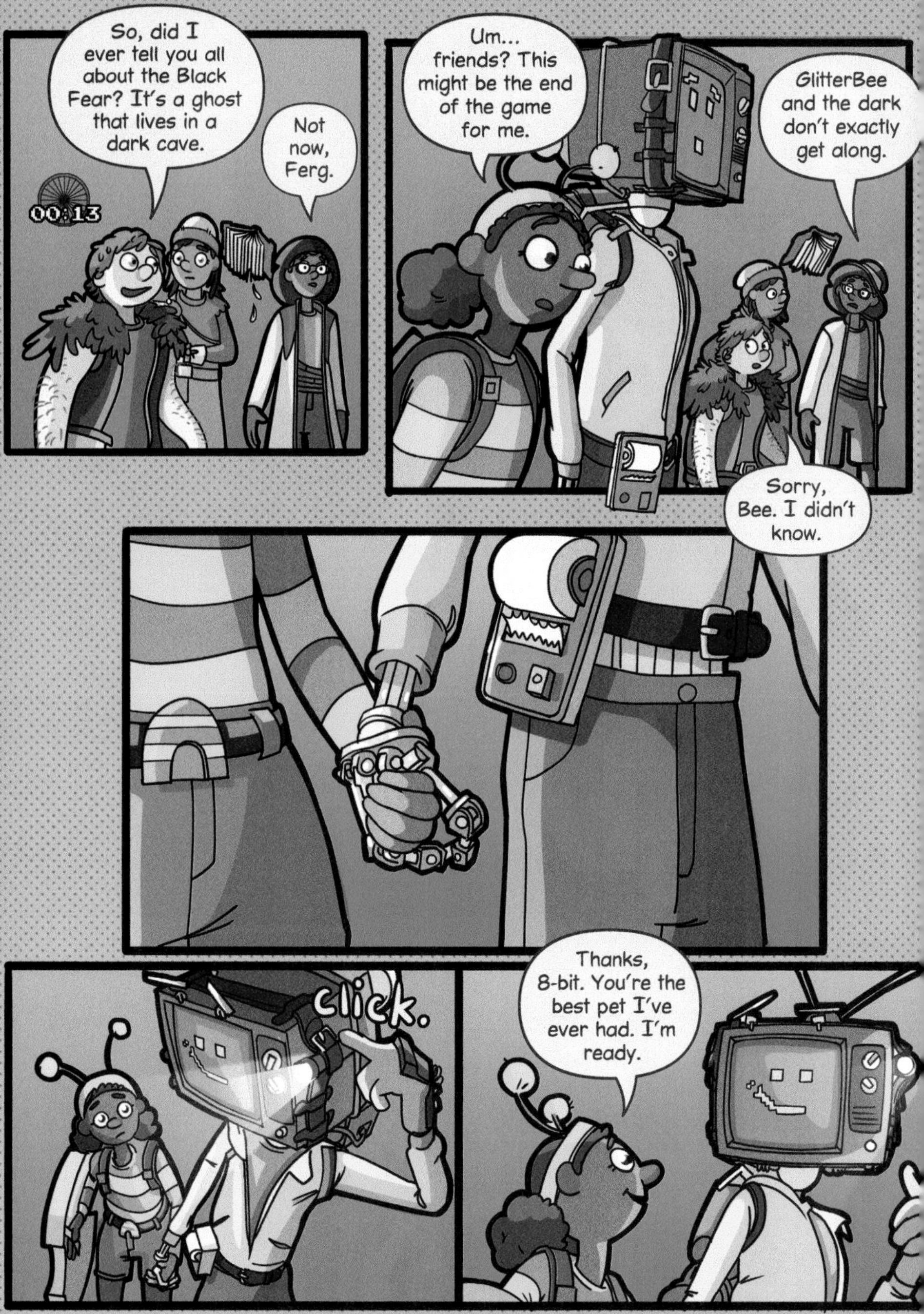
So, did I ever tell you all about the Black Fear? It's a ghost that lives in a dark cave.
Not now, Ferg.
00:13
Um... friends? This might be the end of the game for me.
GlitterBee and the dark don't exactly get along.
Sorry, Bee. I didn't know.
click.
Thanks, 8-bit. You're the best pet I've ever had. I'm ready.

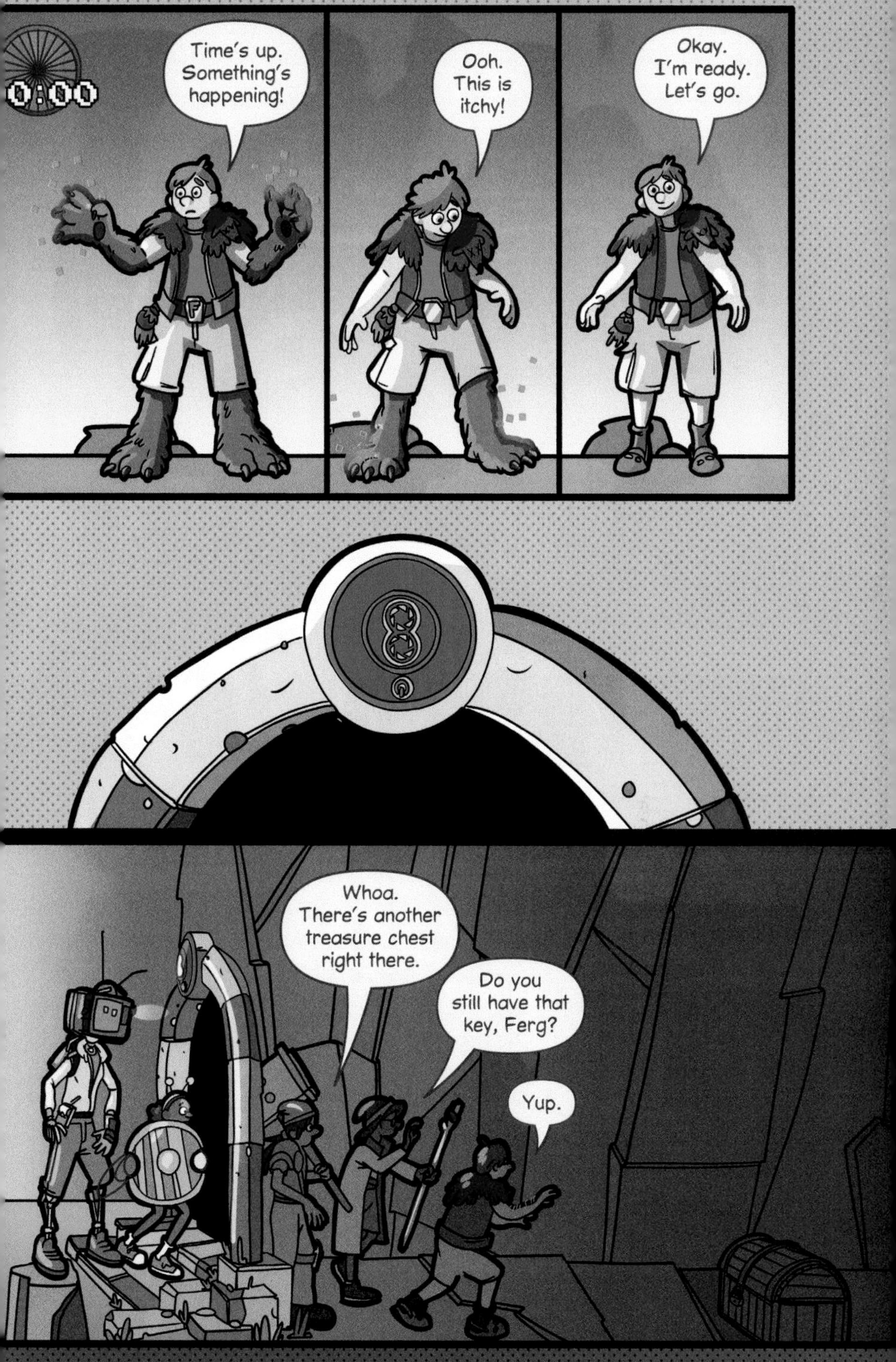
0:00
Time's up. Something's happening!
Ooh. This is itchy!
Okay. I'm ready. Let's go.
Whoa. There's another treasure chest right there.
Do you still have that key, Ferg?
Yup.

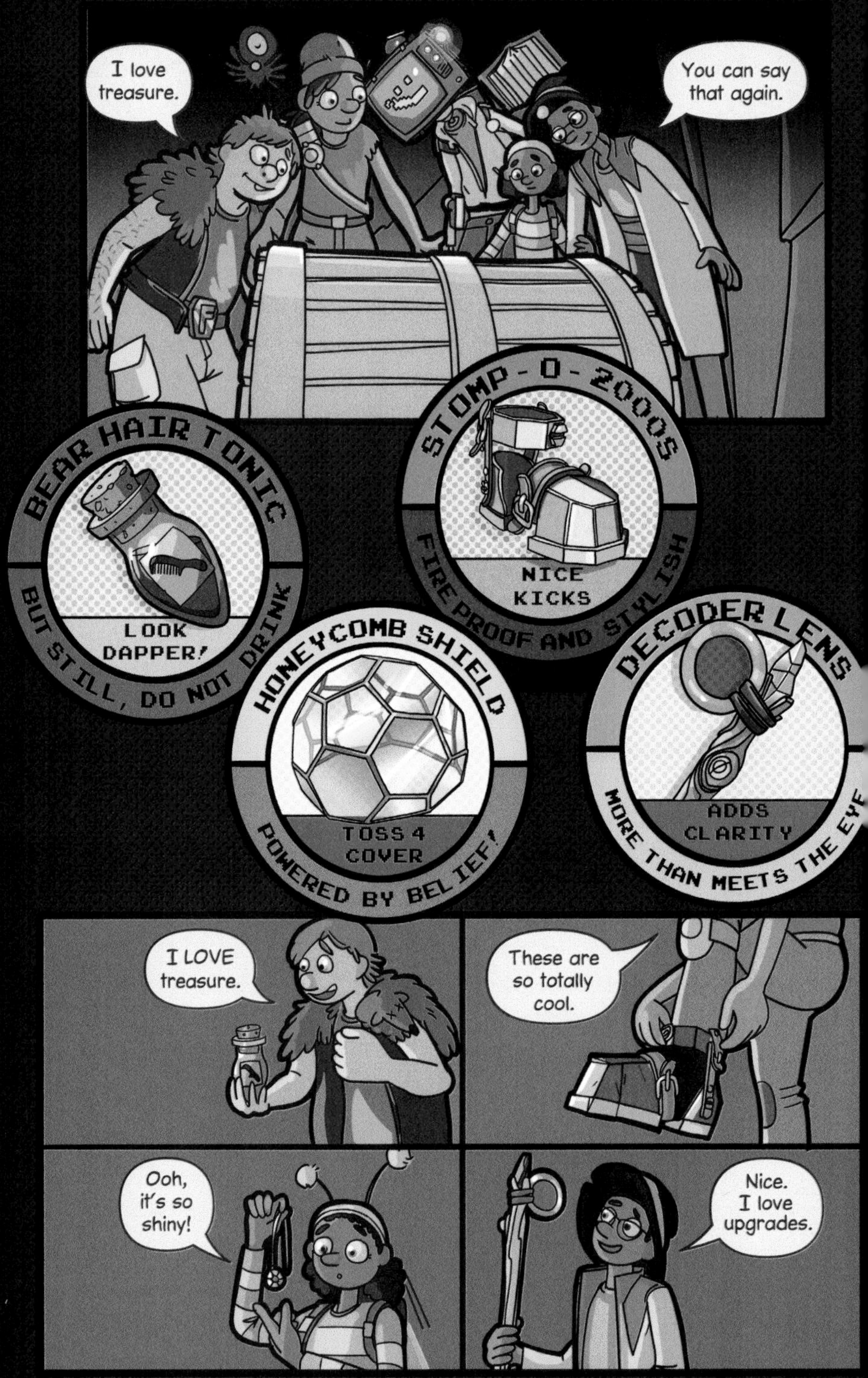
I love treasure.
You can say that again.
BEAR HAIR TONIC
LOOK DAPPER!
BUT STILL, DO NOT DRINK
STOMP-O-2000S
NICE KICKS
FIRE PROOF AND STYLISH
HONEYCOMB SHIELD
TOSS 4 COVER
POWERED BY BELIEF!
DECODER LENS
ADDS CLARITY
MORE THAN MEETS THE EYE
I LOVE treasure.
These are so totally cool.
Ooh, it's so shiny!
Nice. I love upgrades.

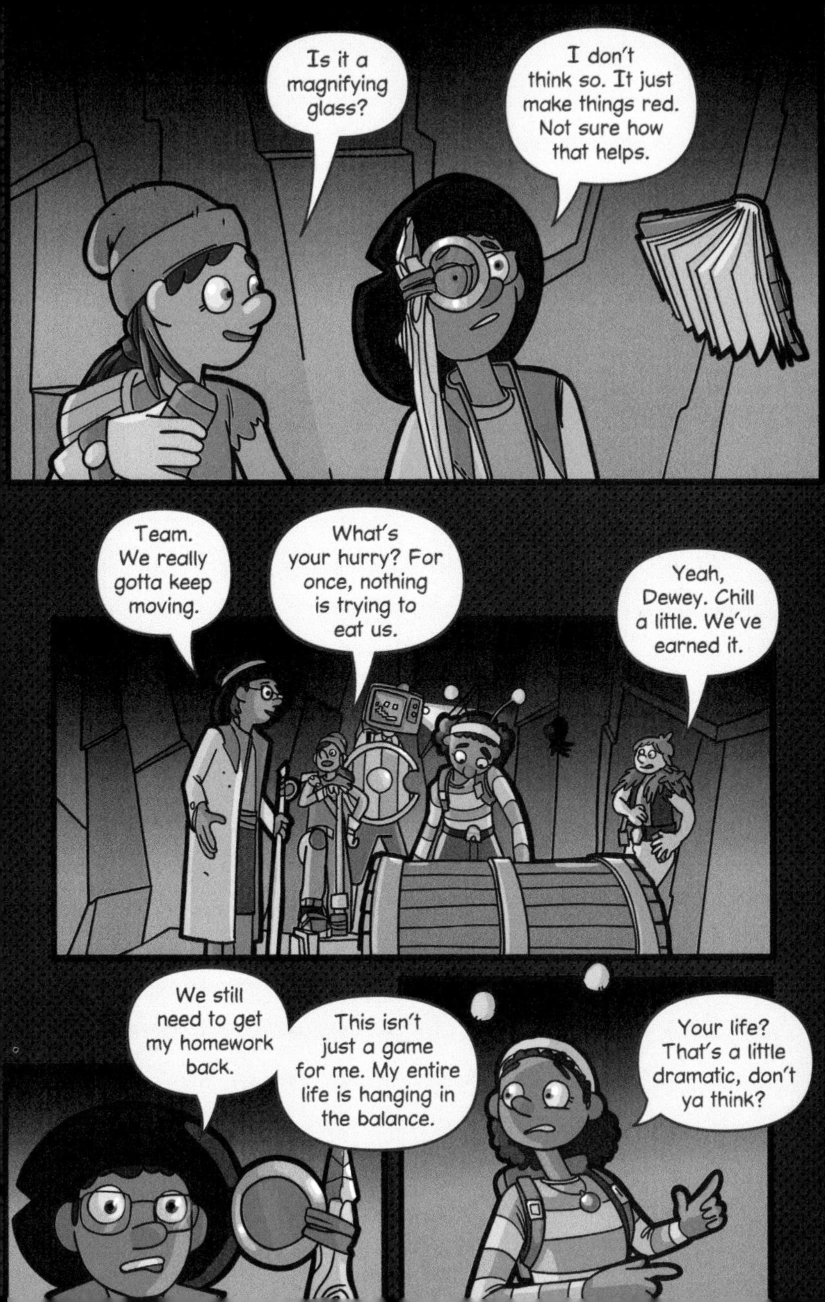
Is it a magnifying glass?
I don't think so. It just make things red. Not sure how that helps.
Team. We really gotta keep moving.
What's your hurry? For once, nothing is trying to eat us.
Yeah, Dewey. Chill a little. We've earned it.
We still need to get my homework back.
This isn't just a game for me. My entire life is hanging in the balance.
Your life? That's a little dramatic, don't ya think?

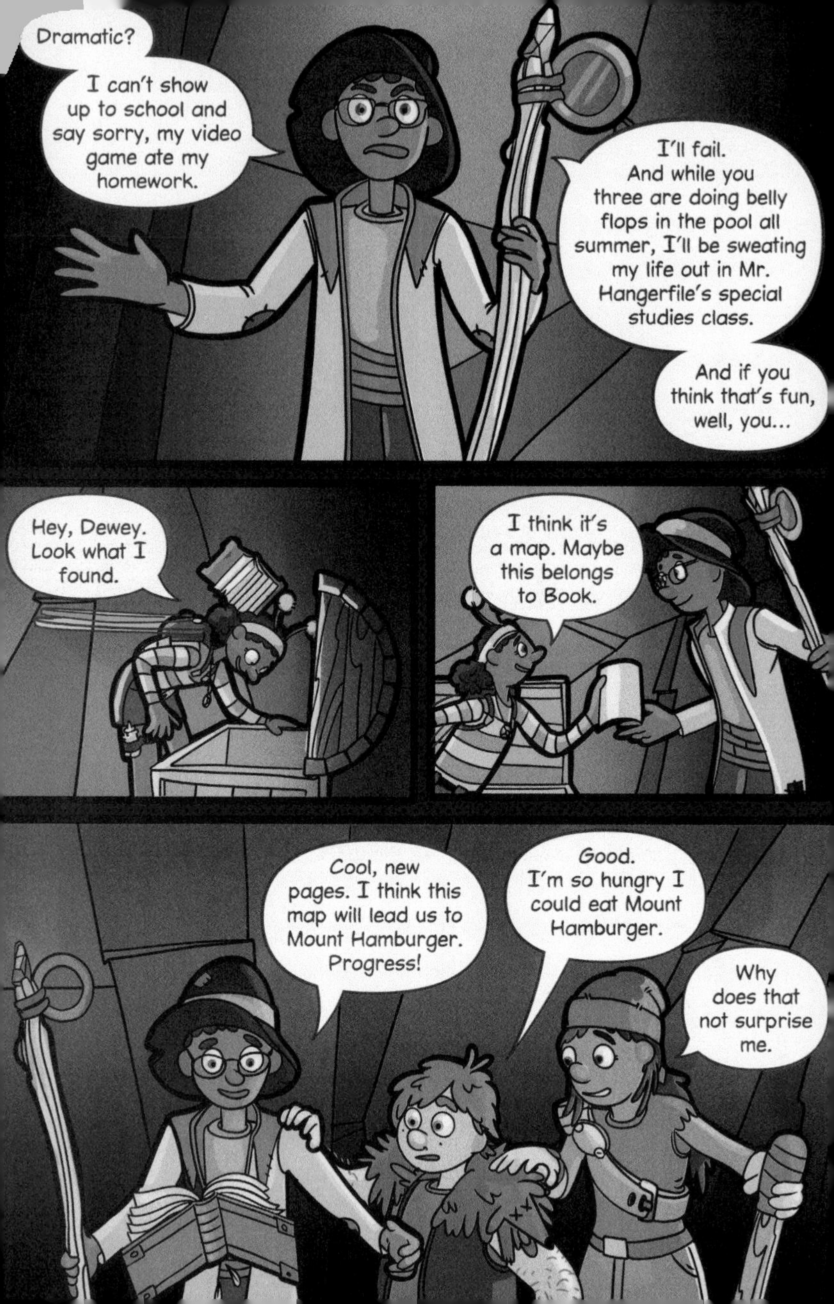
Dramatic?
I can't show up to school and say sorry, my video game ate my homework.
I'll fail. And while you three are doing belly flops in the pool all summer, I'll be sweating my life out in Mr. Hangerfile's special studies class.
And if you think that's fun, well, you...
Hey, Dewey. Look what I found.
I think it's a map. Maybe this belongs to Book.
Cool, new pages. I think this map will lead us to Mount Hamburger. Progress!
Good. I'm so hungry I could eat Mount Hamburger.
Why does that not surprise me.

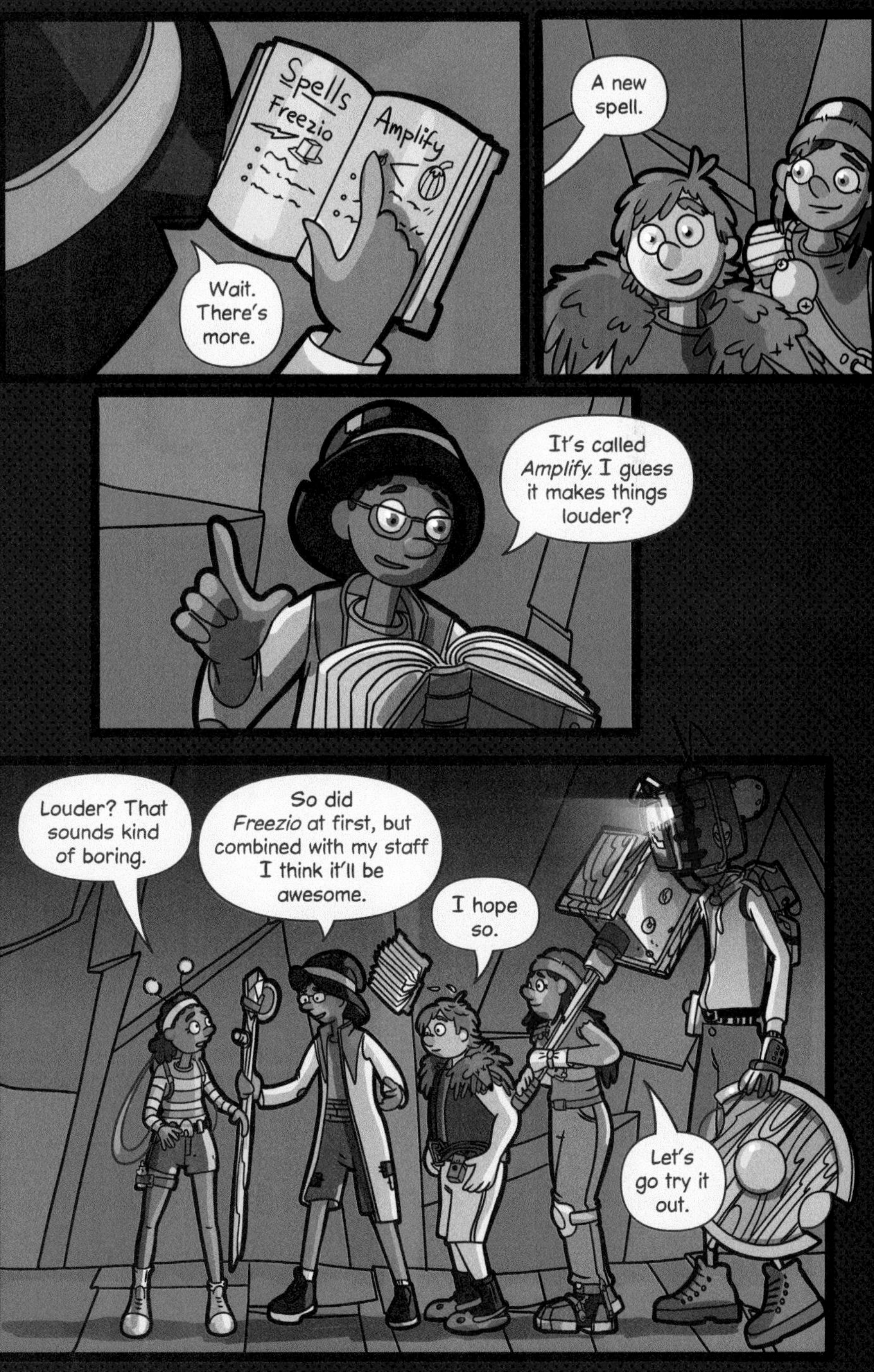

Spells
Freezio
Amplify
Wait. There's more.
A new spell.
It's called *Amplify.* I guess it makes things louder?
Louder? That sounds kind of boring.
So did *Freezio* at first, but combined with my staff I think it'll be awesome.
I hope so.
Let's go try it out.

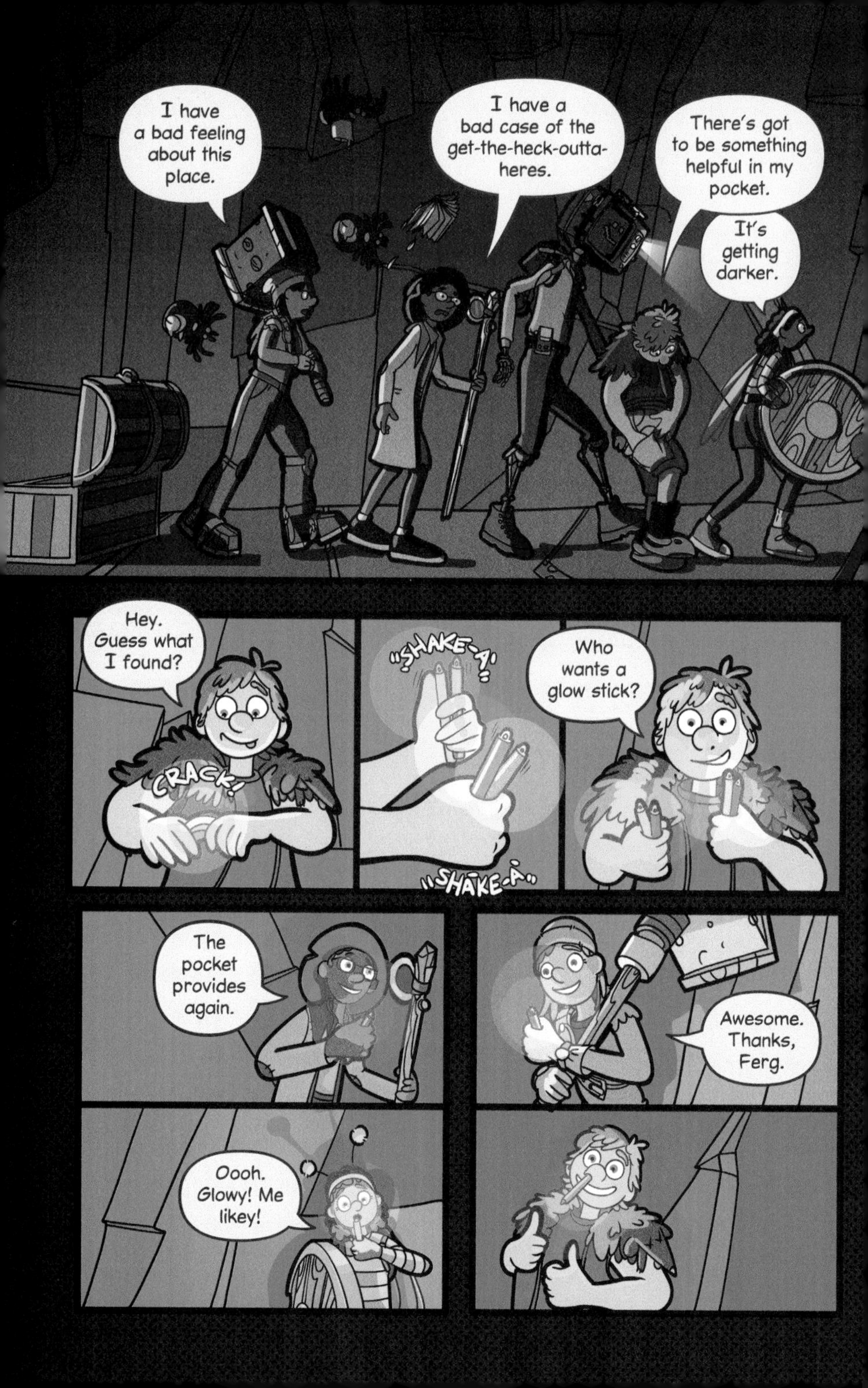

I have a bad feeling about this place.
I have a bad case of the get-the-heck-outta-heres.
There's got to be something helpful in my pocket.
It's getting darker.
Hey. Guess what I found?
CRACK!
"SHAKE-A"
"SHAKE-A"
Who wants a glow stick?
The pocket provides again.
Awesome. Thanks, Ferg.
Oooh. Glowy! Me likey!

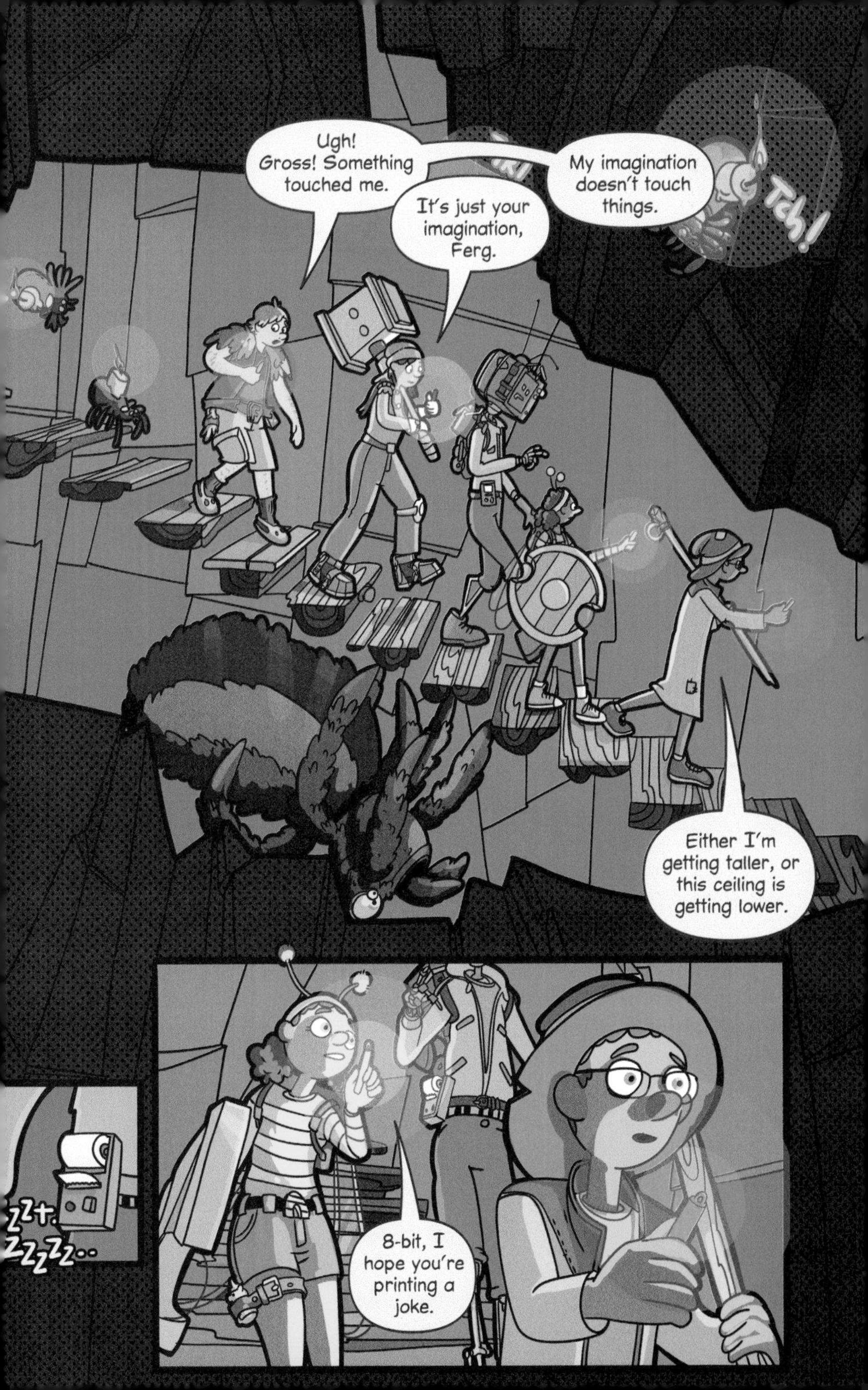
Ugh! Gross! Something touched me.
It's just your imagination, Ferg.
My imagination doesn't touch things.
Tch!
Either I'm getting taller, or this ceiling is getting lower.
8-bit, I hope you're printing a joke.
zzt.
zzzzz..

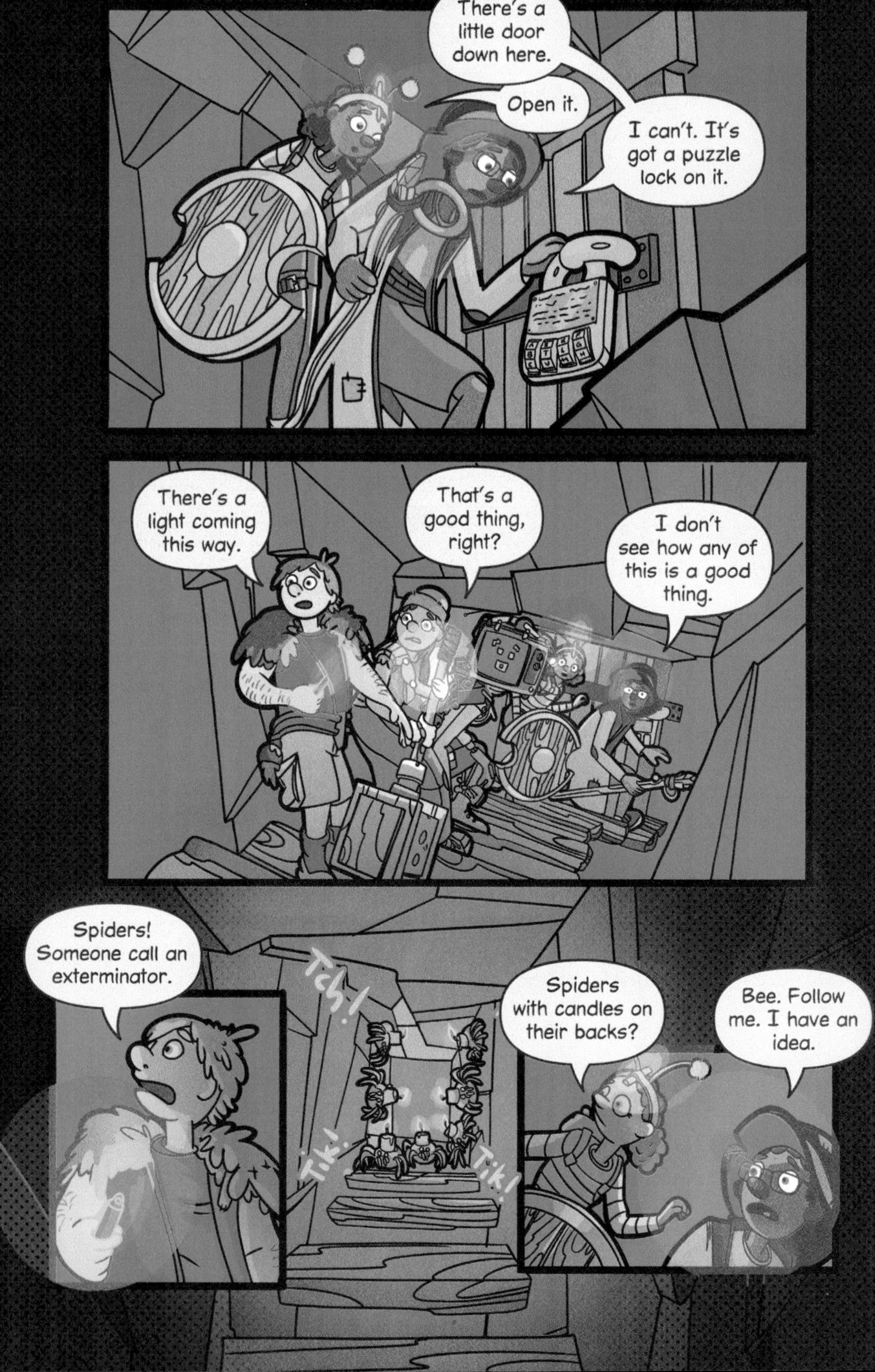
There's a little door down here.
Open it.
I can't. It's got a puzzle lock on it.
There's a light coming this way.
That's a good thing, right?
I don't see how any of this is a good thing.
Spiders! Someone call an exterminator.
Tch!
Tik!
Tik!
Spiders with candles on their backs?
Bee. Follow me. I have an idea.

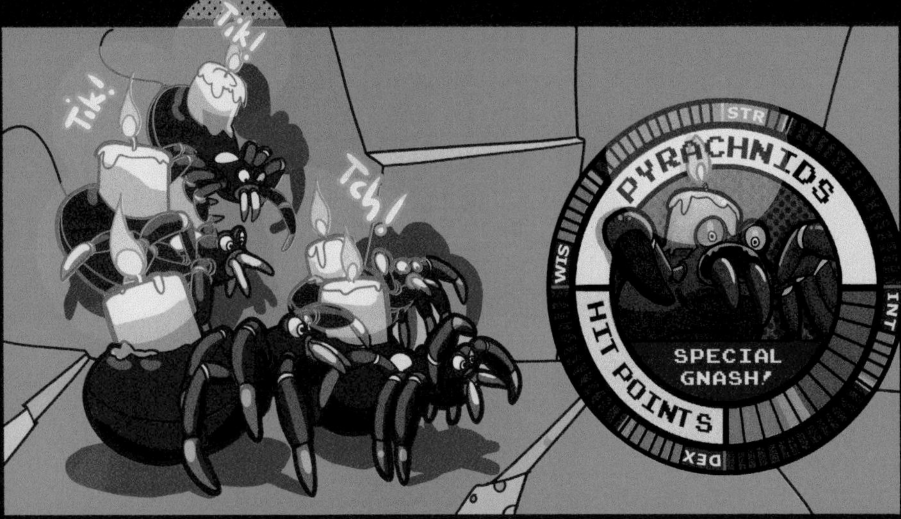
Tik!
Tik!
Tch!
STR
PYRACHNIDS
WIS
INT
HIT POINTS
SPECIAL GNASH!
DEX

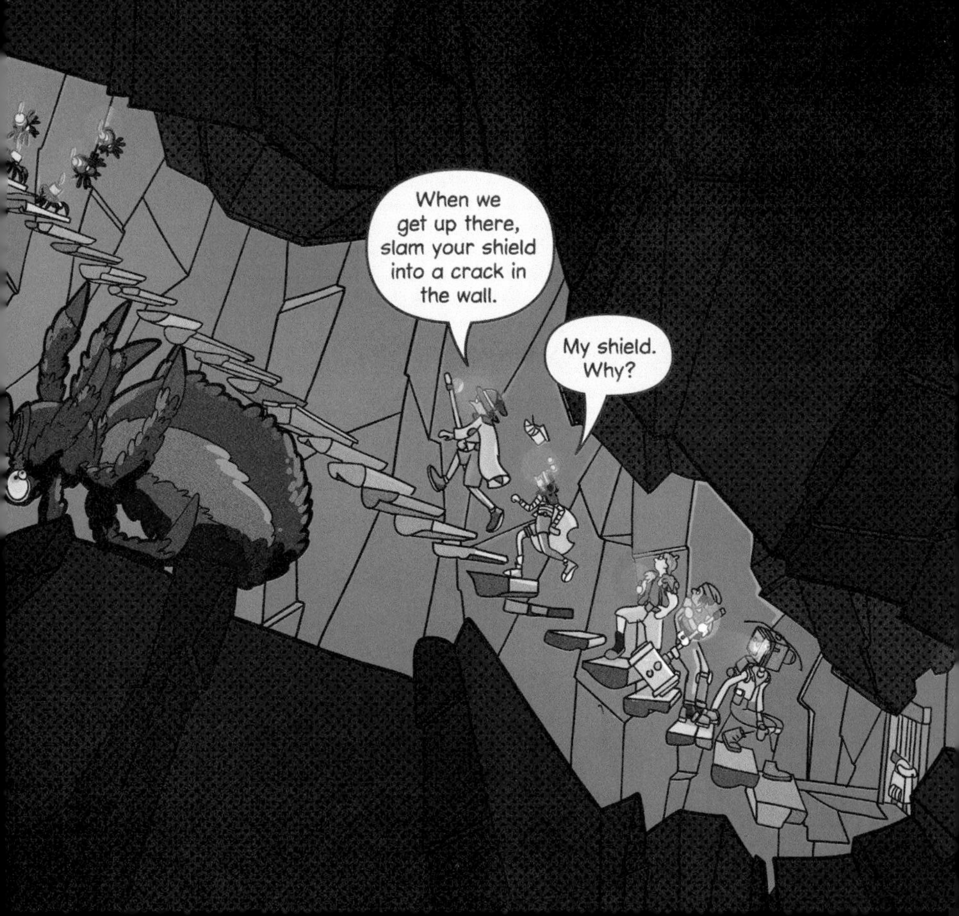
When we get up there, slam your shield into a crack in the wall.
My shield. Why?

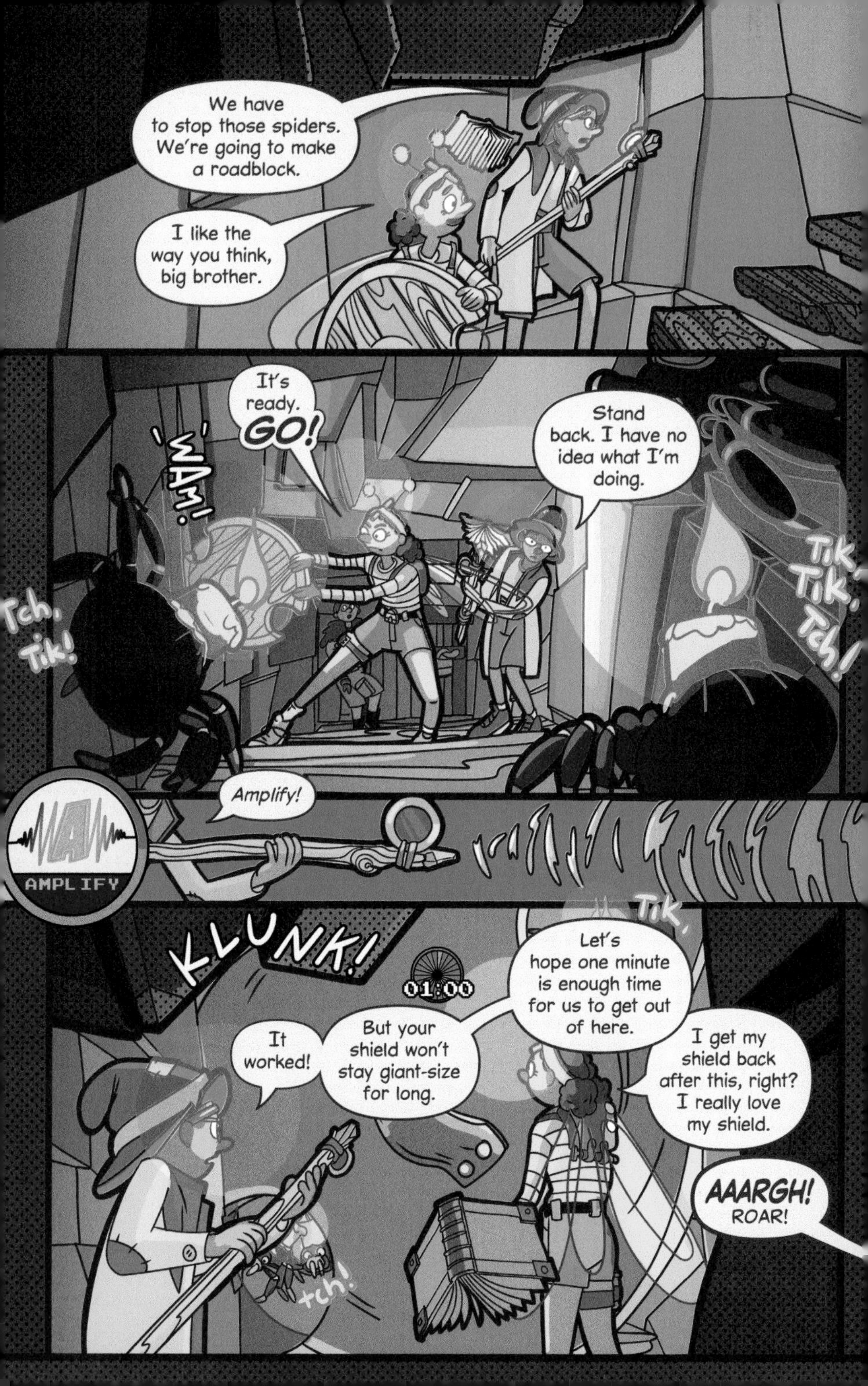
We have to stop those spiders. We're going to make a roadblock.
I like the way you think, big brother.
It's ready. GO!
WAM!
Stand back. I have no idea what I'm doing.
Tch, Tik!
Tik, Tik, Tch!
Amplify!
AMPLIFY
KLUNK!
Tik,
01:00
It worked!
But your shield won't stay giant-size for long.
Let's hope one minute is enough time for us to get out of here.
I get my shield back after this, right? I really love my shield.
AAARGH! ROAR!
tch!

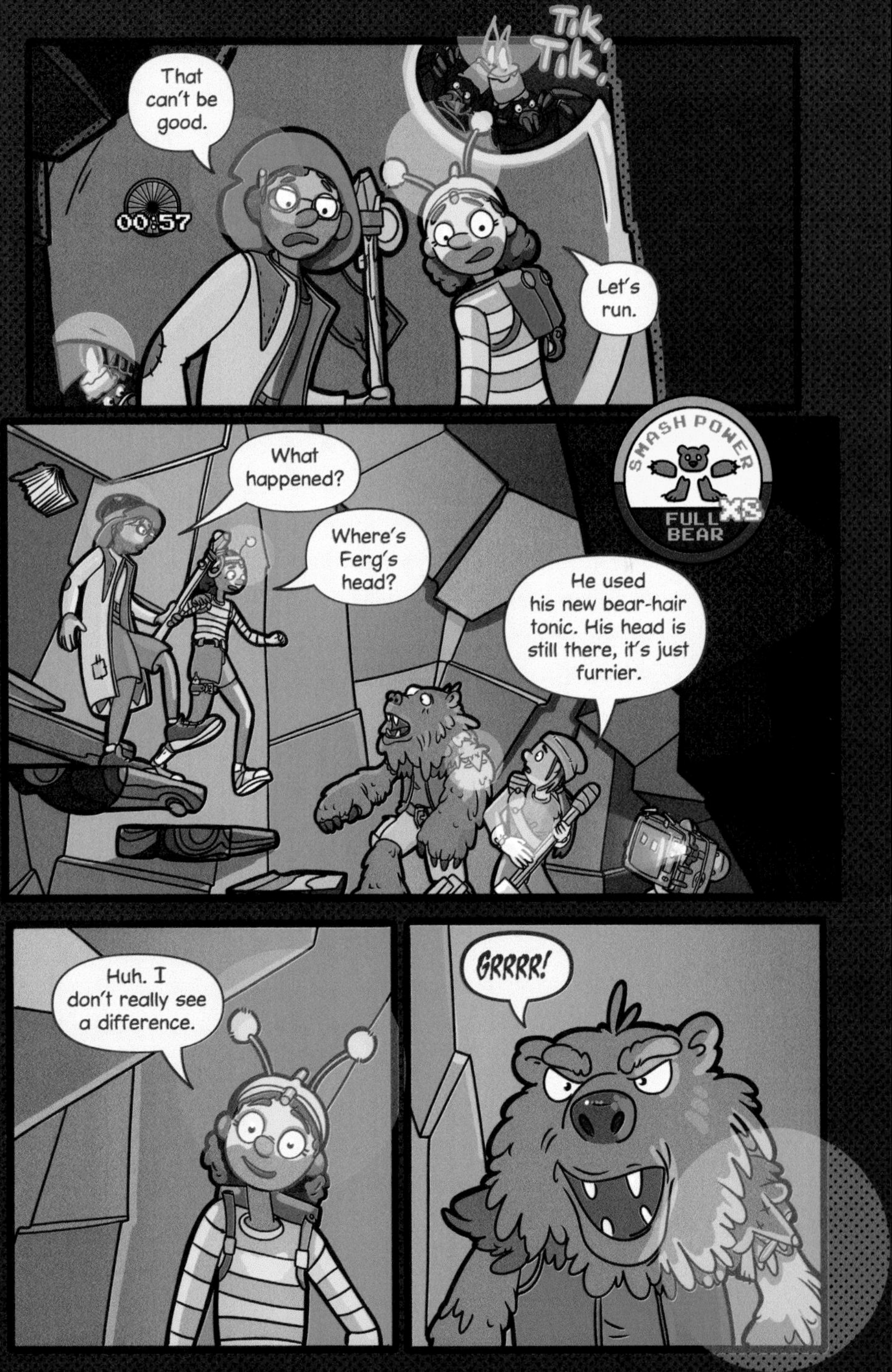
TIK, TIK!
That can't be good.
00:57
Let's run.
What happened?
Where's Ferg's head?
SMASH POWER
FULL BEAR
X8
He used his new bear-hair tonic. His head is still there, it's just furrier.
Huh. I don't really see a difference.
GRRRR!

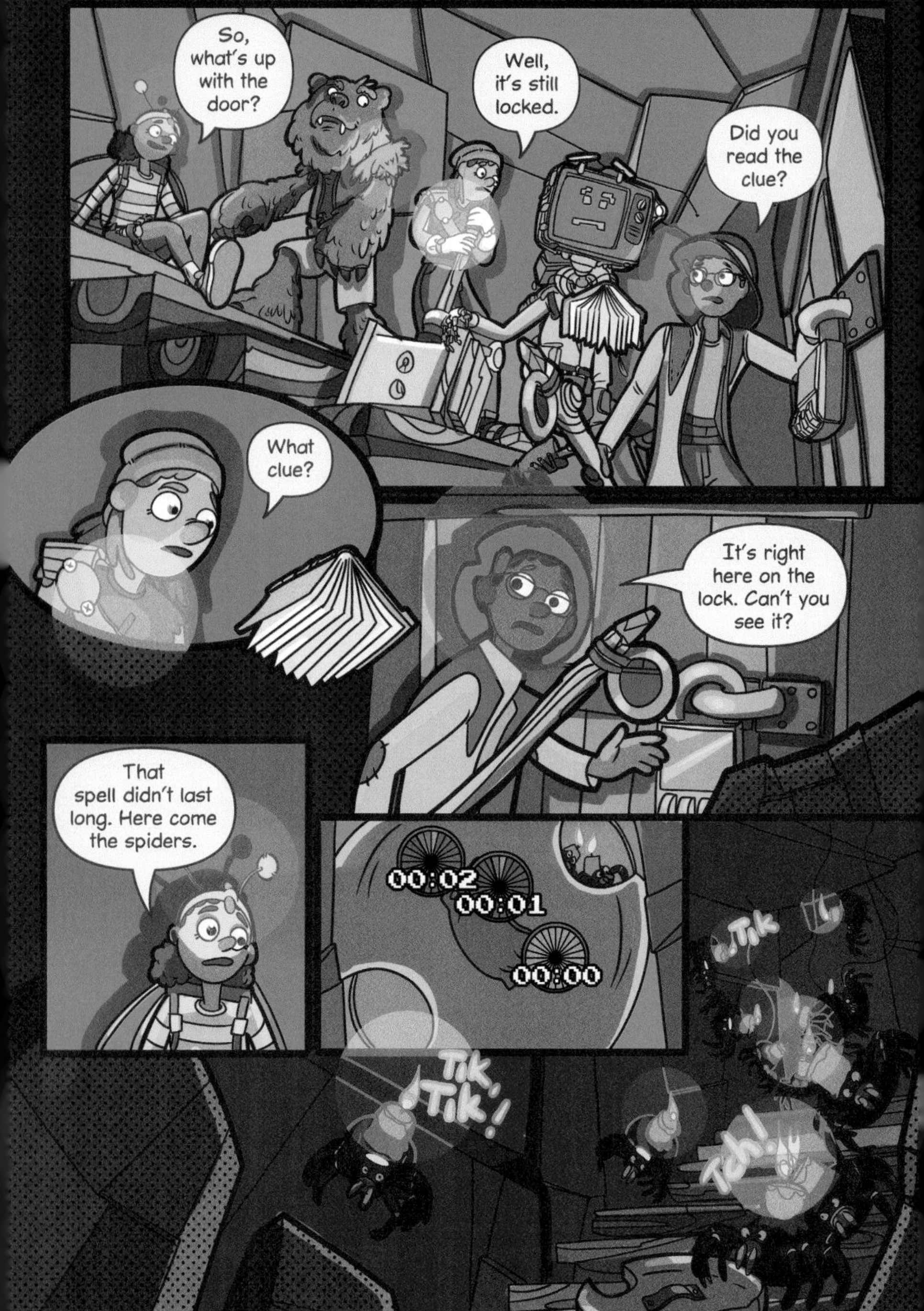
So, what's up with the door?
Well, it's still locked.
Did you read the clue?
What clue?
It's right here on the lock. Can't you see it?
That spell didn't last long. Here come the spiders.
00:02
00:01
00:00
Tik
Tik, Tik!
Tch!

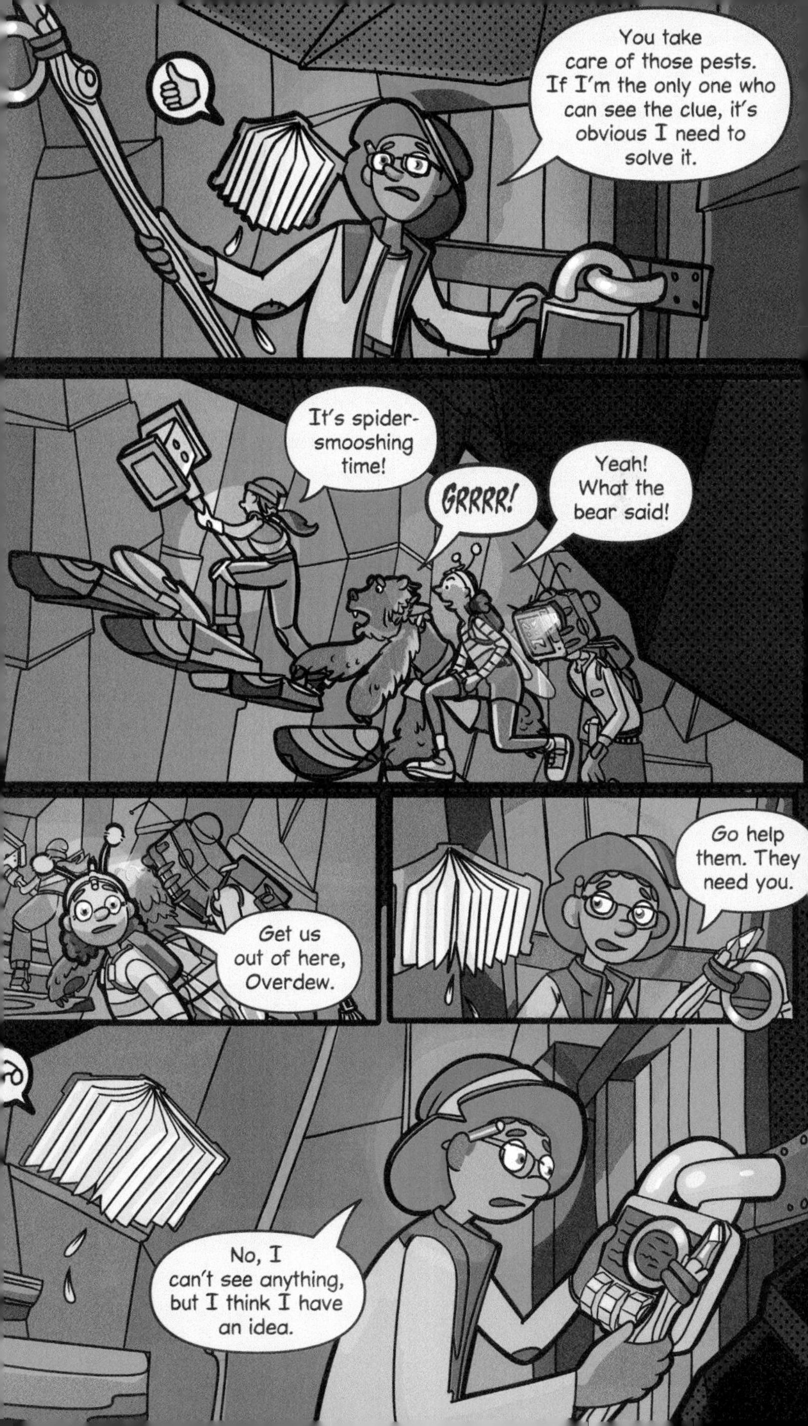

You take care of those pests. If I'm the only one who can see the clue, it's obvious I need to solve it.
It's spider-smooshing time!
GRRRR!
Yeah! What the bear said!
Get us out of here, Overdew.
Go help them. They need you.
No, I can't see anything, but I think I have an idea.

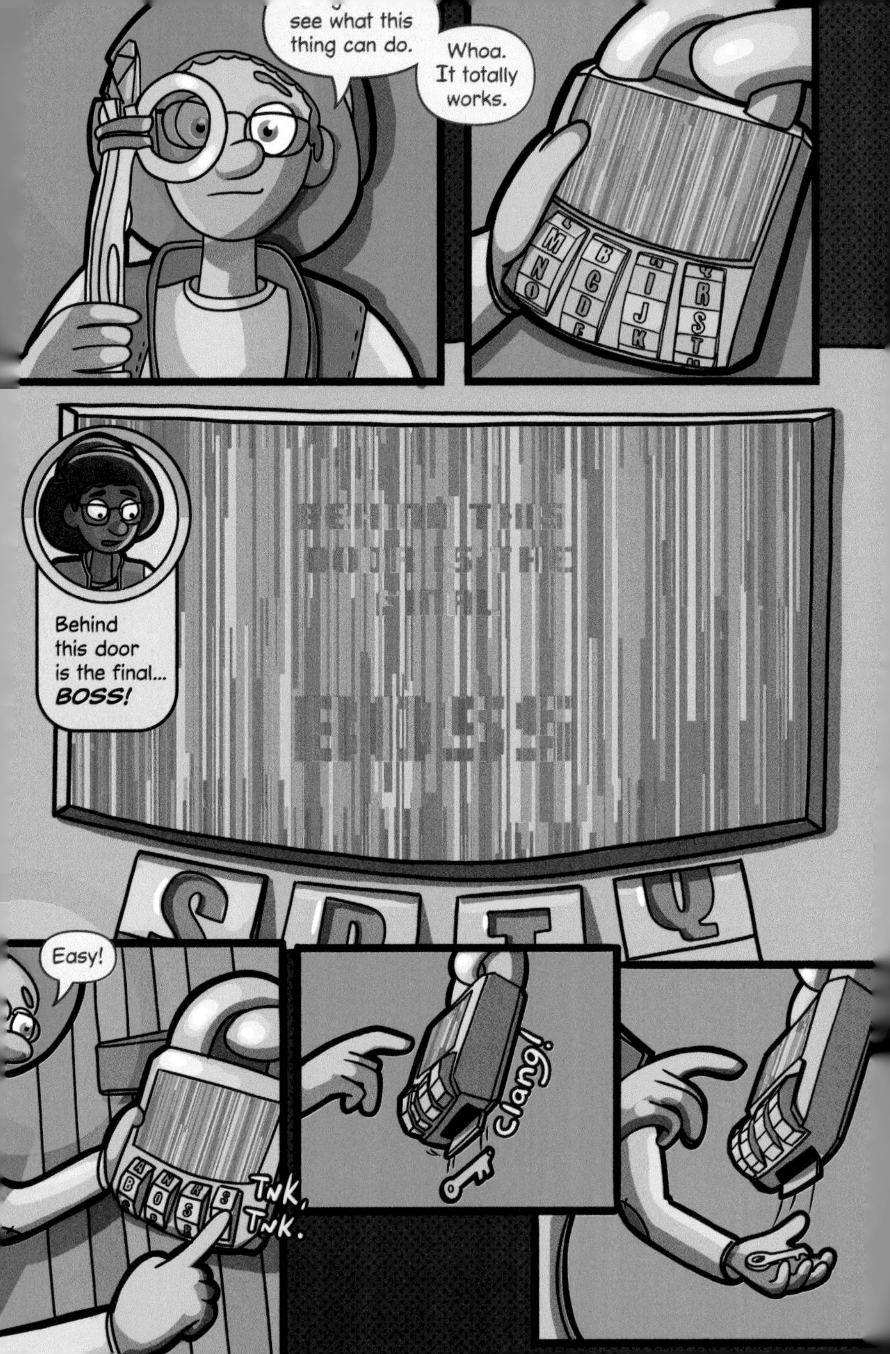
see what this thing can do.
Whoa. It totally works.
Behind this door is the final... BOSS!
Easy!
TNK, TNK.
Clang!

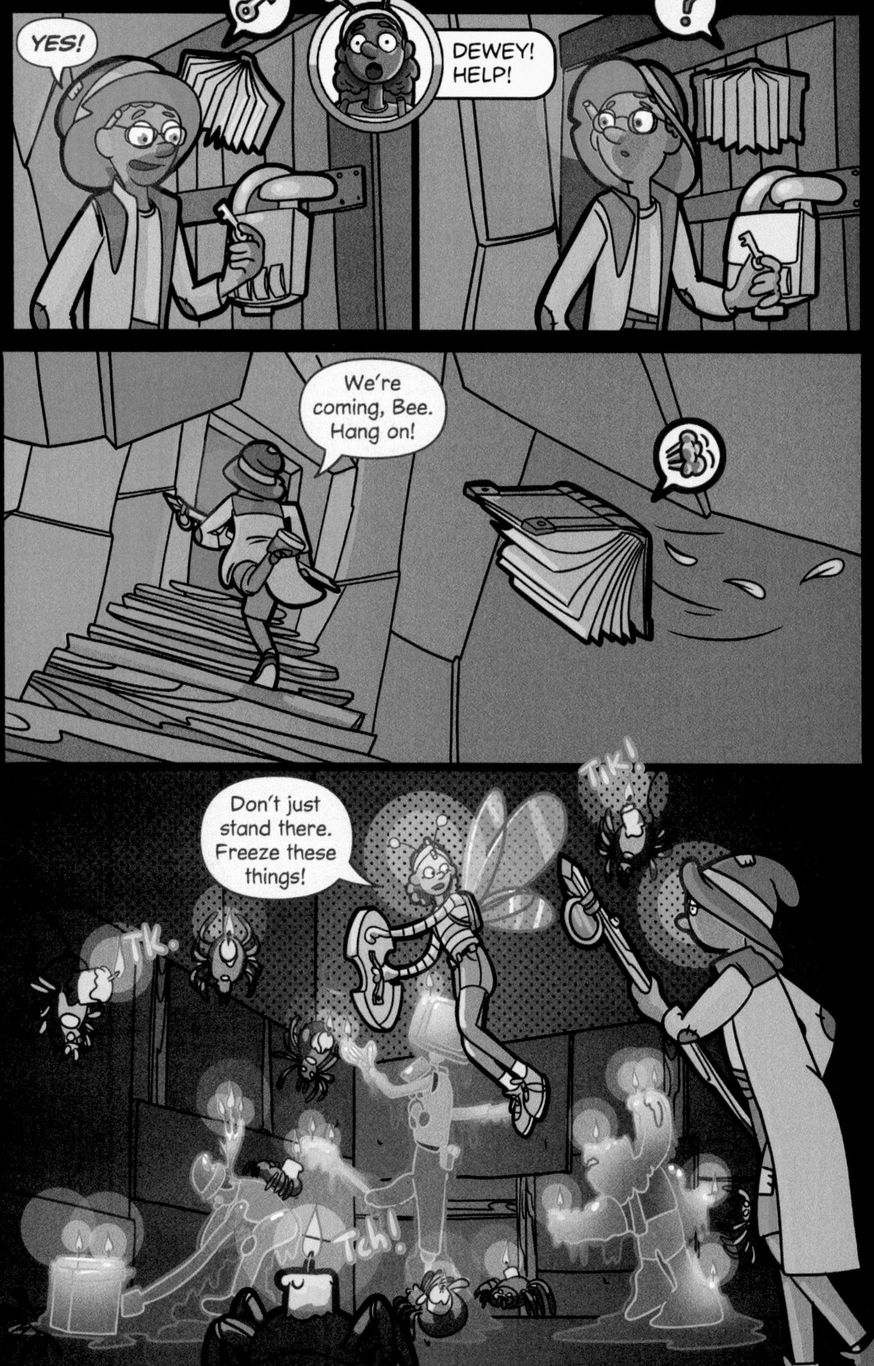
YES!
DEWEY! HELP!
We're coming, Bee. Hang on!
Don't just stand there. Freeze these things!
TIK!
TIK.
Tch!

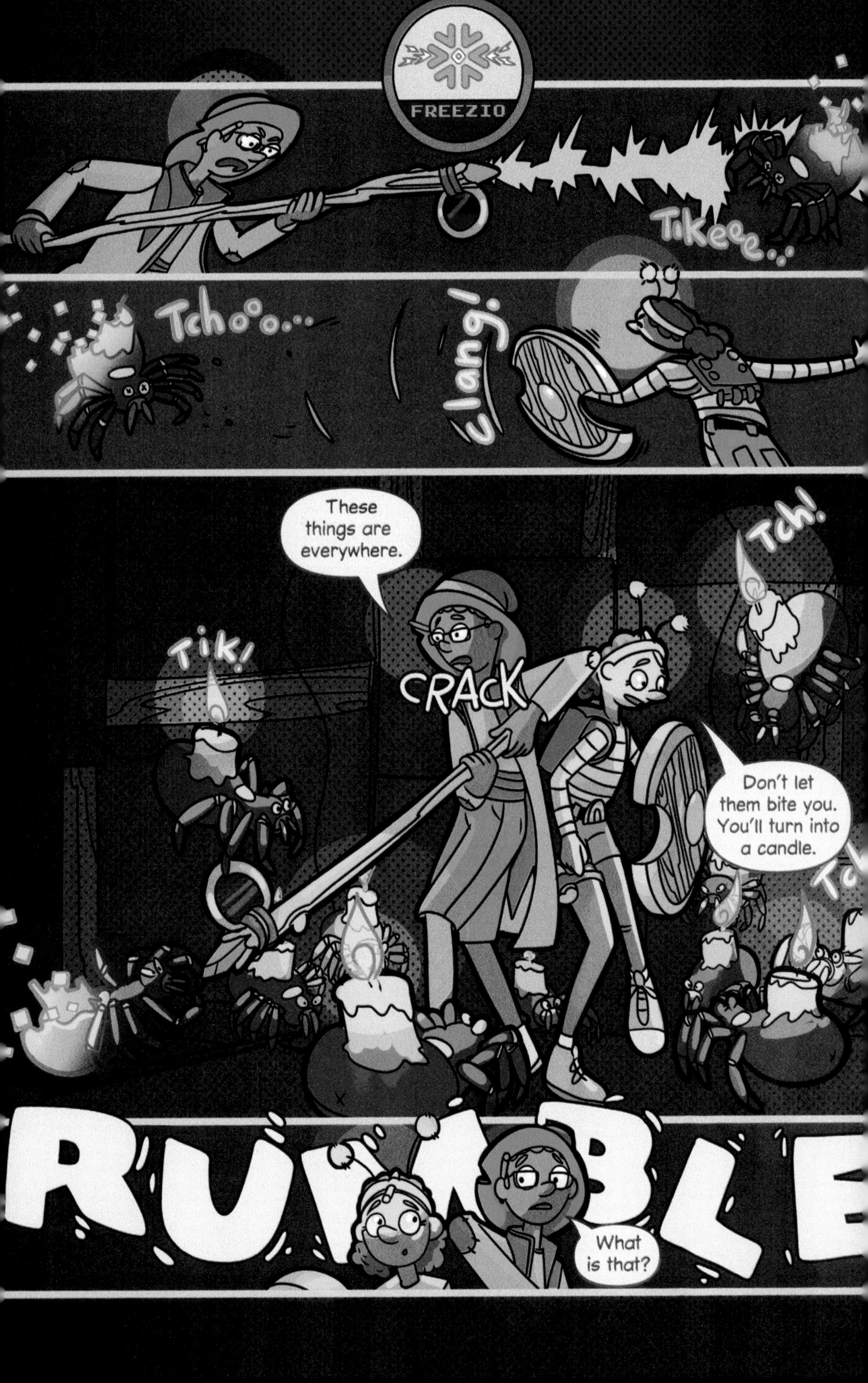
FREEZIO
Tikeee...
Tchooo...
Clang!
These things are everywhere.
Tik!
Tch!
CRACK
Don't let them bite you. You'll turn into a candle.
RUMBLE
What is that?

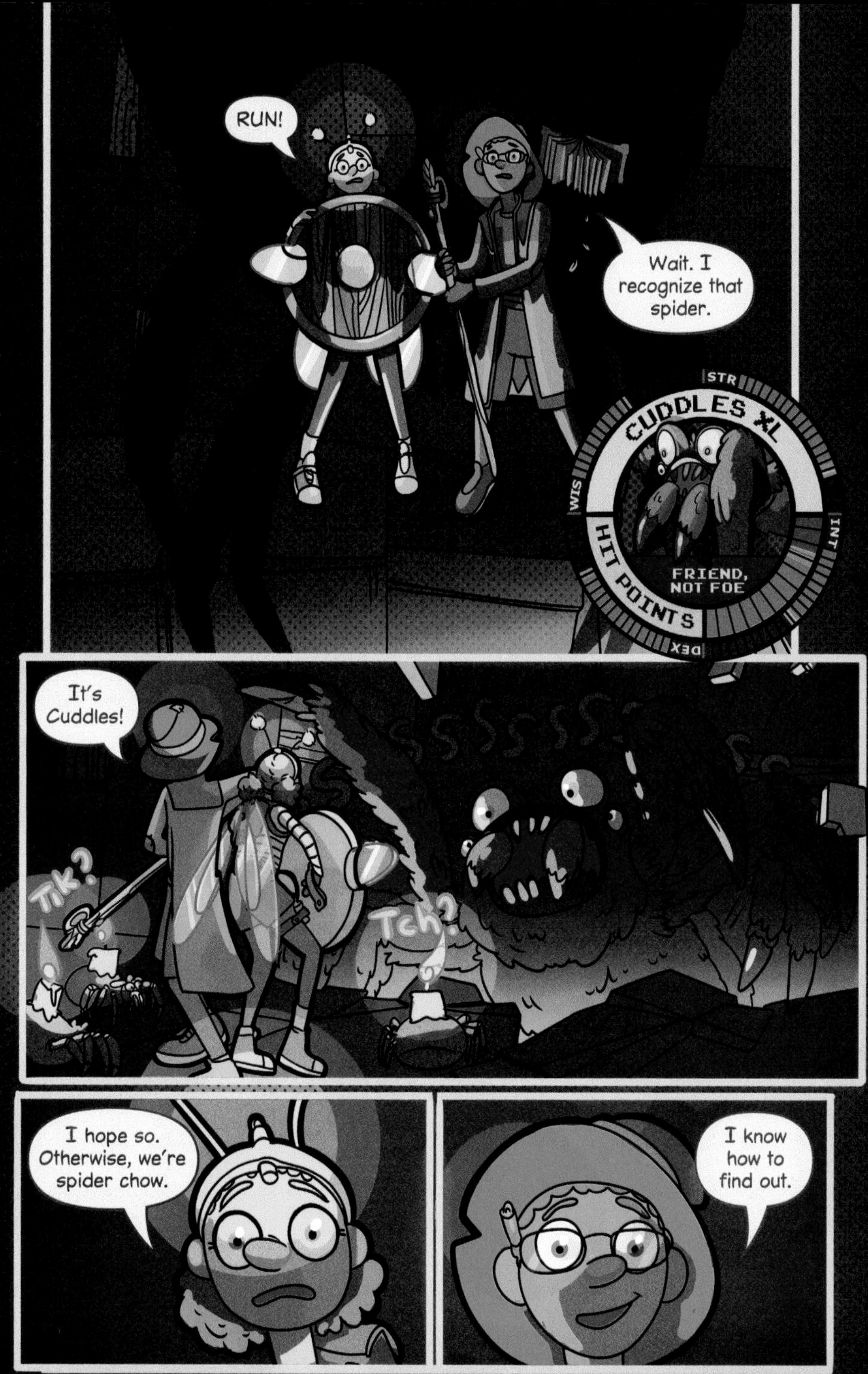
RUN!
Wait. I recognize that spider.
STR
CUDDLES XL
WIS
INT
HIT POINTS
FRIEND, NOT FOE
DEX
It's Cuddles!
Tik?
Tch?
I hope so. Otherwise, we're spider chow.
I know how to find out.

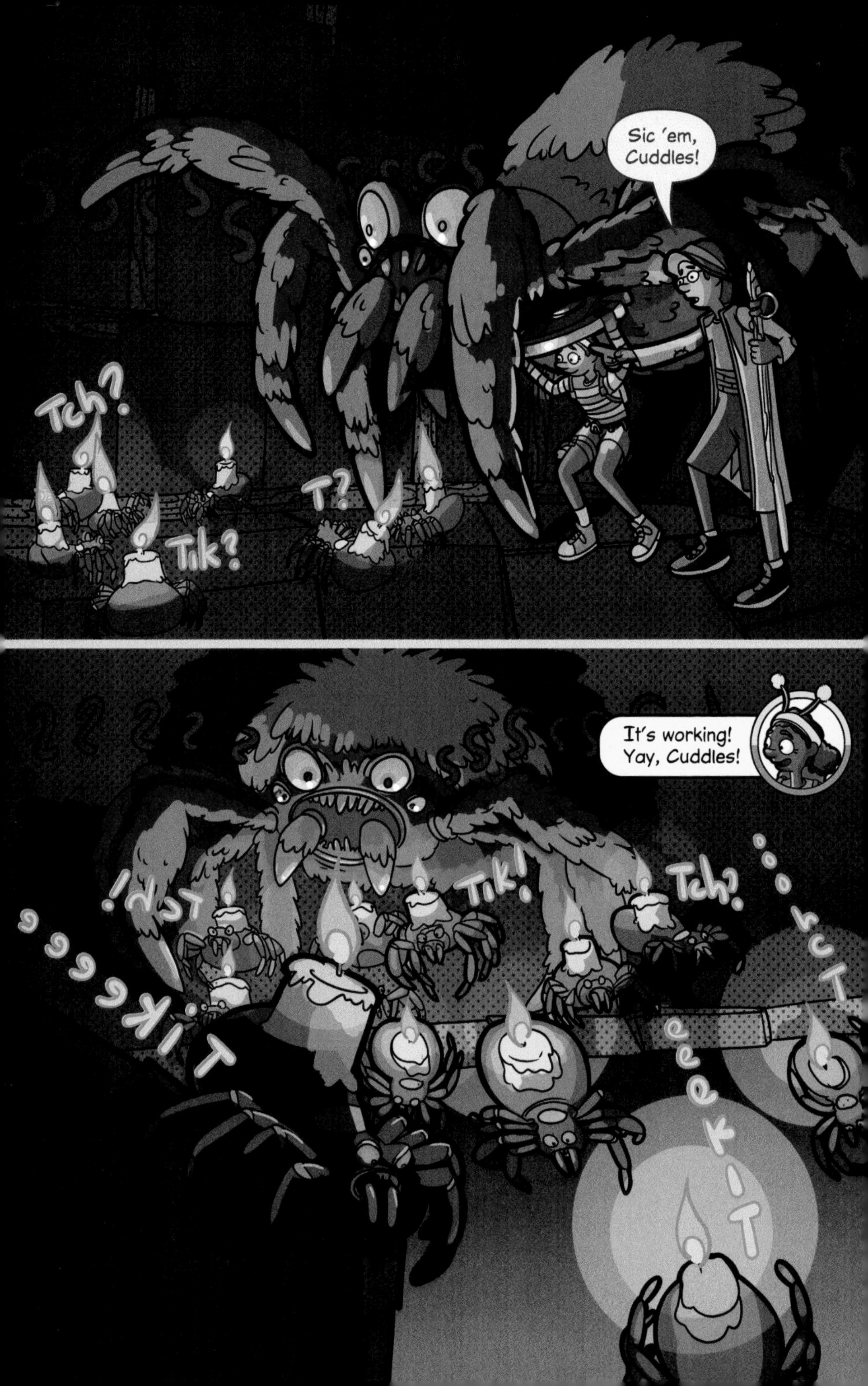
Sic 'em, Cuddles!
Tch?
T?
Tik?
It's working! Yay, Cuddles!
Tch!
Tik!
Tch?
Tikeeeeee
Tikeee
Tchoooo

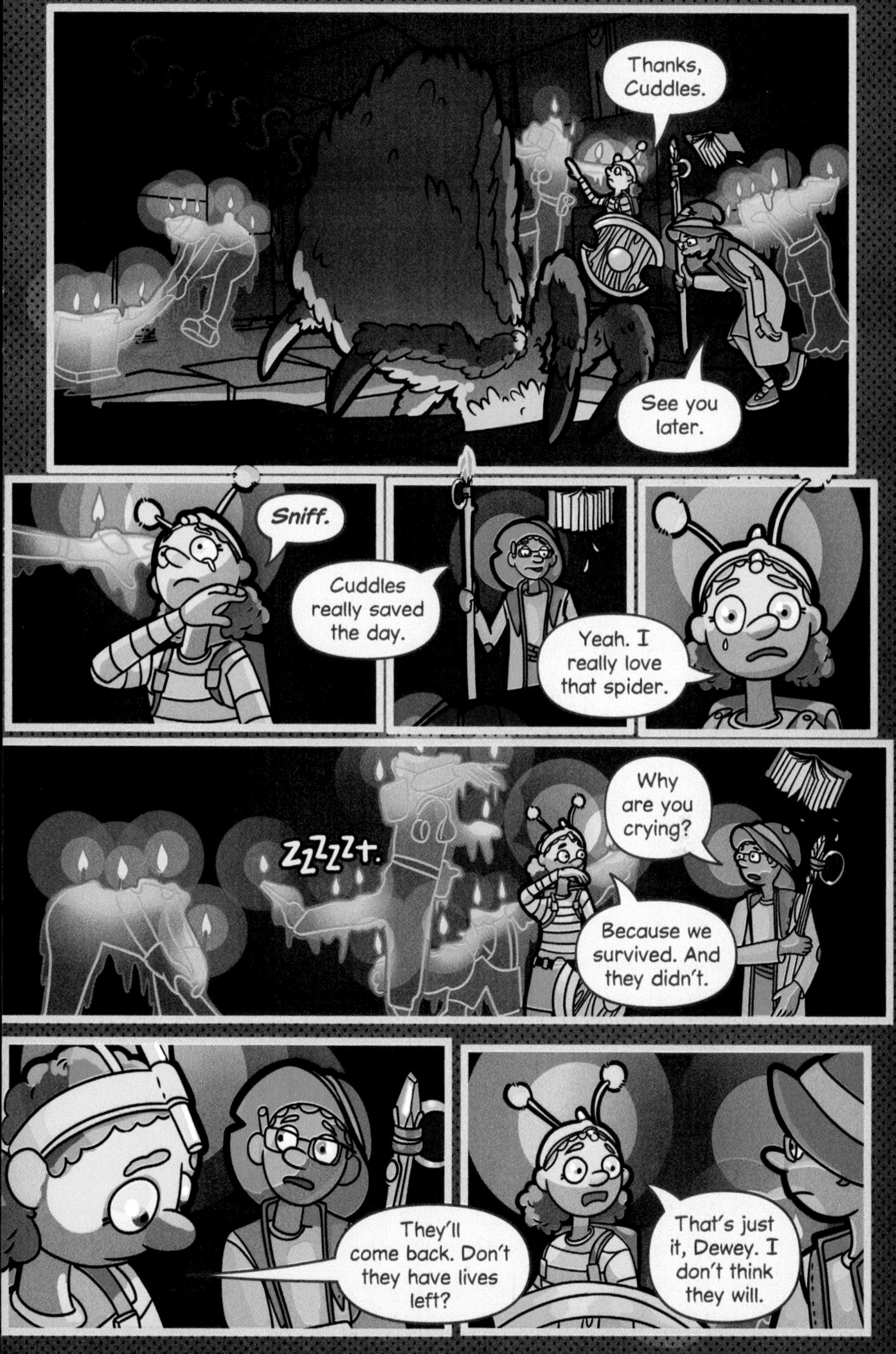
Thanks, Cuddles.
See you later.
Sniff.
Cuddles really saved the day.
Yeah. I really love that spider.
Why are you crying?
ZZZZZT.
Because we survived. And they didn't.
They'll come back. Don't they have lives left?
That's just it, Dewey. I don't think they will.

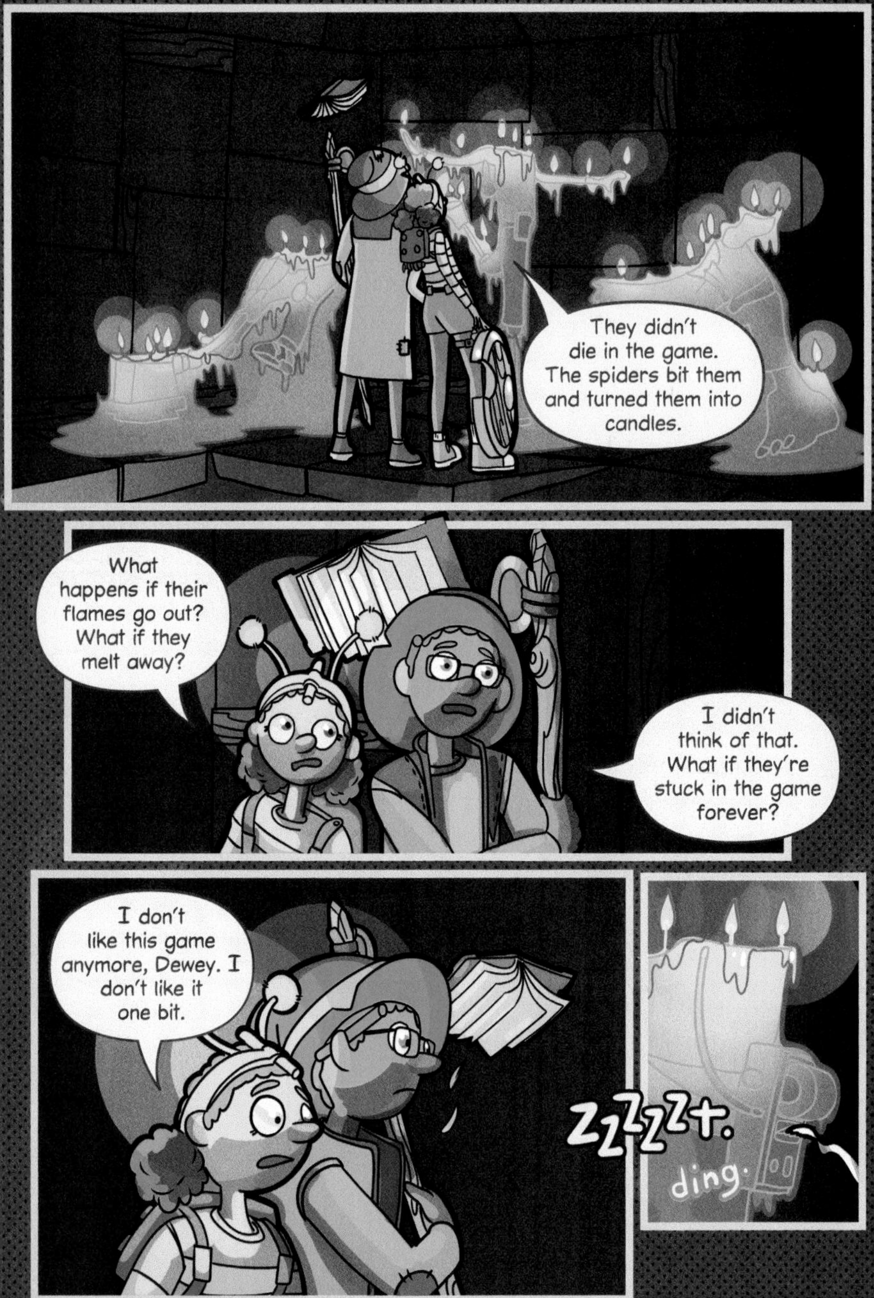
They didn't die in the game. The spiders bit them and turned them into candles.
What happens if their flames go out? What if they melt away?
I didn't think of that. What if they're stuck in the game forever?
I don't like this game anymore, Dewey. I don't like it one bit.
ZZZZZZT.
ding.

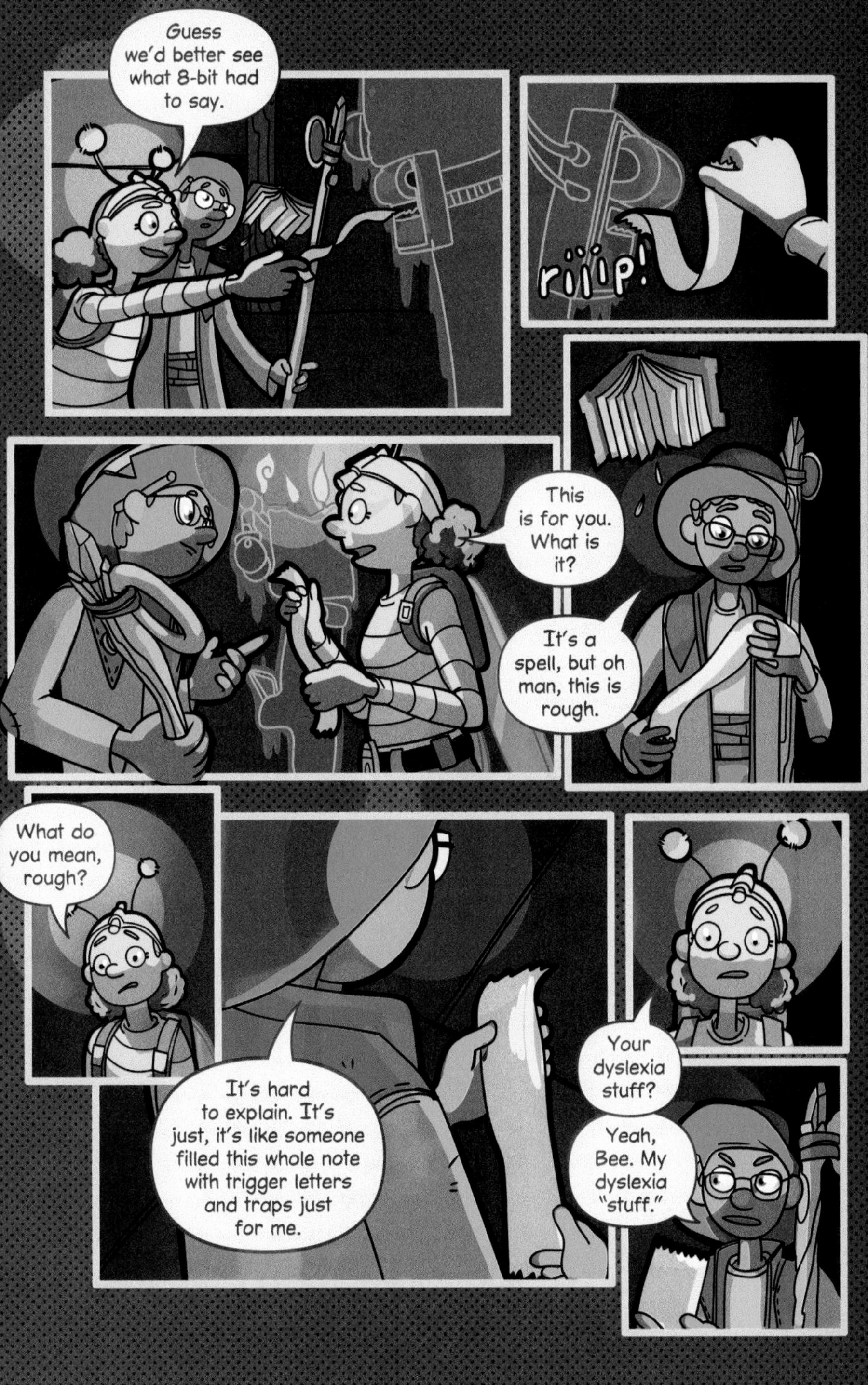
Guess we'd better see what 8-bit had to say.
riiip!
This is for you. What is it?
It's a spell, but oh man, this is rough.
What do you mean, rough?
It's hard to explain. It's just, it's like someone filled this whole note with trigger letters and traps just for me.
Your dyslexia stuff?
Yeah, Bee. My dyslexia "stuff."

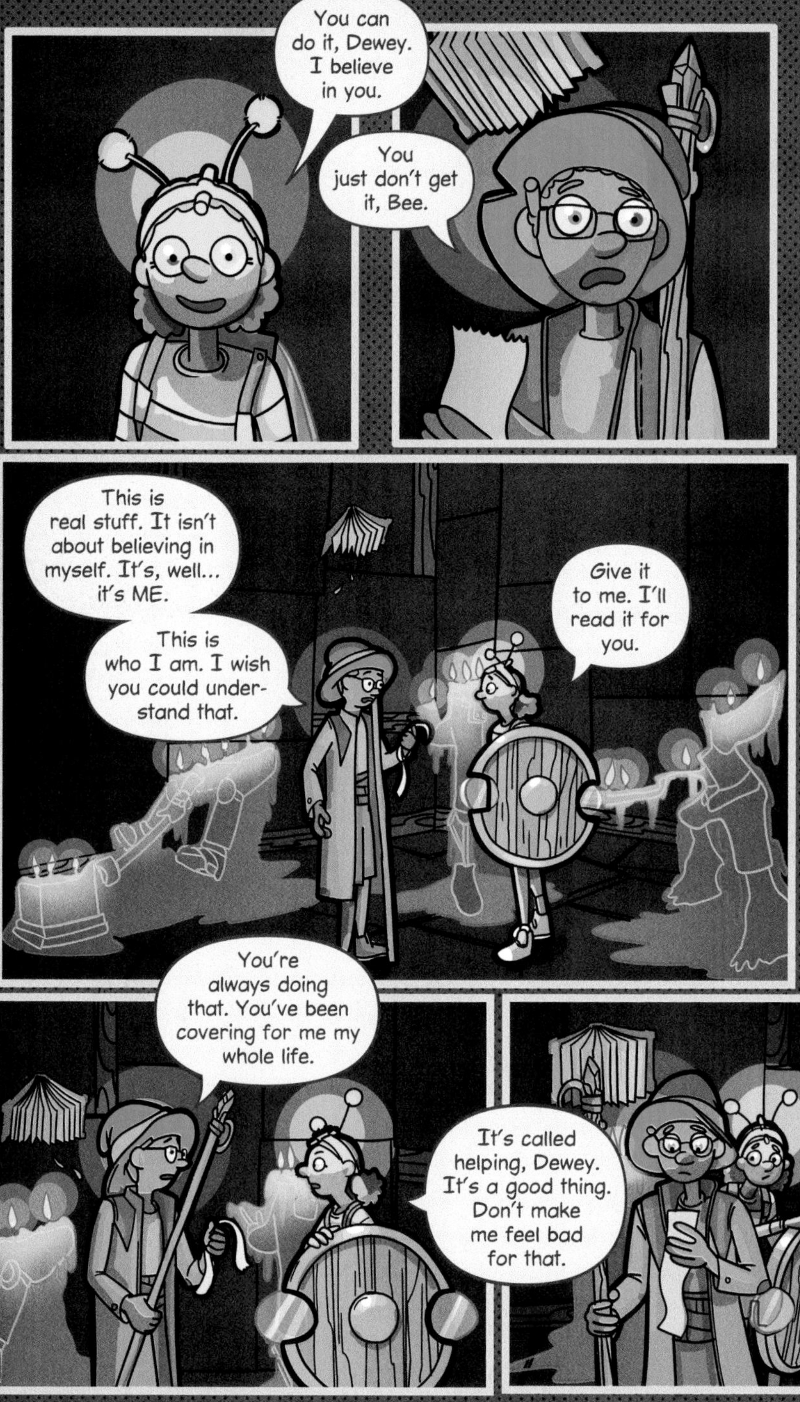
You can do it, Dewey. I believe in you.
You just don't get it, Bee.
This is real stuff. It isn't about believing in myself. It's, well... it's ME.
This is who I am. I wish you could understand that.
Give it to me. I'll read it for you.
You're always doing that. You've been covering for me my whole life.
It's called helping, Dewey. It's a good thing. Don't make me feel bad for that.

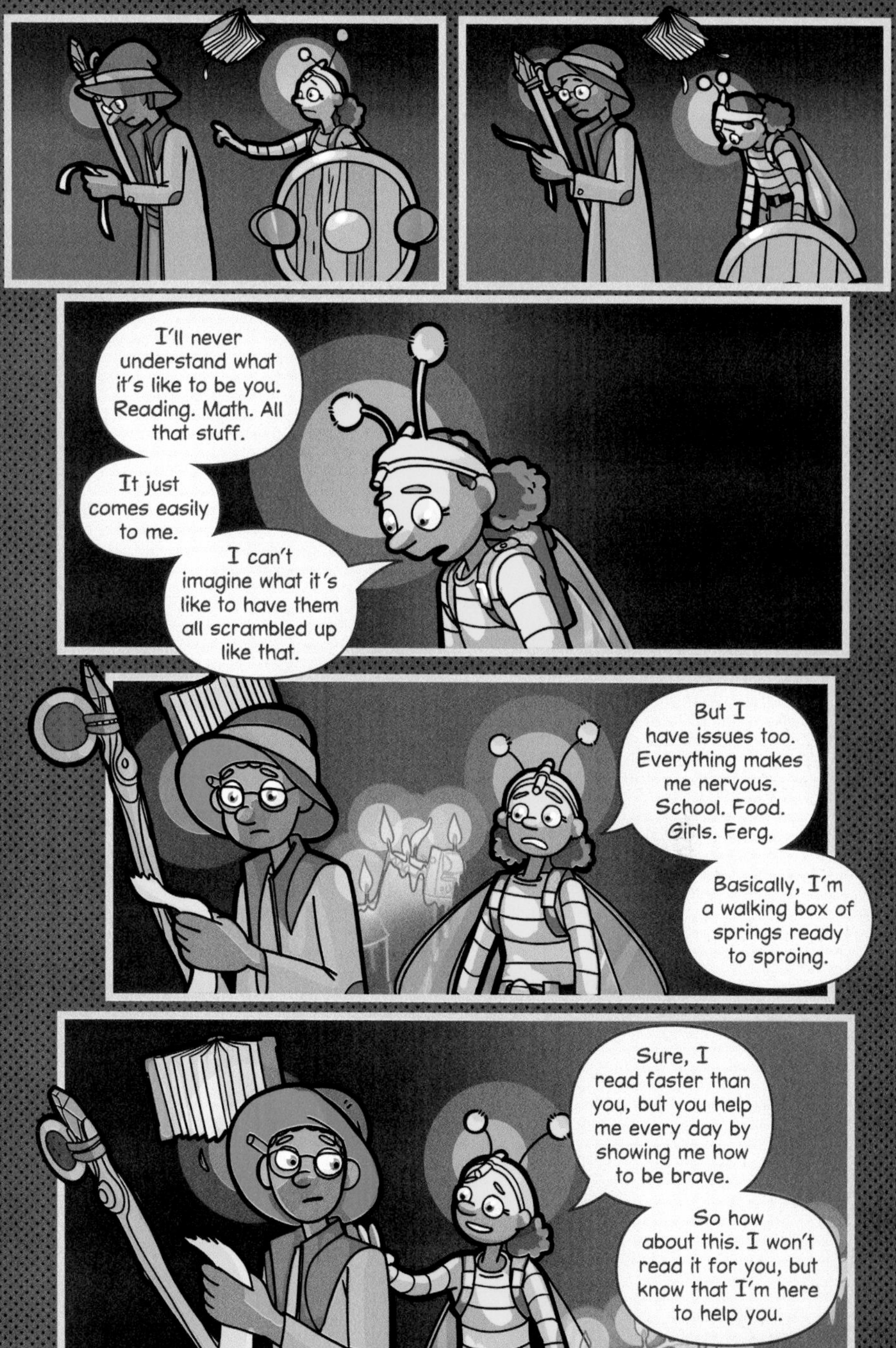
I'll never understand what it's like to be you. Reading. Math. All that stuff.
It just comes easily to me.
I can't imagine what it's like to have them all scrambled up like that.
But I have issues too. Everything makes me nervous. School. Food. Girls. Ferg.
Basically, I'm a walking box of springs ready to sproing.
Sure, I read faster than you, but you help me every day by showing me how to be brave.
So how about this. I won't read it for you, but know that I'm here to help you.

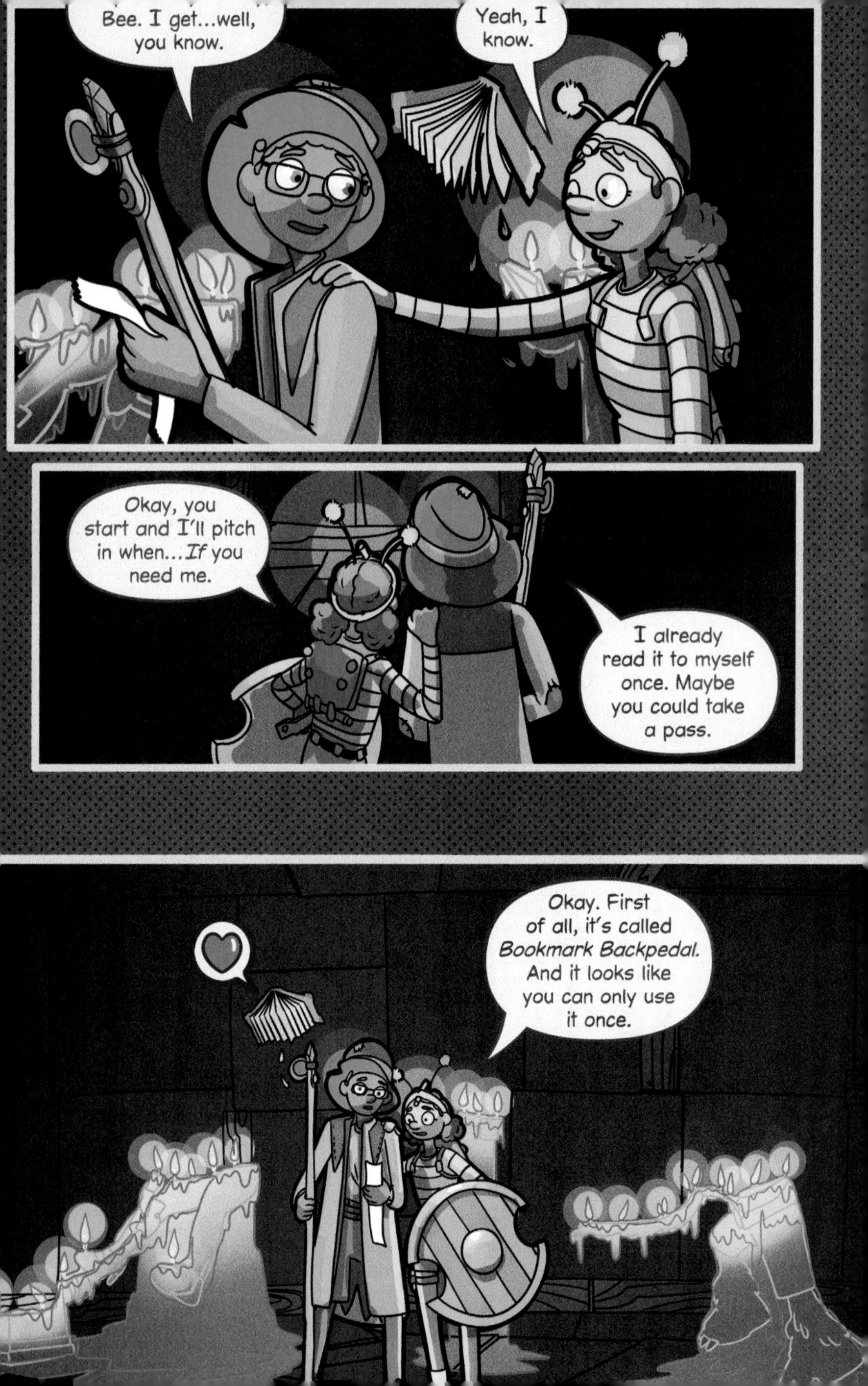
Bee. I get...well, you know.
Yeah, I know.
Okay, you start and I'll pitch in when...*If* you need me.
I already read it to myself once. Maybe you could take a pass.
Okay. First of all, it's called *Bookmark Backpedal.* And it looks like you can only use it once.

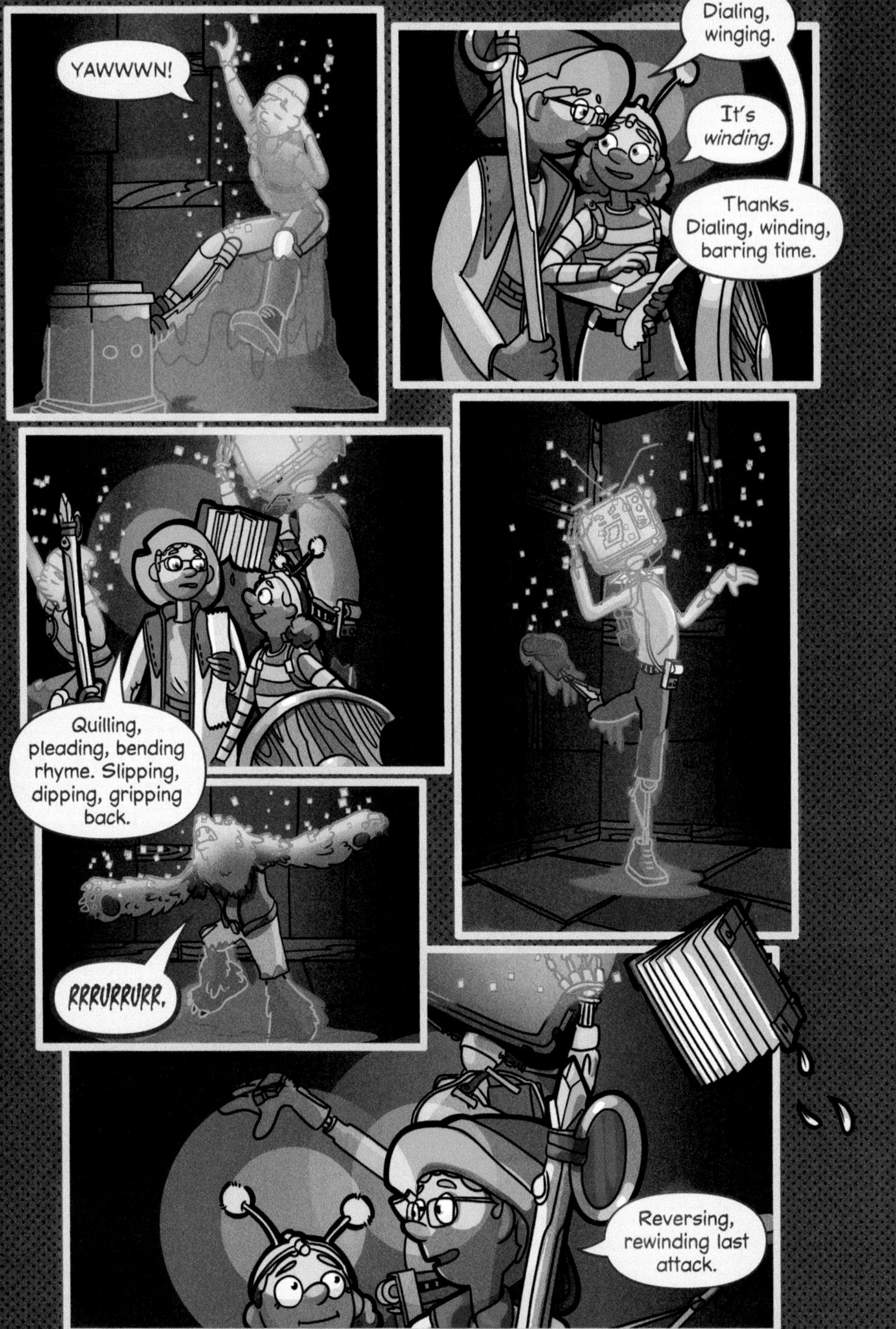
YAWWWN!
Dialing, winging.
It's *winding.*
Thanks. Dialing, winding, barring time.
Quilling, pleading, bending rhyme. Slipping, dipping, gripping back.
RRRURRURR.
Reversing, rewinding last attack.

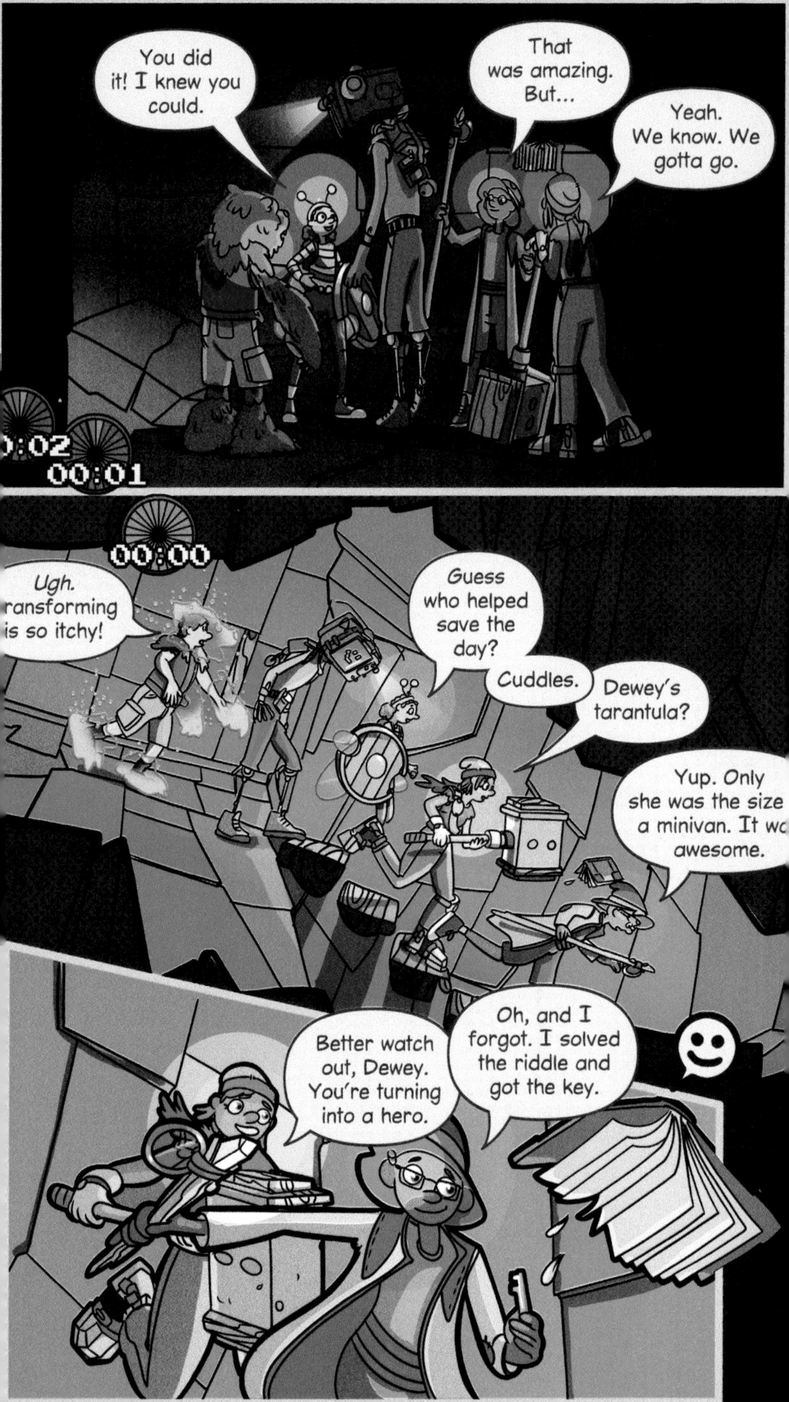
You did it! I knew you could.
That was amazing. But...
Yeah. We know. We gotta go.
0:02
00:01
00:00
Ugh. ransforming is so itchy!
Guess who helped save the day?
Cuddles.
Dewey's tarantula?
Yup. Only she was the size a minivan. It w awesome.
Better watch out, Dewey. You're turning into a hero.
Oh, and I forgot. I solved the riddle and got the key.

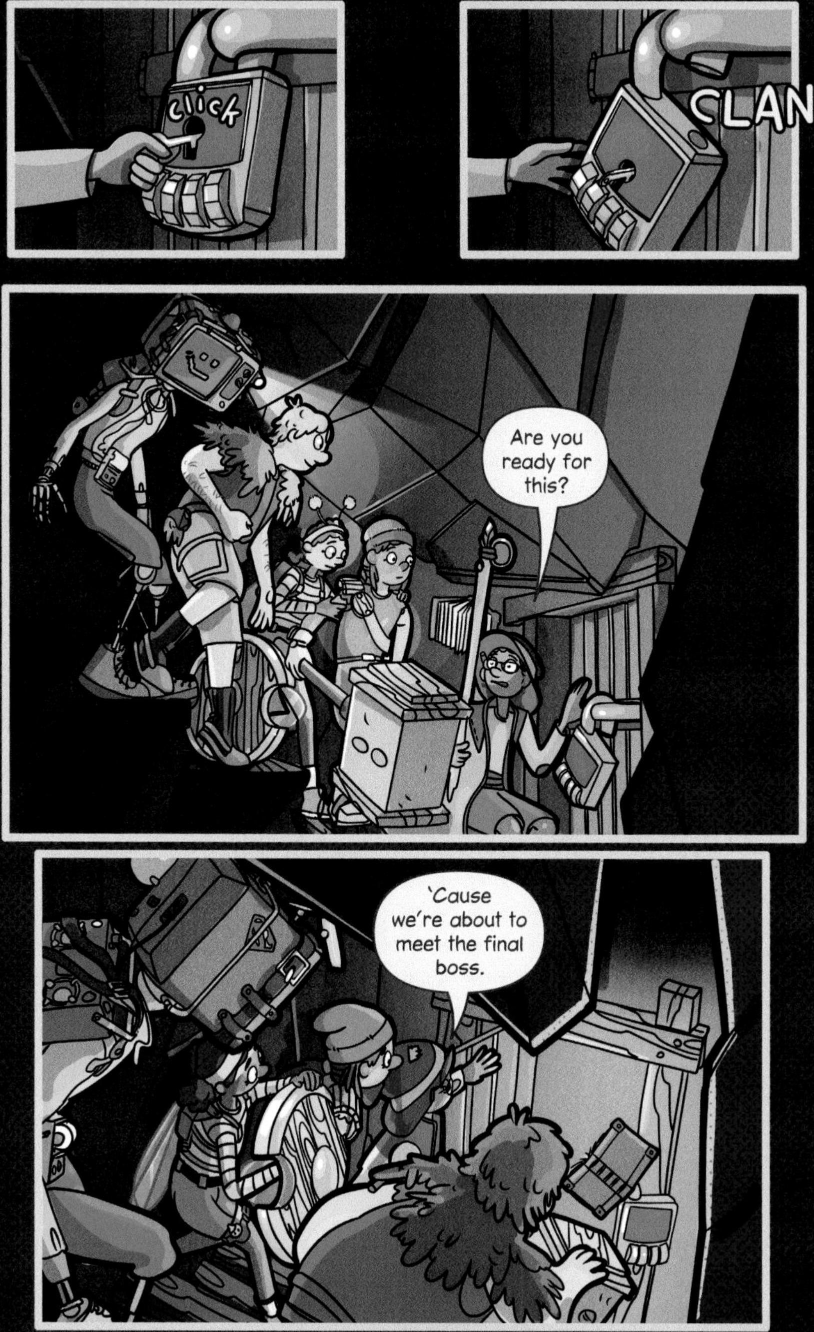
click
CLAN
Are you ready for this?
'Cause we're about to meet the final boss.

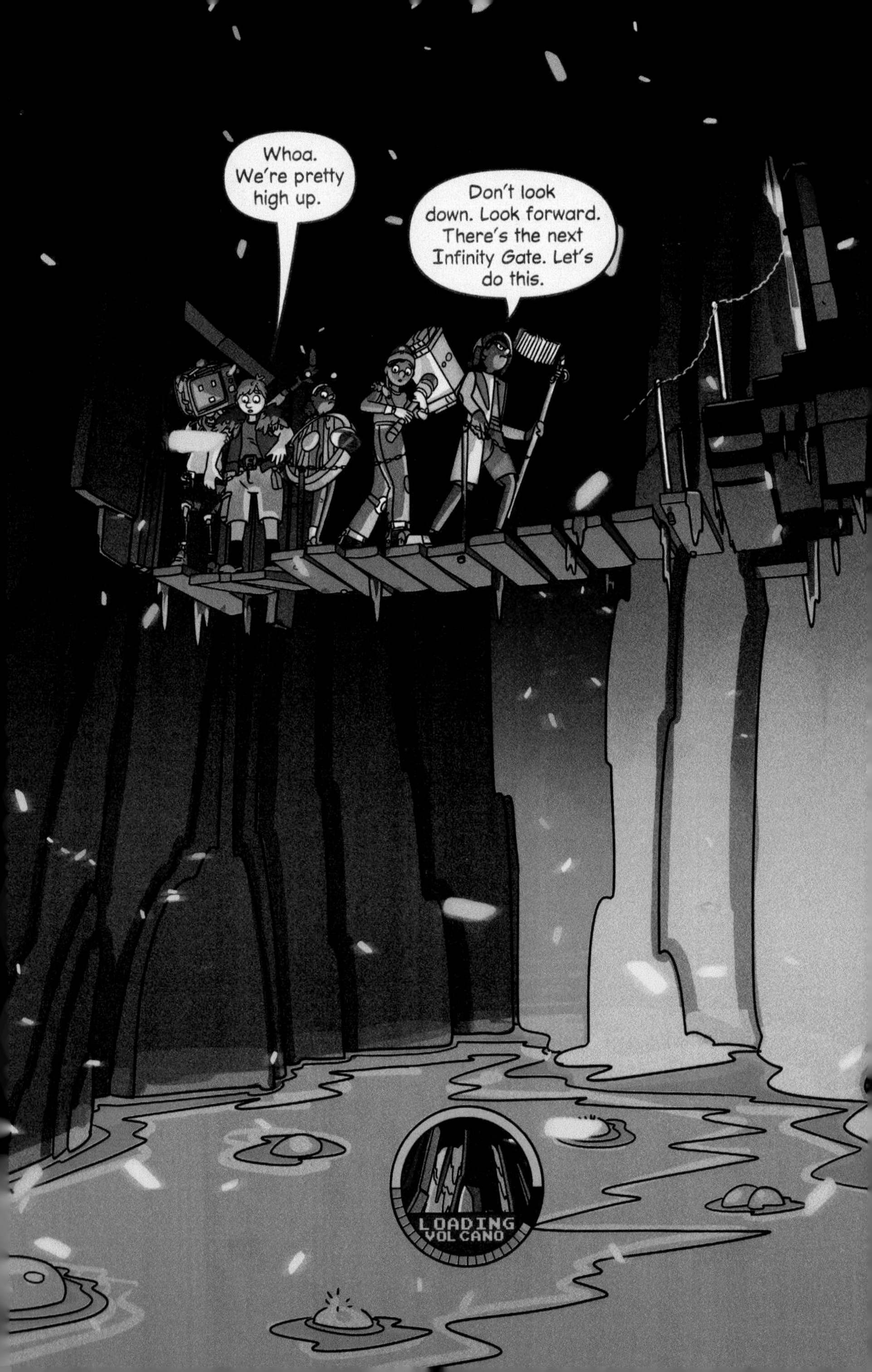
Whoa. We're pretty high up.
Don't look down. Look forward. There's the next Infinity Gate. Let's do this.
LOADING VOLCANO

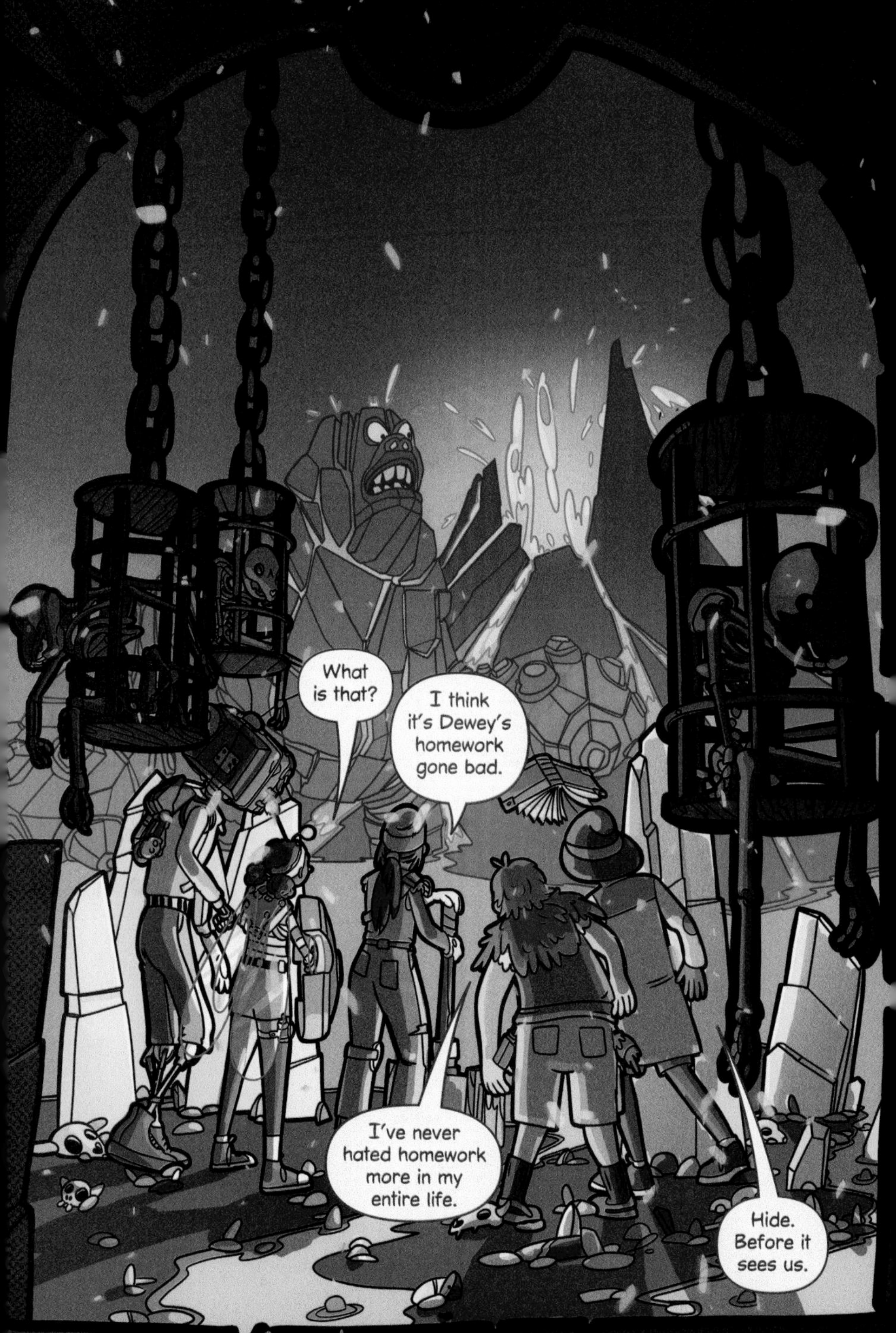
What is that?
I think it's Dewey's homework gone bad.
I've never hated homework more in my entire life.
Hide. Before it sees us.

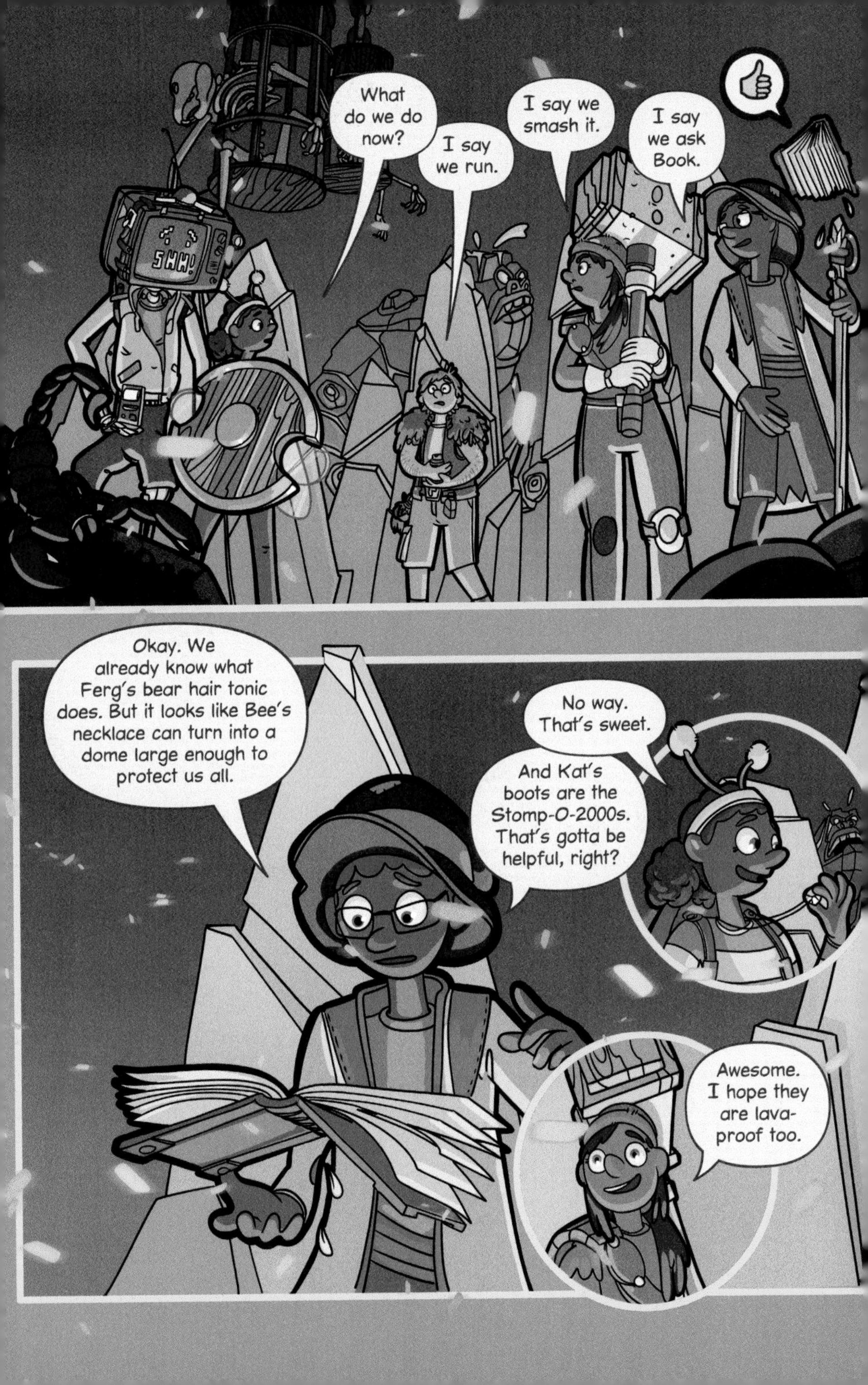
SHH!
What do we do now?
I say we run.
I say we smash it.
I say we ask Book.
Okay. We already know what Ferg's bear hair tonic does. But it looks like Bee's necklace can turn into a dome large enough to protect us all.
No way. That's sweet.
And Kat's boots are the Stomp-O-2000s. That's gotta be helpful, right?
Awesome. I hope they are lava-proof too.

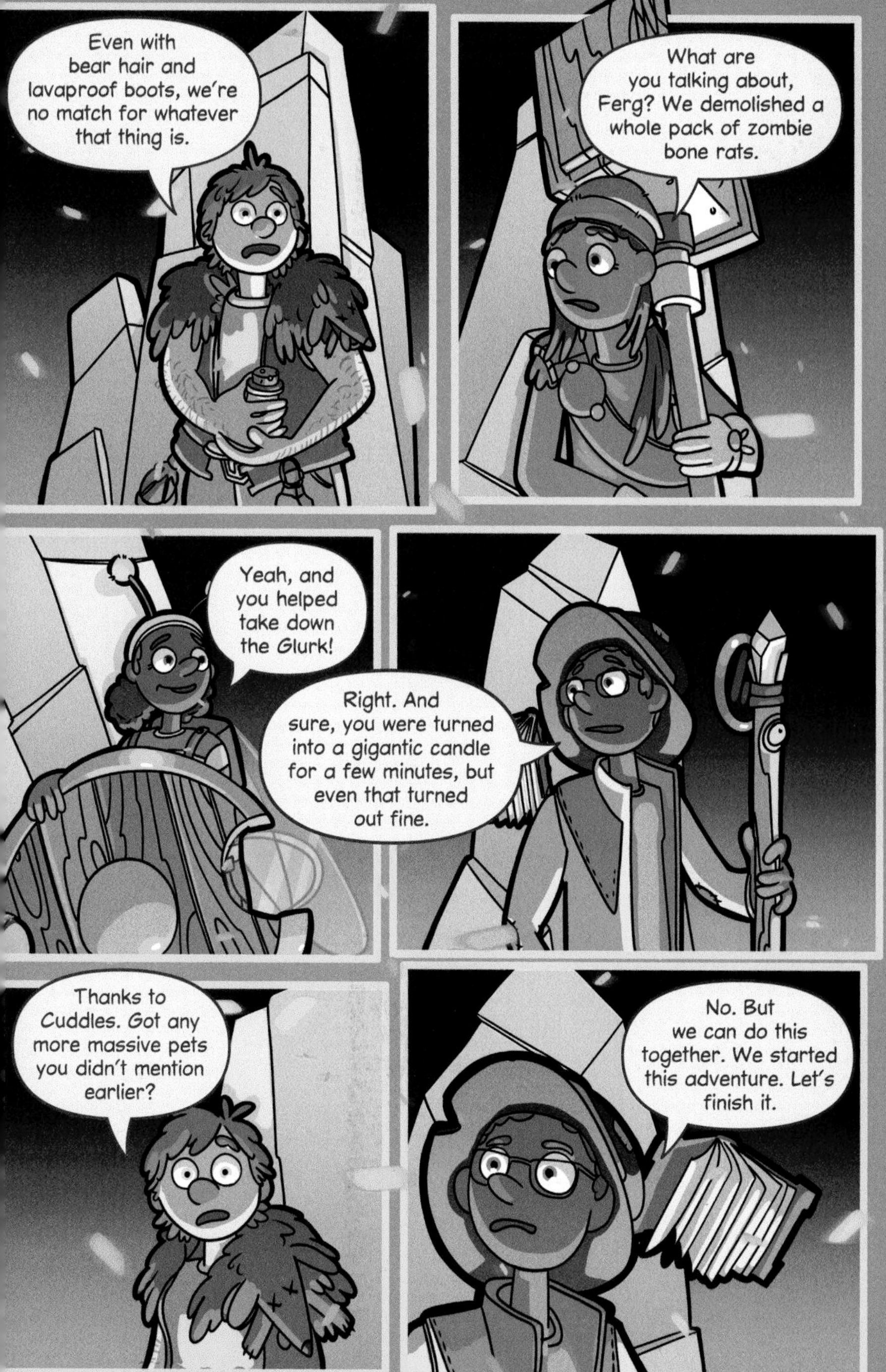

Even with bear hair and lavaproof boots, we're no match for whatever that thing is.
What are you talking about, Ferg? We demolished a whole pack of zombie bone rats.
Yeah, and you helped take down the Glurk!
Right. And sure, you were turned into a gigantic candle for a few minutes, but even that turned out fine.
Thanks to Cuddles. Got any more massive pets you didn't mention earlier?
No. But we can do this together. We started this adventure. Let's finish it.

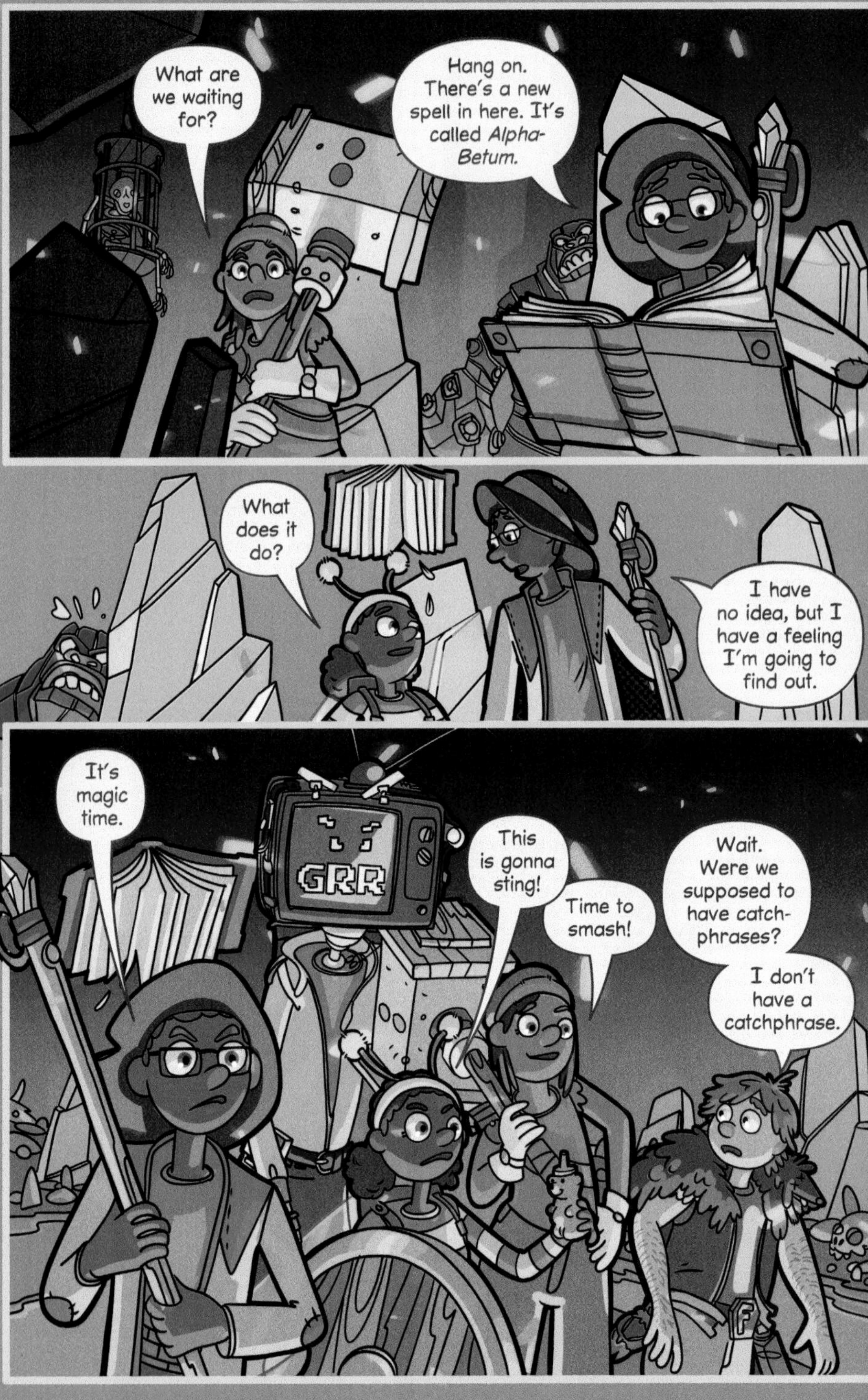
What are we waiting for?
Hang on. There's a new spell in here. It's called *Alpha-Betum.*
What does it do?
I have no idea, but I have a feeling I'm going to find out.
It's magic time.
GRR
This is gonna sting!
Time to smash!
Wait. Were we supposed to have catch-phrases?
I don't have a catchphrase.

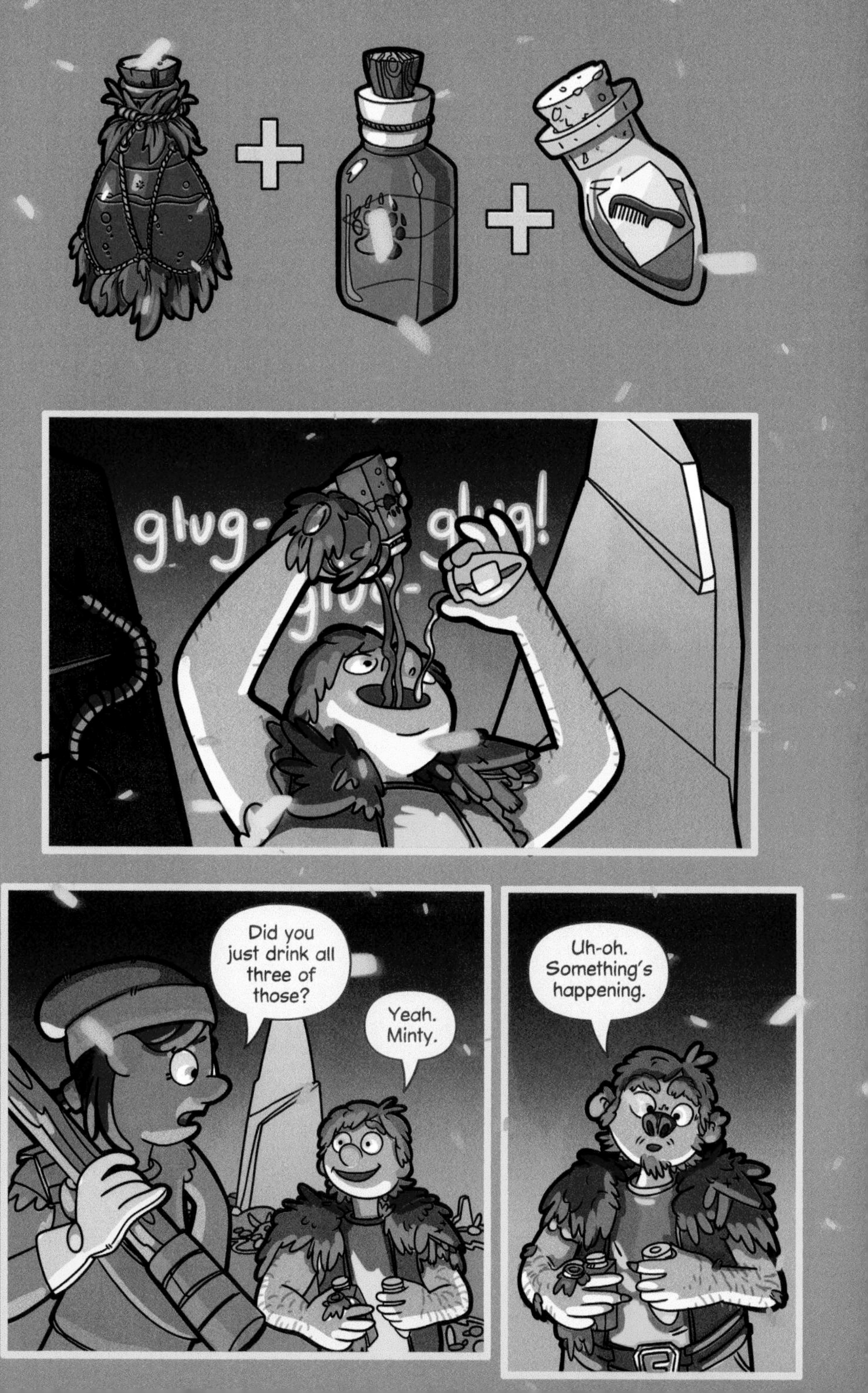
glug-glug-glug!
Did you just drink all three of those?
Yeah. Minty.
Uh-oh. Something's happening.

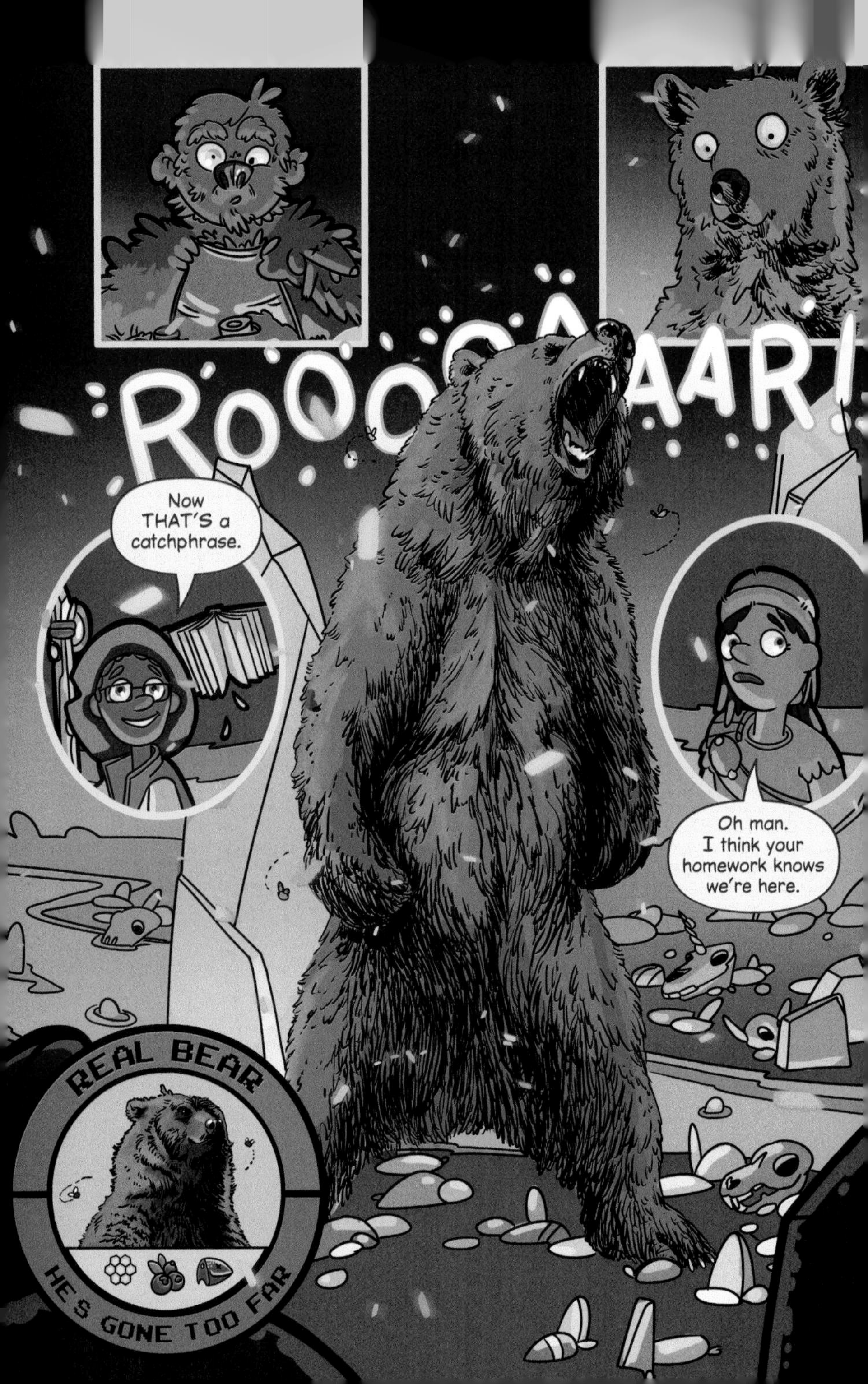
ROOOOAAAR!
Now THAT'S a catchphrase.
Oh man. I think your homework knows we're here.
REAL BEAR
HE'S GONE TOO FAR

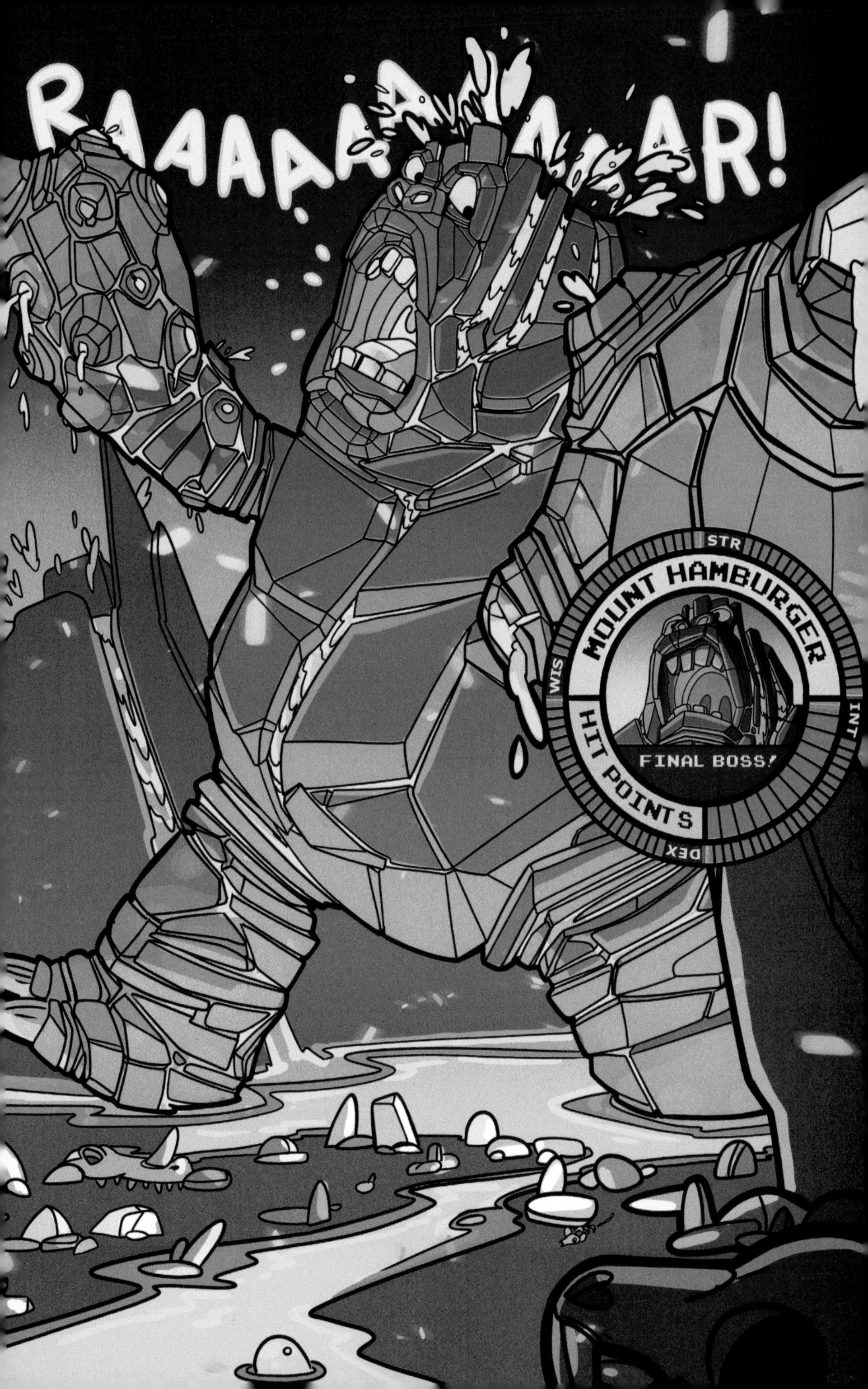
RAAAAAAAAR!
MOUNT HAMBURGER
STR
WIS
INT
DEX
HIT POINTS
FINAL BOSS!

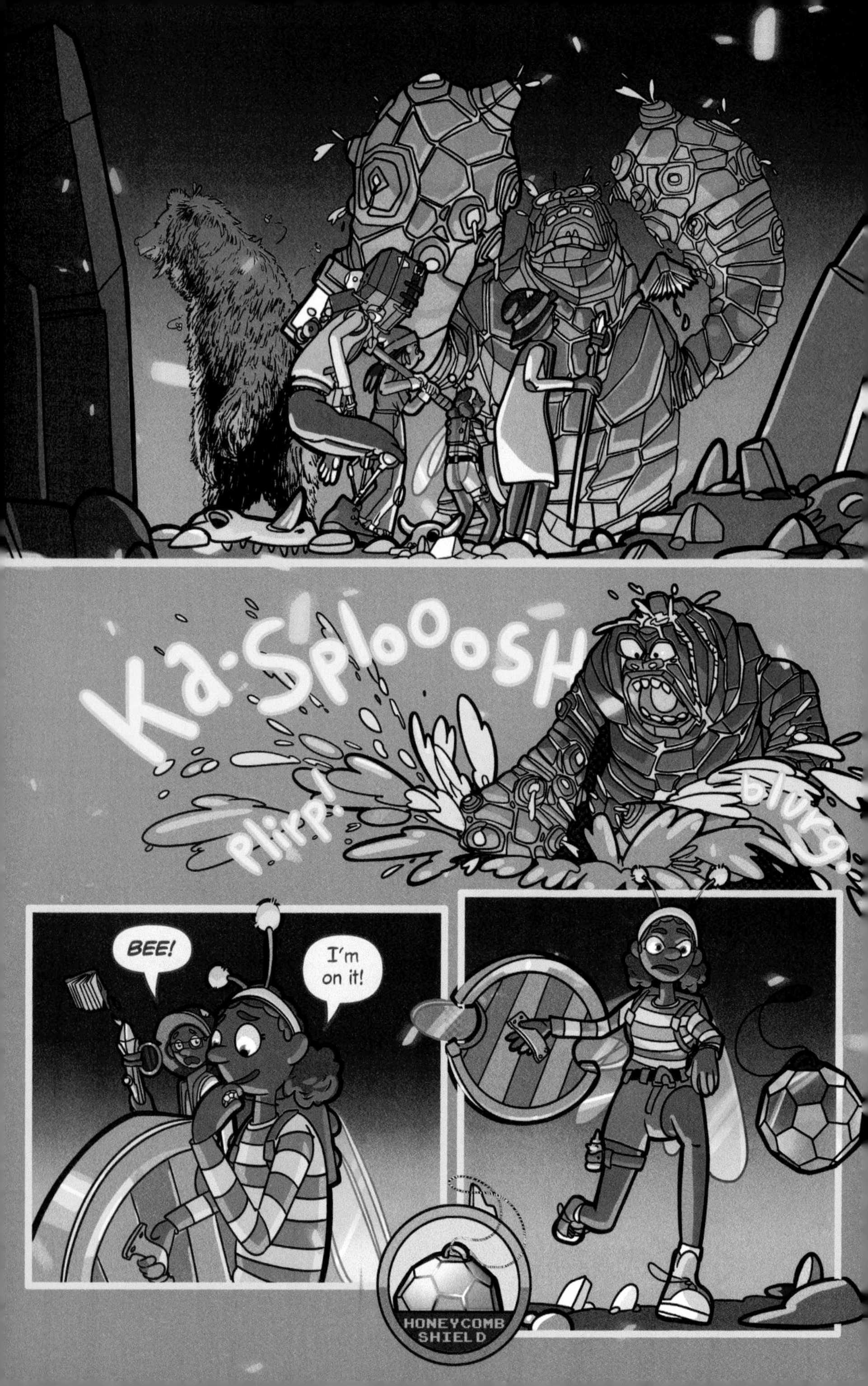
Ka-SplooooSH
Plirp!
blurg.
BEE!
I'm on it!
HONEYCOMB SHIELD

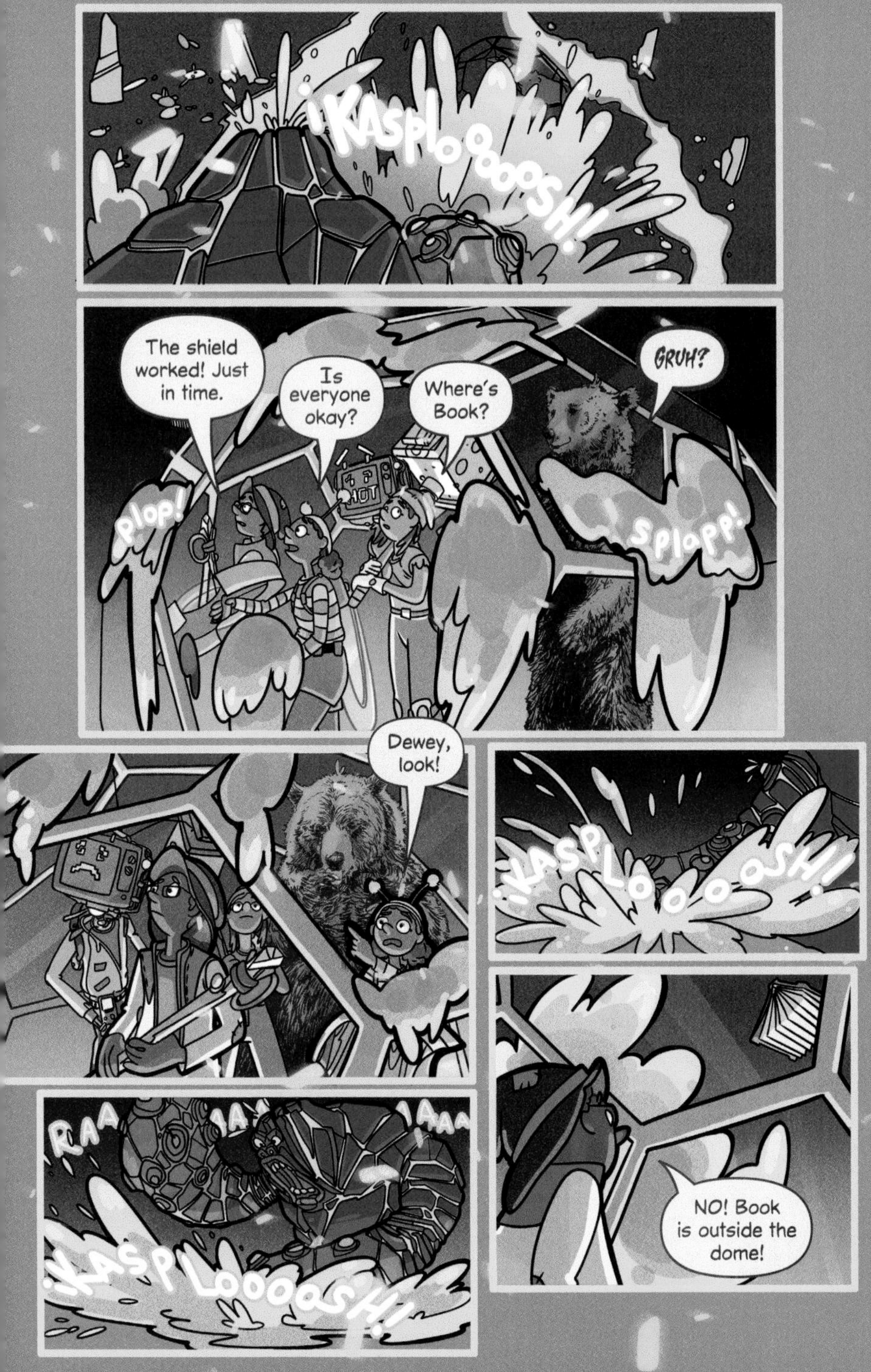
¡KASPLOOOOOSH!
The shield worked! Just in time.
Is everyone okay?
Where's Book?
GRUH?
PLOP!
SPLAPP!
Dewey, look!
¡KASPLOOOOOSH!
RAAAAAAAAAA
¡KASPLOOOOSH!
NO! Book is outside the dome!

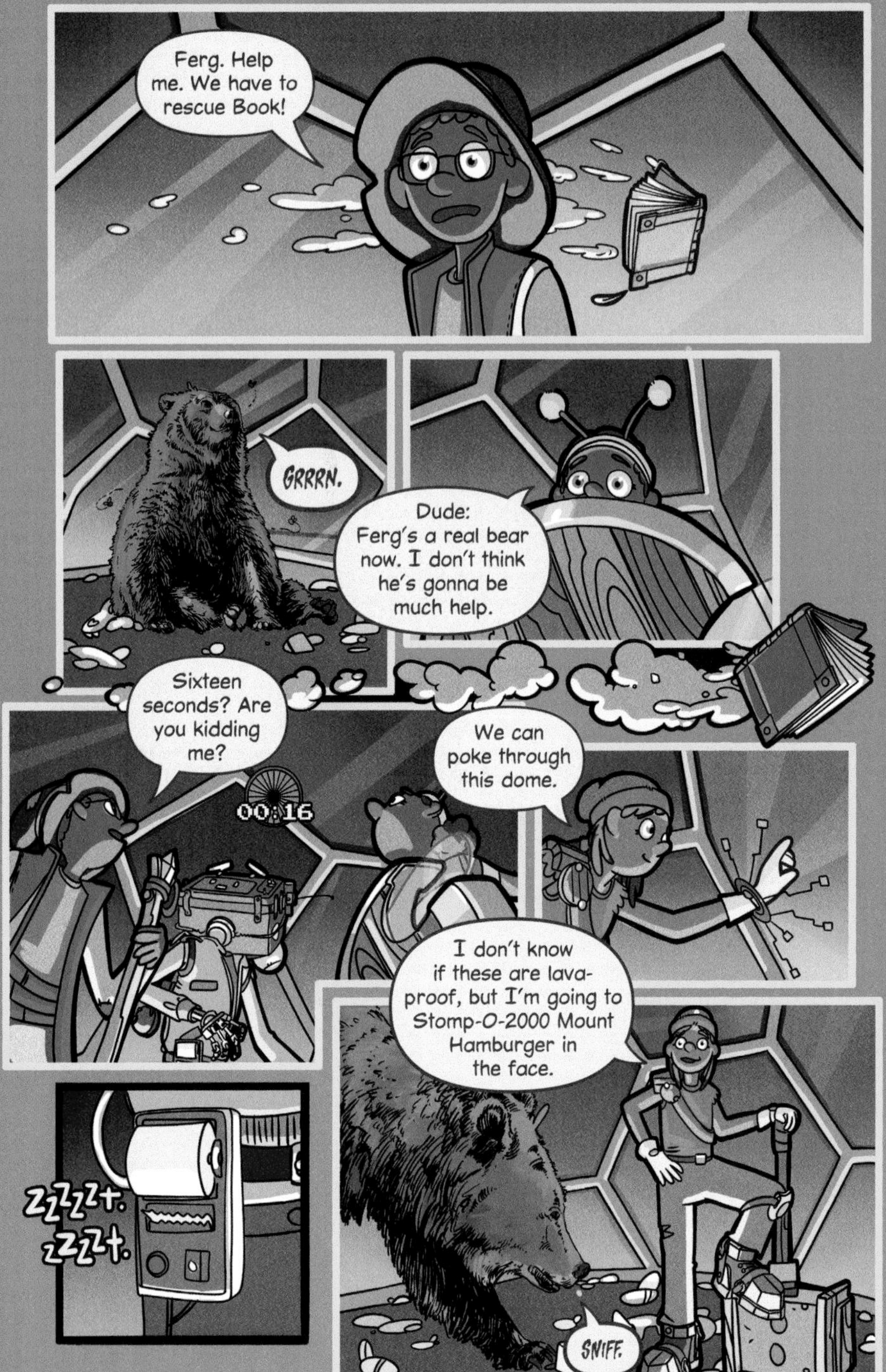
Ferg. Help me. We have to rescue Book!
GRRRN.
Dude: Ferg's a real bear now. I don't think he's gonna be much help.
Sixteen seconds? Are you kidding me?
00:16
We can poke through this dome.
I don't know if these are lava-proof, but I'm going to Stomp-O-2000 Mount Hamburger in the face.
ZZZZZT. ZZZZT.
SNIFF.

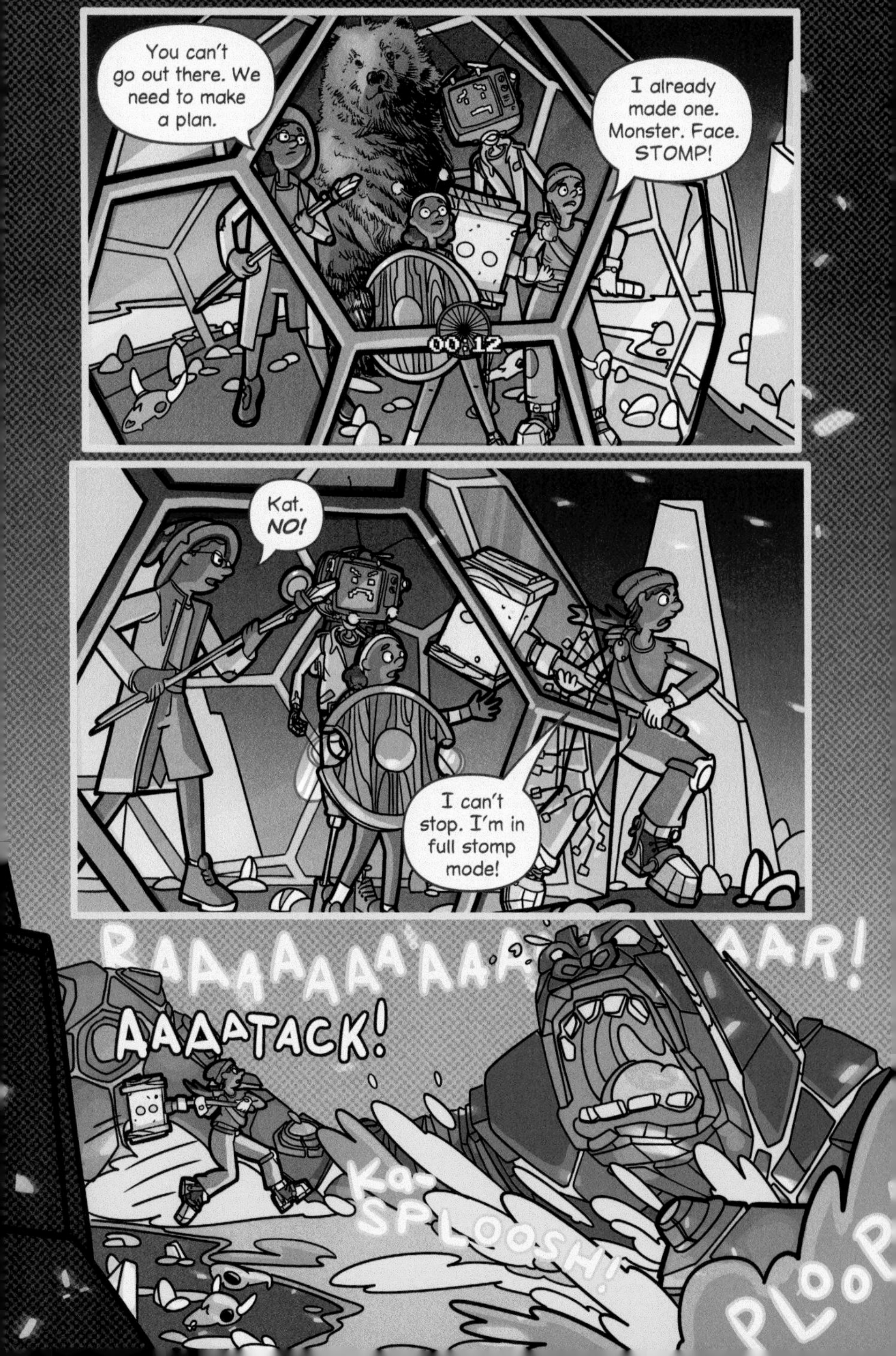
You can't go out there. We need to make a plan.
I already made one. Monster. Face. STOMP!
00:12
Kat. NO!
I can't stop. I'm in full stomp mode!
RAAAAAAAAAAAR!
AAAATACK!
Ka-SPLOOSH!
PLOOP

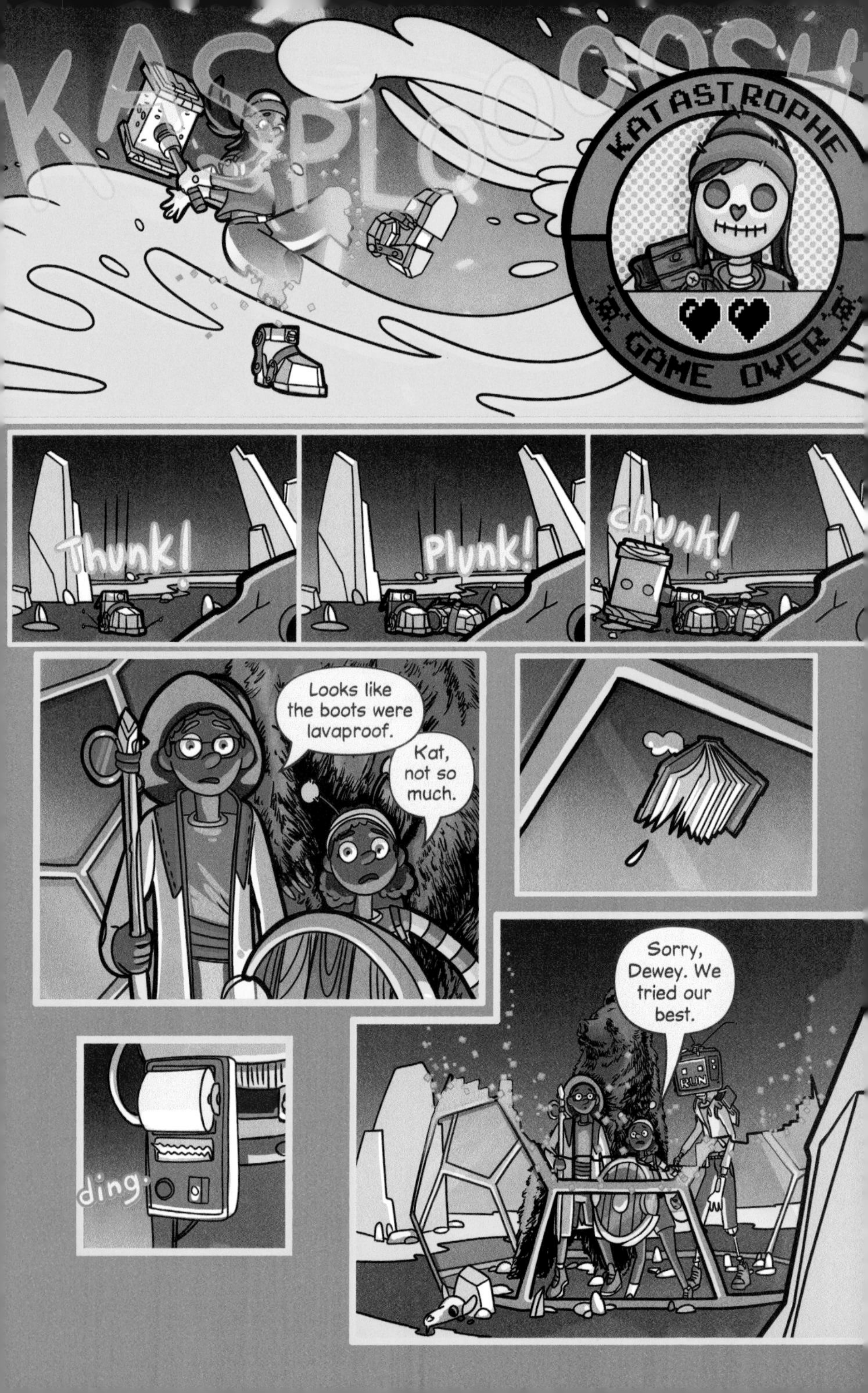
KASPLOOOOSH
KATASTROPHE
GAME OVER
Thunk!
Plunk!
Chunk!
Looks like the boots were lavaproof.
Kat, not so much.
ding.
Sorry, Dewey. We tried our best.
RUN

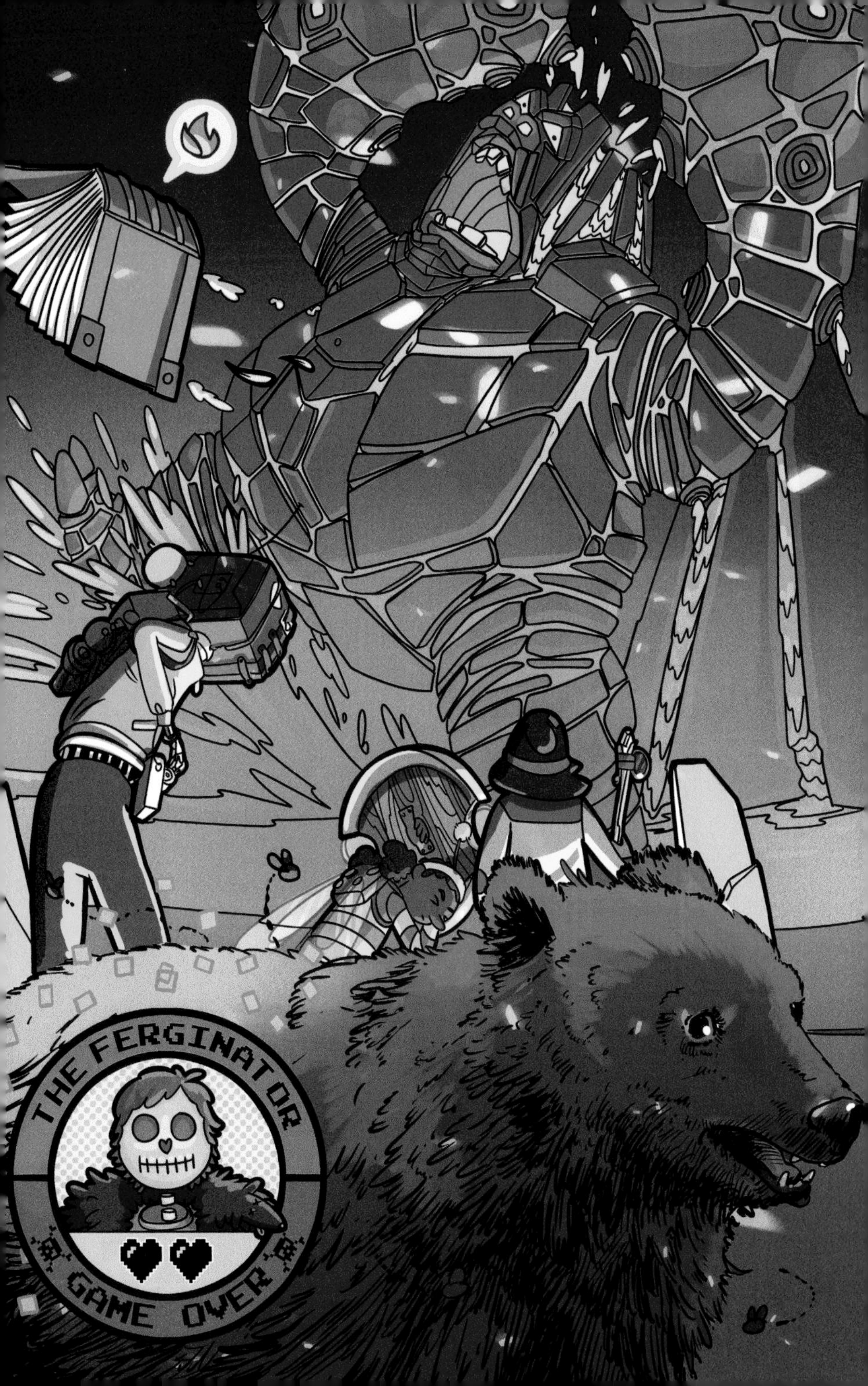

THE FERGINATOR
GAME OVER

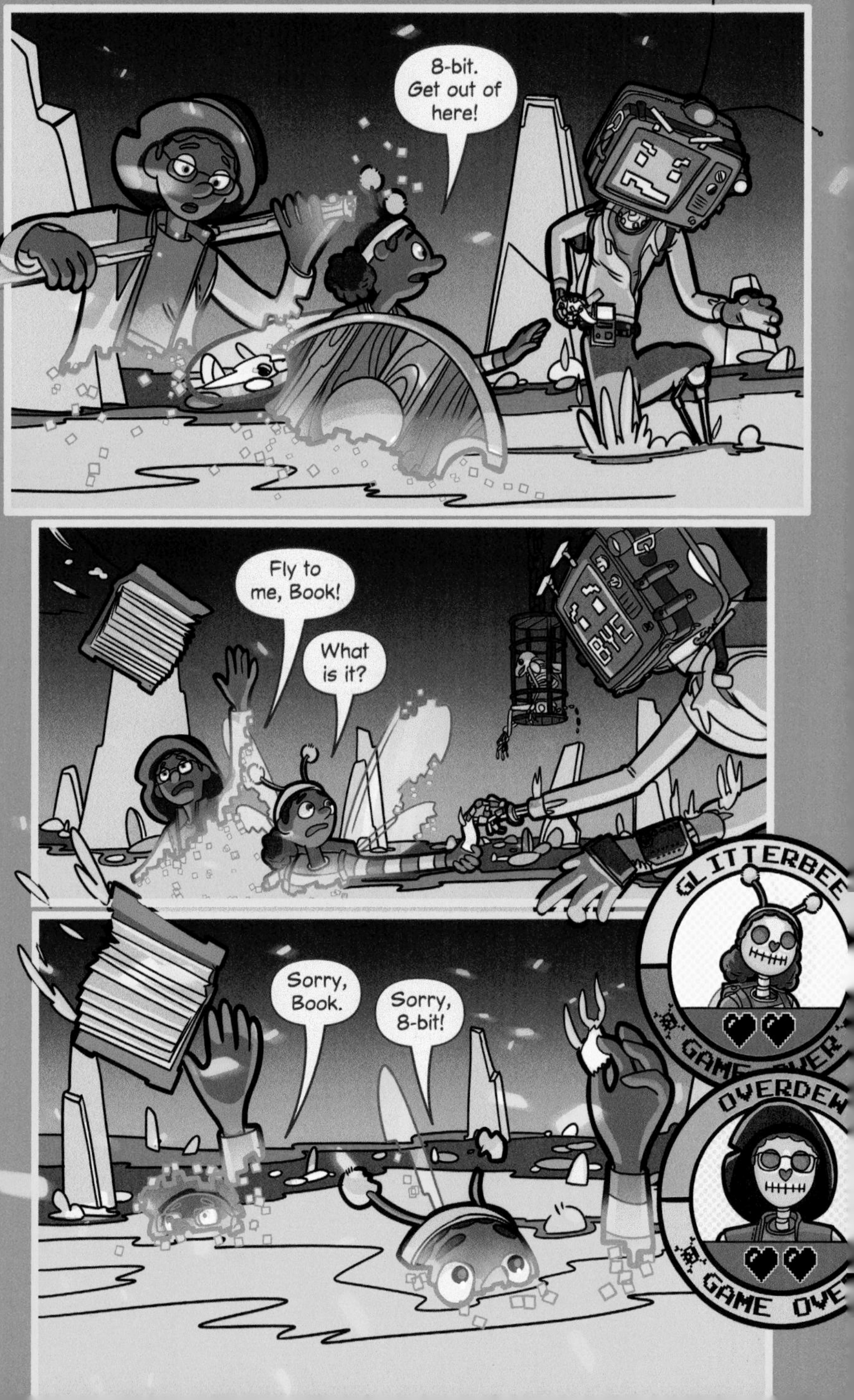
8-bit. Get out of here!
Fly to me, Book!
What is it?
BYE
GLITTERBEE
GAME OVER
Sorry, Book.
Sorry, 8-bit!
OVERDEW
GAME OVE

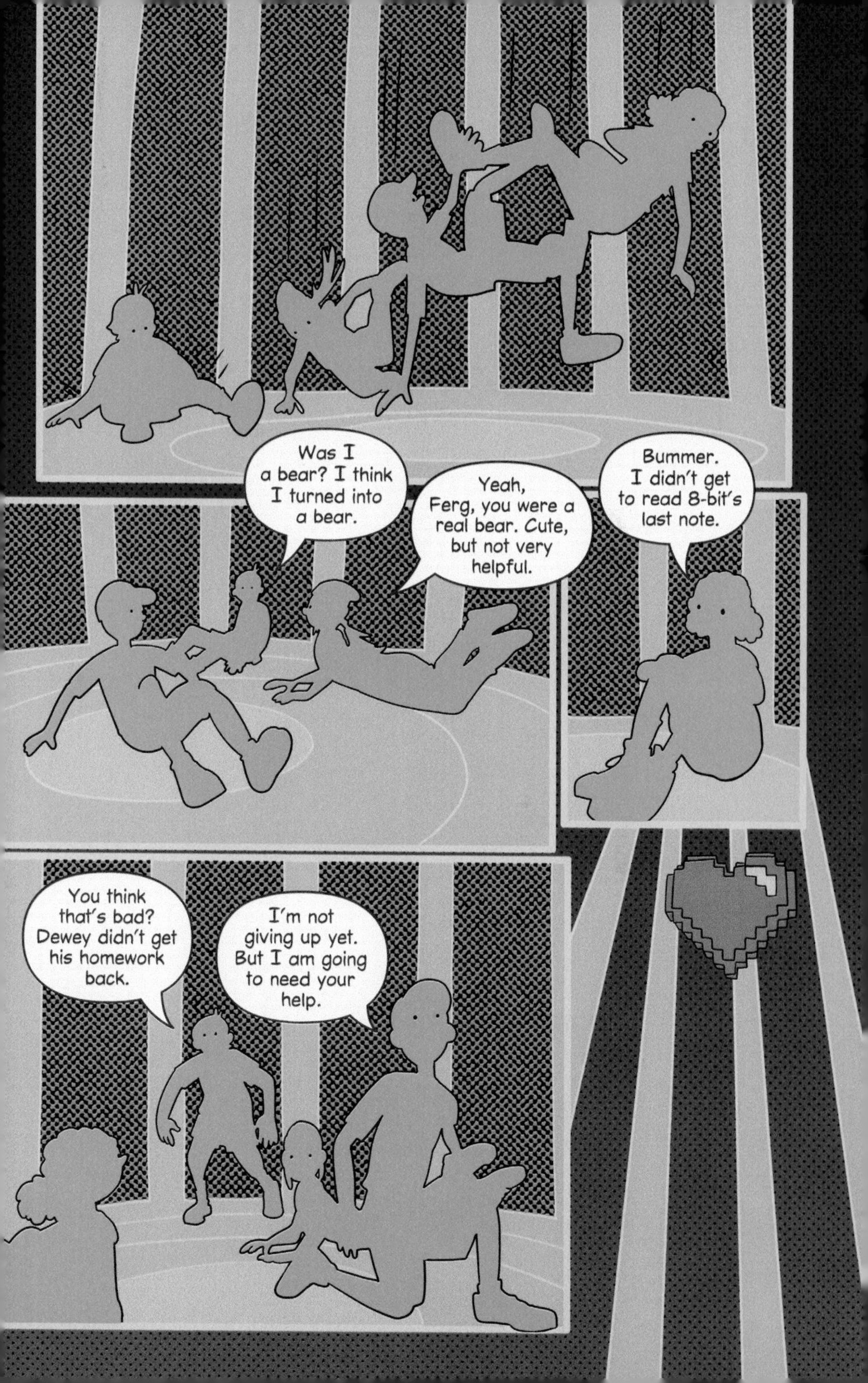
Was I a bear? I think I turned into a bear.
Yeah, Ferg, you were a real bear. Cute, but not very helpful.
Bummer. I didn't get to read 8-bit's last note.
You think that's bad? Dewey didn't get his homework back.
I'm not giving up yet. But I am going to need your help.

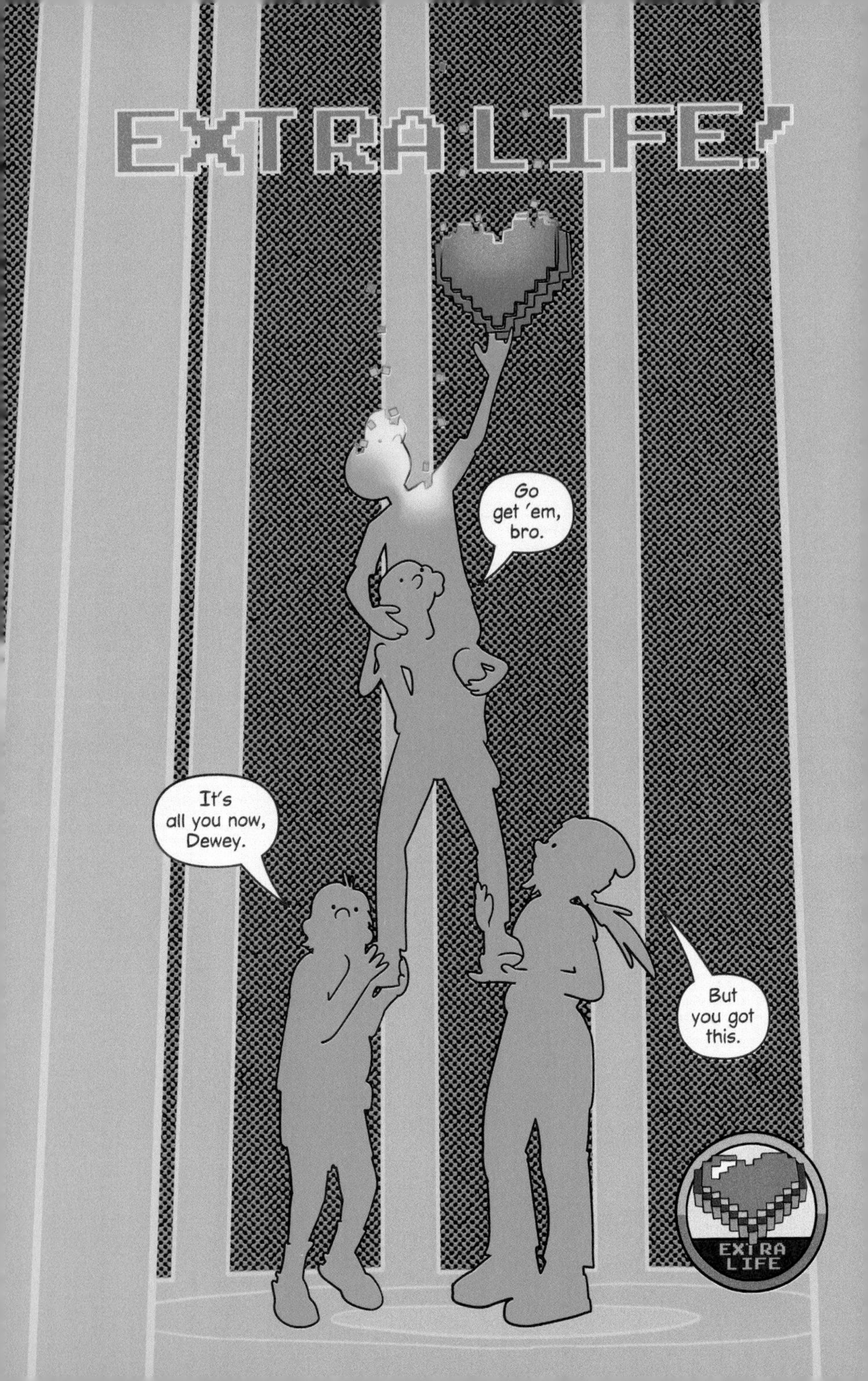
EXTRA LIFE!
Go get 'em, bro.
It's all you now, Dewey.
But you got this.
EXTRA LIFE

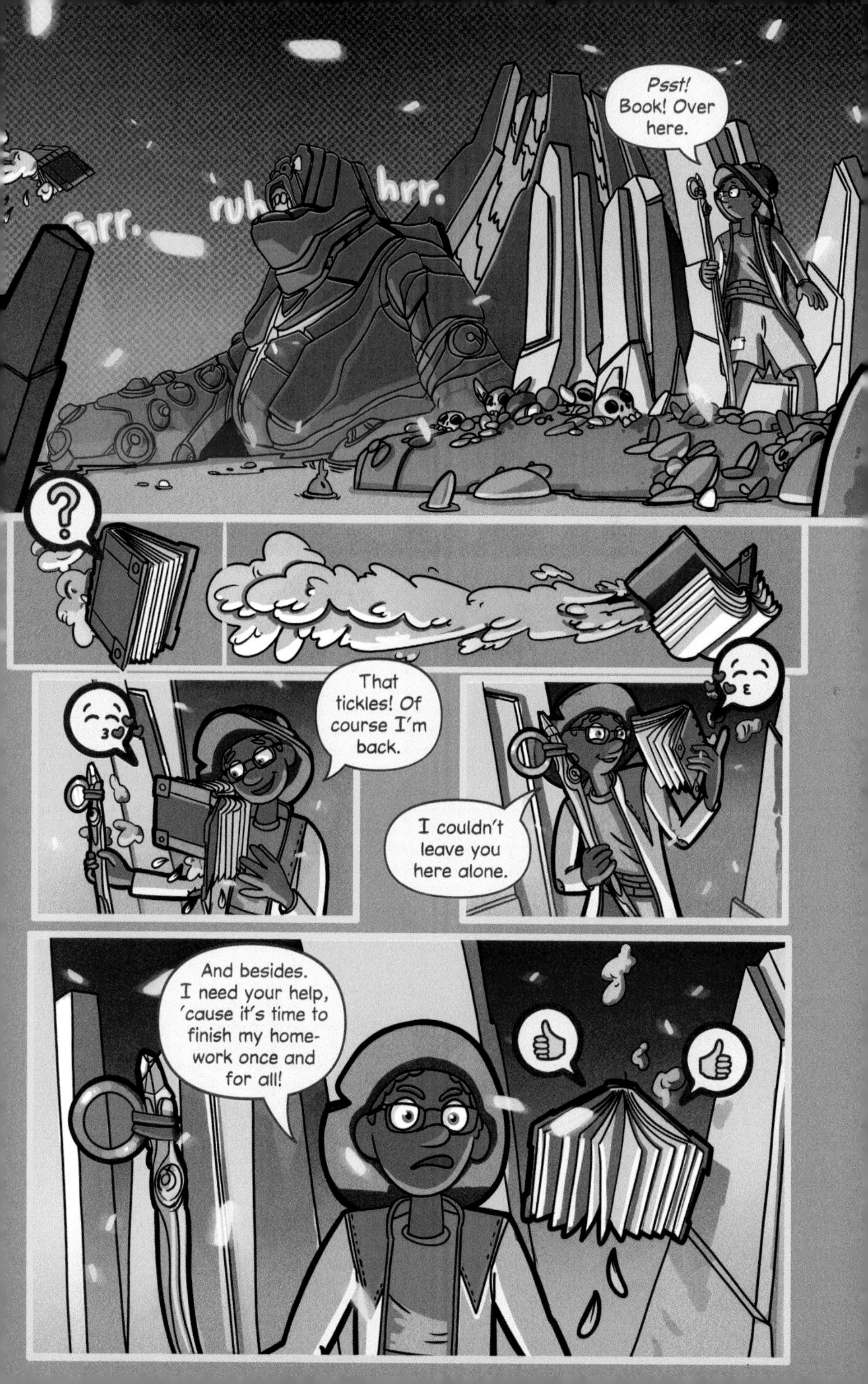
farr.
ruh
hrr.
Psst! Book! Over here.
?
That tickles! Of course I'm back.
I couldn't leave you here alone.
And besides. I need your help, 'cause it's time to finish my home-work once and for all!

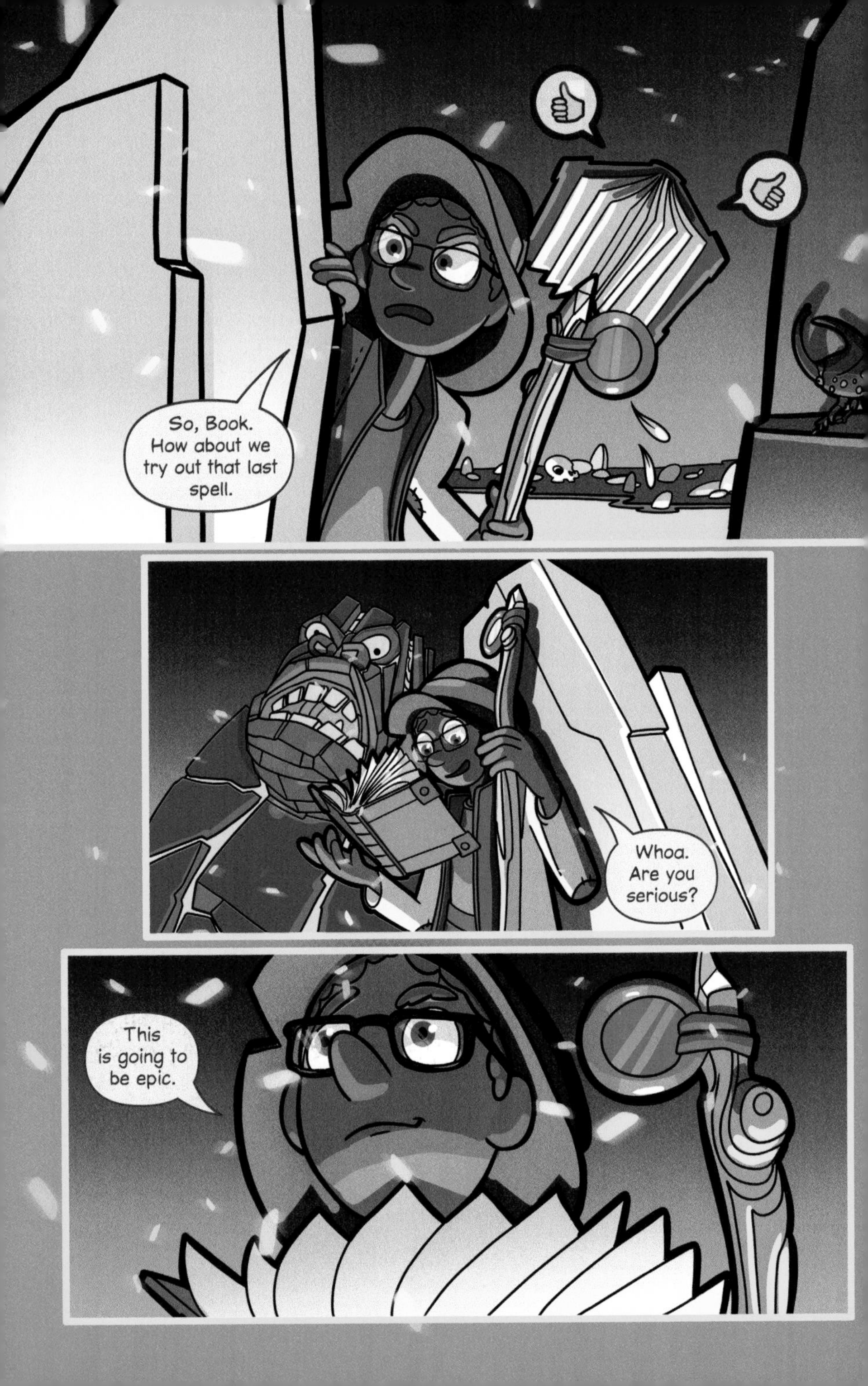

So, Book. How about we try out that last spell.
Whoa. Are you serious?
This is going to be epic.

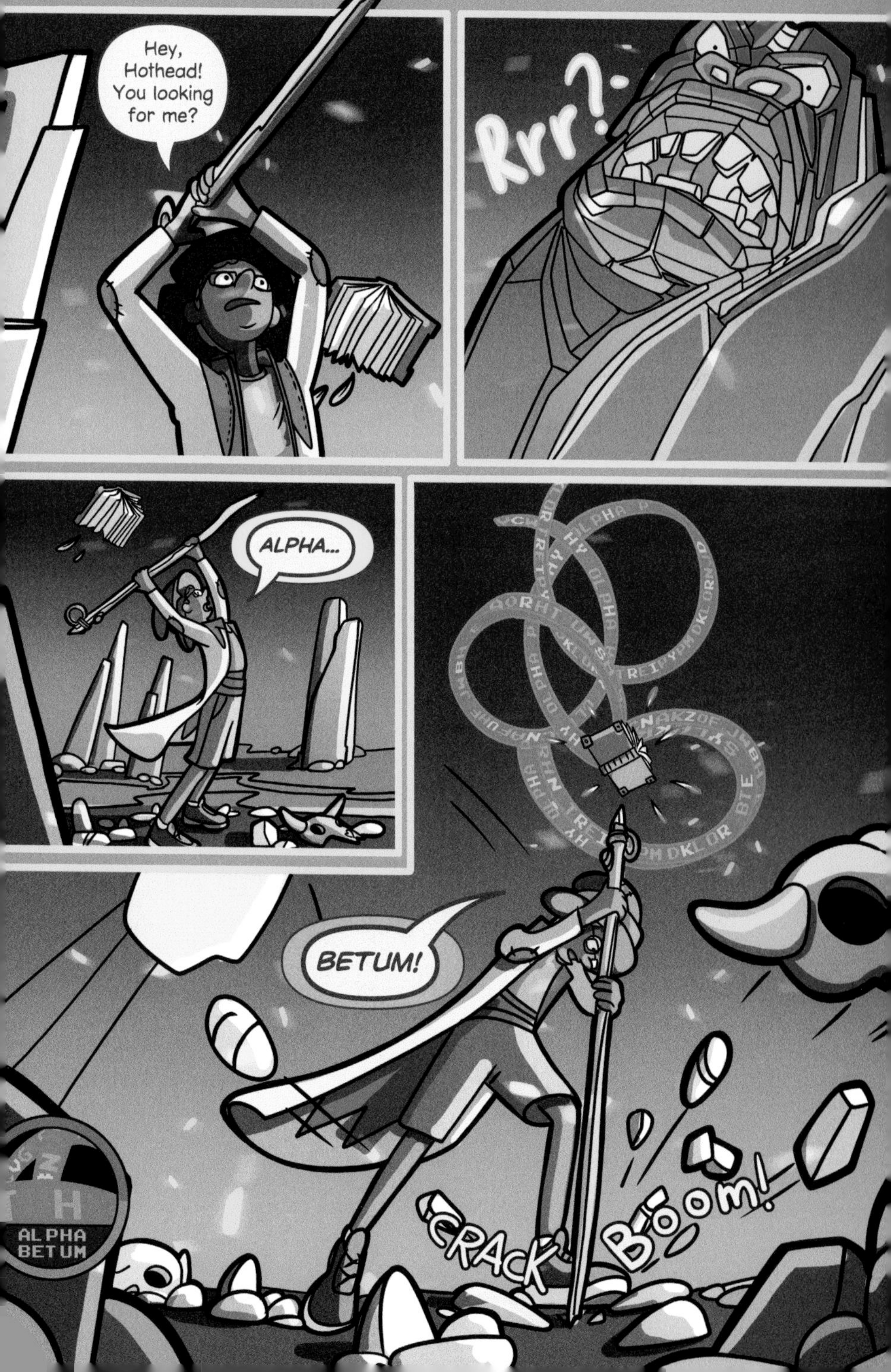
Hey, Hothead! You looking for me?
Rrr?
ALPHA...
BETUM!
ALPHA BETUM
CRACK
BOOM!

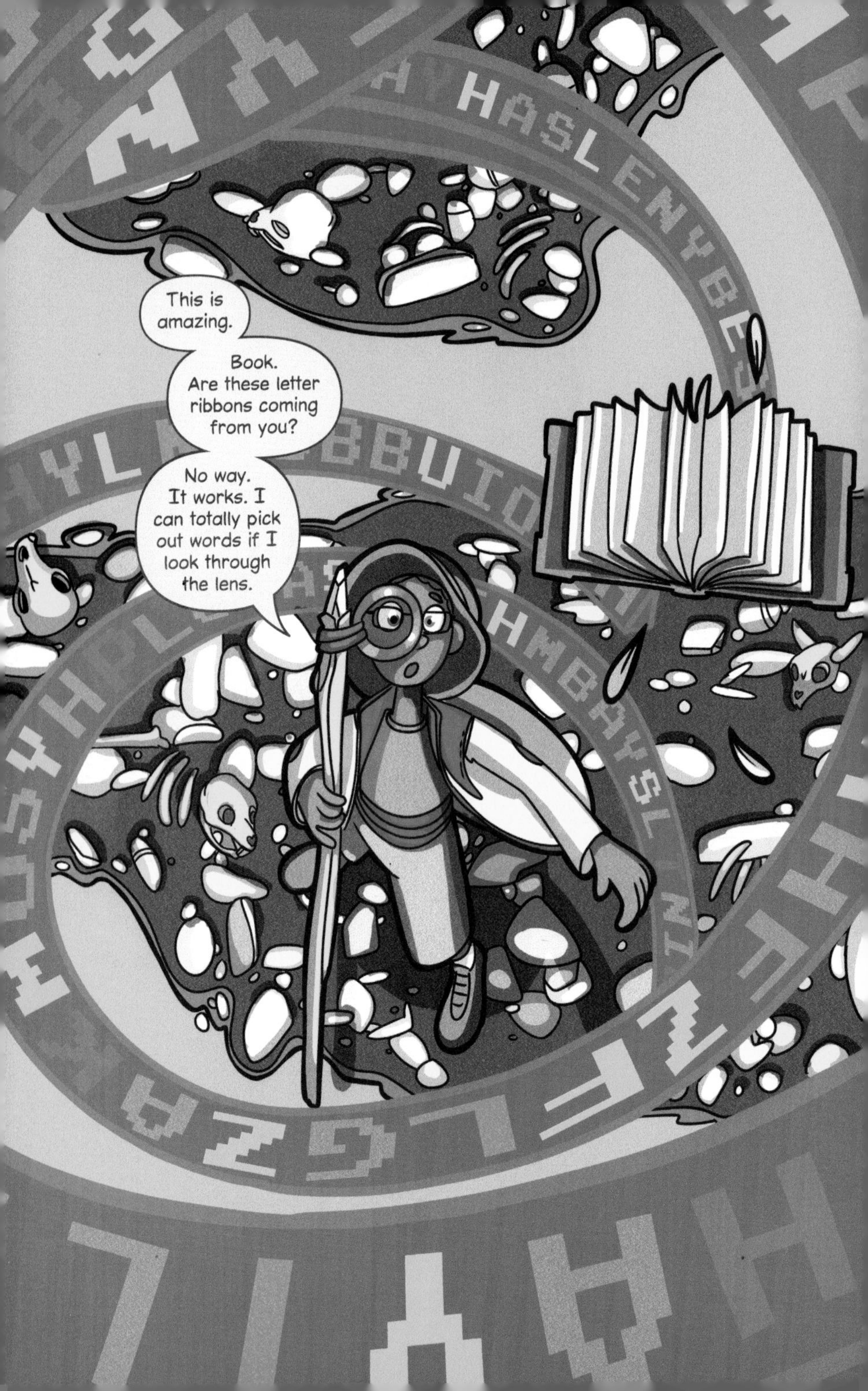
This is amazing.
Book. Are these letter ribbons coming from you?
No way. It works. I can totally pick out words if I look through the lens.

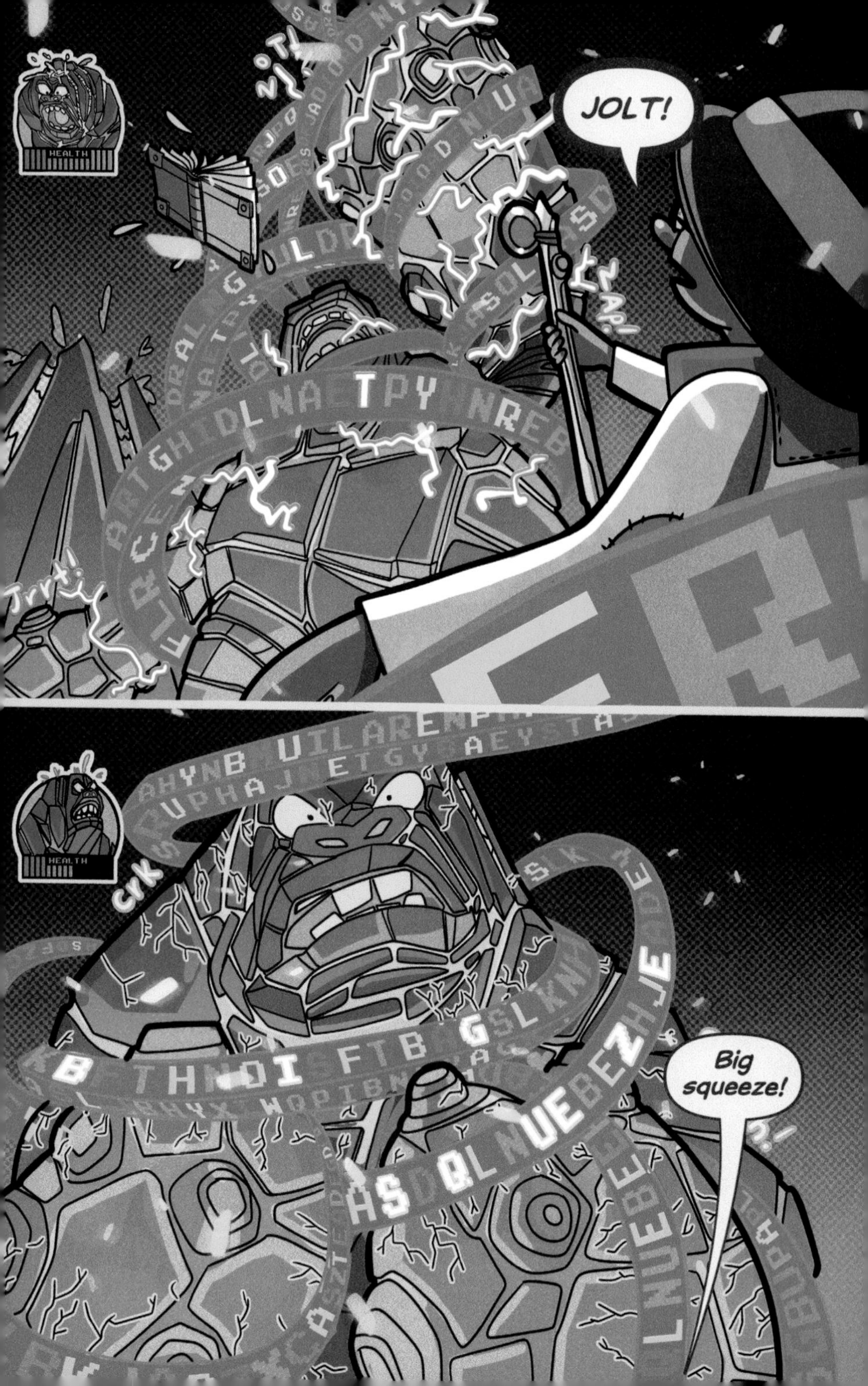
HEALTH
JOLT!
Zap!
Jrrt!
HEALTH
crk
Big squeeze!

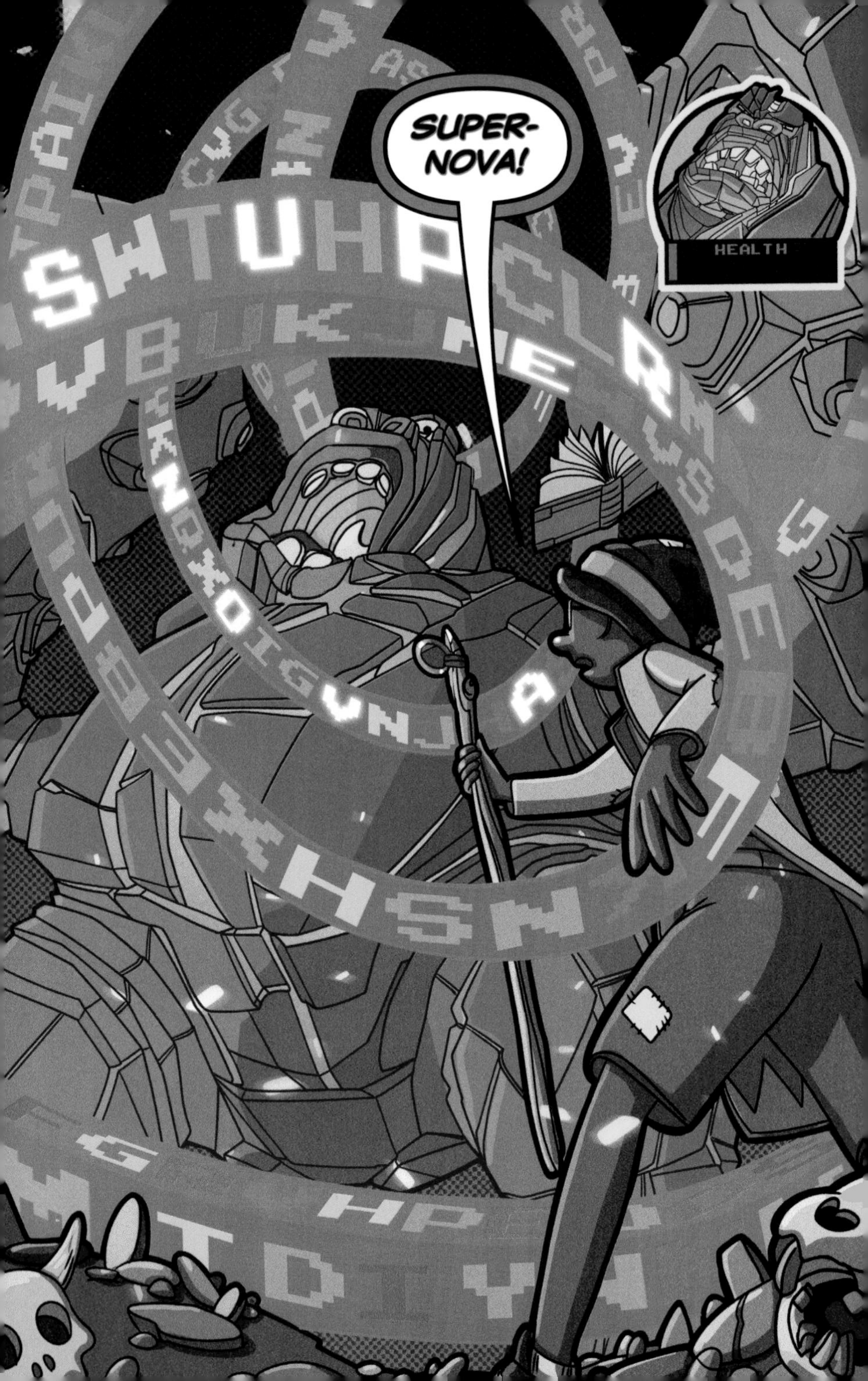
SUPER-
NOVA!
HEALTH

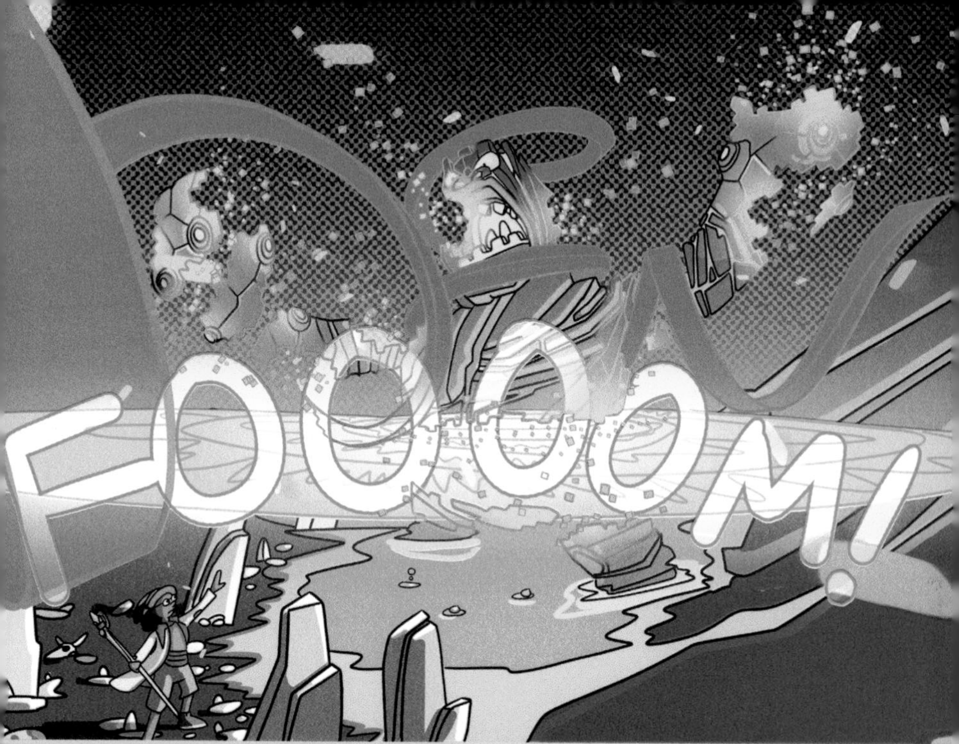
FOOOOOM!

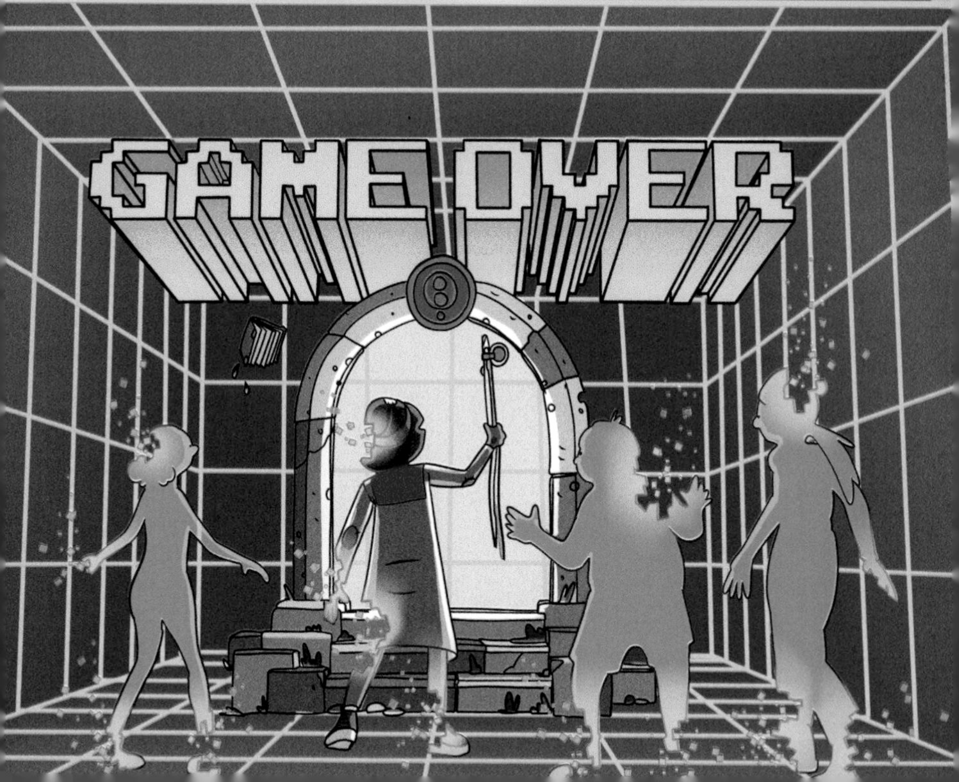
GAME OVER

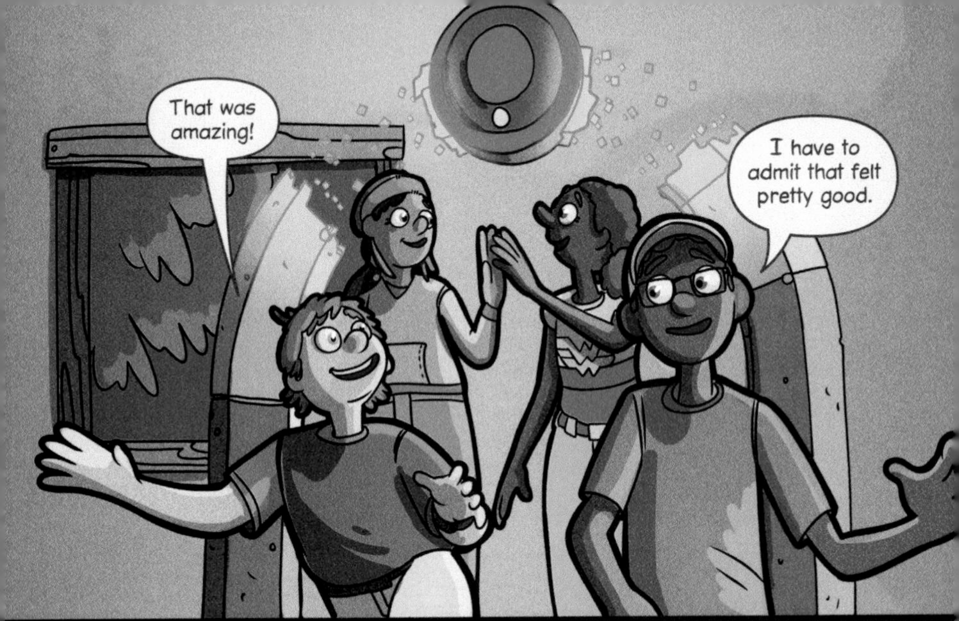
That was amazing!
I have to admit that felt pretty good.

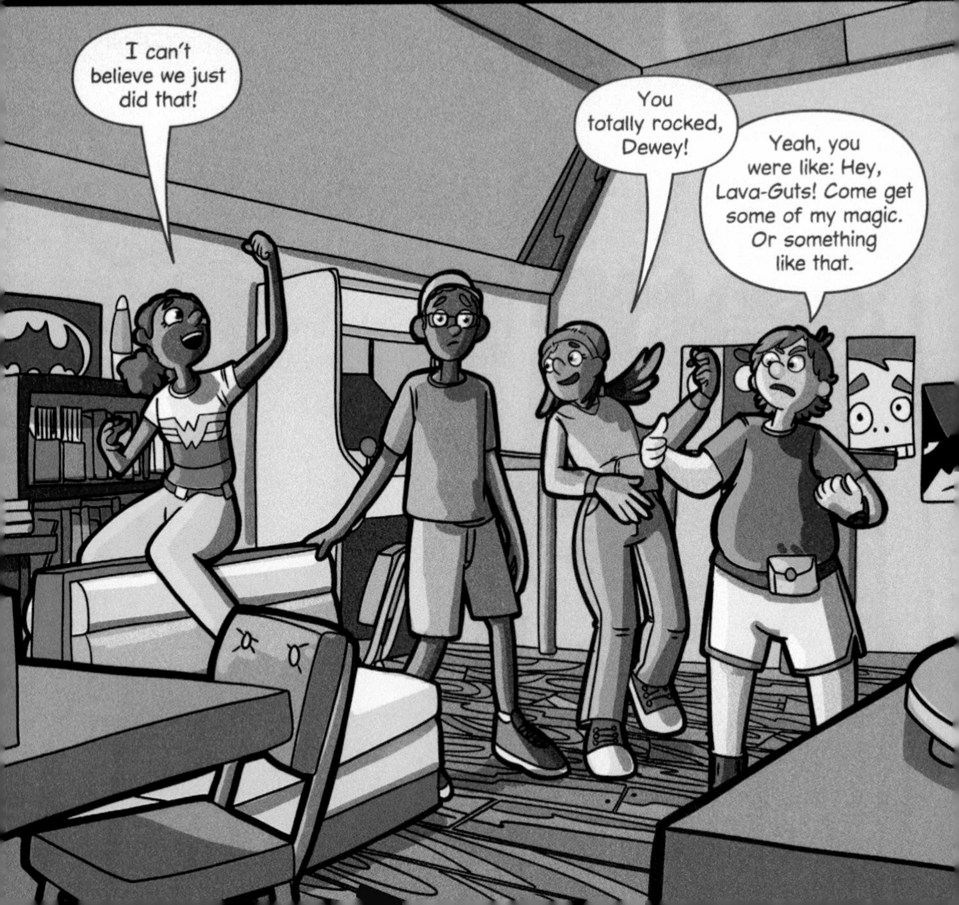
I can't believe we just did that!
You totally rocked, Dewey!
Yeah, you were like: Hey, Lava-Guts! Come get some of my magic. Or something like that.

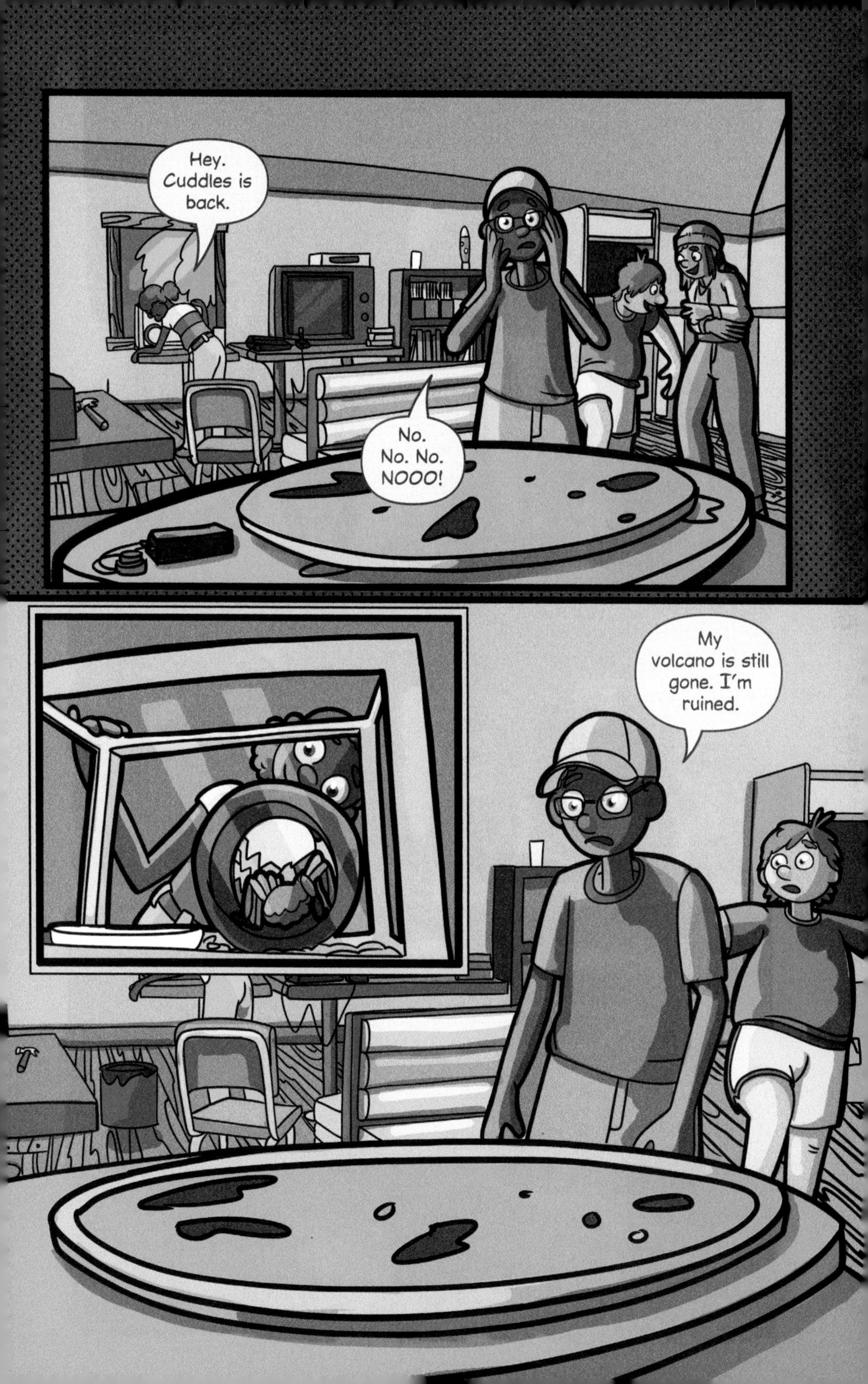
Hey. Cuddles is back.
No. No. No. NOOO!
My volcano is still gone. I'm ruined.

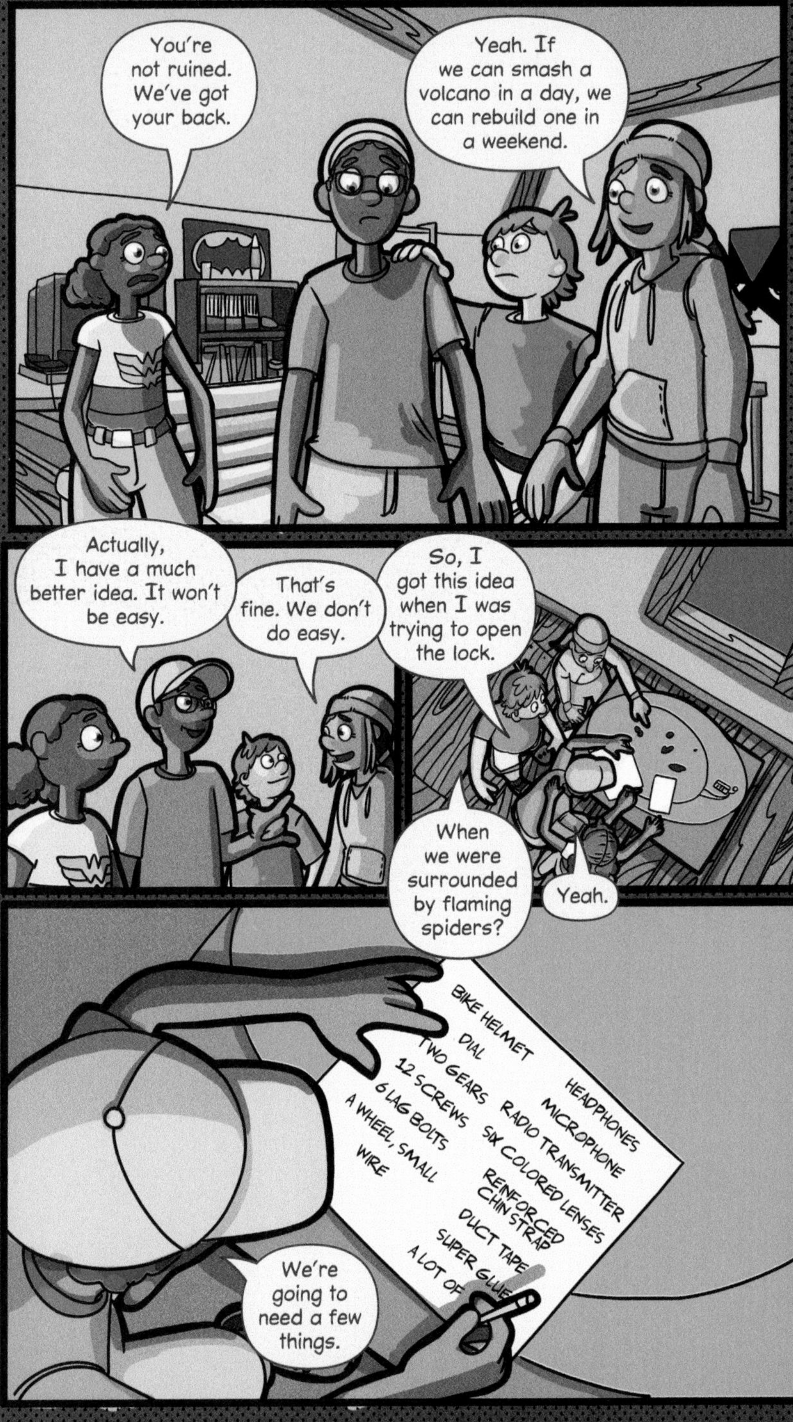
You're not ruined. We've got your back.
Yeah. If we can smash a volcano in a day, we can rebuild one in a weekend.
Actually, I have a much better idea. It won't be easy.
That's fine. We don't do easy.
So, I got this idea when I was trying to open the lock.
When we were surrounded by flaming spiders?
Yeah.
BIKE HELMET
DIAL
TWO GEARS
12 SCREWS
6 LAG BOLTS
A WHEEL, SMALL
WIRE
HEADPHONES
MICROPHONE
RADIO TRANSMITTER
SIX COLORED LENSES
REINFORCED CHIN STRAP
DUCT TAPE
SUPER GLUE
A LOT OF
We're going to need a few things.

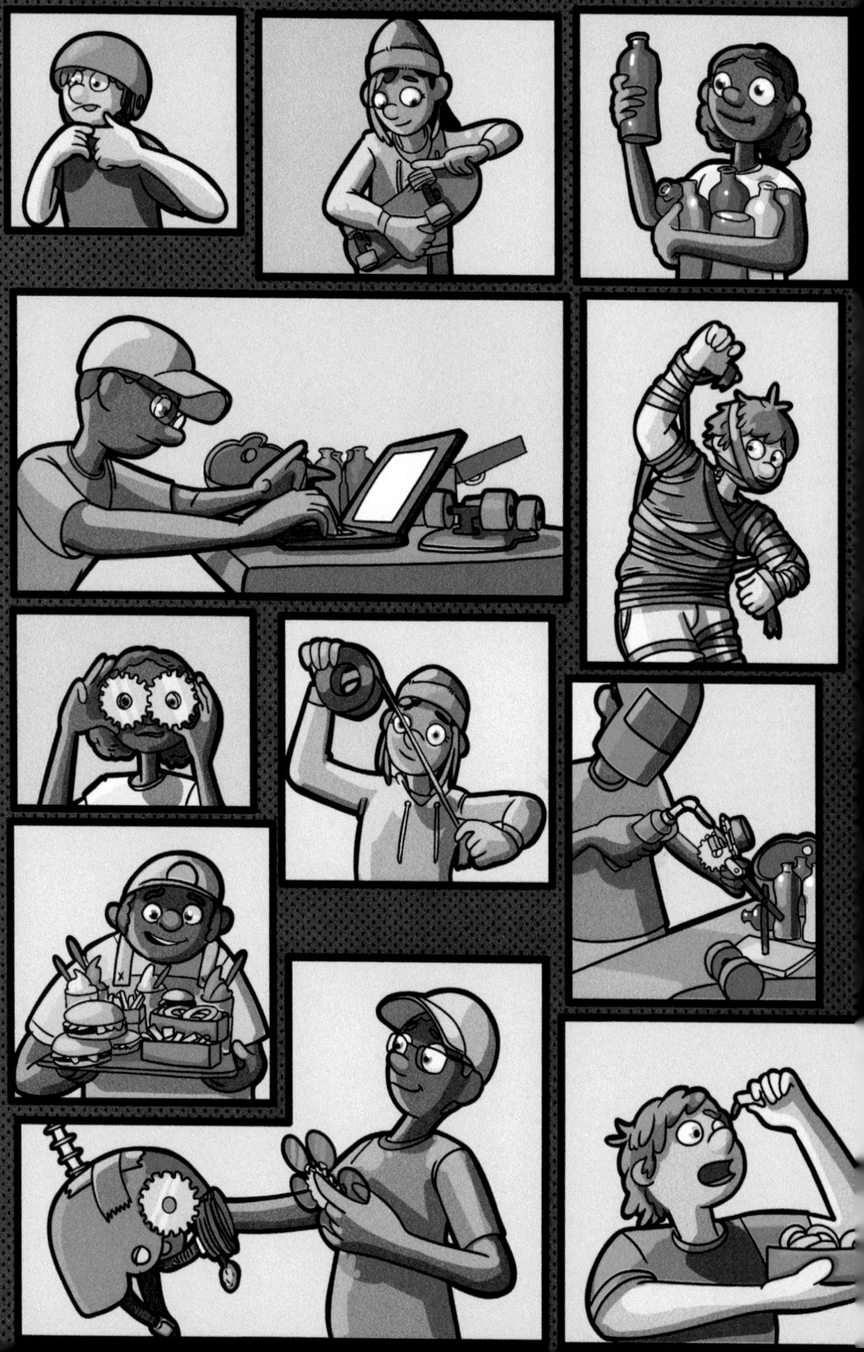

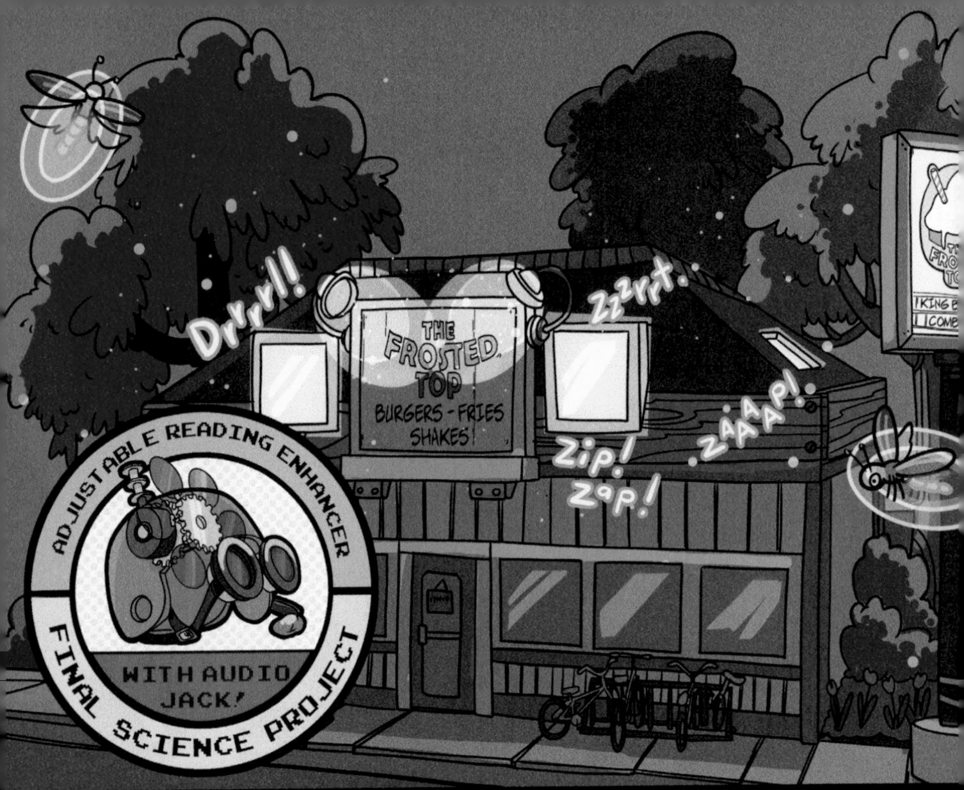

Drrrl!!
Zzzrrt.
THE FROSTED TOP
BURGERS - FRIES
SHAKES
Zip! Zap!
ZAAAAP!
ADJUSTABLE READING ENHANCER
WITH AUDIO JACK!
FINAL SCIENCE PROJECT

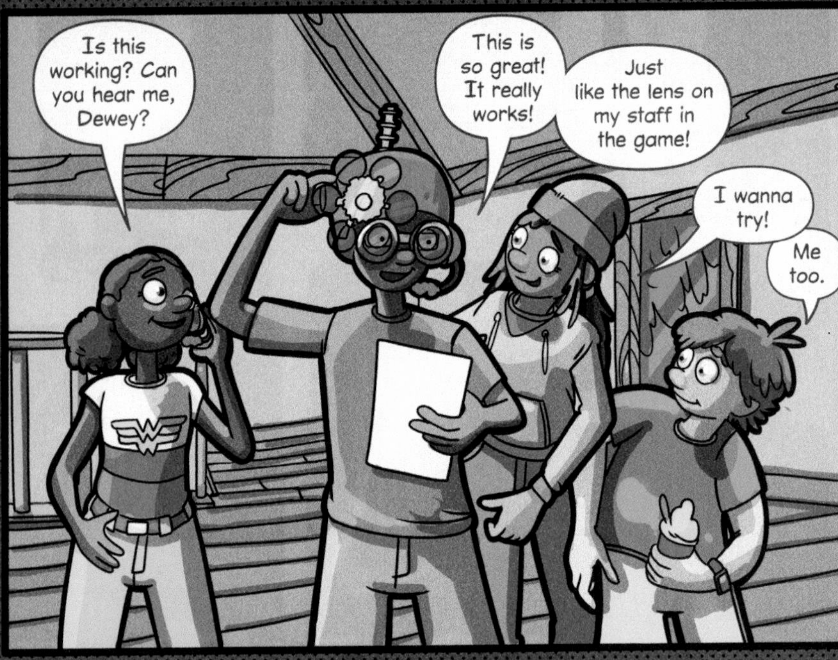

Is this working? Can you hear me, Dewey?
This is so great! It really works!
Just like the lens on my staff in the game!
I wanna try!
Me too.

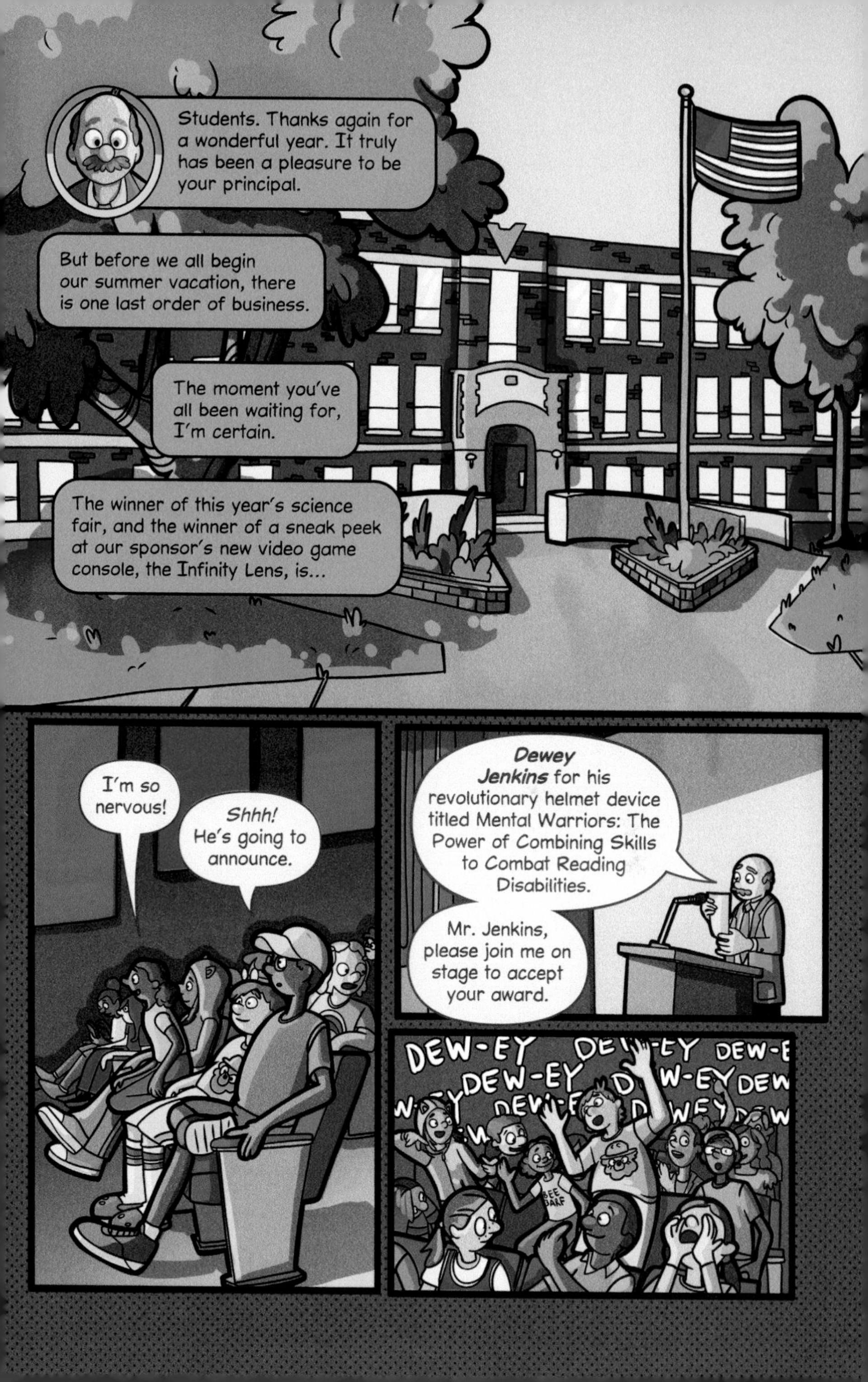
Students. Thanks again for a wonderful year. It truly has been a pleasure to be your principal.
But before we all begin our summer vacation, there is one last order of business.
The moment you've all been waiting for, I'm certain.
The winner of this year's science fair, and the winner of a sneak peek at our sponsor's new video game console, the Infinity Lens, is...
I'm so nervous!
Shhh! He's going to announce.
Dewey Jenkins for his revolutionary helmet device titled Mental Warriors: The Power of Combining Skills to Combat Reading Disabilities.
Mr. Jenkins, please join me on stage to accept your award.
DEW-EY
DEW-EY
DEW-EY

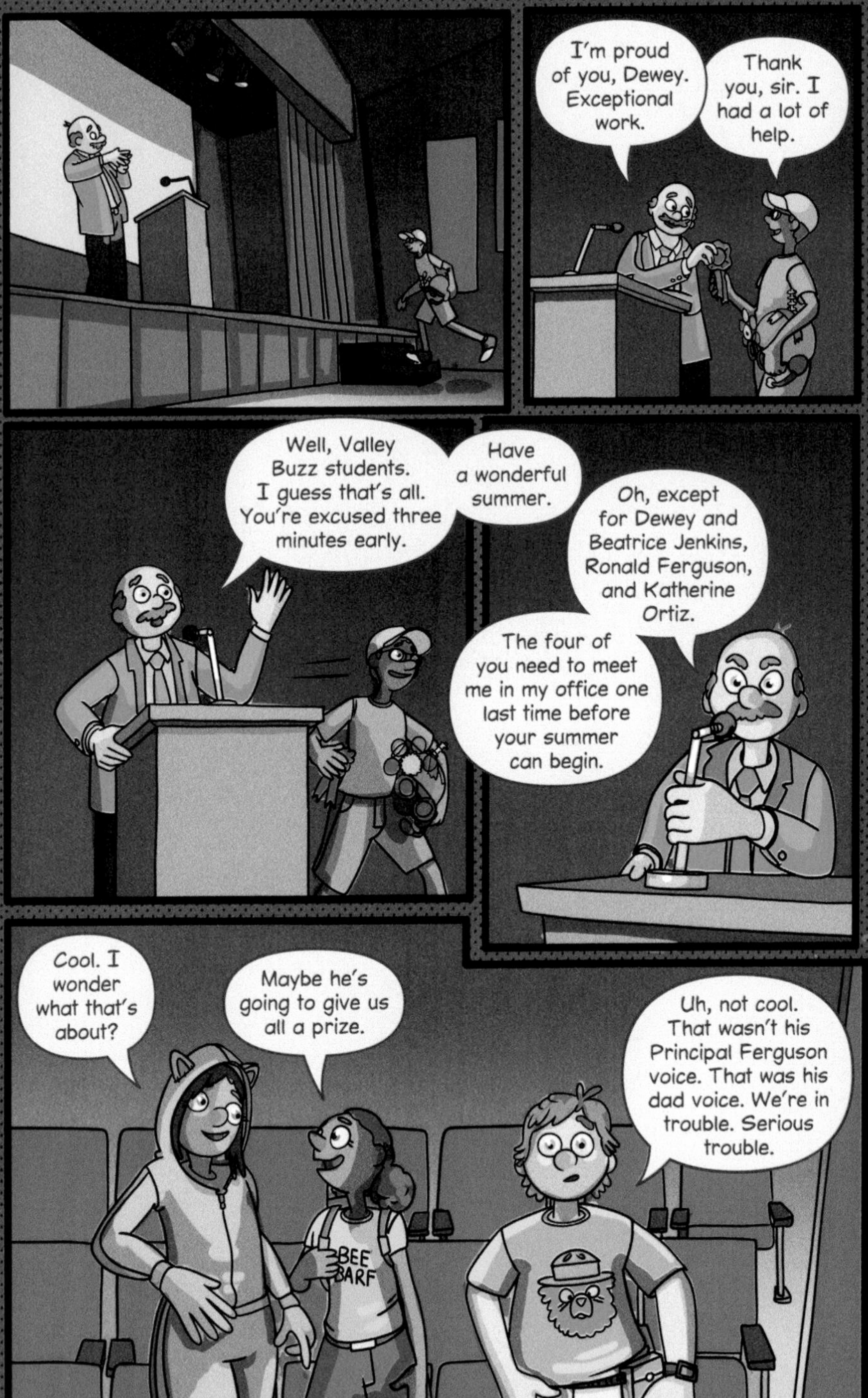
I'm proud of you, Dewey. Exceptional work.
Thank you, sir. I had a lot of help.
Well, Valley Buzz students. I guess that's all. You're excused three minutes early.
Have a wonderful summer.
Oh, except for Dewey and Beatrice Jenkins, Ronald Ferguson, and Katherine Ortiz.
The four of you need to meet me in my office one last time before your summer can begin.
Cool. I wonder what that's about?
Maybe he's going to give us all a prize.
Uh, not cool. That wasn't his Principal Ferguson voice. That was his dad voice. We're in trouble. Serious trouble.
BEE BARF

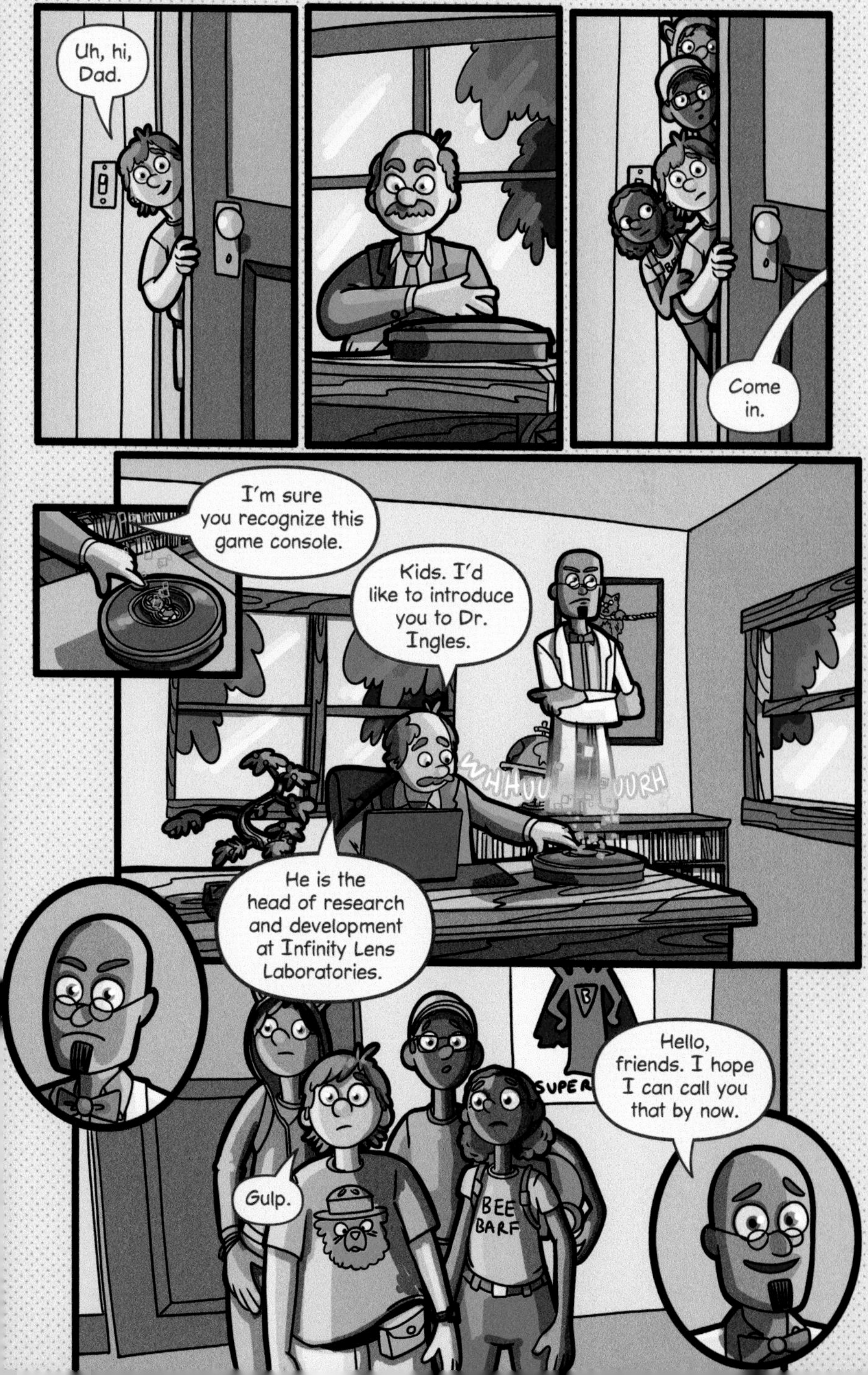
Uh, hi, Dad.
Come in.
I'm sure you recognize this game console.
Kids. I'd like to introduce you to Dr. Ingles.
WHHUU URH
He is the head of research and development at Infinity Lens Laboratories.
SUPER
Hello, friends. I hope I can call you that by now.
Gulp.
BEE BARF

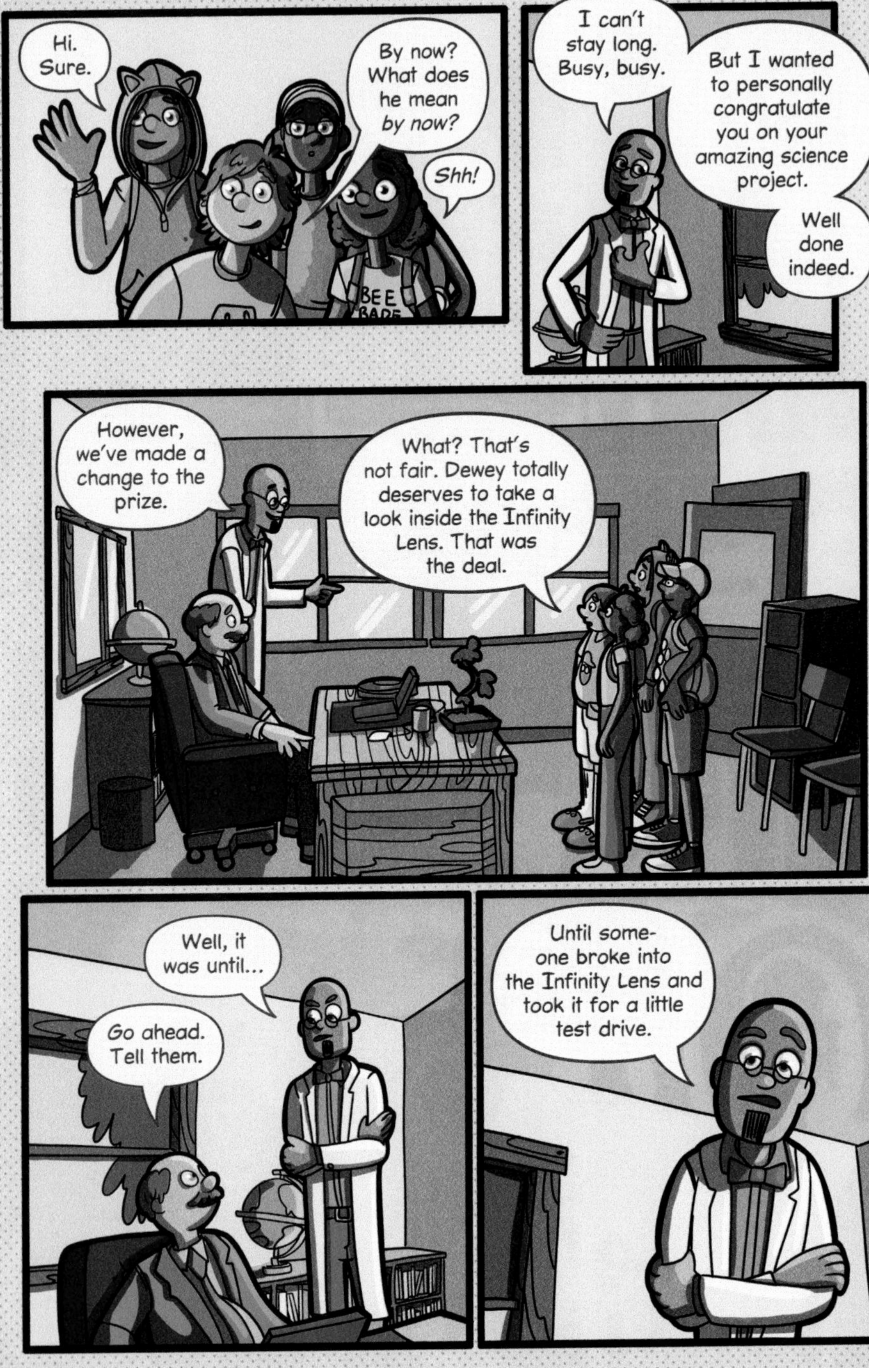
Hi. Sure.
By now? What does he mean *by now?*
Shh!
I can't stay long. Busy, busy.
But I wanted to personally congratulate you on your amazing science project.
Well done indeed.
However, we've made a change to the prize.
What? That's not fair. Dewey totally deserves to take a look inside the Infinity Lens. That was the deal.
Well, it was until...
Go ahead. Tell them.
Until some-one broke into the Infinity Lens and took it for a little test drive.

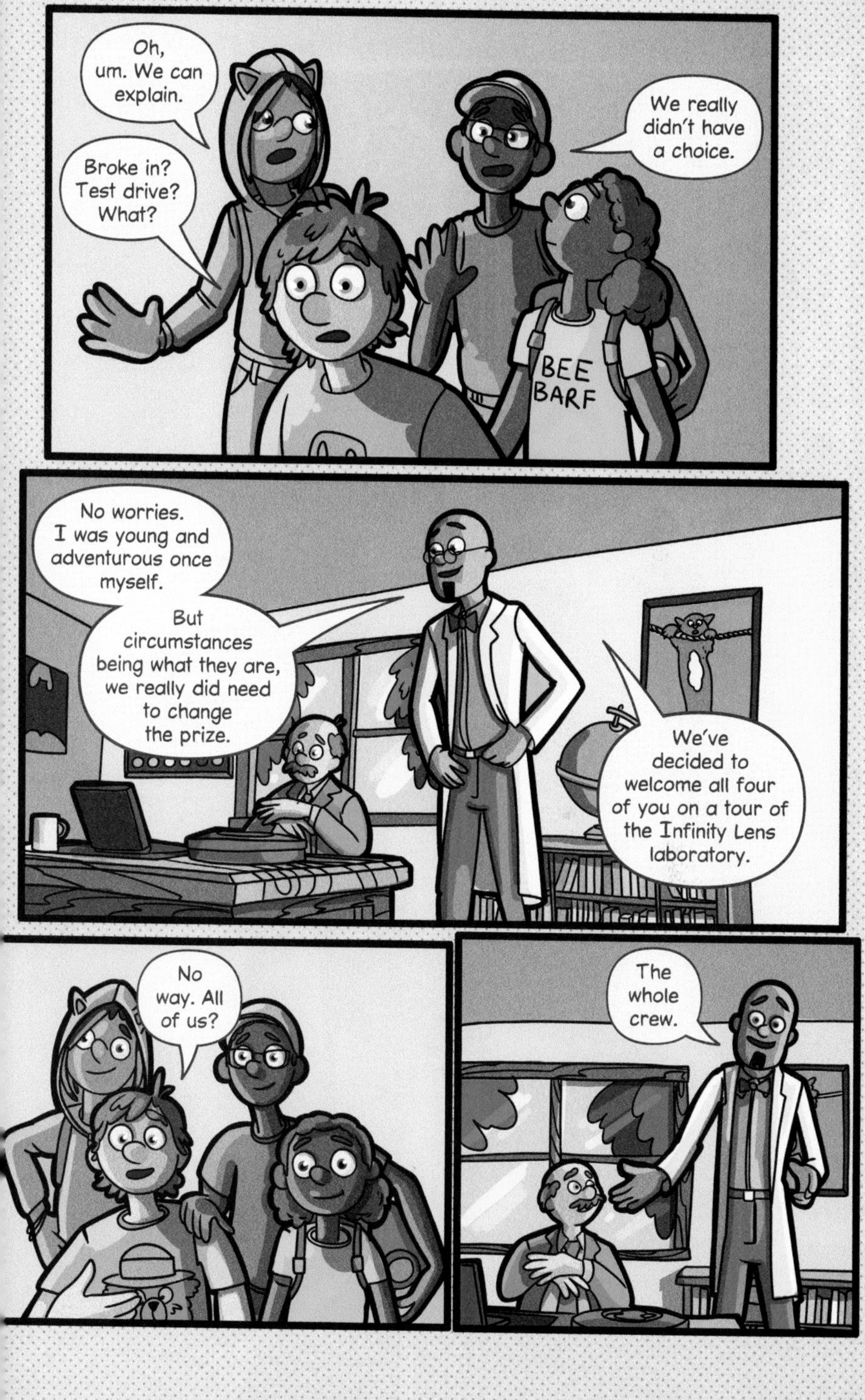

Oh, um. We can explain.
Broke in? Test drive? What?
We really didn't have a choice.
BEE BARF
No worries. I was young and adventurous once myself.
But circumstances being what they are, we really did need to change the prize.
We've decided to welcome all four of you on a tour of the Infinity Lens laboratory.
No way. All of us?
The whole crew.

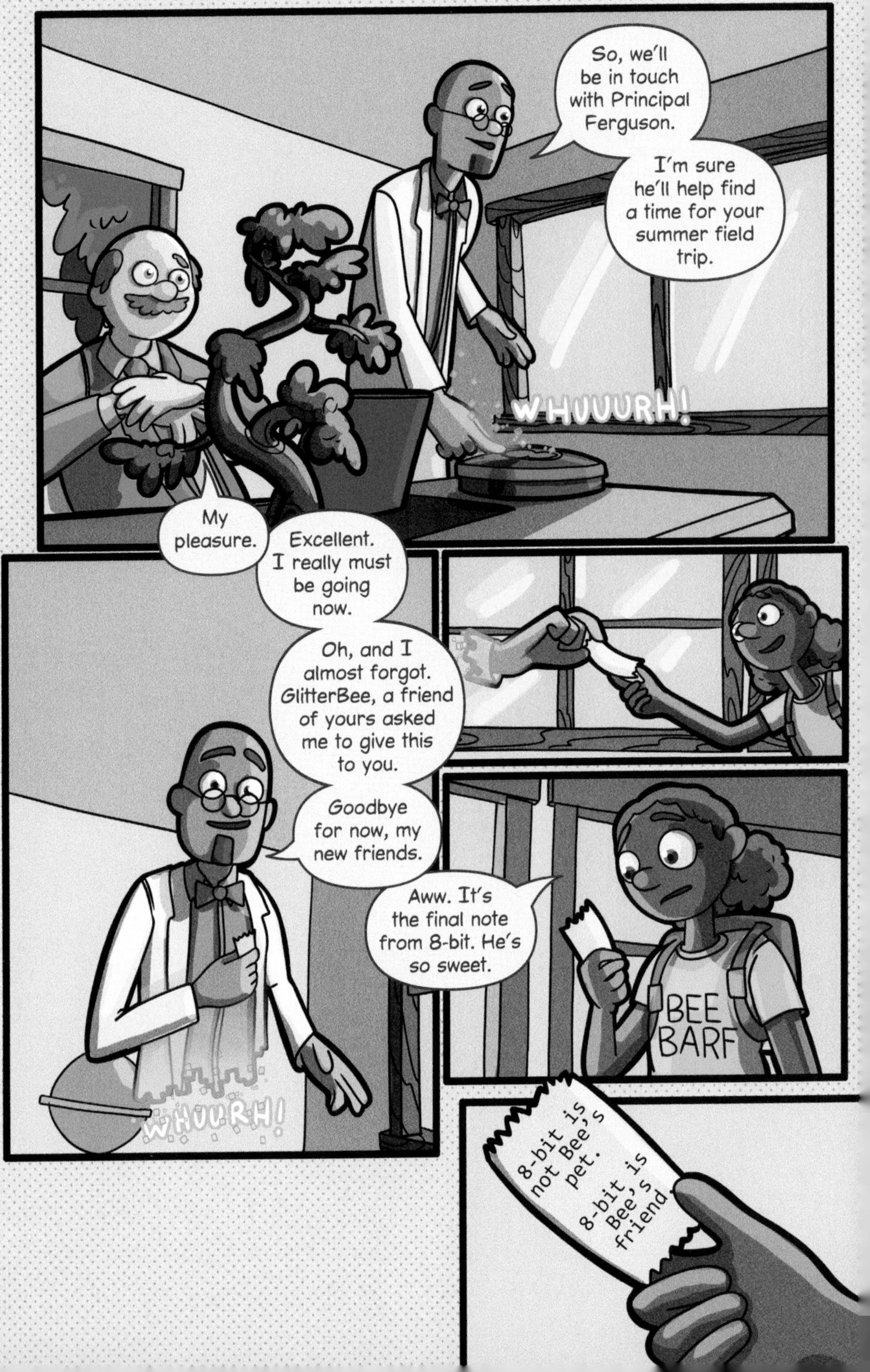
So, we'll be in touch with Principal Ferguson.
I'm sure he'll help find a time for your summer field trip.
WHUUURH!
My pleasure.
Excellent. I really must be going now.
Oh, and I almost forgot. GlitterBee, a friend of yours asked me to give this to you.
Goodbye for now, my new friends.
WHUURH!
Aww. It's the final note from 8-bit. He's so sweet.
BEE BARF
8-bit is not Bee's pet.
8-bit is Bee's friend.

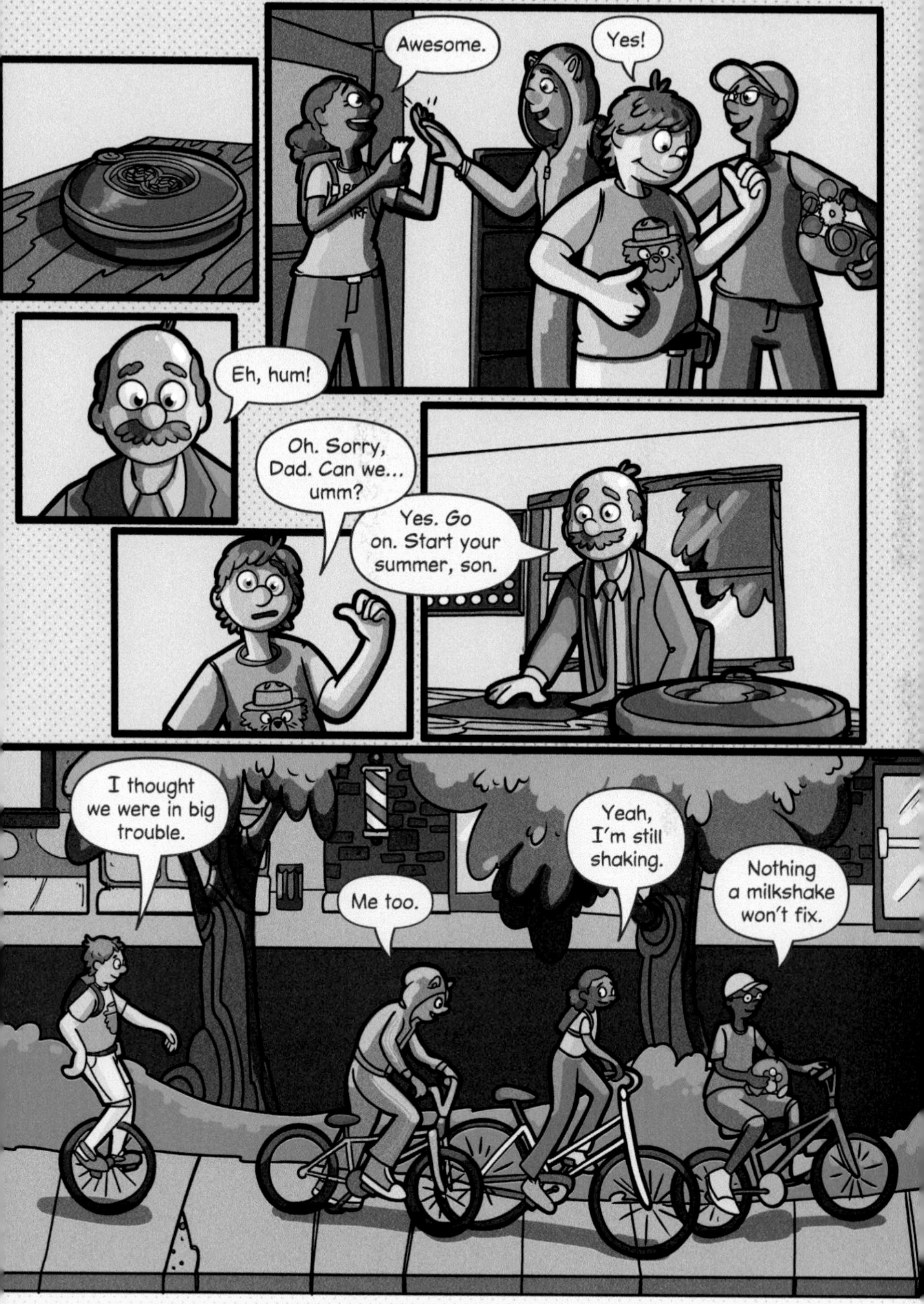

Awesome.
Yes!
Eh, hum!
Oh. Sorry, Dad. Can we... umm?
Yes. Go on. Start your summer, son.
I thought we were in big trouble.
Me too.
Yeah, I'm still shaking.
Nothing a milkshake won't fix.

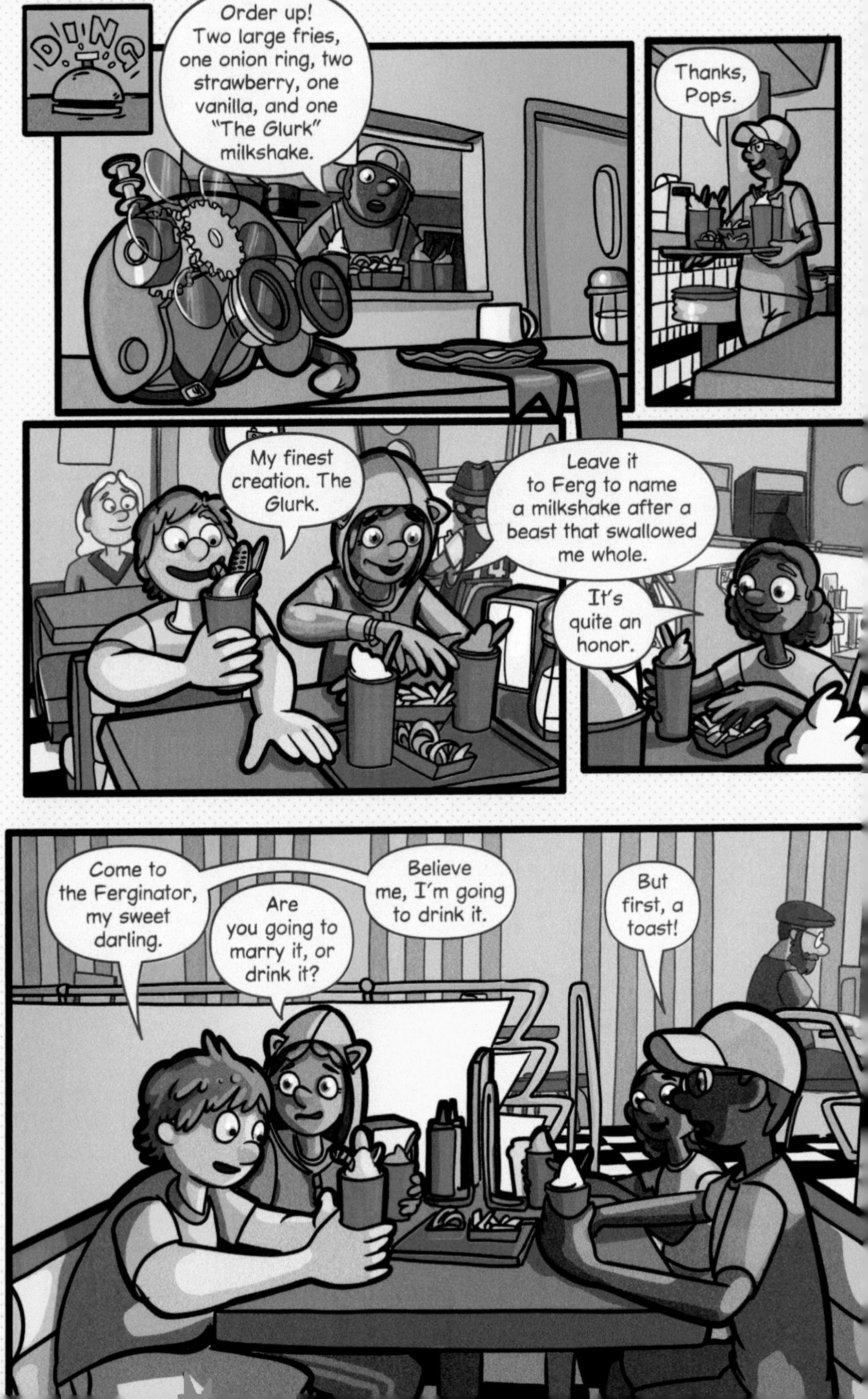
DING
Order up! Two large fries, one onion ring, two strawberry, one vanilla, and one "The Glurk" milkshake.
Thanks, Pops.
My finest creation. The Glurk.
Leave it to Ferg to name a milkshake after a beast that swallowed me whole.
It's quite an honor.
Come to the Ferginator, my sweet darling.
Are you going to marry it, or drink it?
Believe me, I'm going to drink it.
But first, a toast!

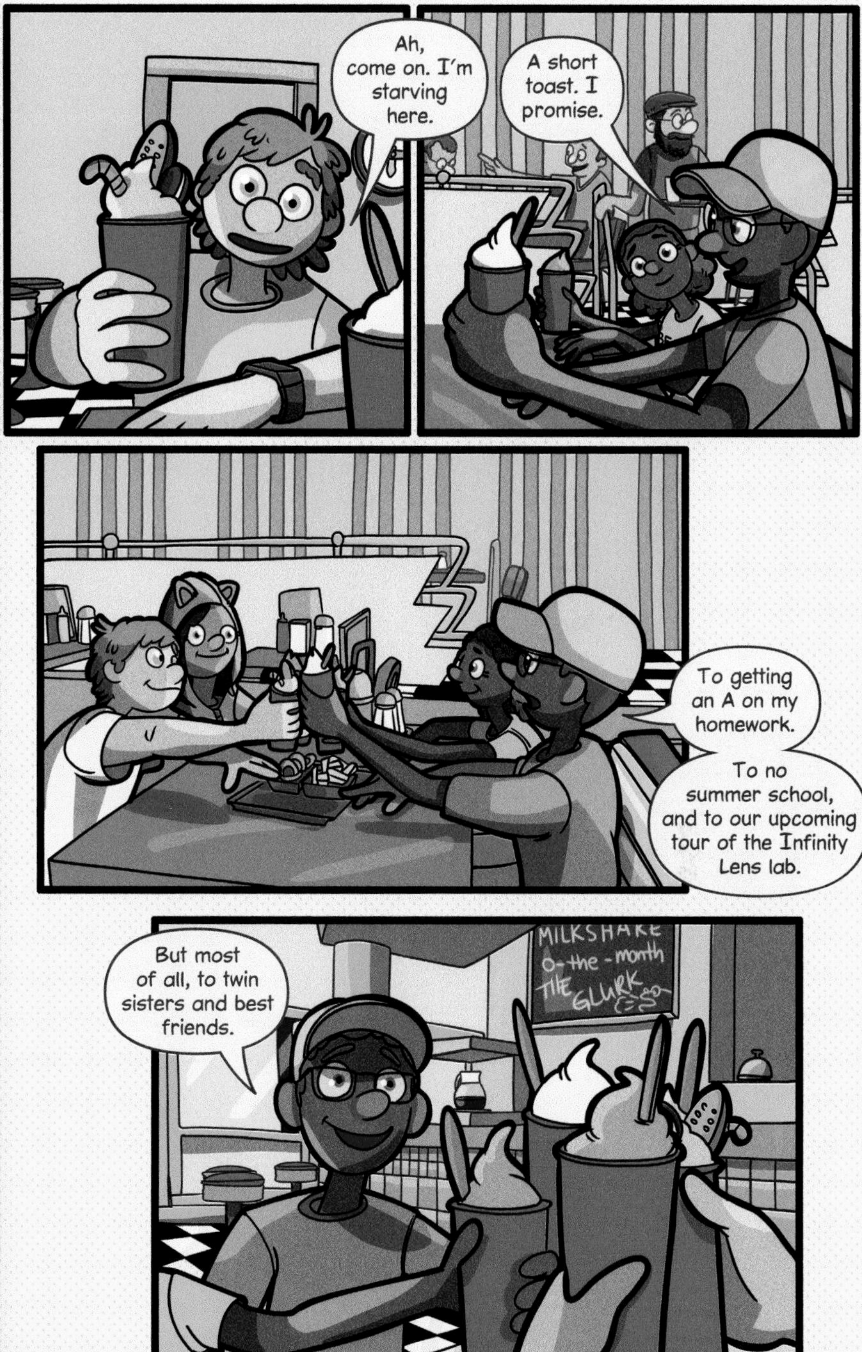
Ah, come on. I'm starving here.
A short toast. I promise.
To getting an A on my homework.
To no summer school, and to our upcoming tour of the Infinity Lens lab.
MILKSHAKE o-the-month THE GLURK
But most of all, to twin sisters and best friends.

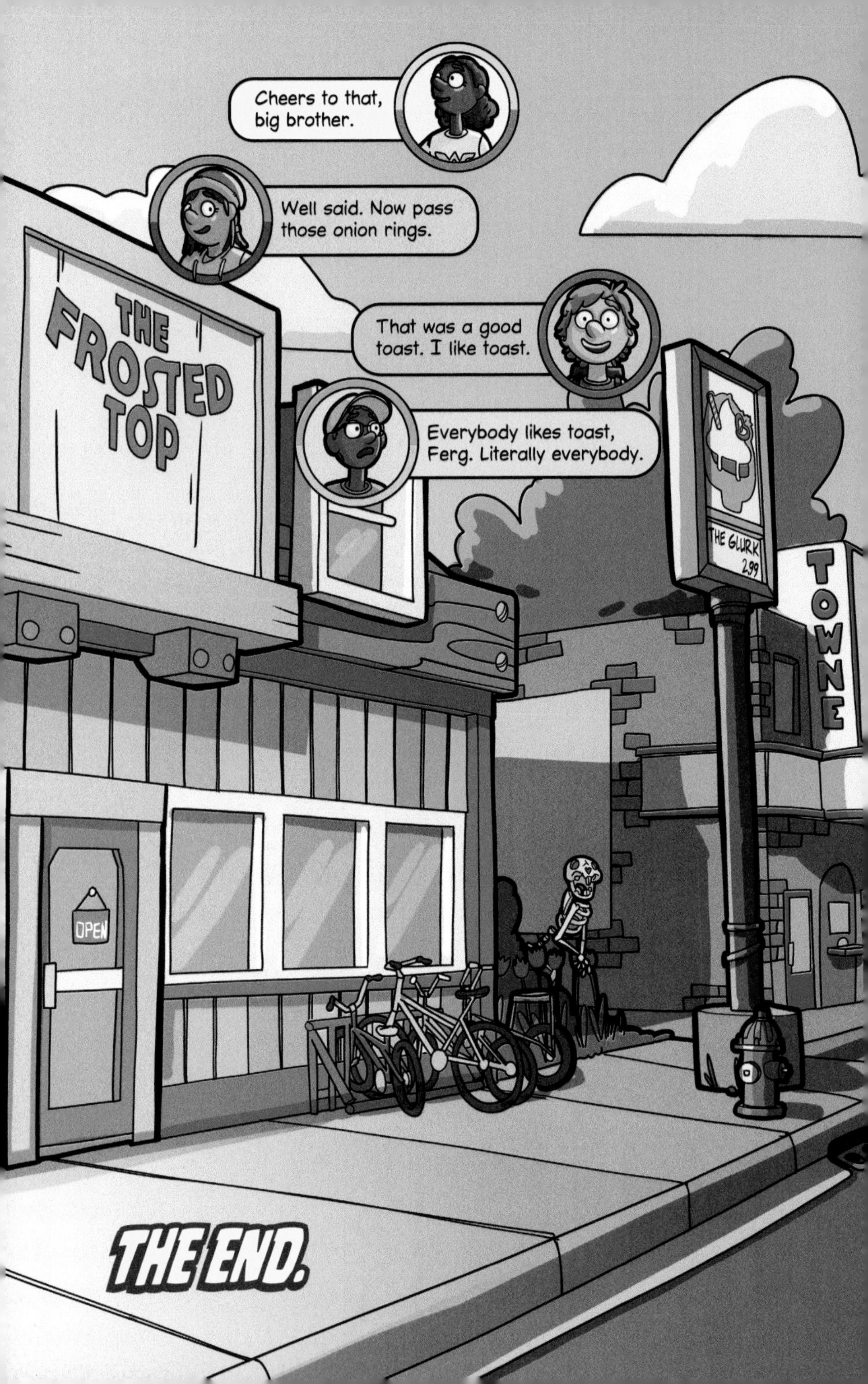

Cheers to that, big brother.
Well said. Now pass those onion rings.
That was a good toast. I like toast.
Everybody likes toast, Ferg. Literally everybody.
THE FROSTED TOP
THE GLURK 2.99
TOWNE
OPEN
THE END.

DUSTIN HANSEN

has been creating story and art for the children's entertainment world for decades. As an international award-winning video game developer, he directed, wrote, and created art for many bestselling games like *The Sims* and *Madder Football* before launching EA's more kid-friendly, story-driven Street Sports franchise.

Dustin's true passion lies with story. And this itch to tell an unbelievable yarn has led him to work in film and theme parks, and as the innovation director for Hasbro Inc.

Recently, Dustin finds himself taking his most direct approach to storytelling as an author and illustrator. His bestselling book *Game On! Video Game History from Pong and Pac-Man to Mario, Minecraft and More* is a hit among reluctant readers, and his illustrated chapter book series, *Microsaurs*, just wrapped up its sixth and final book.

Dustin has always been a comics geek, which isn't a surprise since Dustin is dyslexic and first fell in love with story through comics when he was young. His drive to use visuals to provide clues about the written word has been a thread throughout his career, and nowhere is it more evident than in his work on his debut graphic novel, *My Video Game Ate My Homework*

Thirteen-year-old Ashley Rayburn is an aspiring artist with a troubled past. When she stumbles upon a set of body paints, she assumes it's a gift from her latest foster parents. But it turns out it's really a top secret military weapon, and each color gives the wearer a different superpower. It's not long before the military becomes wise to what happened to their secret weapon. And this spells big trouble not only for Ashley, but for her newfound family and friends, as well.

PRIMER
superhero
a graphic novel
Jennifer Muro &
Thomas Krajewski
art by Gretel Lusky
DC

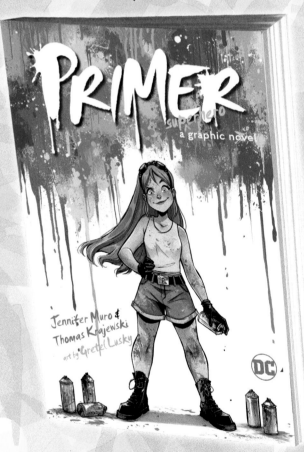

The following is a sneak peek of *Primer*,
written by Jennifer Muro and Thomas Krajewski,
with art by Gretel Lusky.

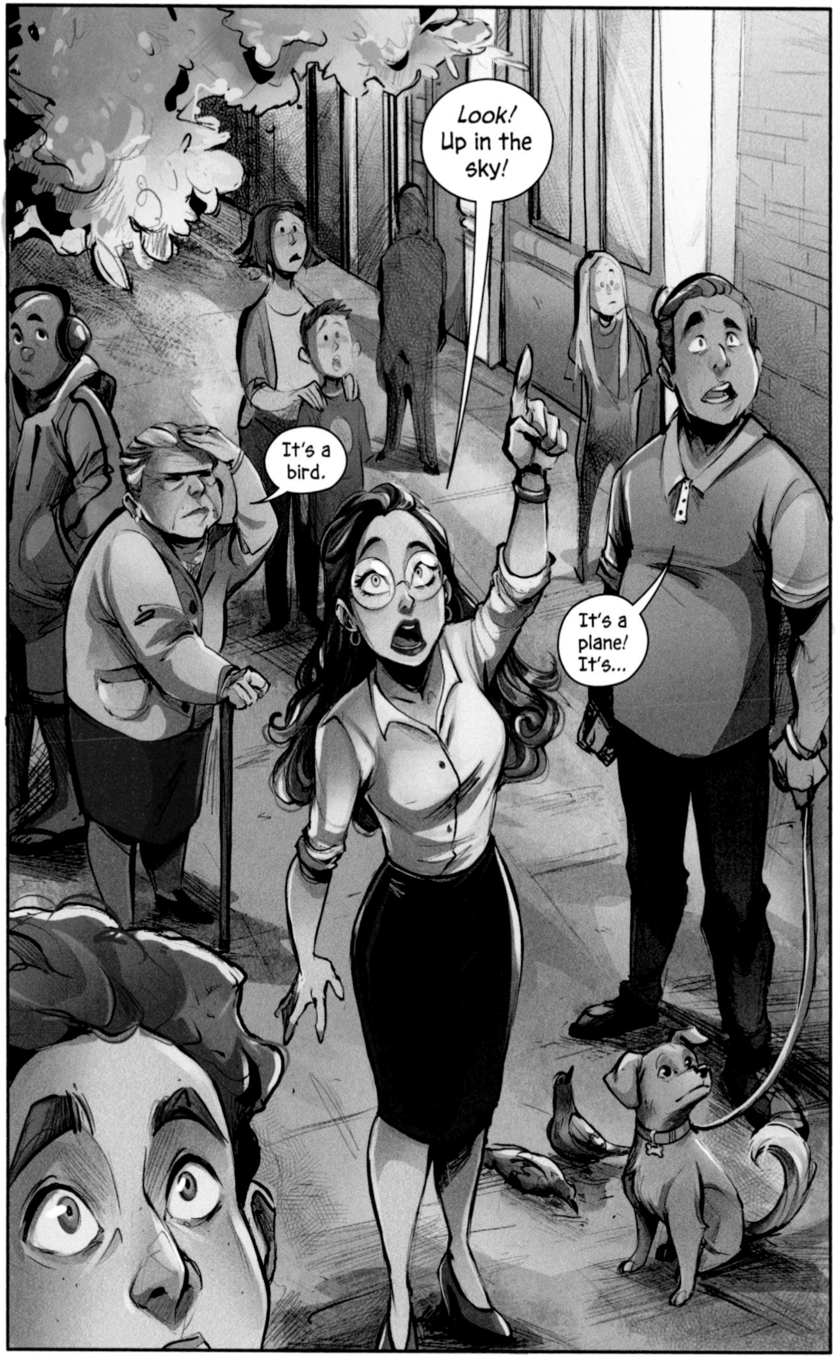
Look! Up in the sky!
It's a bird.
It's a plane! It's...

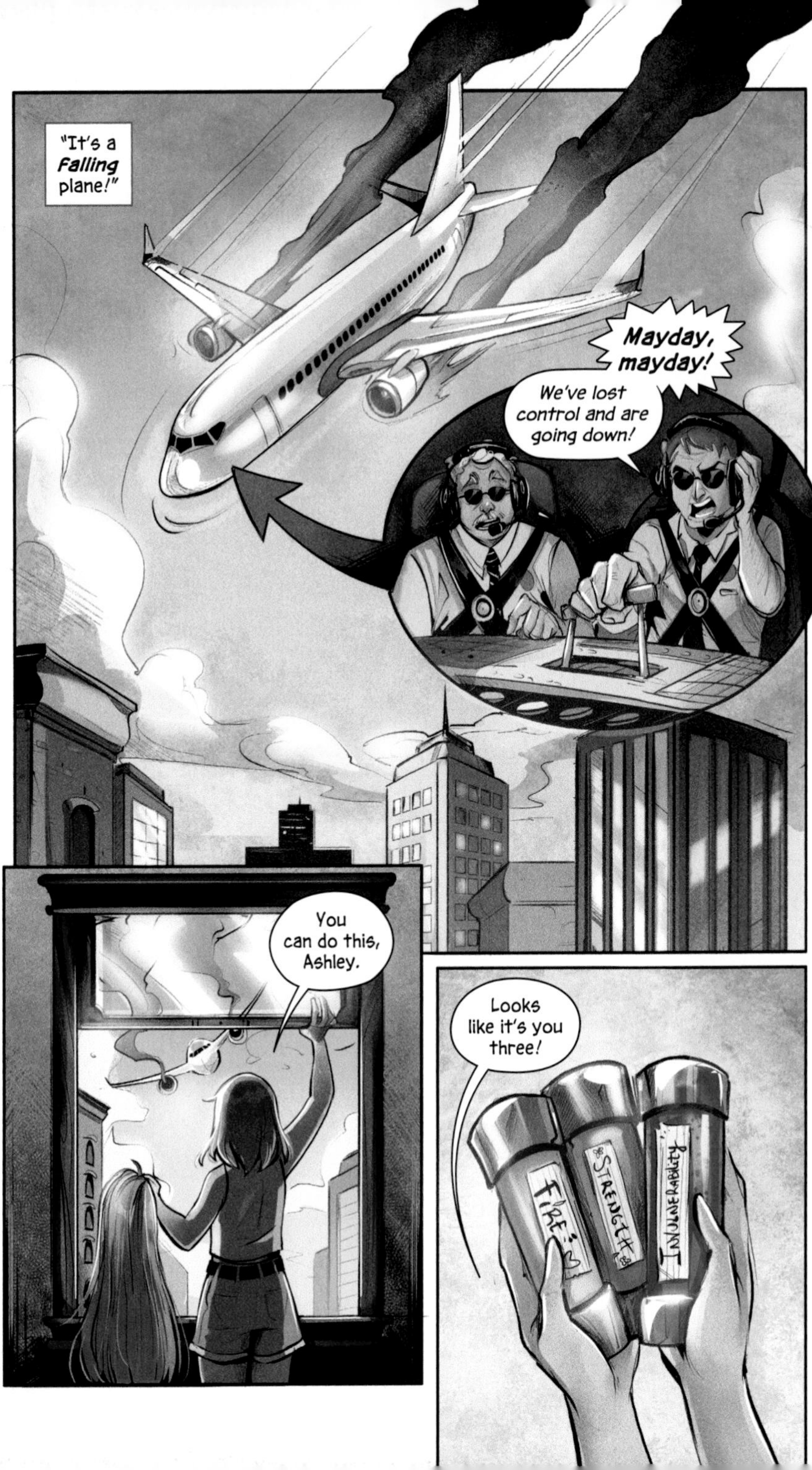
"It's a *falling* plane!"
Mayday, mayday!
We've lost control and are going down!
You can do this, Ashley.
Looks like it's you three!
FIRE!
STRENGTH
INVULNERABILITY

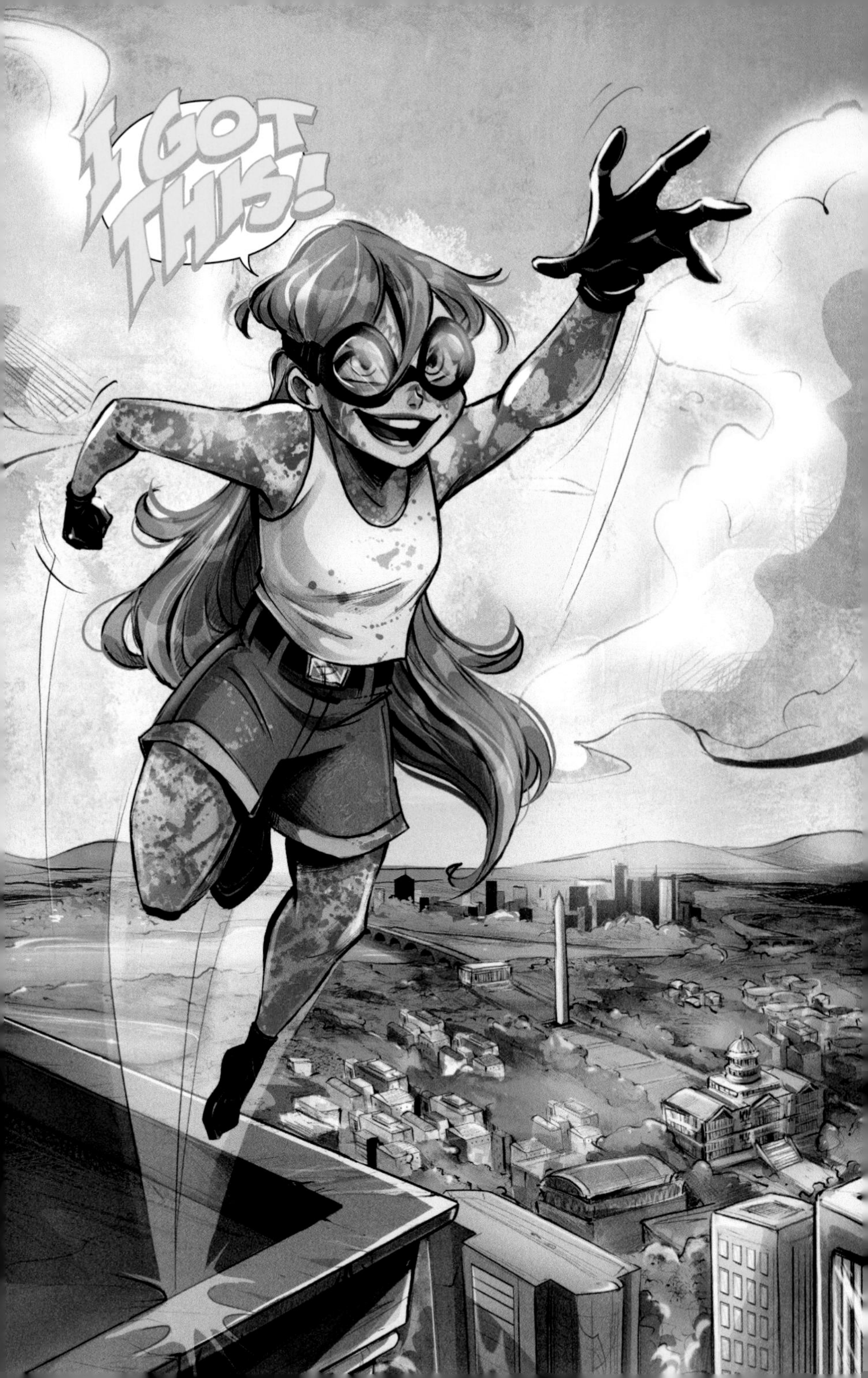
I GOT THIS!

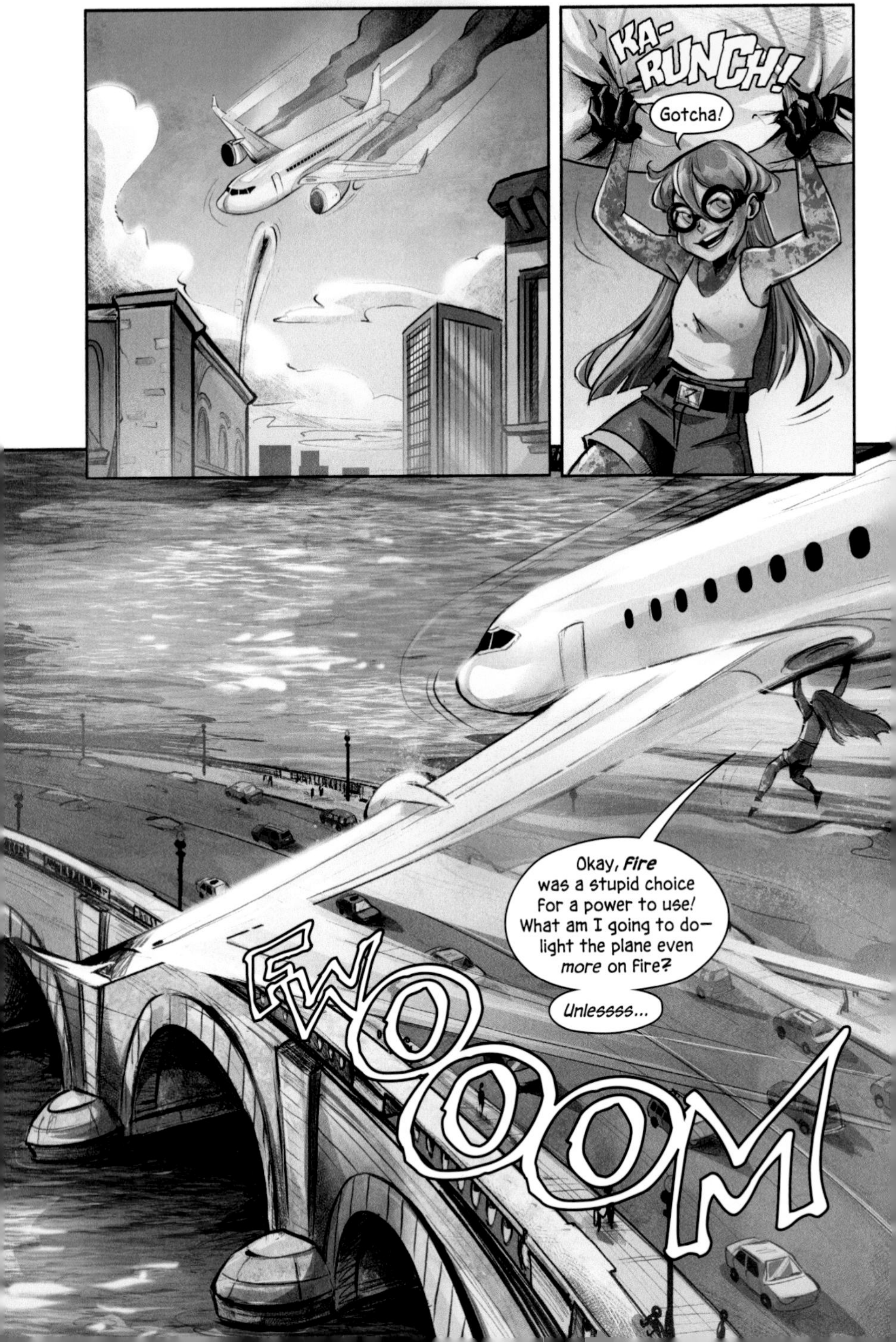

KA-RUNCH!
Gotcha!
Okay, *Fire* was a stupid choice for a power to use! What am I going to do— light the plane even *more* on fire?
Unlesssss...
FWOOOOM

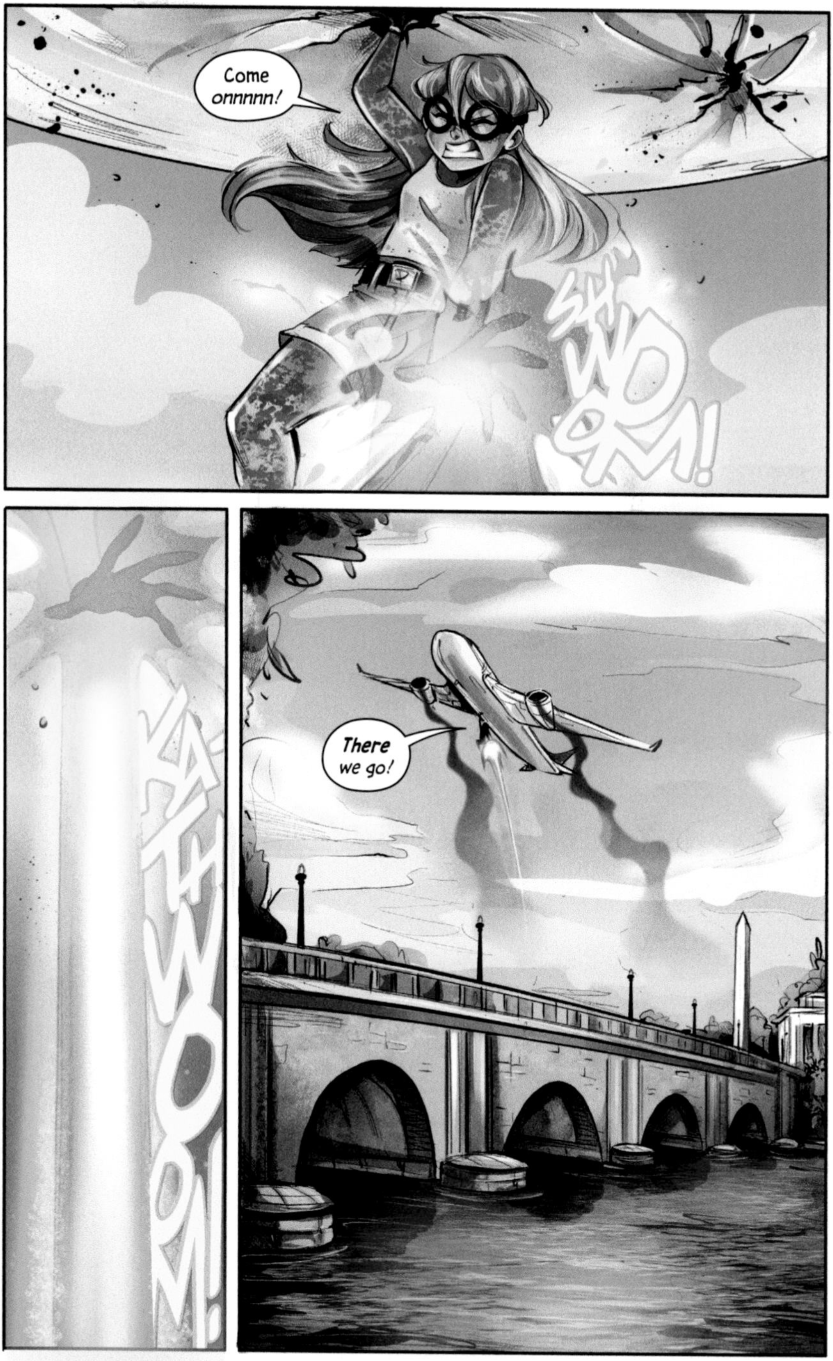
Come onnnnn!
SHWOOM!
KA-WOOM!
There we go!

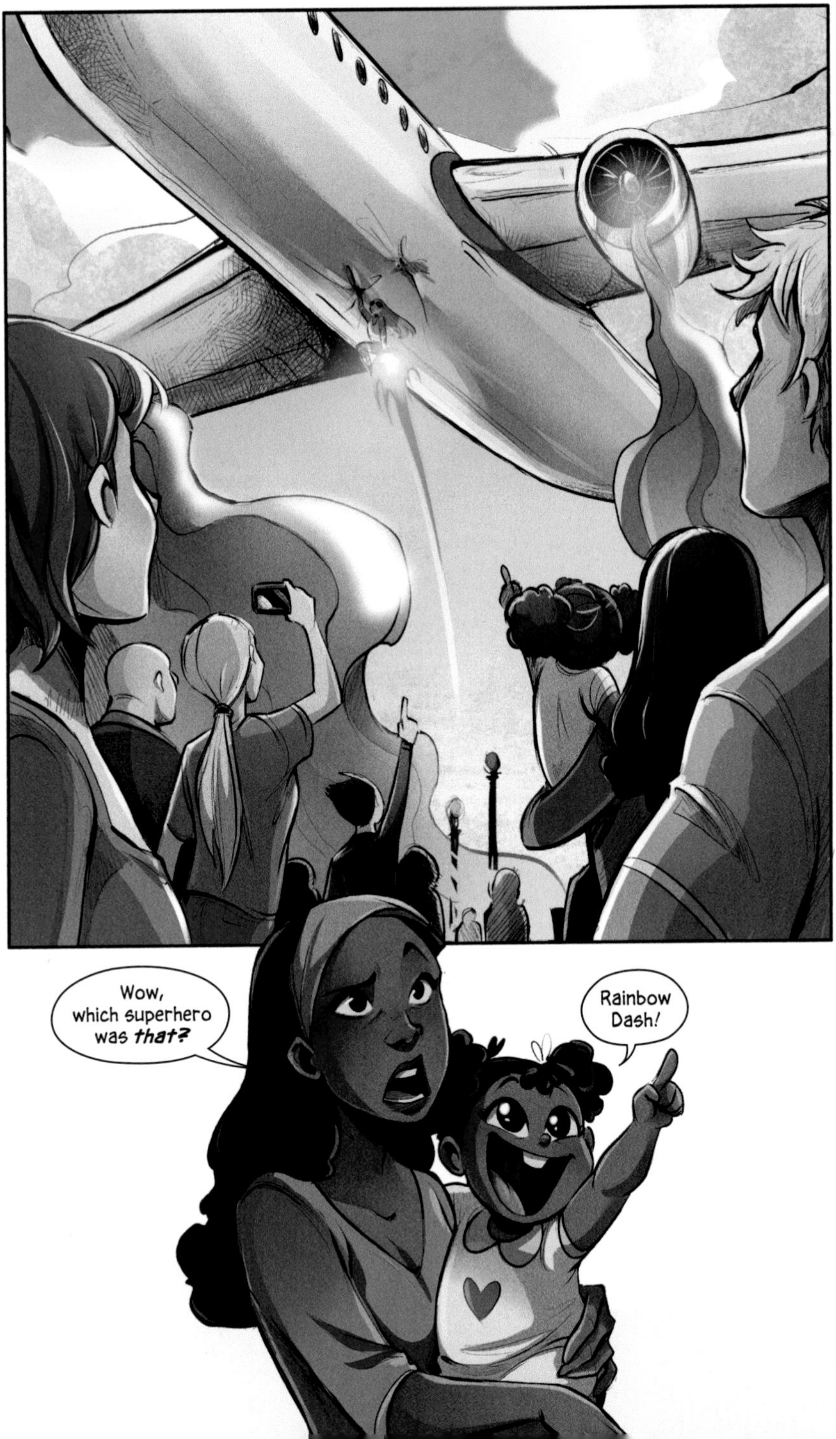
Wow, which superhero was *that?*
Rainbow Dash!

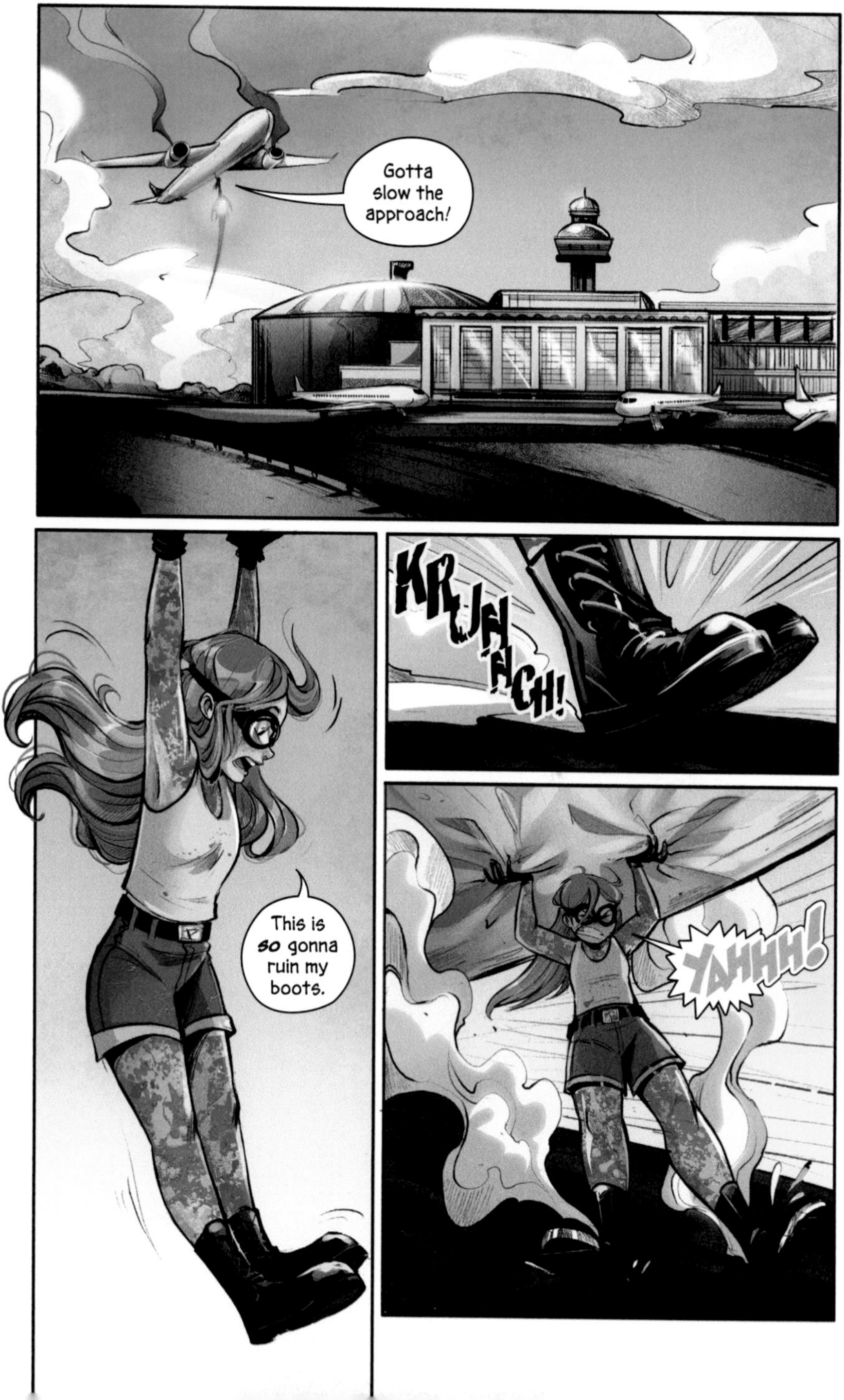
Gotta slow the approach!
This is so gonna ruin my boots.
KRUNNCH!
YAHHH!

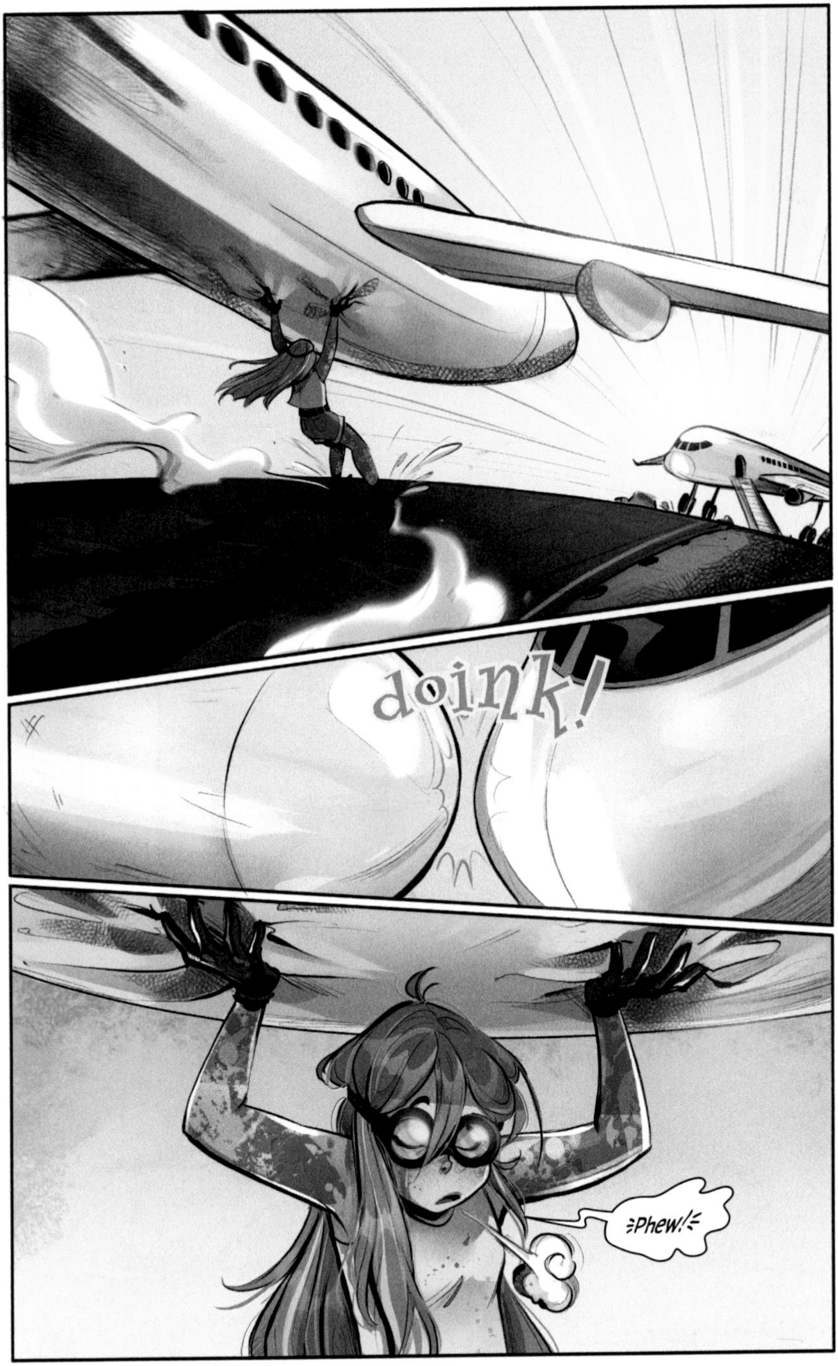
doink!
Phew!

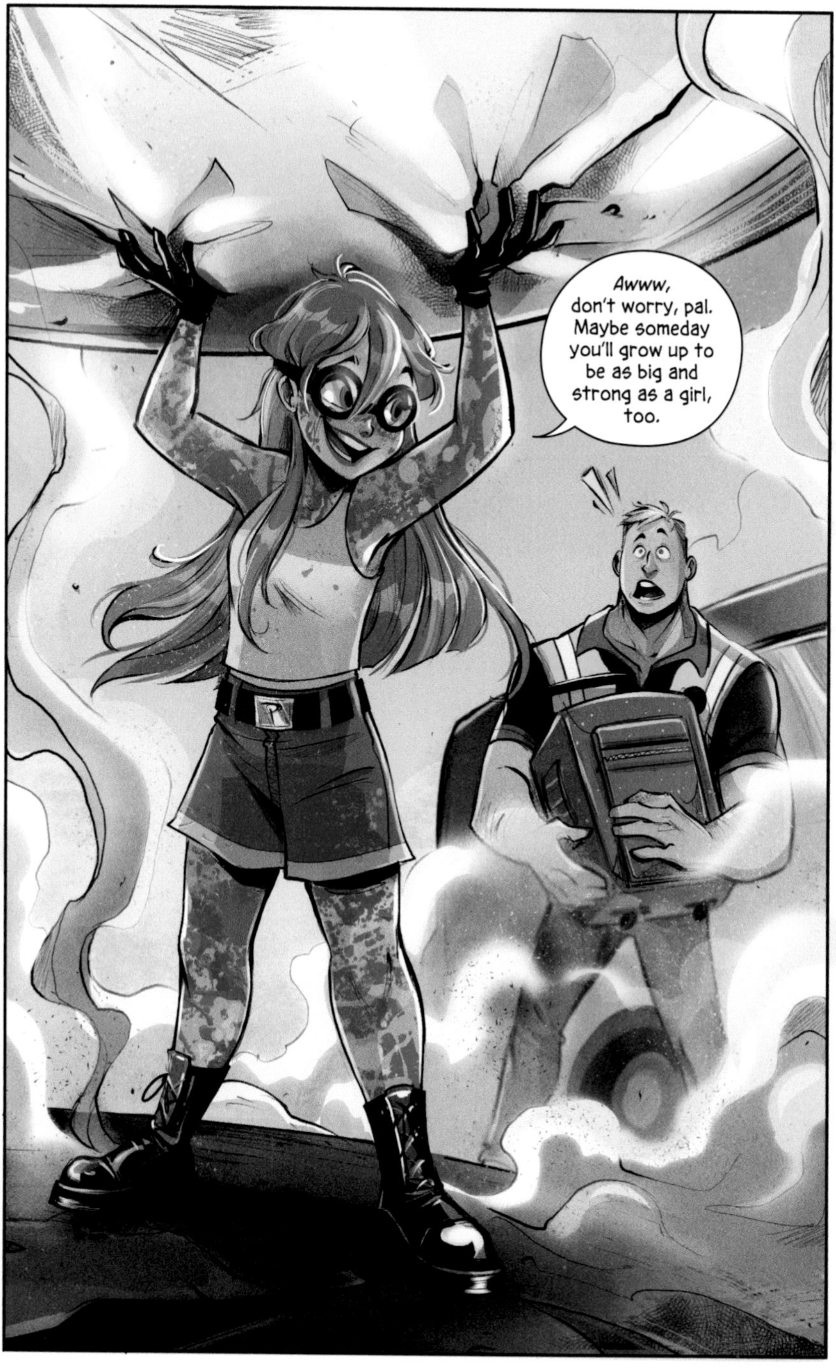
Awww, don't worry, pal. Maybe someday you'll grow up to be as big and strong as a girl, too.

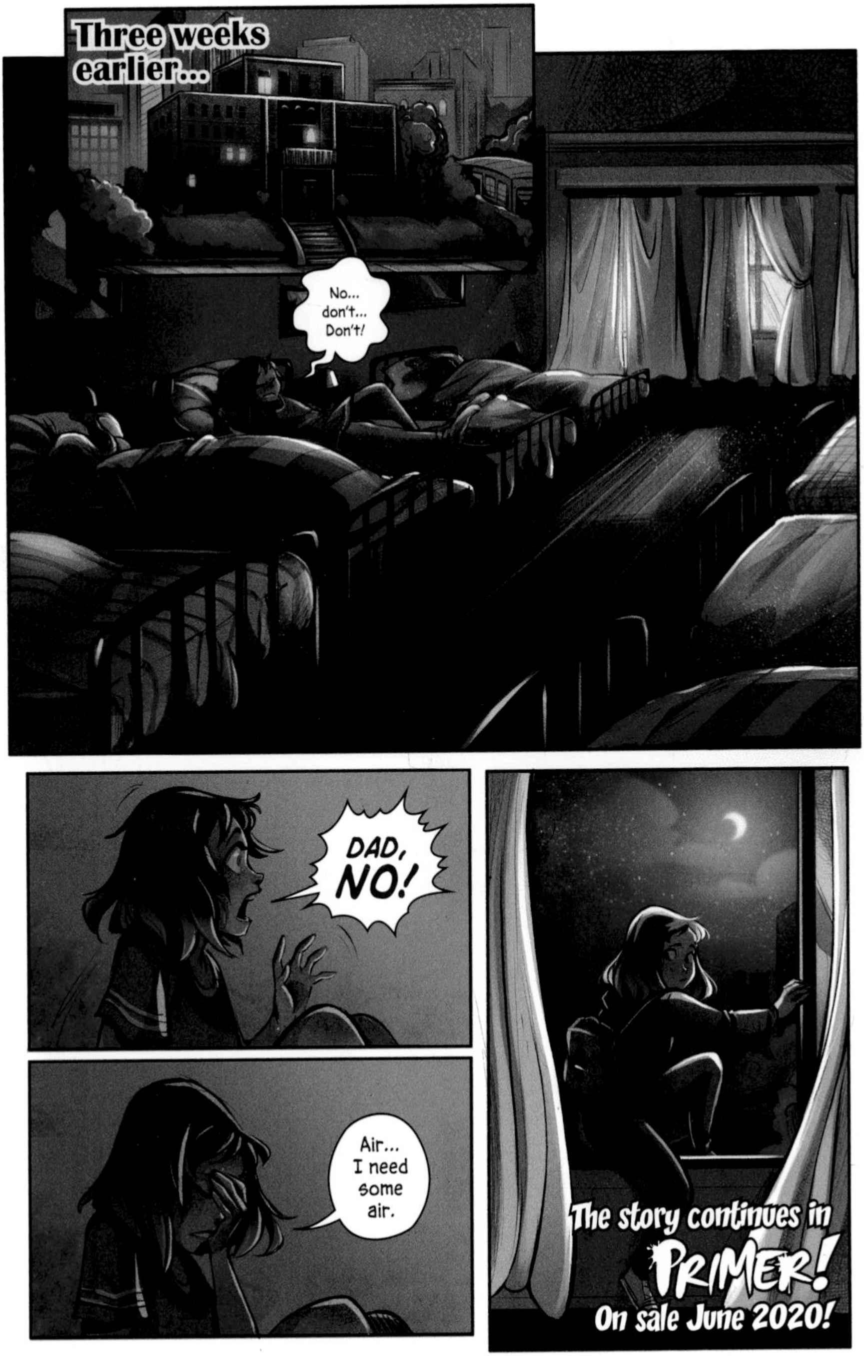
Three weeks earlier...
No... don't... Don't!
DAD, NO!
Air... I need some air.
The story continues in PRIMER!
On sale June 2020!